THE
STOLEN
MARRIAGE

By Diane Chamberlain

The Stolen Marriage
Pretending to Dance
The Silent Sister
Necessary Lies
The Good Father
The Midwife's Confession
The Lies We Told
Secrets She Left Behind
Before the Storm
The Secret Life of CeeCee Wilkes
The Bay at Midnight
Her Mother's Shadow
The Journey Home (anthology)
Kiss River
The Courage Tree
Keeper of the Light
Summer's Child
Breaking the Silence
The Escape Artist
Reflection
Brass Ring
Lovers and Strangers
Fire and Rain
Private Relations
Secret Lives
The Shadow Wife/Cypress Point

The Dance Begins (ebook short story)
The Broken String (ebook short story)
The First Lie (ebook short story)

THE
STOLEN
MARRIAGE

Diane Chamberlain

MACMILLAN

First published 2017 by St Martin's Press, New York

First published in the UK 2017 by Macmillan
an imprint of Pan Macmillan
20 New Wharf Road, London N1 9RR
Associated companies throughout the world
www.panmacmillan.com

ISBN 978-1-5098-0853-3

1 3 5 7 9 8 6 4 2

A CIP catalogue record for this book is available from the British Library.

Printed and bound by CPI Group (UK) Ltd, Croydon, CR0 4YY

*In memory of Lydia Lee Green, fellow author
and loving friend who battled polio as a child
and went on to do so much and be so kind.*

THE
STOLEN
MARRIAGE

JUNE 1944

PROLOGUE

Hickory, North Carolina

It's a terrible feeling, being despised. From the moment I set foot in Hickory, I felt the suspicion, distrust, and outright hostility of most of the people I met. Even my new sister-in-law regarded me with disdain. When Henry told me Lucy was just a few years younger than me, I thought, *How wonderful! We can be friends.* But we were not anywhere close to being friends.

I was making my bed one bright June morning when I heard footsteps in the hall outside the room I shared with Henry. Lucy pushed open the door, walking into the room without knocking, and I tightened the sash of my robe. Neither Henry nor I was happy about living with his mother and sister. In a month or so, we would move into our own home. I hoped that would make things better. Our marriage. My relationship with my mother-in-law, Ruth. My heavy heart. I hadn't been happy in so long. I doubted a new house was going to fix what was wrong with me.

Lucy flopped down on Henry's bed in her coral linen blouse and tan capris. She held a long white envelope, thick with its contents, in her hand.

"Can you drive me to Adora's house in the Buick?" she asked, holding the envelope in the air. "I want to drop off the money for the headstone."

"I thought your mother was going to take the money to her," I said as I tucked the chenille bedspread beneath my pillow. Adora was Ruth's former maid, and her little grandson was one of the first victims of the polio epidemic sweeping through Catawba County.

"She asked me to do it." Lucy patted her hair as if making sure every strand was in place. She was a pretty girl, her dark blond hair perfectly coiffed in a wavy bob. Her blue eyes lit up when she smiled, although I rarely saw that smile directed at me. "Mama doesn't like going to Colored Town," she continued. "But the cab drivers don't like going there either, and we have that car sitting right here in the garage. Please?"

I was surprised by the request. Lucy never made a secret of her disdain for me. Plus, gas was rationed. We didn't drive anywhere unless it was absolutely necessary, and we certainly never drove the Buick. It hadn't been out of the garage in the five months I'd lived in Hickory. Henry had told me right from the start that I wouldn't be driving as long as the war was going on. I knew *how* to drive, but the Buick needed new tires and with rubber being rationed it would be a while, if ever, before Henry would be able to get them.

"I'm sorry, Lucy," I said, straightening up from making the bed. "You know Henry said I can't use the car."

"That's ridiculous." She studied her nails. They were painted coral and perfectly matched her short-sleeved blouse. "The car's sitting right there," she argued. "It still has gas in it. So its tires are old? It's not like Adora lives on the moon. We'll make it to her house and back with no problem."

"Henry said—"

"You're so afraid to do anything on your own!" she interrupted me, those blue eyes darkening. "And why do you still insist on calling him 'Henry'? He's *Hank*. Henry sounds ridiculous."

"He introduced himself to me as Henry, so he'll always be—"

"He was putting on airs. Come *on*," she pleaded. "Please take me. Please?"

I sat down on the dressing-table bench, facing her. "Maybe we could mail the money." I motioned to the envelope. "Adora's family is still under quarantine, aren't they? You won't even be able to go into the house."

"I'm not mailing thirty-eight dollars!" she snapped. "I'll just leave it on their porch for them."

Maybe I should do it. This was a chance to forge a relationship with my sister-in-law. All my attempts at friendship with her had failed, but maybe with only the two of us in the car, I'd stand a chance. We could chat as we drove. We could stop someplace for a milkshake on the way home.

"All right," I said. "Now?"

"If you can bring yourself to get dressed." She nodded toward my robe.

"Of course." I wouldn't be ruffled by her sarcasm. "I'll just be a minute."

Once Lucy left the room, I began dressing. Stockings, girdle, slip, a yellow skirt and white blouse. I missed the dungarees and scuffed saddle shoes I used to wear before marrying Henry, but those casual clothes would never do now.

Lucy was waiting for me next to the detached garage that stood behind the house. I couldn't help the jittery nerves I felt as I opened the double garage doors and approached the driver's side of the car. I was disobeying my husband. I hoped he never had to know. When Henry was angry, I was never sure if he would yell or simply fall silent. Either way, he would be upset to know what I was doing right now.

I opened the car door and slid onto the mohair bench seat, while Lucy got in on the passenger side. She was holding a second envelope, this one large and tan, and it bore a white address label. I'd seen those manila envelopes with their white labels around the house from time to time and thought they had something to do with Henry's furniture factory. I was too focused on the car to ask Lucy why she was bringing this one along.

The Buick came to life instantly when I turned the key in the ignition and pressed the starter. I'd worried Henry might have siphoned the gas out of the tank for the Cadillac, but that didn't seem to be the case. I felt rusty as I explored the dashboard and pedals and gear shift. Lucy seemed to scrutinize my every move, unnerving me. She would report back to her friends. *My moronic sister-in-law couldn't figure out how to drive the Buick,* she'd say, and her friends would agree that I was the most insufferable creature in all of Hickory, the girl who had tricked Henry Kraft into marrying her.

"Make sure you put it in 'reverse' and not 'drive,'" Lucy said.

How stupid do you think I am? I thought, but I said nothing and my hand trembled slightly as I shifted into reverse, my foot pressing hard on the clutch. I backed slowly out of the garage and down the long driveway.

"Turn north when we get out to the street," Lucy commanded.

"North?" I asked. "That's the wrong direction."

"We need to make another stop." She held up the manila envelope. "I have to drop this off at someone's house."

I stopped the car before it reached the street. "Where does this someone live?" I asked.

She hesitated. "Just on the other side of the river. We'll go out 321."

I laughed. "No, we will not go out 321," I said. "You said we'd go to Adora's. Period. We shouldn't be in this car to begin with."

"It's five minutes away, Tess. We drive to this fellow's house. Leave the envelope in his mailbox and then drive to Adora's. Adds ten minutes total to the trip. What's the big deal?"

I looked down at the gas gauge. We were fine as far as gas went. What *was* the big deal?

"What's so important that it can't simply be mailed?" I asked, motioning toward the envelope in her hands.

"It's some boring business document Hank wants this man to have and it'll take too long to mail it. He hasn't had time to get it to him himself. Hank'll be pleased we delivered it."

The day was bright and warm and I wanted to please her. To do something right in her eyes.

"All right," I said, against my better judgment. I backed the car out of the driveway and headed north along our hilly tree-lined street. Driving, I felt the sudden thrill of freedom. We rolled down our windows and the warm air filled the car.

"Hank should let you use this car all the time," Lucy said as I turned a corner. "He's so stingy."

"He's not stingy," I said, thinking I should defend my husband. "He's really a fine man."

I felt her staring at me and I glanced at her. "What?" I said.

"You don't know Hank at all," she said.

"What do you mean?"

She played with the clasp on the manila envelope. "There are things about my brother . . . You have no idea, Tess," she said. "You're so naïve. He's using you, you know. I suppose that's fitting. You used him, so he uses you."

My hands tightened on the steering wheel. She was tapping into a fear that haunted me when I was at my weakest. I would tell myself that Henry was a good man. On my darkest days, I reminded myself that as miserable as I was, I would have been worse off without him. I'd learned to ignore his moodiness. I'd learned to accept his explanations when he came home late at night from work—and on the few occasions when he didn't come home at all.

"I don't understand," I said. "How is he using me?" I ignored the dig about me using him. It was an argument I would never win.

"Never mind," she said. "Let's just drive."

"No, really, Lucy," I said, downshifting as we approached a stop sign. "You can't start a conversation like that and then . . ."

"You don't really know him, that's all." Her voice had a tight, sinister edge to it. "He's not who you think he is."

I laughed uncomfortably. "So mysterious!" I said. We'd reached 321 and I turned onto the wider road in the direction of the river. "I'll have to ask him to tell me all his deep, dark secrets."

"Do *not* tell him I said anything." She leaned her head closer to the open window, the breeze blowing her hair around her head. "Let's just shut up about it, all right?"

"Fine," I said.

We drove for a few minutes in silence. I saw the broad river ahead of us, the sun reflecting off its glassy surface. We were nearing the long bridge when an explosive sound suddenly filled the car and we veered abruptly to the right. I yelped, pressing the brake hard, but the car was no longer in contact with the road. It sailed over the grassy shoulder and down a steep slope, straight toward the river. Lucy screamed, her hands on the dashboard. One of the tires blew, I thought. Maybe more than one? We seemed airborne for the longest time and I grabbed wildly for the steering wheel as it spun out of my control. My foot still pounded the brake, but it did nothing to slow us down as we catapulted toward that blinding sheet of glassy water. I let out my own scream as I glanced at Lucy. She looked stunned, a trickle of blood running from her forehead and down her cheek, her lips forming some sort of prayer.

The Buick hit the water nose first and it felt as though we'd crashed into a wall of concrete rather than a river. The car instantly began to sink, chilly water rushing through our open windows, spilling onto my lap, pooling on the floor of the car. It rose quickly up my calves. My thighs.

"Let me out! Let me out!" Lucy screamed, her arms flailing.

My heart felt like a drum in my chest as I tried to open my car door, but the pressure of the water was far too great. "Climb out!" I shouted to Lucy. She was frantically rolling her window up in a futile attempt to keep the river from pouring into the car. "Don't roll it up!" I shouted. "You need to get out that way!"

She seemed dazed, that prayer or whatever it was still on her lips. The water had quickly risen to my chin and I filled with terror at the thought of it covering my head, stealing my breath. Maneuvering my body onto the seat from beneath the steering wheel, I grabbed the door frame and fought the current of water as I pulled myself through the open window. I gasped for air and realized I'd been holding my breath even though my nose had never been underwater.

The roof of the car was still above the surface of the river. I held on to it as I pulled myself around the car to the passenger side. Reaching blindly into the water, I tried to grab the door handle. Drawing in a breath, I pulled myself below the water's surface. Lucy was on the other side of the window, her head tipped back as she struggled to keep her nose above the rapidly rising water. I knocked ineffectually on the glass, trying to pantomime that she needed to roll her window down. She didn't seem to understand me and I watched the level of the water quickly reach her nose and pull her under. Her blue eyes were wide with terror, beseeching me to save her, her hand pressed flat against the window. I rose to the surface of the water, gasping for breath for real this time, and paddled as quickly as I could over to the driver's side of the car. I would have to go back in through the open window and somehow pull her out. I filled my lungs with air and dove under the water and through the window. My legs still outside the car, I grabbed Lucy's shoulder with one hand, her hair with another. I tugged and only then realized her legs were pinned beneath the dashboard. She turned her terrified face toward me and I watched in helpless horror as the life left her eyes. I was frozen for a moment, my brain numb with fear before I became aware that my lungs were about to burst. In a panic, I retreated through the window, one thought in my mind: *Air. I need air.*

And then I had no thoughts at all.

PART ONE

1

Little Italy, Baltimore, Maryland

"A big piece for the doctor," my mother said as she passed the plate to Vincent across our cramped dining room table. She held the plate in her left hand—her right hand was still a bit weak from the small stroke she'd suffered a few years ago—and the plate sagged under the weight of a slice of her Italian crème cake. She'd been stockpiling our rationed sugar for weeks to make that cake.

"Thanks, Mom." Vincent smiled at my mother. He'd called her Mom for as long as I could remember, something that pleased my mother no end. She adored him as much as I did. He was the son she'd never had. I called Vincent's parents, who now sat across the table from me, Mimi and Pop. The Russos lived next door to us in our Little Italy neighborhood. Our identical brick row houses had identical marble stoops and when I was very small and playing on the sidewalk, I had to concentrate hard to remember which house was mine and which was Vincent's. Our houses were nearly identical inside as well, the rooms filled with crucifixes, statues of Mary, and framed paintings of Jesus's sacred heart, as well as with the scent of tomato gravy and sweet sausage.

On this day, we were celebrating both my twenty-third birthday and the completion of Vincent's hospital residency at Johns Hopkins. I'd known Vincent from the time I was in the cradle, and I'd loved him madly since I was a teenager but I had to admit that even I felt a new attraction to him the first time I saw him in his white coat, *Vincent Russo M.D.* emblazoned on the pocket, a stethoscope slung around his neck. That white coat set off his dark good looks: his thick hair with the slight widow's peak. His wide white smile. His nearly straight nose, just a hint of the aquiline shape that was so prominent in his father's face. We'd been engaged for the last year, and in May, I would become his bride. We'd been planning our future together for a very long time. We knew where we would live: a younger, fresher part of Little Italy, close but not too close to our parents. We would have four children. Both of us had grown up as only children—a rarity in an Italian neighborhood—and we most definitely did not want that lonely existence for a child of ours. With only the rhythm method to rely on, we knew we might end up with many more than four, but that was fine. We fantasized that someday he would have his own pediatric practice and I would be his nurse. In a few months, I'd graduate from nursing school, take my licensing exam, and finally be able to call myself a registered nurse, a career I'd longed for since I was ten years old when my mother developed diabetes and a nurse taught me how to administer her insulin shots. Mom had been perfectly capable of giving herself her own injections, but she'd wanted to plant that seed in me, guiding me toward the career she hoped I'd pick. It worked. Nursing was my passion. How I'd handle being both a nurse and a mother to four-plus children, I didn't know, but I was excited to find out.

"Have you decided on your dress yet, Theresa?" Mimi asked as she swallowed a piece of cake. Like her husband, she had a soft, slight Italian accent. Theirs had been an arranged marriage of sorts. When Pop came over as a teenager from Sicily, he knew the daughter of an old family friend had arrived the year before and was waiting for him. I couldn't imagine marrying someone I barely knew, yet they were devoted to each other. My parents, on the other hand, had been born and raised in Little Italy and met at a dance. My father died when I was four and I barely remembered him. Mimi and Pop had taken my mother and me under their generous wings after his death.

"I can't decide between the two dresses we loved," I said, "but it's still so early." Mimi and my mother had been with me when I tried on the dresses. If I picked one out now, I'd have to be careful not to gain an ounce before May. I wanted Gina Farinola, my closest girlfriend, to go with me to help me make the final decision. Then we needed to find a maid-of-honor dress for her.

"You can't go wrong with either of them," Mimi said.

"I like the one with the little rosettes, Tess," Mom said. She leaned across the table to tuck a strand of my hair behind my ear. I'd inherited her thick, unruly, nearly black hair, the only difference being that her hair was now streaked with silver.

"Oh, the one with the rosettes was beautiful," Mimi agreed.

I caught the smile that passed between Vincent and his father as the girl talk continued. Those two handsome, dark-eyed, dark-haired men stayed at the table, smoking cigarettes and bickering about the Baltimore Orioles, while Mom, Mimi, and I began clearing the dishes and carrying them into the kitchen. Vincent was leaving most of the wedding plans up to me. The wedding would be small. We planned to invite only thirty people to the reception, which would be held in one of our favorite neighborhood restaurants. We couldn't afford much more than that, but I wouldn't have cared if only our families were present. It was the marriage I longed for, not the wedding.

My mother was washing the dishes and Mimi and I were drying when Vincent walked into the small kitchen. "Can I steal Tess away from you ladies?" he asked, his hand already at my waist.

"Of course." Mimi pulled the dishtowel from me. "Go on now." She gave me a little shove toward the door. "You two have fun."

Vincent took my hand and led me through the living room and toward the front door. "Let's go for a walk," he said. Outside, he put his arm around me as we turned left on the sidewalk. Vincent's touch had been electrifying me for years. The first time I'd felt that lightning bolt pass through me when he touched me, I was fifteen years old and he was nineteen and home from college. I'd been trying unsuccessfully to change the needle on the Victrola in the Russos' living room. Vincent had moved me aside, gently, his hands on my rib cage, and my legs went soft in the knees. He'd replaced the needle and turned to me.

"What do you want to hear?" he'd asked. I couldn't respond for the buzzing in my ears. My mind was suddenly mush and my body a solid mass of nerve endings. His smile told me he knew exactly how I felt. Then he asked me to a movie. That was the beginning of everything. Seven years we'd been together now. Seven long, wonderful, love-filled, and sometimes very frustrating years. We wanted more of each other than we could have. I looked forward to the day when we could finally sleep in the same room. The same bed. At last we would be lovers, a thought that filled me with a hunger for him. It was both amazing to me as well as a source of pride that we'd been able to wait this long. We hadn't even come close to making love because Vincent didn't want that temptation. He'd grown up expecting to become a priest, so it made sense to me that he would never pressure me to cross that line before we were married. Gina teased me about it. She and her boyfriend Mac made love before he joined the army and she thought Vincent and I were crazy for waiting. She didn't think sleeping together was a sin. Gina didn't think much was a sin, actually.

"Something's come up that I need to talk to you about," Vincent said now, lowering his arm from my shoulders and taking my hand as we walked. His tone, which had been playful all through dinner and our birthday-and-residency celebration, was suddenly serious and I wondered if I should be worried. My biggest fear was that he would be called up for service. He had a minor problem with his heart—a murmur, his doctor called it—and so far, that had kept him out, a fact he felt guilty about. The heart murmur caused him no trouble at all, thank God. "Why should I get to stay safe at home when so many others have to fight?" he would say. Selfishly, though, I was happy he couldn't be drafted.

"Do I need to be worried?" I asked now.

He gave my hand a squeeze, and in the golden evening light, I saw him smile. "No," he said. "You just need to be a bit . . . flexible."

"I can do that," I said, happy just to be holding his hand.

We walked past the row houses on our block, several of them bearing the red-bordered blue star flags in the windows, indicating that a family member was serving in the armed forces. One of the houses had two blue stars and one gold. It was sobering, walking past that house. This was a costly war.

The air was warm and silky on my bare arms as we headed toward the place we always went to talk: St. Leo's. Our church. The hub of Little Italy. Even as kids, Vincent and I had had whispered conversations in St. Leo's. It was where we made our first communions and confirmations and it was a source of comfort for both of us. It was also where we would become husband and wife.

We reached the church and, once inside, sat down in the last pew, still holding hands. I breathed in the scent of musk and candles and incense that seemed to emanate from the cold stone walls and the smooth wood of the pews. It was a scent I always equated with comfort and safety. As much as I loved St. Leo's, though, I knew it meant more to Vincent than it did to me. While I felt the comfort of knowing I belonged in this church where people loved me and cared for me, Vincent felt something deeper here. Something spiritual. He'd tried to explain it to me, but it was the sort of thing you couldn't force another person to feel—that intense closeness to God. One of the priests at St. Leo's had recognized Vincent's brilliance in math and science early on and encouraged him to go into medicine instead of the priesthood. "There are many ways to serve God," he'd told him. I would be eternally grateful to that priest.

There were only a few other people in the church this evening. They sat or kneeled in the pews much closer to the altar. A few of them were at the side of the church, lighting candles. Since the war began, another bank of candles had been added. We had so many young men to pray for these days.

I leaned my head on Vincent's shoulder. "So," I said softly. "What do I need to be flexible about?"

"There's been a small change in my plans for the next few weeks," he said. "I need to go to Chicago for a little while."

I lifted my head to look at him. "Chicago? Why?"

"There's an infantile paralysis epidemic there," he said. "They're asking for doctors to volunteer."

"Ah," I said, understanding. "You're thinking about your cousin Tony." Vincent's much older cousin had contracted infantile paralysis—polio—as a teenager. He was in his forties now and he wore braces on his legs and needed crutches to help him walk.

"Yes," he said. "I guess I'm a little more sensitive to polio than another doctor might be, but I'd want to help anyway."

That was Vincent. Always first to jump in when someone needed help. "There are so many kids living in poverty in this country," he'd told me once. "I'll devote at least part of my practice to helping them." I had the feeling we would never be rich, but that was fine.

"How long do you think you'll be gone?" I asked.

"I'm hoping only a couple of weeks," he said. "These epidemics tend to happen during the summer and run their course by fall."

I hated that frightening disease. Every summer, it seemed to set a different part of the country in its sights, attacking the children and leaving them horribly ill, sometimes paralyzed, for months or years or even the rest of their lives. As a nursing student, I'd seen a couple of children who'd been devastated by it.

Vincent let go of my hand and put his arm around my shoulders and I snuggled closer. "I don't want to be away from you any longer than that," he said.

A couple of weeks. That sounded like a lifetime to me right then and I felt like protesting, but I needed to support him. "I'll be fine," I said. "I wish I was done with nursing school so I could go with you to help." I had another week in my summer program and the fall semester would start shortly after.

"That would have been perfect." He squeezed my shoulders. "I'll miss you," he said, "but I'll be back in no time."

"I'll be fine," I said again. I was determined to mean it.

2

Vincent's two weeks in Chicago stretched into three, then four and I began the final semester of my nursing program. We'd never been apart for so long. He was desperately needed there, he wrote in his letters, which arrived a couple of times each week. They were short letters, his handwriting sloppy, hurried. He rarely called. The boardinghouse where he was staying had only one phone for eight men to share. Plus, he was so busy. He promised to be home by early October, but I was beginning to doubt his promises. Those few times I spoke with him, I heard something new in his voice. A different sort of energy and excitement. He couldn't stop talking about the children he was seeing and the work he was doing. And he was falling in love with Chicago, he said. Would I ever consider living there? That sort of talk worried me. Chicago? Leaving Baltimore and our families had never been part of our plan.

As for me, I'd talk about my challenging classes and how Mimi and Pop were doing and the plans for our wedding. I'd talk about loving him. About our future, when we would work together in his pediatric practice. About the children we would have. He'd make a gallant effort to respond to what I was saying, but after a sentence or two he'd ease the conversation back to his work. I knew he was committed to me. I knew he wanted a future with me, and yet I felt something like impending doom during those weeks apart. I tried to remind myself that many of my friends, Gina included, had boyfriends thousands of miles away who faced danger and death every single day. My fiancé was safe. How dare I want him even closer to me when he was doing such important work and taking so much satisfaction from it?

The day before he was to come home, he called again. From the moment he said "Hi, Tess," I knew what he was going to tell me.

"I have to stay a bit longer, darling," he said. "I'm sorry."

Words failed me, and he rushed on.

"I've gotten involved in some research here," he said. "You know, into the cause of infantile paralysis? And the various forms of treatment? It's so important. You understand, don't you?"

"You said you'd be home tomorrow." I heard the slightest break in my voice and hoped he hadn't noticed. I would not be a baby.

"I know, and I'm sorry, but this isn't the sort of thing that can be put off," he said. "The work has to happen while the polio virus is still active in the area. Plus most of the other personnel have had to go back to their jobs, but since I'm not practicing yet, I'm free to stay."

"What if our wedding were tomorrow?" I tested. "Would you still stay there?"

He hesitated as though he couldn't believe I'd actually asked that question, and I felt ashamed for doubting him.

"I'm sorry," I said. "I know you'd come home."

"Of course I would."

"Maybe I could come there? I have the weekend off, plus my Monday classes don't start till afternoon."

Again that hesitation. I squeezed the phone cord, waiting tensely for his answer.

"Honey," he said. "Do you know how long that would take you? First, it's nearly impossible to get a train reservation with the way they're moving the troops around. Even if you *could* get a reservation, you'd have to spend twenty hours on the train. And once you got here, I don't have any place for you to stay. I'm in a boardinghouse, remember? Plus I'll be working all hours of the day and into the night."

For the first time in our long relationship, I wondered if he might be seeing someone else. The thought felt like a knife in my chest. He couldn't be, though. Not Vincent. We'd been apart too long. I was losing my memory of who he truly was. I was letting myself get bitter.

"All right," I said, then before I could stop myself, I added, "I'd ask when you'll be coming home, but it doesn't really matter what you say, does it? You'll just change the date as it approaches."

"*Tess*," he chided. "That's not like you."

"I know." He was right. It wasn't like me, but I couldn't help but feel hurt that I seemed to be last of his priorities.

"Look, I need to get off, darling," he said. "Someone else wants to use this phone. Give me two more weeks here, all right? I promise, I'll come home then, no matter what's going on here. Just remember that you and I have our whole lives together. Ten years from now, you'll look back on these few weeks and laugh at how insecure you sound. Keep your chin up for me now, all right, sweetheart?"

"All right," I said after a moment. "I love you."

"I love you too," he said, "and don't you ever forget it."

3

By the middle of October, Vincent still wasn't home. I sat with Gina in her bedroom, both of us in our dungarees and cotton shirts as we smoked cigarettes and drank Pepsi Cola on her twin beds. She'd added a shot of whiskey to my Pepsi. "For your nerves," she'd said.

I usually loved sitting in Gina's room. It hadn't changed since she was a little girl and the pink and white striped curtains and ruffled pink bed skirt were a sweet counterpoint to our cigarettes and whiskey. Today, though, even Gina's room gave me little comfort.

She lit another Chesterfield and turned to face me.

"It's time you opened your eyes, Tess," Gina said after I told her that Vincent had postponed coming home yet again. "He's seeing someone. Even Vincent Russo is a man, not a saint."

"I don't believe he'd ever cheat on me," I said. Most of the time, I didn't. Only when I was lying in bed after another day of not hearing from him by phone or letter did I give in to any doubt about his fidelity. During daylight hours when I was happily absorbed in my nursing program, I knew it was me and me alone that he loved. Nighttime, though, was a different matter.

"It's not so terrible, though, honey." Gina brushed a lock of her dirty-blond hair from her cheek, then took a drag on her cigarette. "He'll be back," she said. "He's probably just nervous about getting married and needs one last fling. Let him get it out of his system and then he'll be yours for the rest of your life."

"He's not having a fling," I said, though there wasn't much power behind my words. I hated that I felt any doubt about him at all.

"I think you're kidding yourself," she said. "Do you think for one minute Mac hasn't had some fun while he's over there?"

I was shocked. "Has he told you that?"

She shrugged. "He doesn't have to." She sipped from her glass, then set it back on the night table between the beds. "He's a man," she said. "It's different for them. They can't go that long without a girl."

"Doesn't the thought of him being with someone else bother you?"

"I just don't think about it," she said. "He's fighting for his country. It has to be terrible, what he's going through. I wouldn't blame him if he could find a little pleasure."

I felt a chill run up my spine. "You're a lot more forgiving than I am," I said.

"You know what we should do?" Gina stubbed out her cigarette and sat up straight, crossing her legs Indian-style on the bed. I'd known her a long time and recognized the look of mischief in her eyes.

"What?" I asked warily.

"We should get out of here for the weekend," she said. "Let's see if we can get on a train to Washington!"

"What if Vincent calls while I'm away?"

She scowled. "What's the likelihood of that?" she asked. "You said he hardly ever calls. And you can't live your life waiting for him to get in touch. Come on. Let's do it."

Washington, D.C., was only an hour train ride from Baltimore. I'd been to the city several times to tour the museums and once to see a play, but never overnight. "Where would we stay?" I asked. "Washington will be a zoo these days with all the government workers and military and—"

"My aunt has that tourist home near Capitol Hill, remember?" she interrupted me. "Maybe she has a vacancy. Let me call her and see if she can put us up. It wouldn't even cost us anything."

"I think I just want to stay home and sulk this weekend," I said, lighting another cigarette.

"No you don't!" She leaned forward, riveting me with her blue eyes. "And really, Tess. You're usually so tough and I love you but now you're starting to get on my nerves with your whining. Think about it, will you? My boyfriend's in harm's way every minute of every day. He can't even tell me where he is. His letters come through V-mail after the censors have gone over them. His life isn't his own right now. Do you hear me complaining? No. Your boyfriend is a few hours away doing something he loves. So you have to stop this griping. All right?"

I was taken aback, first by her criticism and second by the fact that she was right. I'd become self-absorbed in the last few weeks. Gina probably needed an escape for the weekend even more than I did.

"You're right," I said. "I'm sorry. Let's go to Washington."

4

We arrived in Washington at eleven-thirty the following morning after the stifling-hot train ride. The train had been so crowded with boys in uniform that we'd had to stand until two very young-looking soldiers offered us their seats. Union Station was packed wall to wall with travelers. Businessmen in suits and women in their hats and white gloves were lost in a sea of military uniforms. Everyone looked rushed as they swarmed through the massive station. It took us several minutes to work our way through the crowd, our suitcases thumping into the legs of other travelers, before we made it to the exit and out onto the sidewalk. The scent of early fall mingled with the smell of cigarettes and perfume and hair tonic as we joined the mob waiting for a taxi. There was a chill in the air and I drew my coat tighter across my chest. We were both wearing skirts and blouses beneath our lightweight coats, as well as the tams we'd bought on a shopping spree the year before. Gina had lamented that she was completely out of nylons, so she'd carefully applied a line of eye pencil up the back of her leg to fool the casual observer. I still had two pairs of nylons in reasonable condition—not counting the white stockings that went with my nurse's uniform—and I was wearing one of them now.

"We're never going to get a cab." Gina frowned at the sea of people in front of us. "Aunt Ellen's place is about a half hour's walk from here. Shall we hoof it? Are you okay carrying your suitcase?"

"Sure." I nodded and fell into step beside her.

My tan and brown suitcase, the one I'd had since childhood since I so rarely traveled, was quite light. Gina's aunt only had room for us for one night, so I'd packed a nightgown, robe, and slippers, some toiletries and a bit of makeup, and a dress to wear out to dinner tonight. That was all. I hoped we could find someplace reasonable to eat. Gina had a good secretarial job with a weekly paycheck, while I was still paying for my education with a bit of help from my mother. Every spare penny I had, and there were not many of them, would go toward my wedding and honeymoon.

My mother hadn't been at all happy when I told her I was going to Washington with Gina.

"What should I tell Vincent if he calls?" she asked.

"The truth." I shrugged. "That I'm in Washington with Gina."

"Don't you think you should be here if he calls?"

I thought Gina had been right. It was pathetic for me to sit by the phone hour after hour, day after day, on the small chance that Vincent might call. "Mom, it's nearly impossible for him to get to a phone, so I doubt very much that I'll hear from him," I said. "Plus, I'm only going for one night."

"Well," she said, "just remember who you are."

I frowned at her. "What does that mean?"

"Remember you're a girl engaged to be married to a wonderful man," she said.

I laughed. "Have a little faith in me, all right?" I said.

"I can see Aunt Ellen's row house," Gina said after we'd been walking twenty minutes or so. Her hands were laden down by her handbag and suitcase, so she pointed toward the end of the block with her raised chin. "See it up ahead?"

"Uh-huh," I said. My shoulder ached from carrying the suitcase despite its light weight, and by the time we reached the tourist home, I was perspiring. Breathing hard, we set our suitcases on the sidewalk and looked up at the three-story brownstone squeezed between two larger buildings. It was a pretty house with a bay window on each level and stone garlands near the roofline. Neither of us seemed in a hurry to tackle the long flight of stairs to the front door, but after a minute, I picked up my suitcase and headed up the walk, Gina close behind me. We were both out of breath by the time we reached the small stone porch. An envelope taped to the doorbell was addressed to Gina. She tore it open and read out loud.

Dear Gina, I'm distressed to tell you that I need to go to my house in Bethesda to deal with a burst pipe. I tried to reach you at home but you'd already left. I'm beside myself that I'm leaving you and your friend alone, but it can't be helped. The two of you come in and make yourselves at home. You'll each have a room to yourself (2 and 3 at the top of the stairs)—amazing this time of year, so enjoy the privacy! There are good locks on the doors and the two businessmen seem very nice. I'm sure they won't disturb you. If you need anything, call. The phone is on a table by the stairs. Sorry I'll miss seeing you this trip! Much love, Aunt Ellen.

Gina looked at me over the top of the note. "So much for our chaperone." She laughed. Gina's aunt had been reluctant to let us come because she had two male boarders staying with her. *I never mix men and women,* she'd told Gina. *It's not appropriate.* Gina had talked her into it. "You'll be there," she'd said to her aunt on the phone, rolling her eyes at me as I listened to her end of the conversation. "You can be our chaperone."

"I'm sure it will be fine," I said now, unconcerned. My mother would have a fit if she knew.

Gina pulled open one of the double doors and we walked into a small, cozy living room. We set down our suitcases and it took a moment for my eyes to adjust to the dim light after the bright sunshine outside. The air held the delicious sweet aroma of pipe tobacco, a scent I'd always associated with the father I'd lost so young. I remembered the scent better than I remembered him.

"Hi, fellas," Gina said, and only then did I notice the two men sitting in leather Queen Anne chairs near the fireplace. They stood when they saw us, nodding in our direction. One of them, the older of the two, offered a slight bow.

"Welcome, ladies," he said, bending over to stub out a cigarette in the ashtray by his chair. His smile was warm and welcoming. He was probably close to forty with thick hair, nearly black, bushy eyebrows, and a thin dark mustache. He'd loosened his tie and the sleeves of his shirt had been rolled up to reveal muscular forearms dusted with dark hair. "One of you must be Mrs. Foley's niece," he said. With those few words, I could already place his hard New York accent.

Gina smiled, brushing a strand of hair behind her ear in a manner I could only think of as flirtatious. "Yes," she said. "I'm Gina and this is Tess."

"And I'm Roger Talbot and this is Henry . . ." He raised his eyebrows at the other man, obviously not knowing—or recalling—his name.

"Henry Kraft," the second man said with a nod. "How do you do?" His voice was a silky drawl, and he had a scrubbed-clean look about him. His light brown hair was neatly cropped, his build tight and lean. Unlike Mr. Talbot, he was dressed for business in a gray suit that fit him to a T. I knew little about men's clothing. You rarely saw a suit in Little Italy and I knew Vincent owned only one. Nevertheless, I had the feeling that Henry Kraft's suit was expensive and tailored just for him. His shirt was a light gray pinstripe and his blue tie was perfectly knotted at his throat. On the end table next to him, a curl of fragrant smoke rose from his pipe. He looked closer to our age than the other man. Late twenties, I guessed. Even from where we stood, I could see the pale blue of his eyes. I could see, too, that his smile didn't reach them. Those eyes had the slightest downward cast to them and I imagined there wasn't a smile broad enough in the world to lift the sadness I saw in that handsome face.

"Hey!" Mr. Talbot took a step toward our suitcases. "Let us carry them up for you."

"Oh, would you?" Gina said in a saccharine voice I'd never heard her use before. Was she flirting? "We carted them all the way from Union Station and our arms are about to fall out of their sockets."

Mr. Kraft started toward us as well, but Mr. Talbot held up a hand to stop him. "I've got both," he said gallantly. He finished crossing the room in a few swift steps, then lifted our suitcases as if they were made of cotton and marched ahead of us up the stairs. We followed him to the second story, where he set down the suitcases outside the door to room number 3. He turned to face us.

"Hope to see you ladies again later," he said, with a nod. "How long are you in town?"

"Just for the night," I said.

"And you?" Gina asked. "My aunt said you're here on business?"

"Securing a government contract, same as that gentleman down there." He nodded toward the stairs. "Mr. Kraft. He's in the furniture trade in North Carolina. Southern boy." He said the word "Southern" in a way that let us know he thought himself better than the man downstairs. "He already has a contract with Uncle Sam and is hoping to expand on it. I'm in textiles and was getting a few tips from him."

"Ah well," Gina said. "Good luck."

The man turned to face me. "You're a bit of a quiet one, aren't you?" he said, and I simply smiled. "Still waters run deep," he added. "I bet there's plenty going on in that pretty head of yours."

"Thanks for your help," I said, and I moved past him toward the door.

We went into our separate rooms—Gina in 2, me in 3—as Mr. Talbot walked heavily back down the stairs. My very spare room had two twin beds, a four-drawer dresser, and a sink jutting from the wall next to a narrow closet. I hung up the dress I'd packed for dinner and was tucking my nightgown beneath the pillow of my bed when Gina knocked on the door and poked her head inside.

"Come on!" she said. "Let's explore!"

The weather was perfect, the air fragrant and golden from the leaves that were beginning to turn. We walked our legs off, the streets crowded with military men and government girls. We spent hours in the Freer and the National galleries. Some exhibits were closed, as the art had been moved out of the city due to the war, but we still managed to exhaust ourselves. So much reminded me of Vincent. His dark eyes stared out at me from a seventeenth-century painting and I thought I spotted him in one of the galleries, studying a sculpture of a horse. I considered finding a pay phone and calling my mother to see if he might have called, but I knew that would annoy Gina and only leave me more depressed than I already was.

My heels were blistered by the time we headed back to the tourist home, and we both seemed too tired to talk. We were a block away from the house when Gina suddenly spoke up.

"What did you think of those two fellas in Aunt Ellen's living room, huh?" she asked.

I shrugged. "They seemed nice," I said. It did strike me as a bit odd now that we were sharing a house with two men for the night.

"I think that one—Henry—had eyes for you."

I laughed. "I'm engaged, remember?" I wiggled my ring finger with its small but sparkling diamond in front of her face.

"Which is not the same as married," she said. She stopped walking and tipped her head to study my face. "I don't think you know how pretty you are, Tess," she said as she started walking again. "How men look at you."

"What? That's crazy," I said, though I couldn't help but be flattered. When it came right down to it, I knew very few men and had no idea how they saw me. Vincent had been the only man I ever dated. He told me all the time that I was beautiful, but I assumed he was looking through the eyes of love. I knew I didn't look like the average girl. I thought my eyes were too big, too round for the rest of my features, but Vincent always said he loved getting "lost" in them. While I rued how long it took my hair to dry after I washed it and how unruly it was when I struggled to style it, he said he loved getting his fingers tangled up in it.

I thought of that man, Henry Kraft. His gently handsome face. His sad-looking eyes. "I'll have to show him my ring," I said.

"Killjoy," she said. "Maybe those men can suggest a good place for dinner."

"I think there are Hot Shoppes in Washington," I said. "Let's go there." I could afford a sandwich and root beer at a Hot Shoppe.

Gina shook her head. "Can't get a drink at a Hot Shoppe," she said. "Let's find someplace more exciting. It'll be my treat," she added, and when I started to protest she held up her hand. "When you get your RN license and a job, you can take me out, all right?"

"Fair enough," I agreed. It would be fun to go someplace different for a change.

We found the two men in the living room again when we reached the tourist home. They stood near the stairs, their fedoras in their hands as though they were getting ready to go out.

"We're headed to Martin's for dinner," Mr. Talbot said. "How about you gals join us?"

"Who's Martin?" I asked.

Mr. Kraft smiled. "It's the best restaurant in Georgetown," he said.

"We have a reservation," Mr. Talbot added. "I'm sure we can change it from two people to four."

I was about to politely decline when Gina ran right over me. "We'd love to!" she said, grabbing my hand and nearly dragging me toward the stairs. "Just give us a couple of minutes to change."

"You have ten," Mr. Talbot called after us. "Cab's on its way."

Upstairs, I followed Gina into her room. "I don't think we should go out with them," I said. "It feels wrong. Your aunt would have a fit."

"She'll never have to know," she said, opening the closet and taking out her dress. "Go put on your dress and make it snappy. They'll buy us a swell dinner at the best restaurant in Georgetown. Are you going to pass that up?" She saw my hesitancy. "It's not like a date, honey," she said. "After all, there are four of us. You aren't going out alone with someone. It's like four colleagues having dinner together. That's all."

"I insist you gals start calling us by our first names," Mr. Talbot said as we clambered into the cab. "I'm Roger, remember?"

I sat between him and Gina in the backseat, while Mr. Kraft—Henry— rode in front with the quiet, somber driver. The cab smelled of cigars and Gina's perfume, a dab of which I'd put behind my ears since I hadn't brought any of my own. I was stifling in my coat and gloves. Henry was quiet as the taxi made its way through the clogged streets to Georgetown, but Roger filled the air of the cab with his booming voice, telling us how he once saw Speaker of the House Sam Rayburn at Martin's. On another occasion, he said, he spotted Senator Harry Truman sitting at the next table.

"Did you talk to either of them?" Gina leaned forward to speak past me.

"No, though I certainly tried to listen in on their conversations," he said. He went on to talk in detail about every meal he'd eaten at Martin's and I began to think we were in for a very long evening.

Martin's wasn't what I expected. It was more tavern than the posh restaurant I'd anticipated. The walls and the long bar were made of dark, polished wood, the tin ceiling was a bronze color, and there were far more male diners than female. I felt slightly overdressed and out of place. We were led to a wooden booth and Gina and I sat on one side, Roger and Henry on the other.

When the waiter arrived at our table, Roger ordered drinks for all of us. "Spytinis all around," he told the middle-aged man.

"What on earth is a spytini?" Gina giggled at the name. She pulled a cigarette from the case in her handbag.

"Martin's special martinis," Roger said. He leaned across the table to light Gina's cigarette, then lit one of his own. "A spy who used to dine here loved the martinis, so they changed the name. You'll love them, too," he added.

I'd never had a martini and would have preferred a glass of wine, but decided to give the drink a try. This was a night of firsts and I'd be adventurous. Besides, I had the feeling few people argued with Roger Talbot.

As we waited for our drinks, Roger and Gina talked nonstop about politics while Henry and I quietly observed. I had no idea Gina knew a thing about the war or what was going on in the world. At one point, Henry caught my eye and winked. Not a flirtatious wink, no. It was a wink that said, *You and I are the quiet ones and that's fine. Let these two talk their heads off.* It felt a bit conspiratorial and I smiled back at him, suddenly liking him.

Our pretty spytinis were delivered and Roger raised his in a toast. "To the lovely ladies from Baltimore," he said. "May they thoroughly enjoy their stay in the nation's capital."

"Thank you," Gina said, and we all took a sip.

"Oh *my*," I said, my cheeks on fire, my throat ice cold, and the men laughed. I took another sip, fascinated by the taste. All their eyes were on me. "It tastes like, I don't know . . ." I sipped again, licking my lips. "Salt and spice. And pine trees," I said, and the three of them chuckled.

"I think Tess has a new favorite drink," Gina said.

"Careful now, Tess," Roger said. "When's the last time you had anything to eat?"

"I'm fine," I assured him, and I raised my glass to my lips once more.

It wasn't until Henry lifted his own glass again that I noticed he was missing three fingers on his left hand. The sight was so jarring, I had to quickly turn my head away, my heart giving a double thump in my chest. His thumb and forefinger were intact, but the other three fingers were gone, right down to the smooth knuckles of his hand. What had the poor man been through? Did he lose them as an adult or a child? I'd wondered why he wasn't in the military. Now it was clear, and his sad eyes made more sense to me.

Roger suddenly seemed to notice my own hands and he leaned across the table to grab my left, holding it by the fingers so that my ring sparkled in the overhead light.

"Well, what's this?" he inquired, lifting my hand a couple of inches from the table. "You've got a fella?"

"Yes," I said, gently pulling my hand from his grasp.

"Overseas?" he asked.

I shook my head. "He's a doctor volunteering with the polio epidemic in Chicago." I felt my cheeks color with pride.

"A doctor!" Roger said. "He's a fool to let you go running around unchaperoned, beautiful girl like you. Ain't she a lovely one?" he asked Henry, who nodded.

"They're both lovely," Henry said diplomatically.

"I'd love to see that beautiful hair of yours down," Roger said. "How long is it?"

"Long enough," I said coyly. I took another sip of the spytini and felt the icy heat of the drink spread through my chest and work its way into my arms, all the way to my fingertips. I took one more delicious sip before I set the glass down.

"Her hair is a few inches below her shoulders," Gina answered for me. "And her fiancé loves it, so don't get any ideas. Plus, she's a nurse, so they're a perfect couple."

"Certainly sounds like it," Roger said. "Your fiancé's a lucky man." He leaned away from the table as the waiter set another round of spytinis in front of us even though we hadn't yet finished the first.

"So," I said to the men as the waiter walked away. I wanted to get the topic off myself. "You're both here to negotiate contracts with the government. That must be very challenging."

All three of them looked at me as though I'd spoken a foreign language, but then Henry responded.

"My family's factory in Hickory—that's in North Carolina—has built fine furniture for nearly half a century," he said. "But the last couple of years, we've shifted our efforts to producing material for the war effort." It was lovely, listening to him talk. I'd only heard a Southern accent on the radio. It was much more charming in person.

"What sort of material?" I asked.

"Oh, everything from crates for bombs and ammo to mess tables to aircraft parts," he said, then added wistfully, "and precious little furniture these days, I'm afraid."

"Hickory," Roger said. "Sounds like some little Southern backwater."

Henry only smiled at the insult. "The fastest-growing city in North Carolina," he said. "Population fourteen thousand and counting. We have a lake and a river and the mountains are right nearby. And industry is booming."

"It sounds wonderful," I said, annoyed with Roger. I was glad when the waiter finally returned to take our order. The men ordered filet mignon, but Gina and I both ordered the crab cakes, which got a lot of teasing.

"You can take the girls out of Maryland, but can't take Maryland out of the girls," Roger said.

We had yet another round of spytinis when our meals arrived. And wine appeared, although I couldn't remember any of us ordering the bottle. Conversation between Gina and Roger got a bit louder with each drink consumed, while Henry and I seemed to grow quieter. Gina and Roger argued playfully over sports and the décor in the restaurant and whether or not Baltimore was truly a Southern city. Behind the words, I heard the flirting. Gina was good at it. She'd perfected the coquettish lowering of her eyelids. The smile that lifted only one side of her mouth. The tilt of her head. She was playing with fire, I thought. Henry and I exchanged the occasional commiserative look as we sipped our spytinis. It was odd that in our mutual silence I felt a connection stronger than if we'd been speaking to one another.

I knew I'd had far too much to drink the moment I got to my feet at the end of the evening. I didn't feel ill, just unsteady, my knees soft as butter. The colors of the room swirled in my vision. The bronze of the ceiling seemed to drip down the walls, and I heard myself giggle, the sound coming from far away. When Henry offered me his arm, I took it gratefully.

Our cab driver wouldn't let any of us sit in front with him, so all four of us crammed into the backseat. Gina sat on Roger's lap, and when he rested his hand on the fabric of her dress, high on her thigh, I was relieved to see her calmly brush it away. I sat demurely next to Henry, my own hands folded in my lap, my head in a fog that wasn't the least bit unpleasant. I'd only had too much to drink once before when Vincent and I attended a party where drinks were handed out like candy. I'd been miserable after that party. I'd thrown up more times than I could count and then crawled into bed, the covers over my head to block out the light. Was I drunk now? I didn't think so, but I did feel as though, if someone gave me a good pinch, I wouldn't notice.

I looked down at my folded hands, then over at Henry's lap where his hands lay flat against his dark trousers. Seven fingers. I wanted to touch his wounded hand in sympathy. I hoped he hadn't been a child when it happened. How horrid that would have been! More likely, he'd been an adult using some of the equipment in his factory. Child or adult, though, it must have terrorized him. Whatever had happened to him, he'd clearly overcome it. He'd become not only the head of a business, but a man who could negotiate with Uncle Sam, as well.

He lifted his hand, turned it palm side up, and I knew he'd caught me staring. "It happened when I was six years old," he said, only loud enough for me to hear. "I was playing with my father's tools, which was strictly forbidden. I couldn't reach the table saw very well and this was the result." He rested his hand on his thigh again.

I winced. "I'm sorry," I said.

"Our maid Adora saved my life."

I felt myself tearing up as I imagined the terror of that little boy. "Thank heavens your maid was there," I said.

He touched my arm, lightly, gently, and when he spoke again, I heard the smile in his voice. "I bet you're a very caring nurse," he said.

As soon as we reached the tourist home, Roger and Gina headed upstairs without even wishing Henry and me a good night. They were laughing, and I watched Roger pull his tie free from his neck and give Gina a playful swat on the bottom with it before the two of them disappeared onto the second story. I heard Gina say, "Oh, no you don't," and Roger's muttered reply. There was some muted conversation I couldn't understand. Then Gina laughed.

"Go to your own room," she said. "There's a good boy."

I heard her shut her bedroom door, then Roger's heavy, defeated footsteps in the hall, and I was relieved Gina was taking her flirting no further. She would have hated herself in the morning.

When I brought my attention back to the living room, the pictures on the walls grew fuzzy and I had to grab the edge of an end table to keep from toppling over.

"You're unwell," Henry said, taking my arm to steady me.

"I'm all right," I said. "I'm just not used to . . . to those spytinis." I giggled at the name all over again. "Just a bit dizzy. I think I'll go up."

"Of course," he said.

I started for the stairs, and when I lifted my foot to climb the first step,

I tripped, nearly wrenching my arm as I grabbed the railing to stop my fall.

"Whoa," Henry said, rushing to my side. "Let me help you."

I felt his arm around me, his hand tight against my waist. I didn't object. I needed the help.

We climbed the stairs together and he walked me into my room. I couldn't wait to reach my bed. I meant to simply sit down on the edge of the mattress, but my body had other ideas and I lay back, my head against the pillow, my eyes shut. The room spun, but it was a gentle spinning, almost as if I were in a dream, and when Henry leaned down and rested his lips against mine, I didn't turn my face away. What on earth was I doing?

"I can't." My voice sounded like it came from another room. It echoed in my head. "I'm engaged."

"Yes," he said. "I'm sorry. I didn't mean to . . ." His voice faded away, and once more, I felt his lips press against mine, and the room twirled as if I were on a merry-go-round. Was I pushing him away or pulling him closer? Was his tongue teasing my lips apart or was my mouth inviting him in? Everything was happening so quickly. I knew I should resist him, yet I was not. Instead, I felt my body give in. *Not a big deal,* the voice in my head said. *Let it happen. Get it over with.* I felt the pressure of him pushing inside me. Then a sharp pain. The sensation of sandpaper scraping me raw as his body rocked above me. I both knew and didn't know what was happening and I pushed reality away. I was suddenly back in Gina's bedroom. *You need a little whiskey in your Pepsi for your nerves,* Gina said. I held on to the image of her handing me the glass. Everything was pink. Her pink and white striped curtains and pink ruffled bed skirt. *Ruffles,* I thought, my mind full of cotton. *Ruffles. Gina. Whiskey. Pink.*

He stood up. I opened my eyes to see his unfamiliar features. His brown hair jutted in tufts from his head. What was his name?

"Oh," he said. "You should have told me you were a virgin."

I watched him lift the lamp from the dresser and hold it above the triangle of bedspread between my parted thighs, my nylons down around my calves. I sat up quickly, the walls of the room tumbling around me, and saw the small red stain on the blue bedspread. A sickening dizziness took hold of me and with it a terrible shame.

"Oh no," I said. Bile teased the back of my throat,

He didn't seem to know what to say. "Are you all right?" he asked after a moment. He began pulling on his pants.

I scrambled beneath the covers of the bed, wanting to get away from his sight, my cheeks hot with embarrassment. "I just want to go to sleep," I said, squeezing my eyes shut.

I knew he stood there a while longer, watching me. Maybe trying to come up with more to say. All I could think about was how I would scrub the bedspread the moment I woke up in the morning. I would make it very, very clean.

Although my eyes were closed, I felt sunlight wash over the bed the following morning where I lay curled in a fetal position, tasting bile and alcohol at the back of my throat. My head felt cleaved in two. I didn't dare move or I would be sick.

The night before came back to me in a rush and I kept my eyes squeezed tightly closed in regret. What had I done? I'd made love—no, I'd *had sex*—with a stranger. Oh, to be able to take it all back! The drinking, the allowing him into my room, the kissing, the intimate moments that should never have been given to him.

Vincent. I felt a tear run from my eye across the bridge of my nose. In the hallway outside the room, I heard voices and I lay still, very still, until I heard footsteps descend the stairs and had the sense that I was alone on the second story. Then I let it out. The tears. The regret. The terrible grinding guilt. I lay there for the longest time, waiting for the men downstairs to leave the house. I didn't ever want to see Henry Kraft again.

5

I sat in the pew of the unfamiliar church, waiting my turn in the confession. I knew all the priests at St. Leo's. Worse, they knew me. And of course they knew Vincent. I couldn't possibly tell one of them what I had done. I was having a hard enough time admitting it to myself. So I'd taken the bus to a church on the other side of Baltimore where I knew no one and no one knew me. I'd thought of skipping confession altogether this week, since my shame over what happened in Washington was so great I couldn't bear to speak about it out loud. But then I wouldn't be able to receive communion at mass tomorrow and my mother would know something had happened. She would guess I was carrying a terrible sin inside me, and she would be right.

That night with Henry Kraft was all I could think about, and each time it filled my mind, I felt the same nausea I'd fought all that morning. Gina had thought I was simply hungover as I retched and cried in the bathroom of the tourist home. I'd been quiet on the train back to Baltimore, my head resting against the grimy window, my eyes shut but my mind on fire. Gina asked me point-blank if something had happened with Henry and I lied to her. "Of course not," I said. So now I could add lying to my list of sins. One more thing to confess.

I was in desperate need of absolution as I sat there in the unfamiliar church. When it was my turn, I stepped inside the confessional and knelt down in the darkness. I could hear the muffled words of the priest as he spoke to the person on the other side of his cubicle, his voice nearly drowned out by the pounding of my heart.

The priest slid open the window between us and through the screen I saw his blurry features. Thin gray hair. Glasses. A hand on his chin as he leaned his head close to the screen.

"Bless me, father, for I have sinned," I said. "My last confession was two weeks ago and these are my sins." My voice quivered and I took in a breath. "I argued with my mother over some housework I didn't want to do," I began. "I told a lie to my best friend. And I had premarital sex with someone."

The priest was momentarily silent. "Are you engaged to this someone?" he asked.

"No, father. I'm engaged to someone else." I filled with self-disgust as the words left my mouth.

"This is a very serious sin," the priest said. "To have relations outside of marriage is a mortal sin of the gravest degree. You've compounded that sin by betraying your fiancé."

"Yes." I swallowed. "I know."

"How many times did this happen?"

"Just once."

"Was it with a man or a woman?"

I was shocked by the question. "A man, father." I suddenly remembered the way I'd allowed Henry to kiss me. I squeezed my eyes shut at the memory. "I drank too much and—"

"You drank too much?" His voice had grown loud, almost booming, and I shrank away from the screen. I was certain he could be heard outside the confessional. "That too is a sin," he said. "You must confess *all* your sins. You know that, don't you?"

"Yes, father. I wasn't thinking about—"

"Did you engage in any acts with this man other than intercourse?"

I was confused. "We . . . I went out to dinner with him," I stammered.

"During the sex act," he snapped impatiently. "Did you engage in oral sex or other acts of depravity?"

"No, father."

"You have ruined yourself for your future husband," he said with a disappointed-sounding sigh. "He expected and deserved a pure and innocent bride and you have destroyed that for him."

My eyes burned. "I know, father." *Please,* I thought. *Please stop telling me what I already know. Just give me my penance and let me go.*

"For your penance, spend twenty minutes today at the altar of Our Lady," he said. "Recite ten Hail Marys and six Our Fathers while you think about Our Lady's purity and virtue. Pray the rosary daily for a week and attend mass three times this week. And finally, confess what you've done to your fiancé."

My eyes widened in shock. "Father, I can't do that," I said. "I can do everything else, but not that. It will only hurt him and I don't want to hurt him."

"You should have thought of that before you had relations with another man," he said with unmasked disgust. "You can't go into a marriage with this grievous transgression between you. Your fiancé needs to know the sort of girl you really are before he marries you."

I hung my head, humiliated. I knew that, for the first time in my life, I would not be able to carry out the penance I'd been given. I wouldn't hurt Vincent with this. I knew how he felt about chastity. It would be the end of us. I wished then that I *had* gone to one of the priests at St. Leo's. Someone who knew me well and knew I wasn't the terrible person this priest was making me out to be.

"All right, father," I said, and I wondered if that lie constituted yet another sin.

6

_____

My damp fingers stuck to the pages of the magazine I was pretending to read as I sat in the waiting room of the obstetrician's office. I'd always heard that you couldn't get pregnant the first time you had intercourse. I was a nurse; I knew better. Yet I'd clung to that old wives' tale as I waited anxiously for my period to come. One week passed, then another. And another. I knew fear and stress could affect your cycle. *That's it,* I'd told myself. *It's just stress.* But when a full month had passed and I still had no period, I began to face reality. Still, I waited two more weeks before making this appointment, hope getting in the way of reason.

Vincent now had a paying job in Chicago. He'd called to tell me the news a week after my trip to Washington when my guilt was still fresh and new.

"It's very temporary," he'd been quick to assure me. "Just two months. I haven't started it yet, and I *won't* start at all if you're dead set against me taking it, Tess," he rushed on. "I know I've extended and extended our time apart and you've been a real angel about that, but please listen, sweetheart. It makes so much sense."

The Tess of a few weeks earlier would have been too upset to even respond, but the Tess I'd become post–Henry Kraft felt relief that I had a little more time alone. I wasn't ready to face him.

"What makes sense about it?" I asked.

"It's in a pediatric practice here," he said. "One of the doctors is having shoulder surgery and he'll be out for eight weeks, so I'd be gaining experience in a practice and the money is fantastic. We could—"

"Eight more weeks?" I asked. "That's pretty close to the wedding."

He laughed. "I'll be back months before the wedding," he said. "And they're paying for me to take a train home over Christmas, so you and I will have some time together and we can celebrate your graduation. I can't wait to get my arms around you. I'm sorry I've been gone so long, sweetheart. But absence makes the heart grow fonder, right? I love you more than ever."

My eyes had stung. Vincent was the one person I used to be able to talk to about anything. The person who loved me best, flaws and all. I now possessed one flaw I didn't think he'd ever be able to overlook. "I love you, too," I'd said.

So as I sat there in the obstetrician's office, I counted the days until he would be home for Christmas. Eight. Two days ago, I'd graduated from my nursing program by the skin of my teeth, so self-absorbed because of what was happening inside my body that I barely made it through my clinicals and exams. My breasts had an unfamiliar tenderness to them, and every morning I fought nausea as I ate the oatmeal my mother made for us both. Mom noticed the change in my mood. I knew she thought I was simply depressed about Vincent's continued absence and she tried to cheer me up by talking about the fun we'd all have at Christmastime, his family and mine together for the Feast of the Seven Fishes on Christmas Eve and our big Christmas meal the next day, rituals we'd celebrated with the Russos all my life. All the while, I watched the calendar obsessively, hoping the missed periods were simply an aberration and they would return shortly. I refused to think about what I would do if I were actually pregnant. I refused to give the idea that power over me. Yet part of me knew the truth, so I looked up the number for an out-of-town obstetrician, a Dr. Wilson, and made an appointment with him. And here I sat, turning the pages of a magazine, staring at the articles without seeing them.

A young red-haired nurse appeared in the doorway of the waiting room and looked down at the folder in her hands. "Mrs. DeMello?" she inquired, and I got to my feet. I was wearing my late grandmother's wedding band next to my engagement ring, taped in the back so that it fit. I was a married woman for this appointment.

The nurse led me into an examination room and instructed me to undress and sit on the table. I did as I was told. The room was chilly and I shivered beneath the sheet she provided. I didn't have to wait long before Dr. Wilson burst into the room in a ball of energy.

"Good morning!" he said. He had a jovial look about him. Fat red cheeks, silver glasses, white hair, and a cheerful expression on his face. "Have I seen you before?" he asked, as he lifted the folder from the counter near the sink.

"No, I'm a new patient." I tried to return his smile. "I think I may be pregnant." My thumb rubbed against the tape on the back of my grand-mother's wedding band. "I've missed two periods."

"Well!" he said. "That sounds promising, doesn't it?"

"Yes." I felt the crack in my smile and hoped he didn't notice.

"Not seeing as many pregnancies these days," he said, "what with all the men overseas. Your man is home?"

How I wished my man had been home. None of this ever would have happened.

"Yes," I said. "He has a heart murmur and isn't able to serve, much to his disappointment."

"I'm sure, I'm sure," he said, looking down at the folder. He began asking me the expected questions. The date of my last period, which I knew off the top of my head because I'd been counting and recounting the days since that date for many weeks now. How did I feel? Nauseous in the morning. Were my breasts tender?

"Not too bad," I lied.

He motioned me to lie down and I stared at the ceiling as he examined me. I'd never had an internal examination before and it felt humiliating. I wondered if he could somehow tell that I'd only had intercourse one time. That my so-called married state was a sham.

"Congratulations." He smiled down at me, his fingers inside me. "You are indeed pregnant."

"Don't you have to do the rabbit test . . . the Friedman test . . . to know that for sure?" I asked. I knew that was the definitive test for pregnancy.

"Don't need to," he said. "I've been an obstetrician for thirty years and you can take this diagnosis to the bank. You're definitely pregnant." He rolled his stool away from the examination table. "You and your husband can celebrate tonight," he said. "And you can go ahead and sit up." He lifted my chart from the counter and began to scribble a note. "Are you a smoker?"

he asked, his voice so nonchalant. He had no idea he'd just turned my world upside down.

"Yes," I said, struggling to hold the sheet against my body as I sat up. "Not a lot. About ten cigarettes a day."

"That shouldn't be a problem," he said. He wasn't looking at me as he wrote his notes, and I was glad. I had no idea what he would see in my face as I tried to look like a happy-to-be-pregnant wife. "It's not the time to switch to a pack a day," he said, "but not the time to quit, either." He smiled at me, his pudgy red cheeks lifting his glasses a bit from his nose. "That would wreak havoc on your nerves and turn you into the sort of girl your husband wouldn't want to be around, right?"

"Right." I attempted to smile.

"Go easy on salty foods and nibble some crackers and ginger ale in the morning before you get out of bed. The nausea will pass soon." He got to his feet. "And make an appointment with me for a month," he added before leaving the room.

The door shut behind him and I didn't budge from the examining table. I clutched the sheet to my body, torn between self-pity and self-hatred. Seven days until Vincent was home for Christmas. What was I going to do?

7

The day before Christmas, I rode with Mimi and Pop to Baltimore's Penn Station to meet Vincent's train from Chicago. Mimi could barely contain her excitement. "This is the longest I've ever been apart from my son," she said, turning in the front seat to look at me. "I know you must be just as excited as I am," she said.

"I am." I smiled. Excited and terrified. Vincent would be home for three days and three nights. He'd expected it would be four days and four nights, but the trains were packed and he had been lucky to get a reservation at all. I was personally glad he'd only have three days with us. I'd wanted his homecoming for so long, but now that it was finally here, I simply didn't know how I was going to manage it. The secret between us was enormous and insurmountable. How could I possibly act like my usual self around him? How could I think about a wedding when it now seemed like an impossibility? Sometimes I wondered if it was all a crazy mistake. Maybe I wasn't pregnant at all. My stomach was still as flat as it had ever been, and the queasiness I'd experienced in the mornings had lessened dramatically in the past week. Maybe all the symptoms had been the product of anxiety. The doctor had never done the Friedman test. How could he know I was pregnant without it? Any day now, my period would show up and the last couple of months would be a bad dream. That was my fervent prayer.

Penn Station bustled with holiday travelers, many of them in uniform, as we stood on the platform, waiting and watching for Vincent to arrive.

"Oh there he is!" Mimi grabbed my arm, hopping up and down, waving to her son as he stepped from the train a good distance ahead of us. Mimi was fifty years old, but at that minute, she seemed more like an excited little girl than a middle-aged woman. I watched Vincent stride toward us carrying his suitcase, a shopping bag looped over his other arm. He wore an unfamiliar camel-hair coat, and it struck me that he'd left Baltimore in late summer and now it was winter. He would have had to buy a whole winter wardrobe, clothing I'd never seen before. He smiled, quickening his pace to get to us. My heart contracted in my chest and I battled tears. I loved him so much.

Mimi got his first hug and Pop received a handshake and a warm pat on the shoulder, but Vincent's gaze was on me the whole time he embraced his parents, his smile broad. He had never looked more handsome to me, and when he wrapped his arms around me and whispered in my ear, "How's my beautiful nurse?", I rested my head on his shoulder and cried. I'd missed the solid feel of him beneath my arms. I'd missed the woody scent of his aftershave. The slightly rough skin of his cheek against my forehead. He rocked me a little as we stood there. "Shh, sweetheart," he said, holding me tight. "I'm here. I love you."

I couldn't find my voice. I clutched his arm as the four of us walked through the train station and out to the parking lot. In the backseat of the car, I sat close to him, my head against the shoulder of his camel-hair coat, my arm across his body as if I were afraid he might rise out of the car and disappear again if I didn't hold him down. I dared to feel happy. I was right where I wanted to be. Where I'd always wanted to be.

I was quiet during the nonstop conversation between Vincent and his parents. He told us he'd had to stand for ten of the twenty hours on the train. He tightened his arm around me as he spoke. "It was worth every minute," he said, pressing his lips to my temple.

He and his parents talked about their Christmas tree, the best they'd ever had, Mimi said, but she and Pop were waiting for Vincent to put the star on top as he did every year. My mother was preparing the Feast of the Seven Fishes that afternoon. Although she never made more than five fish dishes, we still called the Italian meal by its customary name. For our Christmas dinner tomorrow, Mimi would make her famous roasted pork loin and antipasto platter.

"But only fruit for dessert this year, Vinnie, what with rationing," she said. "We have enough sugar for your coffee, but that's about all."

I only half listened to her chatter, too preoccupied with my own dilemma to really care about Christmas dinner.

In the Russos' house, Vincent set the star on the top of their tree before he even took off his coat, much to Mimi's delight. Then he lifted his suitcase in one hand, took my hand with the other, and we walked together up the stairs to his bedroom. The small room was still filled with pictures and memorabilia—photographs and ticket stubs and restaurant matchbooks—from our years together and I looked at them all with a mounting sense of loss. Vincent closed the door and turned to face me, that smile of his making me weak with desire for him. He unbuttoned my coat, then slipped his hands inside to pull me close. Silently, I breathed him in. I memorized the feeling of being this close to him. This is what I was going to lose because of the baby. Because of my foolishness. All I would have left was the memory of this closeness. The memory of loving him.

"This feels so good," he said after a moment.

"Yes," I agreed. He lifted my chin to kiss me. It was a tender kiss, his lips warm and soft and so familiar, and when I drew away, I discovered I couldn't look him in the eye. "Should we unpack?" I asked, turning toward his suitcase.

He looked at the suitcase himself. "Let's just leave it for now," he said. "Is it too cold for a walk to St. Leo's?"

I smiled, my gaze darting over his, coming to land somewhere in middle of the room. "Never too cold for that," I said.

Our breath formed puffy clouds as we walked to St. Leo's. We held gloved hands, not saying much, eager to get to the church.

We sat in our usual back pew, away from the few people who came and went in the hushed silence. We kept our coats on—it was never warm in St. Leo's—but we took off our gloves to hold hands.

"You're very quiet, Tess," he said. "You usually can't stop talking when we see each other after an absence."

"When have we ever had an absence?" I asked. "I think the longest we've ever been apart were those ten days you spent with your New York cousins when you were twenty years old."

"True," he said. "But what I mean is, even when we've been apart for a day or two . . . or even a few hours . . . you always have plenty to say. Plenty to tell me. All the minutiae of your day." He let out a quiet, teasing chuckle. "I expected you to flood me with information the moment I got off the train."

I sighed. "After all this time apart, maybe there's just too much information," I said. "I don't know where to begin."

"Well, give it a try," he said. "When do you have to take your licensing exam for your RN?"

"March," I said. How I would study for that exam when I had so much else on my mind, I didn't know.

"And how are the wedding plans coming along?" he asked. "Did you decide on a dress yet?"

I didn't think he really cared which dress I selected. He was just trying to get me to talk.

"Not yet," I said. "There's still time. Everything else is in place." Everything, I thought, except the wedding itself. I could think of no way Vincent and I could possibly get married.

"When do the invitations go out?"

"Not until March," I said. My chest contracted. I didn't see how those invitations could ever go out.

He was quiet. After a moment, he put his arm around me. "I'm worried about you, sweetheart," he said. "When we talked on the phone the last couple of times, and now in person . . . you seem withdrawn. I think you're angry with me. Maybe you think I took advantage of your good nature. You've been extremely patient and a big support to me. I know it's been hard on you. If you're angry, just tell me. Yell or whatever you need to do to clear the air. I wouldn't blame—"

"I'm not angry. I'm just . . ." I began to cry softly and he wrapped both his arms around me. Rocked me gently like a child. "I'm just tired and I missed you and it's been hard not having you here," I said.

"I know," he said. "But only a couple more weeks till the doctor I'm covering for is back and then I'm home for good." He gave me a squeeze. "You really have been strong through all this, Tess," he said, "and I appreciate it. And soon, you and I will stand up at that altar"—he pointed toward the front of St. Leo's—"and say 'I do' and have the rest of our lives together."

I pictured the scene at the altar. Standing next to him in my white dress. Maybe the one with the rosettes that my mother loved. Gina by my side.

And I suddenly thought of a way to make marrying him a reality. He was home for three days and three nights. I could sleep with him. I knew that went against everything either of us believed in, and yet . . . I could play on his guilt. Tell him how hard it had been for me, being without him. How desperately I needed him. I could pass this baby off as his. But even as the thought came to me, I knew I couldn't do it, and the fantasy of our wedding slipped away. I couldn't go into our marriage with a lie.

I couldn't go into our marriage at all.

8

I clutched Gina's hand in the back of the taxi as we rode through an unfamiliar Baltimore neighborhood. It was January third and the Christmas decorations that hung in the air above the street looked tired. The chilly gray day didn't help. I felt sick with nerves. I only had to get through this day, I told myself, and I could get my life back on track. If I made it through today, wedding invitations would go out as planned in March. I'd buy the dress with the rosettes. Vincent and I would have a future together, the future we'd always planned for. As long as I made it through the horror of today.

The few days with Vincent had not gone well. I hadn't been able to feign joy over his homecoming and I finally pleaded a headache that simply wouldn't go away. I was sure our parents talked to each other in hushed, worried voices, wondering what was wrong with me, and Vincent sat on the edge of my bed, gently pressing a cool washcloth to my forehead or rubbing my temples. I didn't even go with Mimi and Pop to take him back to the train station. By that time, though, I'd made up my mind. I knew what I had to do. It was a terrible, unthinkable sin but it seemed like the only way out of the dilemma I was in.

"It's going to be all right," Gina whispered to me now as she squeezed my hand in the back of the taxi. Her palm was as damp with sweat as my own. "It'll all be over soon. A bad memory."

I swallowed hard. Gina had been shocked when I finally got up the nerve to tell her I was pregnant.

"Did he rape you?" she'd asked in a horrified whisper. She couldn't believe I would sleep with a stranger after saving myself for my wedding night all these years.

I shook my head. "I was . . . intoxicated," I said. "But he didn't force me." I wished I could blame Henry Kraft for what had happened. I only blamed myself.

"You've got to get rid of it," Gina'd said. We'd been sitting in her bedroom, our voices quiet because her mother was down the hall in the living room. I could barely hold my emotions together.

"Get *rid* of it?" I'd said, shocked. "I can't believe you'd even suggest that, Gina. It's a sin, not to mention it's illegal."

"It's illegal but not impossible," she said. "This girl I sort of know did it. She said it wasn't so bad. I can find out where you can go to have it done." She leaned across the space between her twin beds to look hard into my eyes. "Do you really have a choice?" she asked.

"I can't do that," I said. Yet what option did I have? I had no husband. The man I was engaged to—kindhearted and loving though he may have been—would never marry me if he knew I was pregnant with another man's child. There was no way I could tell him what I'd done. It would kill him.

"I think I'll have to go to one of those homes where you have your baby and put it up for adoption," I said. "Maybe the church can help me find a home like that? Everything would be hush-hush, and my baby would go to a good family. Have a good life." My own well-planned good life would be over, but at least I would have done the right thing by my baby.

Gina looked horrified. "Those places are terrible," she said. "They'll treat you like trash and you'll never know what they really did with your baby. Where they really put it. And what will you tell Vincent? If you have an abortion, you get to move on with your life."

"It's wrong," I argued.

"Why are you making this so hard on yourself, honey?" Gina said. "Right now, what you have inside of you is a fetus. Not a baby. It won't be a baby for months and months."

I wished I could see things as simply as Gina. We'd been raised in the same church. Made our first communions together. Learned about sin and heaven and hell from the same nuns. Yet somehow, with Gina it never took and she was freer for it. Even with the baby gone, I knew I would never feel free of what I'd done. It was the one thing I would never be able to admit to in confession. I'd carry it with me forever, but at least I could marry the man I loved. We would have other children. *Our* children.

Gina was able to get the details from Kathy, the girl she "sort of" knew who'd had the abortion, and she made the arrangements for me, even giving me one hundred of the exorbitant two-hundred-dollar fee. "Will it hurt?" I'd asked her.

"Kathy didn't say," Gina'd said. "Probably just cramping, but it will be worth it. You'll have one bad day and then you'll be free for the rest of your life."

Now, Gina leaned forward to instruct the taxi driver. "I think you make a right here," she said. We turned off the street with the Christmas decorations onto a narrow road lined with dark, three-story brick buildings. Apartments, maybe? Offices? I had no idea. I tried not to notice their ramshackle condition. The sagging shutters. The trash in the street.

"Stop here," Gina said suddenly. "That must be him."

A man stood on the corner near a black sedan. He reminded me of the pictures I'd seen of my grandfather. Iron-gray hair. Rotund build beneath a heavy black coat. The slightest hint of a hunchback. He wore thick glasses in wire-rimmed frames. I knew what would happen now. Kathy had given Gina the details. The man would drive us to the house where the abortion would take place. "His sister does it," Gina had told me. "Kathy said she's really nice."

"Is his sister a doctor?" I'd asked.

"I don't think so, but she has more experience than most doctors," Gina'd reassured me.

I paid the taxi driver, slipped on my gloves, and we got out, shivering in the chill, damp air as we approached the man.

"Which one of you is the girl?" he asked. "Only the girl can come with me."

I grabbed Gina's arm, my grip tight through her coat.

"I have to come with her," Gina said calmly. She patted my gloved hand. "I promised."

"I only have the one blindfold, so only one of you can come," he said.

"Blindfold?" I looked at Gina. I wished our taxi hadn't already driven off. I wanted to get back into it and ride away from this neighborhood.

"It's all right," Gina reassured me, but there was a shiver in her voice. "We can use something as a blindfold for me," she said to the man. "My scarf?" She started to unknot the scarf at her throat.

"No, no." He waved an arm through the air. "Only the girl can come."

I looked at Gina in a panic. "She has to come with me!" I said.

"Keep your voice down," the man snarled, although we were the only people on this sad-looking street.

Gina took my arm. "Look at me," she demanded, and I tried to focus on her blue eyes. "It's going to be fine." She glanced around us at the decrepit old buildings. "I'll wait for you right here and we'll find a cab to take us home."

"You can't wait here," I said. "This is a terrible area."

"Look." The man's eyes were buggy, magnified by his thick glasses. "Do you want to do this or not?"

"I'll wait on this stoop." Gina motioned toward the dirty gray granite stoop of the building behind us. "I have a book in my handbag to read. I'll be fine. I'll be right here when you get back."

The man frowned at Gina, his bushy gray eyebrows knitting together. "Anyone ask you what you're doing waiting here, you make something up, all right?"

"Of course." She smiled, but the quivery tone was back in her voice and that scared me. I was completely dependent on Gina's calm.

The man looked at me. "You got the money?" he asked.

I nodded.

"Get in, then." He strode toward the sedan and opened the passenger door for me.

I mustered all my courage and slid into the seat. The car smelled of tobacco and something else. Some food smell I couldn't place but that turned my stomach. He got into the driver's seat and handed me a black blindfold. "Put this on," he said, "but give me the money first."

I fumbled in my handbag for the ten twenty-dollar bills, my fingers trembling, and handed them to him.

He counted them, folded the bills in half and stuck them in his inside coat pocket. He watched as I wordlessly put on the blindfold. I heard him start the car and we were off.

"Hello, dear." An old woman greeted me with a smile as I took off the blindfold. I'd been led up a short flight of stairs and now saw that we were in the tiny foyer of a house or apartment building. I couldn't be sure, since I hadn't been able to see the building from the outside. All I knew was that my teeth were chattering and my knees trembled. The woman reached out to hold my gloved hands. "Tess, is it?" she asked.

I nodded. She looked like someone's grandmother, her dull gray hair pulled back in a bun. Her legs were as thick as posts and her black shoes big and solid. She wore a bibbed pink floral apron over her blue dress as though she was about to bake a batch of cookies. I felt both reassured by her kind manner as well as anxious, because she looked like the last person on earth who could perform a medical procedure.

"I'll be working in the shed," the man said, and he disappeared down a long hallway carpeted with a ratty-looking brown rug.

"I'm Edna," the woman said. I wondered if that was her real name. "Let me take your coat."

I slipped off my coat and scarf, my gloves and hat. She took everything from me, laying it all on top of a large wooden chair in the corner.

"Let's go in here." She gestured toward a room off the foyer and I followed her in. A heavy wooden table stood in the middle of the room covered with a sheet. A pillow rested on one end of the table, and a kitchen chair was set on the floor at the opposite end. The carved wooden table legs exposed beneath the sheet looked somehow obscene. On a wheeled tray next to the table lay a basin, a speculum, a long, thin metal rod, and a few other items I didn't recognize. I'd heard about botched abortions done with coat hangers and was relieved that none were in sight.

"Take off your panties," Edna said. "You can just unhook your stockings."

"No coat hanger." I smiled nervously, gesturing toward the wheeled tray.

"Oh, good heavens, no," she said. "I've found this works perfectly." She picked up the metal rod. "A bicycle spoke," she said. "Does the job every time."

A bicycle spoke. Good Lord. Had it been sterilized since the last time it was used? Shivering, I slipped off my shoes and panties, and she helped me climb onto the table, rock hard beneath the sheet. I tried to ignore the small brown stain on the pillowcase as I lay back on the table. It was cool in the room and my body trembled almost spasmodically.

"This will be over in a jiffy," Edna said. "Now open your legs for me." She sat down at the foot of the table as I bent my knees and spread my legs, my eyes on the stained plaster of the ceiling.

"There's a good girl," Edna said. "Now hold very still."

I held my breath, waiting for the cramping to begin. On the plaster ceiling, as if by magic, I saw the image of my tiny, helpless, baby. He—I was certain it was a boy—was nestled inside my body—the body that was supposed to protect it and nurture it, not allow it to be pierced by a bicycle spoke. Gasping, I sat up quickly, pulling away from Edna and her tools. She was wide-eyed, her mouth a small, surprised O.

"I haven't even touched you yet," she said.

"I can't do this," I said, my hand on my flat belly. "I just can't!" I was suddenly crying.

Edna stood up with a heavy sigh. "Oh, for pity's sake," she said. "You won't get your money back, you know." Her sweet grandmotherly demeanor had suddenly disappeared.

"I don't care." I didn't look at her as I climbed awkwardly from the table, my stomach turning at the sight of the basin. The spoke. How could I have thought I could go through with this? "I can't do it." In spite of the fact that I knew I was ruining my life for good, forever, I felt weak with relief. Yes, this spelled the end of my engagement. Yes, it was the end of my future with Vincent. But I had not harmed my child.

Edna stared at me as I looked around the room, unable to remember where I'd put my panties. "Meet me in the foyer when you're dressed," she said after a moment.

I found my panties beneath the table and pulled them on. I could hear Edna talking to the driver—most likely her brother—but couldn't make out their words. Both of them met me in the foyer.

"You can find your own way back to your friend," the man said. He was drinking a beer.

"You have my money," I said, lifting my coat from the chair in the corner and putting it on. I'd stopped shaking. Stopped crying. I felt suddenly strong. "You owe me a ride back," I said to him.

"Take her," Edna said.

With a sour look, he handed her his beer, opened a closet near the front door, and grudgingly got into his coat.

Once settled in the passenger seat of the car, I slipped my hand inside my coat to rest on my belly. I would not have this baby only for it to be put up for adoption. This was *my* child. My son or daughter. I'd saved its life and I was going to be with it, always. I would have to move away from Baltimore. Someplace where no one knew me. Someplace where I wouldn't be the object of scorn and shame or have to worry about bumping into Vincent or his family. I would start a fresh life. I would tell people my husband was overseas. No one would be any the wiser. The only thing standing in my way was my lack of money. I had a hundred and seventy dollars in my bank account that I'd earned when I'd worked at the grocer's to make money for school. Hardly enough to start a new life.

I thought of Henry Kraft and his well-tailored suit. He owned a furniture factory and had government contracts. He would have to give me money. I hoped it would be out of a sense of responsibility, but at that moment, when I felt I could move heaven and earth to protect the life inside me, I was not above threatening to tell everyone he knew that he'd impregnated me and then left me high and dry. I would do whatever it took to protect my baby.

Henry Kraft. I whispered the name to myself. *Hickory, North Carolina.* Wherever that was.

9

The grueling journey from Baltimore to Hickory involved three packed trains and one miserable night. I sat up all that night, my head knocking against the window each time I drifted into an uneasy sleep. At least I'd had a seat. A few soldiers had to stand the entire time.

The third train, a short trip from Salisbury to Hickory, was the worst. I was beyond exhaustion by that point. The heat wasn't working properly and I couldn't stop shivering as my anxiety mounted with each passing mile. In spite of the chill, my palms were sweating and the hankie I clutched for most of the trip was damp. I'd told my mother I was visiting a friend from nursing school who was ill. She'd asked many questions about my friend, expressing concern, and my lies mounted as I invented this girl and her troubles. I couldn't look my mother in the eye as I talked to her. I didn't like the dishonest, calculating person I'd become.

Gina thought I'd lost my mind. She cried when I told her my plan. "You're going to move away?" she asked, incredulous. "Please don't! I don't think I can stand it if both you and Mac are gone." She promised me she wouldn't breathe a word about my plan, though, and even offered to skip work and go with me to Hickory. I told her no. This was something I needed to do on my own.

Although I'd brought a book with me to study for my licensing exam while on the trains, I never even cracked it open. Instead, I rehearsed what I would say to Henry Kraft, smoking the occasional cigarette to calm my nerves. I had no intention of milking Henry dry. I only wanted enough money to support myself and a child in a modest lifestyle. I worried he might react with anger instead of civility or that he might not believe that the baby was his. I'd left my engagement ring in my top dresser drawer, hoping Henry wouldn't recall that I was engaged. I didn't want him to guess the baby might be Vincent's. I couldn't turn off my worries and they mounted steadily as the third train traveled through North Carolina and I smoked the last of my cigarettes.

It wasn't until we were close to Hickory that I began to think about how I would find Henry Kraft's furniture factory. I didn't know the name of it. I knew Hickory was a small town, though. I would also have to find a place to spend the night. The first train I could take out of Hickory wasn't until the following afternoon.

When I got off the train with my handbag and small suitcase, my legs were wobbly from nerves and exhaustion. The cold air was numbing and I wished I had a more substantial hat than my little tricorner beret. The wind cut through my coat and I tugged it tighter around me as I walked out to the curb where a cab was parked. The driver waved me over as if he'd been expecting me.

"Lookin' for a ride, young lady?" he asked as I walked toward him. He reminded me of the abortionist's brother, round and bespectacled. I didn't want to remember that man or anything else about that day. It was behind me. I needed to move on.

"Well, I have to figure out where I'm going first," I said, offering him a tired smile. "Is there a phone booth around here?"

"Ain't a big town," he said. "What are you lookin' for?"

"A furniture factory."

"We got plenty of them," he said. "Hickory Chair. Kraft Furniture."

"That one!" I said. "Kraft Furniture. Can you take me there?"

"Ain't far." He looked me up and down. "You look like you need to go to a hotel first, though, miss. With that suitcase and all? Want me to take you to one?"

"No, thank you. I need to see someone who works at the factory first."

"Ain't none of my business," he said with a shrug. He took the suitcase from me and put it in the taxi's trunk and I got into the backseat.

We rode along the railroad tracks for a while before turning onto a side street. After a short distance, I saw a long, two-story redbrick building that took up at least half a block. Tall white letters painted above the front door read KRAFT FINE FURNITURE. I drew in a long breath, trying to get my courage up. The driver parked in front of the building and I fumbled with my purse as he lifted my suitcase from the trunk. I handed him a bill, thanked him, and headed toward the front door of the building. *This is really happening,* I told myself, but my idea suddenly seemed poorly thought out. Henry Kraft could be up in Washington right now, for all I knew. He could be anywhere other than in this building.

I walked through the main entrance and found myself in a small, square foyer. The walls were covered with framed articles about the history of Kraft Furniture, but I barely noticed them. The black-and-white tiles on the floor blurred in my sleep-deprived eyes, and although the foyer was separated from the rest of the building by a set of double doors, a strong chemical smell nearly overwhelmed me. Varnish, maybe. Paint. Glue. Somewhere beyond those doors, machinery whirred and thumped and clicked. I wondered how the workers stood the assault on all their senses.

There was no directory on the wall, but as I took a step toward the double doors, a woman stepped through them. She wore a hairnet and a leather apron and she looked surprised to see me. I suppose I looked completely out of place in my coat, hat, and gloves, carrying a suitcase.

"Can I help you?" she asked.

"Yes." I smiled. "Can you tell me where I can find Henry Kraft?"

"Upstairs." She pointed to a door I hadn't noticed until that moment. "His office is at the top of the stairs," she said. "Can't miss it."

I thanked her and opened the door to the stairwell. At the top of the stairs, I found another set of double doors. I pushed one of them open and saw a door directly in front of me, the name HENRY KRAFT painted on the wood. The sounds of the factory were muted up here, no more than a distant hum. I walked up to the door and could hear laughter coming from inside the room. Taking off my gloves, I lifted my hand to knock.

"Yes?" a voice prompted.

Tentatively, I pulled the door open and poked my head inside. Henry Kraft sat behind a large, elaborately carved desk, leaning back in his chair. Smoke rose from the pipe on his desk and the scent of tobacco seemed to erase all chemical smells from the air. A light-skinned colored man sat in a chair opposite Henry, holding a broom upright at his side. He'd been smiling, I could tell. Both men still had laughter in their eyes. The colored man got to his feet when I entered, though Henry remained seated.

"Yes?" Henry said again. He glanced at my suitcase, then back at my face. I could tell he didn't recognize me.

"I wondered if I might speak with you?" I asked.

"And you're . . . ?"

"Tess DeMello," I said.

I saw the recognition flash across his face. He stood up, his expression giving nothing away to the other man, who hadn't budged from his stance by the chair.

"Come in." He motioned me toward the desk, then turned to the colored man. "That will be all, Zeke," he said.

The man began walking toward the door. "Miss," he said, tipping an invisible hat to me as he passed. He had a limp, I noticed, and remarkably long, thick black lashes above his dark eyes.

"Shut the door on your way out," Henry said to him. His gaze never left my face. I could tell he was not pleased to see me. His outside world was suddenly colliding with his home turf.

"I'm sorry to just barge in this way," I said.

"Don't you live in Baltimore?" he asked, and I nodded. At least he remembered that much about me. "How did you get here?"

"I took the train," I said. "I needed to talk to you and it was something I didn't want to discuss over the phone."

His eyebrows shot up for a second before falling into a frown. "Oh no," he said, and I knew he already understood the purpose of my visit. "You're . . . ?"

I nodded and lowered my voice on the chance someone might be listening. "About two and a half months," I said.

For a charged moment, he said nothing and I stood up straighter. I would not let him wheedle his way out of his responsibility. Finally, he motioned toward the chair the other man had vacated. "Please," he said. "Sit down. You look exhausted. That's a terrible train ride. You had a roomette, I hope?"

"No, unfortunately," I said. I could barely afford the train ticket, much less the cost of a roomette. I put down my suitcase and crossed the room to sit on the very edge of the chair. I could imagine how I looked. The little bit of makeup I'd put on the day before had to have worn off by now. My hair probably looked a sight beneath my hat and I surely had bags under my eyes. "I didn't sleep well on the train," I said. It was warm in the room and I was beginning to perspire beneath my coat. I folded my hands in my lap. "I don't want to make things difficult for you," I said. "I only—"

He held up a hand to stop me, then sat down and pulled open one of the top drawers of his beautiful desk. "I'll give you a check for you to have it taken care of," he said, pulling out a checkbook.

I was taken aback. "I've decided to have it," I said quickly. Firmly. "The baby. I tried, but I couldn't go through with . . . getting rid of it."

His face clouded, his hand frozen on the checkbook. "What do you want from me, then?"

I licked my lips, preparing my speech. "I'll have to move away from my . . . from where I live. I can't have a baby out of wedlock where everyone knows me. I thought I'd move somewhere else and say my husband is in the army. But I need money to be able to do that. I'm sorry to ask." I cringed at my apologetic tone. I hadn't meant to grovel. This situation wasn't entirely my fault. "It's a terrible dilemma, but—"

"How much do you think you'll need?" He interrupted again. He wanted to be done with me, I could tell. He was not a patient man, but it was clear he would help me, if only to shut me up. To get me out of his office. Out of his life.

"I don't know, exactly," I said. "Enough to rent an apartment and support myself and a baby until I can find work, I guess. I have a nursing degree, but I probably won't be able to work until he or she's old enough to leave with a sitter. And then I'll need to pay the sitter. And of course I'll need to be able to pay for—"

"Where will you live?" he asked. "Geographically?"

I imagined he was worried I'd want to live close to him. "I haven't figured that out yet," I said. "Probably in Maryland, but far from Baltimore." How would I ever leave my mother? I was going to break her heart, in so many ways.

"Are you sure the baby is mine?" he asked. "I remember your ring." He looked at my bare hand. "You were engaged, weren't you?"

"My fiancé and I never had . . ." My cheeks burned. "You were the only one." I wondered if he remembered that small, bright red stain on the bedspread.

"Have you told him?"

I shook my head. "He would never understand. I'll need to break off our engagement." I was amazed my voice didn't crack. If Henry had any idea what that meant—my life as I knew it coming to an abrupt, sad end—he gave no indication.

"Let me think about this," he said. "I'll help, of course," he reassured me quickly, then lowered his voice. "I regret that foolish night more than you could possibly know," he said. "I'm . . . ashamed of it. We'd both had far too much to drink. I should never have let it happen."

I was surprised—touched, actually—that he took responsibility for that night, and relief washed over me. He wasn't going to fight me about my plan for the baby. My need for help.

"But I have to think of the best way to arrange the money," he continued. "To figure out the amount you'll need. Are you staying in town?"

The tension in my body was slipping away. "I need to find a hotel," I said. "Just for tonight. I have to get back to Baltimore."

"Go to the Hotel Hickory," he said, reaching for the phone. "I'll call you a cab. The hotel's back in town." He pointed to my left. "You should be able to get a room now that the holidays are over. If they give you a hard time, say Hank Kraft sent you." He looked out the window for a moment and I saw those downturned eyes that had struck me when we first met, the eyes that gave him a sad look despite his handsome features. "Actually," he said, "better not use my name, all right?" He gave me a quick, anxious smile, and for the first time I saw his nerves betray him.

He spoke into the phone, arranging the cab, then got to his feet. "I'll call you at the hotel," he said. "Tonight, or more likely in the morning. Stay by the phone if you can."

I nodded. "Thank you, Mr. Kraft," I said, getting wearily to my feet. He seemed like a stranger to me. It was nearly impossible for me to believe I'd been intimate with him.

I waited only a minute or two outside the building for the cab to arrive. Thank God. It was so cold and I needed to lie down. I was glad when the driver turned out to be the quiet type. I didn't have the strength for conversation.

We pulled up outside the tall, handsome redbrick hotel. The driver carried my suitcase inside for me, and I was given a room without any questions being asked. It was two in the afternoon and the exhaustion caught up with me as I lifted my suitcase onto the dresser in my room. I undressed down to my slip, then crawled into the bed, my eyes on the phone on the night table. What if I didn't hear from him? What if he'd told me he would help with no intention of doing so? But I knew where he was. I wouldn't leave without some money in hand. I shut my eyes and was asleep within seconds.

10

At nine the following morning, the hotel manager called to tell me "Hank Kraft" was waiting for me in the lobby. "He says to bring your coat," he said.

Henry wore no smile when I came into the lobby in my coat and gloves, my handbag over my arm. No greeting at all. Instead he took my elbow and pointed me toward the door.

"We can't talk here," he whispered. He led me out the front door and onto the bustling street, where he pointed to a butter-yellow Cadillac parked at the curb. It was without a doubt the prettiest car I'd ever seen. He opened the passenger side door for me and I slid in. The car smelled of his delicious pipe tobacco and I breathed in the comforting scent. Henry said nothing as he got into the driver's seat, and he remained silent as he drove a couple of blocks from the hotel. Then he turned onto a side street and pulled to the curb.

"Are you cold?" he asked, his hand on the key. "I can leave the heater going."

"Thank you," I said. I folded my gloved hands in my lap, apprehensively waiting for his decision.

He studied my face for a moment, long enough to make me squirm under his scrutiny. "I believe we should get married," he said finally.

I stared at him in shock. "Get married!" I said. "We don't even know each other."

"Well, we knew each other well enough to . . ." He motioned toward my stomach.

"But that was—"

"I thought about it all night long," he interrupted. "I don't want you going off to who-knows-where with my son or daughter. Someday you'd meet and marry another man, and I don't want that man raising my child. This child"—he motioned to my belly again—"is my rightful heir. I can afford to take care of you both. Very well." He looked hard at me as if to be sure I understood exactly how well my baby and I would be able to live. "You'll have no worries. You'll never have to work. I recently bought land near the house I grew up in, and my architect has finished drawing up plans for a house of my own. Until that house is completed, we'd have to live in my family home with my mother and sister, but—"

"Henry," I said, shaking my head in astonishment. "That's so kind of you, but it's . . . it's unrealistic."

"*Your* plan is unrealistic," he argued. "Moving somewhere where you don't know a soul? Inventing a husband in the military, a husband who will never come home? You'll be living a lie for the rest of your life. How realistic would that be?"

"Don't you already have someone special?" I asked. He was good-looking. Clearly wealthy. He obviously had power and prominence in this town. I was—and we both had to know this—far beneath him when it came to social status.

"No one special," he said, so sharply that I knew there was a story there. A story he did not want to tell.

He reached into the pocket of his tweed coat and withdrew a small black box. Holding it in front of me, he opened it. The sunlight caught the glitter of the largest diamond I'd ever seen. I sucked in my breath.

"You already bought a ring?" I was shocked.

"Please marry me, Tess," he said. "Let's raise our son or daughter together."

I was too stunned to respond. This was crazy! Yet, as I sat riveted by the ring, I thought of Mimi and Pop. Their marriage had been arranged. They hadn't even met one another until a month before the wedding when Mimi was introduced to Pop at a family gathering, knowing he was to be her husband whether she liked him or not. And look at them now. One of the most loving couples I'd ever known. They'd started out as strangers but the love grew between them.

Vincent's smile slipped into my mind and I pushed it out. I couldn't afford to let him into my thoughts right now. There was no hope there, and thinking of him would only derail the future I needed to make for myself and my baby.

I looked into Henry's blue eyes. There was hope in them. How many men would respond this way, wanting to take responsibility for their mistake and make things right? Henry wanted our child in his life. He wanted *me* in his life. This was more than a way out, I thought. It felt like an extraordinary sign from God.

"Yes." I let a smile come to my lips. "Yes. I'll marry you."

11

We spent the rest of the day making plans in his office. Henry had locked the office door, opening it only to answer questions from a few employees and to speak briefly to the custodian, that colored man Zeke, who seemed overly interested in my presence. Henry sat behind his desk while I perched on the hard wooden chair, making the whole exchange feel like a business transaction. Which I supposed, in reality, it was.

"We need to get married quickly," he said, "if we hope to convince people that the baby was conceived after our marriage. It's unlikely anyone will believe us, but at least we can put on a front," he added with a smile I could only interpret as sheepish.

I nodded, ignoring the feeling of being swept into something outside my control. He was right. If we were going to do this, we needed to do it fast.

"Are you sure you don't want to wear the ring?" he asked.

I shook my head, looking down at my bare ring finger. There was a slight pale strip of skin where Vincent's ring had sat for so long. I couldn't replace it with this new ring from Henry. Not yet. I would have felt as though I were stealing it. Sitting there, I thought about the strangeness of our plan. He seemed almost happy that I'd shown up in his life. He was becoming more attractive to me every minute, especially when he smiled, lifting the downcast look of his eyes. Certainly he didn't possess Vincent's head-turning good looks, but he had beautiful, symmetrical features and a gentle countenance. And yet there was no woman in his life?

Perhaps he'd been hurt in love. The way I was about to hurt Vincent. My stomach twisted at the thought.

"I'll pick up wedding bands for us both," he said, then added with a chuckle, "Obviously, I'll have to wear mine on my right hand." He held up his two-fingered left hand.

I smiled, uncertain quite how to respond to his openness about his missing fingers.

"I'll arrange a roomette for you on the train back to Baltimore," he said, "and another when it's time for you to return, which I hope will be very soon."

"Thank you," I said. A roomette would make the long hours on the train more bearable.

"We'll need to get blood tests," he said, "so do that as soon as you can. Hopefully we can have this all sorted out by next week. Give me your phone number and I'll call with the details."

I felt momentarily overwhelmed. He was a take-charge man, no doubt about it, and protective to boot. Already he was taking my needs into account and I didn't know whether to be pleased or resentful that he thought I needed to be coddled. I remembered the licensing exam I'd been studying for. I'd need to look into the requirements for licensing in North Carolina.

"I'll want to get my nursing license here," I said. "Then when the baby gets a little older, I can work."

He looked surprised. "Tess, don't you understand?" he asked. "You don't need a degree or a nursing license, or any other license for that matter. Other than a marriage license," he added. "You are never going to need to work."

"I'd be bored."

He laughed. "I don't think you have any idea how busy you'll be with a baby. Although we'll have a nanny for him. Or her. Of course. But my mother will get you involved in all sorts of clubs and such. You won't have a minute to breathe once you're involved in Hickory life."

"A nanny?" I was stuck on the word. "I don't think we'll need a nanny. I don't know anyone who has one."

"Well, you're going to meet plenty of people who do now," he said. "So listen. Give me your phone number in Baltimore and I'll let you know when you should come. Bring whatever belongings you want to have with you in Hickory, but you don't need much. We have department stores and you can find anything you need here."

"All right," I said.

"I'm afraid I won't have time for a honeymoon or anything like that," he said. "I assume that's all right with you, given the"—he motioned toward the middle of my body—"pressing circumstances?"

I nodded. Vincent and I had talked about Niagara Falls for our honeymoon. That was the most we could afford and I'd been looking forward to it.

"Once we're married, we'll move into the house I grew up in, as I said. It shouldn't be too awkward. There's plenty of room. My mother has a bad knee and almost never comes upstairs, where Lucy and I have our bedrooms." He looked toward the window, thoughtful, then spoke as if thinking out loud. "There's just a twin bed in my room," he said, "but I'll bring in a second twin, and as I said, it will only be six months or so before my new house is ready to move into."

"Have you cleared this . . . living arrangement . . . with your mother?" I asked.

His expression was a little bit haughty. "I don't 'clear things' with my mother," he said. "I've been the man of the house for the ten years since my father's death. Since I was seventeen." Apparently, he ruled the roost and was proud of it. I pictured his mother as a sweet woman who bent to her beloved son's every wish.

"How old is your sister? Lucy?" I asked.

"Twenty," he said. "She's in college."

"You said a girl doesn't need a degree," I said, baiting him.

He looked at me. "Are you the argumentative type?" he asked. I couldn't tell if he was teasing or expressing a genuine concern.

"No," I said. "I'm just trying to understand."

"Education is always good," he said. "Women need to be able to carry on a conversation about something other than diapers and housecleaning. But I can't picture my sister actually working."

"Well, I can't wait to meet her," I said. A sister-in-law. I imagined having a warm relationship with her that would last all our lives. I knew I was romanticizing my future, but it felt like the only way to endure this huge, irreconcilable step I was agreeing to take.

"And *your* mother?" Henry asked. "How will she take this? If you want to invite her to the wedding, you can, of course, though it will only be with a justice of the peace. He's a friend of mine."

I shook my head. "No," I said. "I don't think . . . She's not going to be happy about this." How would I ever tell her about my plans? How would I ever tell *Vincent*? I would write to him. Somehow, I would have to find the words that would end both our romance and our friendship. I couldn't bear to think about it. My heart pounded hard in my chest, painfully so, at the thought of writing that letter.

"Tess DeMello," he said suddenly, looking thoughtful. "Is that your full name?"

"Theresa Ann DeMello," I said.

He shook his head with an uncertain smile. "DeMello," he repeated. "I can barely believe I'm marrying an Italian girl." I could tell that the idea didn't please him. "You'll stand out in Hickory with that thick black hair and those exotic big brown eyes."

"Where I live," I said, "everyone looks like me." I raised my chin an inch, challenging him to make an issue out of my heritage.

"Well, it's all right," he said, getting to his feet. "You'll be a Kraft soon enough."

12

Henry planned to take me to the train station late that afternoon for my return trip to Baltimore, but as we were leaving his office, a very young man—a boy, really—burst into the room.

"We've got a problem with the power in the kiln room!" he said, his blond hair flopping over his forehead.

Henry wore a look of dismay. "I'll be right there, Mickey," he said, and the boy left the office at a run. Henry looked at me apologetically. "I need to deal with this," he said. "I'll call you a cab, or"—he looked thoughtful—"wait a minute." He motioned to the chair. "Have a seat. I'll be right back." He left the office at a run, just like the boy. I sat down and waited, hoping I wouldn't miss my train. A few minutes passed and Henry returned with the boy—Mickey—at his side. Mickey wore a wide grin.

"Mickey here is going to drive you to the station," Henry said, and I noticed the reason for the boy's grin: the Cadillac's keys were in his hand.

"All right." I smiled at Mickey and got to my feet. Henry had pulled his wallet from his pants pocket and counted out a few bills which he pressed into my hand. His fingers brushed mine, the touch of a stranger. "This is enough for a roomette on the train from Salisbury to Washington. Get some sleep, all right?"

I nodded. "Thank you," I said.

"I'm going to see if I can get the power back in the kiln room." He headed for the office door again. "Have a safe journey."

Mickey carried my suitcase out to the small parking lot at the side of the building and put it in the Cadillac's trunk. I got into the passenger seat beside him. He was still grinning as he ran his fingers tenderly over the dashboard. "I always wanted to drive this car," he said.

"It's beautiful," I said.

He turned the key in the ignition and pressed the starter button and the car came to life. "Purrs like a kitten," he said.

"How long have you been working for Mr. Kraft?" I asked, making conversation as we drove toward the station.

"Two years," he said, "since I was fourteen when my father enlisted. I quit school and started working. Got a bunch of little sisters and we needed the money. Hank pays good." He glanced at me with a grin. "He says you're his fiancée."

"Yes," I said, still filled with disbelief that this was happening. If Henry was telling people, it made it even more real.

"Does Violet Dare know about that?" Mickey asked.

Who on earth was Violet Dare? I thought Mickey was carefully keeping his eyes on the road as he asked the question.

"Who is Violet Dare?" I asked.

He gave me a quick glance. "I reckon Violet's fancied herself Hank's fiancée most of her life," he said.

Oh no. Henry *did* have a girl in his life. I had no idea how this news was going to complicate our plans. I would have to ask him about her. Was I stepping on another girl's toes?

"Well," I said, "Henry told you we're engaged and I'd say he should know best." Why was I talking to this forward little teenager about my private life? His probing had made me feel defensive. I was relieved to see the station come into view. "And here we are," I said, sitting up straighter.

Mickey parked in front of the station and got out of the car. I didn't wait for him to open my door, and once I was on the sidewalk, he lifted the trunk lid and handed me my suitcase.

"Good luck with Violet, now," he said, giving me a little salute as he turned, grinning, to get back in the Cadillac. I watched him go, wondering what he knew that I didn't.

13

————————

I was exhausted when I arrived home on Saturday. Even with the roomette, I'd barely been able to sleep on the train as I tried to think of how I would tell my mother my plans. There were no words to soften the blow. In each imagined scenario, I saw her hurt and her anger. I certainly wouldn't tell her about the baby. I would simply have to find a way to make her understand that I was going to marry Henry Kraft no matter what she said.

I'd hoped she would be out, but as soon as I let myself in the front door, I heard water running in the kitchen and knew she was home. I left my suitcase by the stairs and walked into the room. She stood at the sink washing snap beans from our small victory garden. The sound of the running water must have masked my footsteps because she didn't turn around and, for a moment, I simply observed her. She wore her blue floral housedress, a navy blue apron tied at her waist, and her silver-streaked black hair was in a bun at the nape of her neck. I loved her so much. She was my only family. She thought she knew what her future held—what *both* our futures held—and I was going to destroy her hopes and dreams.

"I'm home," I said, walking into the room. I set my handbag on the table. "Can I help?"

She glanced up from her task at the sink and turned off the water above the colander. "Oh my," she said, drying her hands on a dishtowel. "You look like you haven't slept in days! How is your friend? Is she still very ill? I don't believe you told me her name."

I'd never told her the name of my imaginary friend, and I wasn't about to make one up now. Now was the time for the truth. At least, for part of it.

"Mom," I said, "can you sit for a moment? I have some news."

She looked instantly worried. Her round brown eyes, so much like my own, were hooded with concern. Draping the dishtowel over the faucet, she came to sit kitty-corner from me at the table. "Are you all right, honey?" she asked. "You look so pale."

"I'm fine." I folded my hands in my lap. "But I wasn't being honest about why I went away," I said. "I didn't have a sick friend. I went to see a man I met when I was in Washington with Gina a few months ago." Her brow furrowed and I rushed on. "I've fallen in love with him and plan to marry him," I said.

She stared at me in disbelief. "What are you talking about?" she asked. "Have you gone mad?"

I shook my head. "I know it seems crazy," I said. "I just . . . I fell for him."

She said nothing, her eyes wide and her mouth slightly open as though she'd forgotten how to blink. How to swallow.

"I know it's a shock," I went on quickly. "And I've had a hard time figuring out what to do about it, but . . ." My voice faded away. I wasn't sure what more to say.

"What about Vincent?" Her voice took on an hysterical edge when she said his name.

"I realized that Vincent is more like a brother to me than a—"

"*What?*" She slapped the table with her open palm. "Tell me you're joking. You're pulling my leg, right?"

"No, Mom. I'm very serious. I'm sorry. I know you—"

"What does this man do that makes him so special?" she said. "He's better than a doctor?"

"It has nothing to do with his occupation." My voice sounded far calmer than I felt.

"Vincent, who has loved you with all his heart since he was a boy?" she continued. "You'd give him up for someone you've known a couple of months?"

"I can't help how I feel," I said. "I'm very attracted to him. To this . . . new man." At that moment, I thought of how I felt in Vincent's arms. How

I longed for him to kiss me. To touch me. I'd felt little of that with Henry. I doubted I ever would. "He'll be a good provider," I said, as though that was the thing I cared most about. "He owns a furniture company in North Carolina."

"North Carolina! Is that where you've been the past few days?"

I nodded. "Yes. And I'll have to move there, since that's where his business—"

"You'll leave me here all alone?" She pushed back her chair with an angry scrape as she got to her feet. "North Carolina!" she said again.

"I'm not leaving *you*." I looked up at her. "I'll always be your daughter and I'll visit as often as I can. And you can visit me. You can meet Henry. I'm sure you'll—"

"I won't allow it!" she barked. "I will *not* allow you to throw away the boy you've always loved for this—" Her face suddenly paled and she grabbed the back of the chair she'd been sitting in. I stood up quickly, reaching for her arm, afraid she was about to pass out. That had happened a couple of times when her diabetes was out of control, but she drew away from me as if repelled by my touch. Her eyes were wide, her expression stricken. "You're pregnant!" she said, the words exploding from her mouth.

I sucked in my breath. I would have to lie, but I waited a second too long before opening my mouth to answer her, and she raised her hands to her face in horror.

"That's it, isn't it? It was this man . . . this *furniture* man . . . Oh dear God in heaven!" She crossed herself and sank once more onto the chair. "What have you *done!*"

"I'm sorry, Mom," I said, sitting down again. I leaned across the table, reaching for her hand, but she drew it away as if repulsed by my touch. "I'm ashamed of myself," I said. "It was terrible of me, I know, but it happened and I . . ." I shook my head, unsure what else to say.

"You are a horrible person, Tess DeMello." Her nostrils flared and she looked at me as if I were a despicable stranger. She pressed her fists to her temples. "How could you let this happen?" she asked. "Your poor father!" She leaned across the corner of the table to slap my arm. "He's looking down at you right now, so ashamed!" She raised her eyes to the ceiling. "Dear Lord in heaven, what did I do wrong?"

"Mom." I grabbed her hand, but she yanked it away from me. "You didn't do anything wrong," I said. "You're a wonderful mother. I'm the one who—"

"How could you do this to Vincent? To me? To Mimi and Pop? How could you do it to *yourself*, you stupid, stupid girl!"

In all my life, I'd never heard her talk to me this way. I'd never heard her talk to *anyone* this way. I straightened my spine. "I'm going to marry Henry, Mother," I said firmly. "I have to think about the baby now, and I want him or her to have a name and a future."

"My daughter." She rocked on the chair as though she hadn't heard me. "I can't believe my daughter would do something like this. You'll go to hell. You know that don't you?"

"Mother, I—"

"You belong with Vincent." Her voice took on a pleading tone. "You always have. My sweet boy. My Vincent." Tears spilled from her eyes and trailed down her cheeks. I couldn't bear that I was the cause of them. "What are you going to tell him?" she asked. "He left to do volunteer work, the biggest heart any man ever had, and you cheat on him like a whore."

I began to cry myself, unable to keep up my resolute façade any longer, because she was right. Vincent was so good and I was going to hurt him terribly. "I know I made a mistake," I said. "I'm trying to find a way to live with it. I'm going to write to Vincent and tell him I fell in love with someone else. Please don't tell him about the baby, Mom." I pleaded again, my hand on her arm. "*Please*. It would kill him."

"It would kill *you* for him to know what a tramp you've become, isn't that it?"

"No, I—"

"Don't worry," she said, picking up my hand from her arm and dropping it to the table as if it were a piece of rotten fruit. "I certainly *won't* tell Vincent. How could I? How could I admit to him . . . to *anyone* . . . that my daughter is a tramp?" She shook her head, looking suddenly exhausted and far older than her forty-eight years. "Can't you just go away to a home for unwed mothers?" she pleaded. "Maria Lucarelli's girl did that. You could have the baby with the nuns. They'll find it a home. We can ask Father Longo where you should go." Her voice grew more hopeful with each sentence. "We'll make up some reason you had to go away for a while.

Vincent won't need to know. You don't have to marry this other man. You belong with Vincent. You know that, don't you?"

I shook my head. "I'm not going to the nuns, Mom. I want this baby. It's not as though I'm fifteen years old."

She lowered her face into her hands and made a sound deep in her throat, a keening as if she were in mourning. "I don't know you," she wailed. "I don't know the girl who could do something like this." She lifted her tear-streaked face. "You need to leave my house," she said, her voice determined. "Now. Today."

"What? Mother, I just got home. I'm not going anywhere until I—"

"You're a disgrace to me," she said. "I want you gone. Out of this house. You're so in love with this man? Go to him, then. Just go." She stood up and walked over to the sink. She turned on the water again and began washing the beans.

"Mom?" I said, getting slowly to my feet. I hung back, suddenly afraid to approach her. "Mother?"

She didn't respond. I knew she wouldn't. She was finished with this conversation. I had the terrible feeling she was finished with *me*.

In my room, I struggled to write the letter to Vincent. I cried so hard as I wrote it that I could barely catch my breath. The letter had to be cut-and-dried. A little mean. I wanted to make him angry enough to forget me. I wouldn't mail the letter until I was ready to leave for Hickory. The last thing I wanted was for him to rush home to try to change my mind.

> *Dearest Vincent,*
>
> *This letter is so hard for me to write. I'm afraid I need to break off our engagement. I met someone else while you've been away and I fell deeply in love with him and plan to marry him. You worried that I seemed different when you were home for Christmas and you were right. I was struggling with my feelings as I tried to figure out what to do about loving two wonderful men. Now I've made my decision. I'm sure it seems terribly sudden to you and you're probably worried about my sanity, but you needn't be. I'm fine, just heartsick at the thought of hurting you as*

well as your dear parents and my mother, who is terribly disappointed in me. Please don't try to find me. Instead, move on with your life. I know it will be splendid. You are a wonderful person, dear Vincent. I will always care about you, and I pray you quickly find someone worthy of you.
With love and admiration,
Tess

It was a letter full of lies and omissions, but it was the only way.

14

"She still won't answer the phone?" Gina asked from beneath the pink and white quilt on her bed. She was already tucked in for the night.

I shook my head as I sat down on the spare twin bed in her room, still in my dungarees and cardigan. I'd been at Gina's house for two full days and nights, trying to call my mother every few hours, but she refused to answer the phone. I was hurt and angry and scared. I'd certainly known my mother would be upset. I'd known she'd be furious with me. But I never thought she would actually kick me out.

"She'll come around," Gina assured me with a yawn. "She's your mother."

"I don't think she *will* come around, Gina." I remembered my mother's words: *I don't know you anymore.* "I think I've lost her," I said. "I've lost everyone I love."

"You still have me, honey." She propped herself up on her elbow, her nightgown slipping over one shoulder as she leaned across the space between the beds to touch my denim-covered knee. "You'll always have me," she said. "I understand how she feels, though. I don't want you to leave either, but I know you don't have much choice. If you get lonely or scared when you're down in North Carolina, I'm a phone call away."

I barely heard her, I was so lost in my gloom. "I think she actually loves Vincent more than she loves me," I said. "Maybe she always has. She kept calling him 'my Vincent.' She adores him." I leaned back against the headboard and lit my fourth or fifth cigarette of the evening. I remembered the obstetrician telling me ten cigarettes a day was fine. I seemed determined to smoke them all in a row tonight. "Are you sure it's okay for me to stay here a while longer?" I asked.

"It's fine," she said, stifling another yawn. She had to get up early to go to work in the morning and I felt guilty I was keeping her awake with my chatter. "My mother loves you," she added, "though if it turns out you're here for a long time, we'll have to make up some good reason you can't go home."

"I don't know if Henry's going to call me in four days or four weeks," I said. "Or if he's changed his mind altogether," I added, giving voice to my latest worry.

"He'll call," she said, as though she knew him better than I did. The truth was, neither of us knew Henry Kraft at all.

The Monday after I'd arrived at Gina's, I'd called the factory in Hickory and asked for him. I needed to let him know where he could reach me—that I was no longer at home—but the switchboard operator told me he wasn't in. I left Gina's number with the operator, then began to worry. Maybe he was having second thoughts. He'd certainly been impulsive, asking me to marry him. Had he been leading me on, humoring me while he waited for the train to take me away from Hickory? Away from him? The twenty-four hours I'd spent in Hickory were taking on an unreal quality in my mind and the craziness of his proposal was setting in. It was probably setting in for him as well. And there was that Violet Dare girl. The one who fancied herself his fiancée. Who was she? Did Henry tell her about me? How he asked me to marry him? Were they both laughing about me now?

"Get some sleep, honey," Gina said with a yawn. "You need it. Your baby needs it. You can resume worrying in the morning."

I stubbed out my cigarette and stood up from the bed, heading for the bathroom where I'd left my nightgown and toothbrush. I would go to bed as Gina had advised, but I doubted very much that I'd be able to sleep.

A phone rang. In the darkness, I lifted the receiver to my ear.

"Hello?" I said.

"This is Violet Dare," a woman hissed in an angry whisper. "What the hell do you think you're doing with Henry?"

"Tess?"

I opened my eyes, groggy and confused. I looked over at Gina, thinking she'd spoken, but she was burrowed under her covers sound asleep.

"Tess, wake up."

I sat up and saw Gina's mother standing in the doorway, illuminated by the streetlight outside the bedroom window. Her hair was tied up in rags beneath a hairnet. I stared at her blankly, still lost in my dream.

"Your fiancé is on the phone," Mrs. Farinola said, then added, "He says it's urgent, honey."

Vincent? Calling me at Gina's in the middle of the night? My mother must have gotten in touch with him. *Talk some sense into her,* she'd tell him. I only hoped she hadn't told him about the baby.

I got out of bed, pulling on my robe and stepping into my slippers, and followed Mrs. Farinola to the kitchen. My brain still felt muddy with sleep and I half expected Violet Dare to be on the line when I lifted the receiver to my ear.

"Vincent?"

"Thank God you're there," he said. I hadn't heard his voice in a week and a half and the sound of it filled me with heartbreaking love. "We didn't know where you were," he said, "and it finally occurred to me to try Gina's."

I was confused. If he'd called my house, wouldn't my mother have told him I was at Gina's? "I've been here a couple of—"

"It's your mother, Tess," he interrupted. "Mom hadn't heard from her in a few days and she went over there and found her on the floor in the living room."

My mind snapped into focus, my heartbeat suddenly pounding in my throat. "Oh no," I said. "She fell?"

He hesitated. "She passed away, honey," he said finally. "I'm so—"

"What?" I nearly screamed the word. I felt Mrs. Farinola's hand on my shoulder as if to hold me up, and I knew Vincent must have already told her why he was calling. "How could she . . . pass away?"

"They think it was either another stroke, or possibly a seizure from the diabetes. Either way, she hit her head on the coffee table. Mom is devastated that she didn't go over there sooner. They think it happened two days ago. Have you been at Gina's all this time?"

Two days ago! I couldn't answer him. Tears slipped down my cheeks and over my trembling fingers where I held the receiver. "I . . . yes," I finally managed to say. I couldn't tell him my mother kicked me out. "I should go home. Right now." I looked through the kitchen window into the dark night. "But the bus doesn't run till morn—"

"I'll drive you home," Mrs. Farinola said quickly.

"I'm so sorry, sweetheart," Vincent said. "There's no need for you to rush home in the middle of the night. She's . . . she's not there, honey. She's at the funeral home. Cito's. They're waiting till we could find you to make arrangements."

Cito's. Oh my God. That made it all so real. I lowered myself onto one of the kitchen chairs.

"I've been trying to find a train home," Vincent continued, "but they're all booked up and I'm out of gasoline coupons because of my job, plus we're so short staffed right now, that I . . ." His voice drifted off for a moment. "I'm driving all over town during the day, making house calls," he continued. "I don't know if I'll be able to get home, Tess. They're moving troops around right now, and the trains are full. I'm sorry. I hate to leave you alone to deal with this. Go see Father Longo tomorrow. He'll help you with arrangements. And my parents will help. You know they'll always be there for you. I'll do my best to get on a train, all right?"

I barely heard him as he spoke. *Mom.* "I just can't believe it," I said. I remembered my last conversation with her. The argument. The anguish in her face. The shame and disbelief. I stood up abruptly. "I need to get home," I said. I had the irrational feeling that I would walk in the house and find her sitting in her favorite chair in the living room, the floor lamp illuminating a magazine in her lap.

"All right," he said. "Go. I'll call you tomorrow and give you an update on the train situation. Okay, darling?"

I nodded as though he could see me, then stood up and set the receiver back in the cradle on the table. I was dazed, unaware of anything around me. Gina's mother may have offered condolences. Gina herself may have come into the kitchen to ask what was wrong. I didn't know or care. I stood there numbly, feeling sick, my heart as heavy as an anchor. My mother was gone. And it was my fault.

15

Vincent didn't make it home. I should have been angry that he didn't try harder to get a seat—or if necessary, standing room—on one of the packed trains out of Chicago, but instead I was relieved. How could I talk to him? What could I say? I was afraid if I saw him face-to-face, I would reveal too much.

Mimi and Pop and Father Longo helped me make the arrangements for my mother's funeral, and the church overflowed with her friends. I sat with Mimi and Pop in the front row of St. Leo's and when I chanced to look behind us, I was overwhelmed by the sea of people. Even our milkman was there, along with the ladies from the Italian bakery on the corner, our butcher, and the nurse from our doctor's office. All those people who had cared about my mother and who now stood ready to help me, feed me, hold me up. My throat tightened with tears, as much from this outpouring of community love as from the loss of my beautiful, too-young-to-die mother.

People flooded our little kitchen with food that evening. There was so much ravioli, gnocchi, eggplant parmesan, and lasagna that I didn't know what to do with it all. I crammed what I could into our small refrigerator and gave away what wouldn't fit. Mimi stayed by my side nearly every minute, stroking my back and my hair, mothering me now that I had no mother of my own. I was so focused on my grief that I nearly forgot about the baby. About Henry. I nearly forgot about my predicament.

The day after the funeral, our landlord stopped over to tell me my mother had been behind on our rent.

"I hate-a to tell you tis at-a tis terrible time," he said in his thick Italian accent, "but your mama? She owe me for two mont."

I was shocked. That was so unlike my responsible mother. I found her checkbook in her night table drawer and saw the reason she was in arrears. My tuition had gone up and she hadn't told me. We never talked about finances and I felt selfish now for taking any money from her when I was twenty-three years old and should have been making my own. If I'd known the dire straits we were in, I could have dropped out of school and found a job to help out.

I paid our landlord with eighty-two dollars from my savings account, leaving less than a hundred dollars for me to live on. I didn't tell him I would be leaving. He owned the Russos' house as well and I didn't want him to tell them anything. Besides, I hadn't heard a word from Henry and it was beginning to look like I was back to being on my own again. I imagined Henry was struggling with second thoughts about his impulsive proposal. Maybe he'd never been serious about it in the first place. I lay awake two nights in a row, trying to figure out what to do. On the third day, though, he called.

"Sorry it's taken me a bit to get back to you," he said, "but I've managed to get a train reservation with a roomette for you for this Wednesday and we should be able to meet with the justice of the peace immediately after your arrival on Thursday. I'm not sure of the time yet, but—"

"Henry," I interrupted, both relieved and frankly terrified of suddenly stepping into that unfamiliar new life. "I . . . I can't do it this quickly. My mother died last week and I have to deal with the house and—"

"Your mother died?" He sounded stunned. "How terrible for you. I'm so sorry."

"Thank you. I know we have to . . . I know we should get married quickly. But it's just me here, and I need to clean out my mother's . . . things."

"How long will that take you?" he asked.

"I'm not sure," I said. "Maybe a week?"

He didn't respond right away. "Make it sooner," he said finally. "It's best if people think you, you know. That you conceived on our wedding night."

I was nearly three months along. We weren't going to fool anyone. "I know," I said. "I'll hurry. I'll do my best."

"Do you need money?" he asked.

I hesitated. Yes, I needed money, but I wasn't ready to take his. Not yet. "No, thank you," I said. I was pleased that he offered. He was going to be someone I could count on, and right then, I needed that more than I could say.

Henry's call energized me but not nearly as much as the call I received from Vincent that evening.

"I got a ticket, finally," he said. "I'll be home Friday night and can stay the weekend."

"You don't need to come home," I said, panicking. "I'm doing all right and I know it's difficult for you."

"No, I'm coming," he said. "I keep picturing you going through your mother's things alone. How hard that's got to be. I don't want you to be alone, honey."

"Your mother's helping," I said, which was a partial truth. Mimi *wanted* to help, but I was shutting her out. I couldn't bear to have her close by any longer. I felt as though every word that came out of my mouth was a lie. Plus, I was not only emptying the house of my mother's personal belongings, carting bags of clothing and books to the donation center at St. Leo's. I was also emptying it of everything we owned. Everything I could carry.

"I'm coming and that's final," Vincent said.

Oh, Vincent. To see him one more time. To touch him. Wrap my arms around him. I couldn't let it happen.

I would have to be gone by the time he arrived.

16

Hickory, North Carolina

I spotted Henry and his butter-yellow Cadillac the moment I stepped off the train into a biting cold wind. Despite the roomette, I'd slept little and my nerves were on fire as I tried to absorb the fact that, in a few short hours, I would be married.

I'd left the letter for Vincent on the kitchen table in my nearly barren house, along with my engagement ring. I pictured him standing in the empty kitchen, reading the letter, staring at the ring. I felt his confusion. His hurt. I imagined him walking back to his own house where he would tell Mimi and Pop I was gone and wouldn't be coming back. He would call Gina, who had promised me she would never tell him—or anyone else—where I was. The whole scenario was unbearable to think about, so I tried to wipe the images from my mind during the trip and focus on the future awaiting me in Hickory. *You're strong*, I told myself as the train chugged through the bleak winter countryside. *You can do this.* It was the truth. I'd been strong all my life, and in spite of everything I'd been up against the past month, I'd still managed to graduate from nursing school. I would be strong now, too, for the sake of my baby. I thought about that little one, the cause of everything. The *reason* for everything. And for the first time in many days, I smiled to myself. *You will have a daddy,* I said to him, my hand resting on my belly. *You will have a wonderful life. I promise.*

Henry greeted me from where he stood next to his Cadillac. He smiled his handsome smile, held my shoulders lightly, and planted a swift kiss on my cheek. "How was your trip?" he asked, lifting my suitcase from the ground and setting it in the trunk.

"Good," I said. "I appreciated the roomette."

He shut the trunk and gave me a sympathetic look. "I know it's been a difficult week for you," he said. "And I'm terribly sorry about your mother."

He was so kind. "Thank you," I said, watching as he opened the passenger side door for me.

"Come on." He guided me into the car, his hand on my elbow. "Let's go get married."

We drove directly from the train station to the justice of the peace's office in an area called Union Square. For the first time, I got a good look at Hickory's downtown and found it charming. There were shops of all variety, large and small, and the streets were alive with cars, the sidewalks bustling with people. Henry found a parking place half a block from the office. I felt conspicuous as we walked that half block. We didn't speak and we might as well have been two strangers for the lack of physical closeness between us.

The justice of the peace was a dark-haired, dark-eyed man named Franklin Carver and it was clear from the moment we entered the reception area that he knew Henry well. He greeted him with a hearty handshake and me with a curious smile.

"You're a lucky girl," he said as he ushered us into his office. "I've known Hank since we were five years old and can tell you for a fact that plenty of girls have wanted to get their hands on him over the years. He's a pillar of the community." He clapped Henry on the shoulder as he smiled at me. "There must be something very special about you to finally get this boy to settle down."

I squirmed with embarrassment, in way over my head. I didn't know Hickory or those "plenty of girls," though I imagined that Violet Dare was one of them. I didn't know "Hank's" history. I didn't even really know "Hank." But I assumed the man was paying me a compliment, so I smiled at him.

"Thank you," I said. I noticed his gaze dropped to my stomach. I was wearing a pale yellow skirt and matching jacket that I was certain masked any telltale bulge.

"There's definitely something special about Tess." Henry rested his hand on my arm. He looked at me admiringly and I wondered for the first time if he actually *did* see something in me other than just my status as the mother of his child. I wasn't sure what that could be, since he barely knew me.

"Y'all have a seat while we wait for our witnesses—my office staff—to join us," Franklin said as he settled in behind his desk. "You have the documents?" He looked at us as we sat down across from him. "Blood tests and medical examinations?"

Henry reached into his jacket pocket as I reached into my handbag and we slid the papers across the desk to Franklin, watching as he gave them a cursory once-over. I'd managed to get the blood test and physical exam just in time for this trip. I'd gone to yet another unfamiliar doctor in Baltimore. This one told me I was fit to get married, "and the sooner the better."

Franklin leaned back in his chair, his gaze on Henry. "Things aren't looking too good for Gaston," he said. "Did you hear?"

I thought this was idle chitchat between friends as we waited for Franklin's receptionist, but Henry sat up straighter, as though the news had great meaning to him.

"What's happened?" he asked.

"Byron Dare brought in a doctor who knew Loretta's daddy. He testified that Loretta's definitely half colored, as if it weren't obvious enough." He pronounced the word colored, "cuh-luhed." It would take me a while to get used to the accent down here. "So the charge against Gaston is now fornication and adultery." He glanced at me. "Pardon my French," he said, and returned his gaze to Henry. "Both he and Loretta are going to land themselves in prison."

"They should never have come back," Henry said.

I looked questioningly at him.

"Gaston Joyner's an old friend of ours from our school days," he said. "He fell for this colored gal and they went up North—Pennsylvania—so they could get married legally, but then they came back to North Carolina hoping to live here."

"Oh," I said, trying to sound engaged in the conversation. I thought this Gaston Joyner didn't sound very smart. First, getting mixed up with a colored girl and second, coming back to the South where they would never be welcome. I thought it was crazy that any state in the country allowed colored and white to get married in the first place. It only created problems for everyone.

Three women, two of them gray-haired and the third about my age, walked into the room.

"Sorry to hold you up," the younger woman said. She nodded at Henry. "Hank," she said in greeting. Then she looked at me. Or rather, she glowered at me. That was the only word I could think of for the expression on her face. The older women barely gave me a glance as they stood next to Mr. Carver's desk. One of them kept glancing at her watch.

"This is my fiancée, Tess," Henry said to them. He rattled off the names of the older women, then turned to the one who was close to my age. "And this is Jeanetta Gill," he said.

"How do you do?" I said to the three of them.

Jeanetta Gill offered a stiff smile. "So you're marrying our Hank," she said. Her gaze was now on my left hand where I wore the engagement ring Henry had handed me in the car on the way over.

"Yes." I gave her the friendliest smile I could manage. "And moving to Hickory from Baltimore. It's a big step. I don't know a soul here other than Henry."

"Well, bless your heart," she said. "I hope you'll find our sleepy little town to your liking."

I tried to hold on to my smile, but it was difficult. Her words were kind but the tone behind them was not. "I'm sure I will," I said.

Franklin Carver instructed us to stand in front of him while Jeanetta Gill and the other two women stood to his left, and the ceremony, such as it was, began.

I choked up when it was time for me to say "I do." I'd imagined this moment so many times, saying those words, looking into Vincent's loving eyes as we faced our future together with my mother and Mimi and Pop looking on. This was so very wrong and yet I would need to make the best of it. I was marrying a pillar of the community, wasn't I? Surely Henry was someone I could come to love.

Henry gave me a very chaste kiss when we reached the end of the ceremony. I barely felt his dry lips on mine. That was all right. I felt awkward kissing him at all, particularly in front of the four strangers, one of whom already seemed to dislike me, for whatever reason. I wondered if I'd only feel like kissing Henry when I'd had too much to drink. How I was going to make it through our wedding night, I didn't know.

17

After the wedding, Henry drove us to the Hotel Hickory, where he'd reserved the honeymoon suite. We would spend the night in the hotel. Tomorrow, he'd take me to his house, where I would meet his mother and Lucy and figure out how to fit into this family. I should have guessed by the fact that neither his mother nor Lucy came to our wedding ceremony that it wasn't going to be easy.

We had dinner in the hotel's restaurant. The maître d' led us to a table by the window, and although it was dark outside and our view was only of the streetlights and passing cars, I had the feeling the table was the best in the house. Henry ordered filet mignon and potatoes for both of us. As he had at that restaurant in Washington, Henry had managed to get steak despite the war rationing, and our meal was another reminder that he was no ordinary citizen. But it didn't matter what was on my plate. Nerves had stolen my appetite. I nibbled small bites of the meat while I studied Henry's face, trying to get it into my head that he was now my husband. Was this how Mimi felt when she married Pop? Strange and uncertain and scared of the future?

"How did your mother and sister react when you told them you were getting married?" I asked as I cut another tiny morsel from my steak.

Henry looked away from me, a small, hard-to-read smile on his face. "I won't sugarcoat it, Tess," he said. "They aren't happy. Mama has always wanted me to marry a particular girl in town and now her plans for my future have taken an unexpected turn."

"Violet Dare?" I ventured, and his eyes widened in surprise.

"How could you possibly . . ." His voice trailed off.

"The boy who drove me to the train station in your Cadillac," I said. "Mickey? He said Violet Dare was engaged to you. Or at least, she expected to be engaged to you."

His smile was dismissive. "She's a dreamer," he said, cutting a bite of meat.

"Did you want to marry her? Have I broken something up?"

He hesitated, then drew in a long breath and let it out as a sigh, setting down his knife and fork, which, I'd noticed, he used easily despite his missing fingers. "No, you haven't broken anything up," he said. "But some people may think you have."

I thought of the woman who had treated me so coolly in Franklin Carver's office.

"Jeanetta Gill," I said.

He nodded. "She's one of Violet's friends, yes," he said. "I'm afraid Violet has many friends." It sounded like a warning. "And Mama . . . she was understandably shocked when I told her I was marrying you. I told her I met you on a trip to Washington and that we've known each other for quite some time and finally decided to make the move, so let's keep to that story, all right?"

I nodded.

"Mama can be a difficult person," he added, "and I'm sorry we'll have to live with her until the house is built."

Oh no. This was the first time he'd mentioned his mother being difficult. "And your sister?" I asked.

He picked up his knife and fork again and cut into his steak. "Lucy is a spoiled princess," he said before slipping a bite of meat into his mouth.

"Did she want you to marry Violet, too?"

He looked out the window into the darkness as he chewed and swallowed. "Everyone expected me to marry Violet," he admitted. "All of Hickory." He gave me a determined look. "They will all just have to get used to the idea that it's not going to happen."

"Were you officially engaged?" I really needed to know where I stood in this town.

"No." He looked at me. "I don't love her, Tess. I never did love her. I can assure you of that."

"Then why would everyone expect you to marry her?"

He shrugged. "The right age. Right social status. Right family connections. Her father is the district attorney, and—"

"Oh!" I suddenly remembered the name of the attorney Franklin Carver had mentioned in the case against that interracial couple. "Dare?" I asked. "The man prosecuting your friend Gaston?"

He looked impressed. "Very observant!" he said. "Yes, Byron Dare. The district attorney and a big name in Hickory. My father was also a big name, being the owner of Kraft Furniture. Violet and I have known each other since we were children, so it was always assumed we would marry. I never did give her much encouragement, though."

"The engagement ring." I looked down at the enormous diamond on my finger. "Did you buy this for her?" I felt sorry for Violet. I didn't even know her, yet I regretted hurting her.

He shook his head. "It was my grandmother's. I was saving it for the right girl." He smiled at me as though I were that girl, but there was a hollowness in that smile. How could there not be?

"They're not going to like me," I said. "Your family. Everyone in Hickory."

"Oh, they'll like you well enough once they get to know you."

"*You* don't even know me," I said.

He smiled again. "You do have a point," he said. Then he reached across the table to cover my hand with his good right hand. "We'll take things one step at a time," he said. "You'll settle in just fine. We'll have a healthy son or daughter. We'll move into a beautiful house. I look forward to showing you the plans and the lot where it will be built. I hope you like plenty of trees." He gave my hand a squeeze. "Be strong now, Tess, all right?"

I smiled. His words were kind and encouraging and I did feel stronger, hearing them.

"All right," I agreed. "I'll certainly try."

I took a bath in the roomy tub of the hotel's honeymoon suite. I'd felt less nervous the night we'd made love in Washington. I'd been too tipsy that night to worry about anything. Tonight, though, was different. I felt as though my whole marriage, my whole future rested on this night. Henry and I needed to grow close. We needed to be lovers. Sober, attentive, caring lovers. My heart pounded at the thought. I wished I felt more of an attraction to him. Would lovemaking feel different to me now? Would it hurt less? Was I going to break down after it was over because it was Henry I was married to and not Vincent?

Gina had given me a beautiful blue satin negligee when I first got engaged to Vincent and I put it on once I got out of the tub. I studied myself in the mirror. I'd taken my hair out of its bun and victory roll and the moist air of the bathroom had made it wild with waves that spilled over my shoulders. Tendrils of it curled at my temples, and I tried to smooth it into submission with my hands. Where the negligee fell over my breasts, I could see the curve of my nipples. I shut my eyes. I felt naked. How was I going to get through this? I thought about my mother. What had her wedding night been like? Had she been nervous? We'd never had a chance to talk about that sort of thing and now we never would. Tears stung my eyes and I blinked them away. I couldn't let myself think about my mother tonight.

I drew in a long breath, turned out the light, and left the bathroom.

Henry was propped up in the bed wearing blue pin-striped pajamas, a book open on his lap. He smiled at me. "You look lovely," he said.

"Thank you." I slipped into the bed next to him. My hands and feet felt ice-cold.

"Your hair is quite remarkable," he said.

I wasn't sure if that was a compliment or not. Not everyone found thick, wild black hair attractive. I would pretend he meant the comment in a positive light.

"Thank you," I said again.

He lifted the book a few inches. "I like to read in bed," he said. "Do you?"

"Yes," I said. I'd read in bed since I was old enough to turn the pages.

"Do you have a book with you?" he asked.

I nodded.

"Why don't you get it?"

I hesitated. This was hardly what I'd expected on my wedding night, but I got out of bed and walked barefoot over to my suitcase. I hadn't bothered to unpack anything other than my negligee and toiletries, knowing I'd be moving into Henry's house the following day. I reached beneath a stack of clothes for the Agatha Christie novel I'd been attempting to read over the last few nerve-racking days. I returned to the bed, propped my pillow behind me, and the two of us read for the next twenty or thirty minutes. Or at least Henry read. I stared at the pages but couldn't concentrate. I wanted to get this night over with.

"Ready for lights out?" Henry finally asked.

"Yes," I said, setting my book on the night table and switching off the lamp.

"Good night," he said. A soft glow from the streetlights filled the room and I saw him roll away from me, pulling the blanket up to his neck. I was mystified. Mystified and horribly alone. I stared at the dark ceiling. Was he angry? Or was it the baby? Did the thought of making love to a pregnant woman disturb him? I rested my hand on my stomach. I felt the unmistakable swelling of my belly, and I smiled to myself in the darkness. I was not alone after all. I would never be alone again.

18
_____

During our quiet breakfast in the hotel restaurant the following morning, dozens of questions ran through my mind. I wanted to find a way to ask him why he hadn't touched me the night before, yet I couldn't imagine a more awkward question to ask of a man I barely knew. I played with how to word it, but every combination of syllables seemed like a minefield. I had no idea how he would react or if he'd grow defensive. He didn't seem angry in the least, but he was closed up this morning, preoccupied, barely touching his breakfast, his jaw tight. When I would catch his eye, he'd smile at me, but return his gaze to his untouched food or the window. Anywhere but my face.

"You're very quiet this morning," I said finally.

He gave me a weak smile. "I'm thinking about taking you home," he admitted. "About Mama and Lucy. I'm trying to figure out how to make an awkward situation easiest for all three of you."

"Ah," I said, pleased to finally know what was going through his head. "How can I help?" I asked. "I promise to be on my best behavior."

"Just try to endure them," he said. He gave me that anemic smile again. "And whatever you do, don't mention the baby."

"Of course not." I could tell he was genuinely anxious and it made me feel sympathetic toward him. Maybe that had been the problem the night before: he couldn't stop worrying about today. "It will be all right," I reassured him. Most people liked me. I couldn't think of anyone who didn't, for that matter, except perhaps that Jeanetta Gill, and she didn't know me. I determined to win his mother and sister over.

If I hadn't truly realized I was marrying into money, I knew it the moment we turned into the driveway of the house in the beautiful Oakwood neighborhood where Henry had grown up. Two stories tall and painted a pale green with black shutters, it was one of the most beautiful houses I'd ever seen. I was struck by its symmetry, the right side a mirror image of the left, from the windows to the double chimneys to the porches that graced either side of the building. A wide brick walkway extended from the sidewalk to a pillared front porch topped by a small balcony. The house was surrounded by trees, most of them leafless at the moment, but I could imagine the lush backdrop they'd create in the spring.

"This is breathtaking," I said, leaning forward to get a better look, my hand on the dashboard.

"The house I'm building is a bit more modest," Henry said. "A brick colonial. I hope you'll like it. I've never been that interested in all the trappings."

"I'm sure it will be lovely."

He stopped the car just shy of a detached two-car garage. To our right stood a small cottage painted to match the house.

"What is that little building?" I asked.

"Our maid, Hattie, lives there," he said, opening his door. He circled the car to open my door for me before collecting our suitcases from the trunk. Together, we walked to the front door of the house. My future was inside that house and I had no idea what it held.

A maid dressed in a gray uniform and white apron opened the door as we climbed the two steps to the small stone porch.

"Mornin', Mr. Hank." She stepped back to let us into the house, her eyes on me with frank curiosity. She was slender, almost reedlike. Her black hair was tucked under a ruffly white cap, and she looked to be in her late thirties.

"This is Tess, my new wife," he said, as he set our suitcases on the gleaming hardwood floor of the wide foyer. "Tess, this is Hattie."

"Hello, Hattie." I smiled.

"Miss Tess." She nodded. "They in the livin' room waitin' for you, Mr. Hank. I'll carry them suitcases up to your room?" She didn't move her gaze from my face for a single second.

"I'll see to the suitcases," Henry said. "You can get us some tea?"

"Yes, sir," she said.

Henry guided me by the elbow toward the closed door to our right. "Courage," he whispered in my ear as he opened the door, and we walked into a beautiful sun-filled room adorned with pink and gold floral wallpaper and thick oriental rugs. Henry's mother and sister sat in wing chairs flanking a white brick fireplace. His mother rose to her feet and came toward us. She was fiftyish, a bit older than my own mother had been, and she wore a beige wool skirt, white blouse, and handsome blue and green patterned scarf. She had Henry's blue eyes, and her well-styled chin-length hair was completely white. She was quite beautiful.

"Hello, dear," she said to her son, kissing his cheek. Then she held her hand out to me. Her smile struck me as practiced and warm, but her hand was ice-cold.

"This is Theresa Kraft," Henry announced and I nearly corrected him. It would take me a while to get used to my new surname. "She goes by Tess."

"I'm happy to meet you, Mrs. Kraft," I said.

"Call me Miss Ruth, dear," she said. She was holding both my hands now. "Welcome to our home, Tess. Come sit with us. Lucy, aren't you going to greet your new sister-in-law?"

Lucy hadn't bothered to get up from the wingback chair. She looked over at us. "Hi," she said. The hooded look she gave me told me she'd already made up her mind that she wouldn't like me. She was going to be my challenge.

"Hi." I gave Lucy my warmest smile as I sat down on the nearby sofa. She was a pretty girl who looked younger than twenty. Her hair, cut in a bob that nearly reached her shoulders, was the same dirty blond as Gina's. She wore a dark blue skirt, navy cardigan over a pale blue blouse, and pearls. "It's so good to meet you both," I added, hoping I was the only person in the room to pick up the shiver in my voice. I noticed the painting hanging above the mantel. Lucy and Henry as children. They sat on a bench in front of a body of blue water. "What a beautiful painting," I said.

All three of them looked up at the painting as though they'd forgotten it was there.

"Yes," Ruth said. "Lucy was three there and Hank, ten."

"It's lovely," I said.

Hattie came into the room carrying a tray with a silver tea service and a plate of small chocolate cookies. She was older than I'd thought at first— somewhere in her early forties—but her dark skin was as smooth as satin and she carried the laden tray as though it were made of paper. She set it down on the coffee table in front of me, and everyone was quiet as she poured us each a cup. I longed to simply lean forward and do it myself. I didn't like being waited on.

"No tea for me, Hattie," Henry said when she started to pour the fourth cup. He got to his feet. "I'll let you gals get to know each other while I take the suitcases upstairs." He and Hattie left the room together, and I was alone with my new in-laws. I took a sip of tea from my cup, then set it on the end table next to a multicolored glass vase. I noticed those glass vases were everywhere in that room.

"This is pretty," I said, gently touching the lip of the vase. I looked at Ruth. "You must be a collector."

"Of Tiffany vases, yes I am," she said, and I saw Lucy roll her eyes. "I received one as a wedding present and I've been collecting them ever since." She set her saucer and cup on the table next to her chair and smiled at me. "Tell us all about yourself, Tess," she said. "Hank said you grew up in Baltimore?"

"Yes." I had the feeling I shouldn't mention Little Italy.

"Brothers and sisters?"

"No," I said. "A very small family. It was just my mother and me, since my father passed away when I was young. And," I added, "I recently lost my mother, as well."

"Oh no." Ruth looked pained. "I'm so sorry to hear that. Was it sudden?"

"Yes," I said. "She had a fall and hit her head."

"Tragic," Ruth said, her hand to her cheek. "You must be reeling."

"I am," I admitted. What would my mother make of this house? These people?

"What sort of work did your father do?"

I knew better than to say he'd been a plumber. "He had a home repair business," I said.

Her face lit up, ever so slightly. "Ah, so he was a businessman," she said. "How many employees did he have under him?"

I could see no way around the truth. "It was just him," I said. "He did everything himself." I knew she now pictured him in grimy work clothes, crawling around under people's houses to work on their pipes. Which would be completely accurate.

"I understand you and Hank have known each other quite a while," she said, changing the topic.

"Yes, we met in Washington a while back," I said, hoping I didn't need to be more specific. I wasn't sure exactly when Henry had told her we met.

"You were in Washington because . . . ?" she prompted.

"I was with a girlfriend," I said. "We wanted to visit the Smithsonian."

"And you met Hank and charmed him off his feet." She gave me a smile I couldn't read.

I frankly didn't want to remember meeting Henry or anything else about that visit to Washington. "He was very nice," I said weakly.

From her chair in front of the fire, Lucy snorted. "Try being his sister," she said.

"Lucy!" Ruth snapped with a frown. "Please act your age."

I turned to Lucy, wanting to get the questions off myself. "Henry says you go to college, Lucy," I said. "What are you studying?"

"This and that." She shrugged.

"Lucy is an English major at Lenoir-Rhyne, our excellent local college," Ruth said.

"Wonderful," I said. "Will you teach after you graduate?" I remembered Henry saying he couldn't picture Lucy working.

"Hopefully, I'll get married after I graduate," she said.

"So, you have a suitor then?" I smiled.

"Not yet. Hard to have a suitor when you haven't come out."

"Come out?" I didn't know what she meant.

"No debutante balls with the war going on," Ruth said.

Oh, *that* sort of coming out. The sort a girl from Little Italy knew nothing about.

"They would have to have a war just when it was my turn," Lucy said sulkily. She was really quite an unpleasant girl.

"Oh, Lucy," Ruth said with a tired smile. "And how about you, dear?"

she turned to me again. "Hank said you were going to school before he stole you away. What were you studying?"

"Nursing," I said. "I finished my degree and I'm gearing up to take my licensing exam in March." I'd learned that the RN exam would be held in Winston-Salem, a few hours' drive from Hickory.

"Oh, for what reason?" she said. "You won't need to work, and nursing is such messy business."

I felt insulted and annoyed. "I think I'd be bored if I didn't work." I said, then realized I was probably insulting *her*.

"Well, there are many lovely ways to while away the time here in Hickory," she said. "Do you play bridge?"

"I never have, but I'd love to learn." I'd never given a thought to bridge in my life.

"We also have many book clubs. Do you like to read?"

"Oh yes. I'm reading an Agatha Christie novel right now."

"And you can join Mama's Ladies of the Homefront organization," Lucy said with a hint of sarcasm.

"And hopefully you'll take to it more easily than my daughter," Ruth said.

"What is 'Ladies of the Homefront'?" I asked.

"It's not a group so much as a movement," Ruth explained, leaning forward with some enthusiasm. "Another woman and I became concerned with what's happening to the women in our country while their men are away fighting. Wearing slacks. Smoking to excess. You don't smoke, do you, dear?"

"Occasionally." I smiled apologetically, thinking of how much I'd like a cigarette at that very moment.

"So unfeminine." Ruth appeared to shudder. "I worry the men will come home to a country full of manly women. I do hope you'll come to our meetings. I'll introduce you around. And then there's our wonderful church and all the activities there. You're Baptist, of course?" She looked at me as though the answer were a foregone conclusion.

I shook my head. "Catholic," I said, and her eyes widened before she had the chance to catch herself. "Well," she said, apparently shaken by my answer. "You're Baptist now, dear."

———

I was relieved when Henry returned to the room. He held out a hand to me. "Let me steal you away to show you around the house," he said.

I excused myself and left the room with him, taking in a relieved breath when we shut the living room door behind us. We walked across the foyer and into a beautiful library, the walls covered from floor to ceiling with shelves of books. Two leather wingback chairs were angled against one wall.

"How lovely!" I exclaimed. "You'd never run out of things to read in this house."

"I helped my father build these shelves when I was just a boy," Henry said, smoothing the fingers of his right hand over the edge of one of the shelves near the fireplace. "And my desk, as well." He pointed toward the massive desk that faced the front window. His voice sounded different than I'd heard it before. He loved this room.

"That's wonderful," I said. "And soon you'll be able to build things with your own child."

He gave me a smile that told me how much he liked that idea. "I admit, I'm hoping for a boy," he said, almost shyly.

"I think it *is* a boy," I said, then prompted, "but if it's a girl?"

"I fear I'll turn a daughter of mine into a tomboy." He laughed. "She'll be fit for no man."

"She'll be lucky to have her father's time and attention," I said, but he had moved on to the shelves nearest the side window. He motioned me over.

"This is my favorite section," he said. He pulled one of the huge, heavy volumes from a shelf and walked across the room to set it on the desk. I followed him and watched as he opened the book, which was filled with pictures and illustrations of early American furniture. He turned a few of the pages almost reverently and I could see how much he enjoyed creating furniture. I remembered the smells and sounds of his factory and knew he belonged there. I gently touched his arm.

"You love your work," I said.

He looked up at me. "Yes," he said. "I'm fortunate to have a job I love."

He closed the book and slipped it back into its place on the bookshelf while I wandered through the room, touching the spines, reading titles. I spotted a thick scrapbook on a small table in the corner and touched the corner of it with my fingers.

"Mama's scrapbook," he said. "Some family photographs. Newspaper articles. That sort of thing."

I would have liked to look through the scrapbook. Get to know my new family. But it didn't seem the time, and I returned my attention to the bookshelves. I spotted several Bibles and a whole shelf devoted to the Baptist faith.

"I think your mother is upset that I'm Catholic," I said.

Henry raised his eyebrows, then began guiding me out of the room. "Not many Catholics around here," he said, as we walked through a small sitting room. "Just a tiny congregation and they mostly keep to themselves." He stopped walking when we reached a closed door and turned to face me. "You won't be able to go to the Catholic church, Tess," he said. "You're going to have to fit in here in Hickory. Fit in with my family and our way of life. And of course our child will be Baptist. It's best you don't tell anyone that you were a Catholic."

"*Were* a Catholic?" I said. "I don't know anything about being Baptist. Even going to a Baptist service is a sin."

"That's ridiculous." He shook his head with something close to a chuckle. "You'll have to give up all that hocus-pocus that comes with Catholicism."

I said nothing. I thought of the priest who'd loudly blasted me for sleeping with Henry. Had I deserved that much vitriol and humiliation? I was angry at that priest. Angry at the church that would make me feel so dirty and guilty. Yet my life had centered around my beloved St. Leo's. I wasn't sure I could break away. Already I felt an ache in my heart that I would miss mass tomorrow, not to mention all the tomorrows to come.

Henry pushed open the swinging door and we walked into the largest kitchen I'd ever seen in a home, all done up in white and a deep, rich blue. The whole downstairs of my Baltimore house could fit inside that kitchen. The cabinets were white metal, the countertops a pale blue laminate with dark blue trim. The floor was a blue and white checkerboard. Even the large white porcelain enamel table was trimmed with blue. The whole kitchen was spotless.

Hattie walked into the room from the outside door, a wicker laundry basket in her arms, white sheets spilling over the rim. The smell of sunshine followed her into the room.

I smiled at her. "That looks heavy," I said. I thought Henry should help her with the basket, but he made no move toward her.

"Ain't bad," Hattie said. "Used to it." She rested the basket momentarily on the kitchen table.

"Let's continue our tour," Henry said.

"Excuse us," I said to Hattie. It was going to take me some time to get used to having a person in the house whose role was simply to clean up after us.

Henry put his hand on my elbow and guided me into a hallway papered with pink cabbage roses on a gray background. He pointed to a closed door. "That's Mama's room," he said. "And by the way," he added, "you don't need to excuse yourself from Hattie, or sympathize with her about her work. She knows her place. You have to learn what yours is."

I felt scolded. "I've never had a maid before," I said.

"You'll adjust," he said, leading me back to the foyer. He motioned toward the broad staircase. "Let me show you upstairs," he said.

I gripped the smooth dark banister, which was almost too thick to get my hand around, and followed him up.

"There are three more bedrooms up here," he said, when we reached the upstairs hallway. "Mine, and Lucy's, and one for guests. And then there's this parlor." We stepped into a small living room. The flocked wallpaper was a pale blue and the overstuffed sofas and chairs were upholstered in a bold multicolored floral print. I instantly loved the room. I could picture myself sitting in one of those comfortable-looking chairs, studying for my licensing exam as I sipped a cup of coffee and smoked a cigarette. I recalled Henry telling me that his mother rarely came upstairs because of a bad knee. I would be free to smoke up here without her knowing what a "manly" girl her son had married. I chuckled to myself.

"What's so funny?" Henry asked.

"Nothing," I said. "I love this room, that's all."

Back in the hall, we passed the closed door to Lucy's room and then Henry opened the door opposite hers. "My room," he said. "Now *our* room, at least temporarily. Sorry about the mismatched beds. Hideous. Some of my workers brought the extra one from the factory so we'd have two in here. Again, temporary, trust me. It makes my stomach turn to see these beds together." He motioned toward the two twin beds, one with tall carved posts at the head and foot, the other with a headboard made of wooden slats.

I laughed. "They make your stomach turn?"

"A pineapple bed and a mission-style bed right next to each other?" He gave a visible shudder and I laughed again.

"You're going to have to teach me about furniture," I said. To be honest, I barely saw the beds. I was taken by the armoire on the opposite wall. It was enormous, very tall, shaped like an elongated pentagon. The mirrored door was a long graceful oval and small floral carvings ran in a narrow line across the arched top and down each sloping side. "I don't know a pineapple bed from a . . . what did you call it? Mission bed? But I do know that this is beautiful," I said. "Did your father make it?"

He laughed as he came to stand beside me. "You have good taste," he said, "but I can see you have a lot to learn about furniture. This is Victorian. Made even before my father's time." He ran a hand over the smooth wood. "Mahogany exterior." He turned the key in the lock and opened the door. "Cedar interior covered in turquoise satin. It's where I keep my good clothes, as you can see." Suits and shirts hung neatly from the brass bar that ran across the interior of the armoire. He shut the door and carefully turned the key. "You will have the use of that entire closet." He pointed to a nearby closet door. "I'll move the rest of my things from there into the spare room."

Back in the hall, Henry showed me a bathroom that, while small, contained a deep claw-foot tub I would have liked to sink into right at that moment. "You and I will use this bathroom," he said. "Lucy has one next to her room. Hers is larger. I had no need for all that space, but we'll have a good-sized bathroom in my—*our*—new house."

We walked to the end of the hall and stood at the window that overlooked the backyard. I could see the garage and Hattie's little cottage.

"We added the garage onto the old woodworking shed several years ago when we got a second car." He looked at me. "Do you drive?" he asked.

"I have my license," I said. My mother and I had shared an old Ford until, with the gas and tire rationing, we decided it had become more trouble than it was worth and sold it to Vincent for a small sum. It was quite easy for us to take the bus wherever we needed to go, and a friend had often given me a ride to nursing school.

"Unfortunately we just have the Cadillac running now," he said. "There's a '39 Buick in the garage, but the tires are in terrible shape, and as long as rationing continues, we won't be able to replace them. Otherwise,

I could let you use it. But you're welcome to take a cab wherever you want to go."

"Are there buses?" I asked.

He smiled at me. "You're a frugal one, aren't you?" he said. "Yes, there are buses, but please feel free to take a cab."

"All right," I said, returning my gaze to the little cottage. I noticed the window boxes, empty now for the winter. "I bet that cottage is adorable in the warmer months," I said.

"Hattie's lived there the past two years," he said, "but I still think of it as Adora's cottage."

"That was the maid who saved your life?"

He nodded. "She worked for us for more than twenty years."

"Twenty years!"

"She was like part of the family," he said. "Her son and daughter too. But she's about fifty now and crippled with rheumatism, so she had to stop working. Hattie's her niece."

"Where did Adora go?"

"She's still in Hickory, living with her daughter and her grandchildren. I hired her son and daughter on at my factory. Zeke is our maintenance man and Honor works part-time as a housekeeper."

"Wasn't Zeke the colored man in your office when I came to the factory?"

"That's right."

"How come he's not in the military?"

"He was." Henry shrugged. "He volunteered for the Marine Corps and broke his leg last year while he was in training at Camp Lejeune. He's doing well though. Walks with a limp and I'm sure he has more pain than he lets on." He put his hands in his pockets. "We still look in on Adora. Make sure she's got enough to eat, what with the rationing and all."

I followed his gaze toward the cottage. "How did it happen?" I asked. "How did Adora save your life?"

He shook his head as though he were tired of talking. "Not now." He turned to face me. "You look a bit wrung out," he said. "I know this must be a lot to take in. Would you like a nap?"

The thought of lying down, closing my eyes, and escaping from everything new and unfamiliar was seductive. "I would," I said.

We walked back to his room, where he told me the pineapple bed would be mine. "You can unpack and have a good rest," he said. "I'm going to drive over to the factory."

"It's Saturday," I said.

"Yes, but I wasn't there yesterday and I want to make sure everything's in good shape."

I must have looked panicky at the thought of being in the house alone with his mother and sister, because he rested a hand on my shoulder. "Don't worry," he said. "I'll be back before you even wake up."

19

I woke to the sound of muffled voices on the other side of the bedroom door. It had to be nearly five o'clock, the room filled with a dusky twilight. I raised my head an inch from the pillow to try to make out the voices. Henry and his mother? So much for "Miss Ruth" rarely coming upstairs.

"She doesn't play bridge and I'm hardly going to put everyone in the bridge club through the agony of tutoring her," Ruth said.

I couldn't hear Henry's response, though his voice sounded calm.

"She looks foreign," Ruth said. "Like a Gypsy. Is she Italian or . . . ?"

I wasn't sure, but I thought Henry said, "What does that matter? She's a Kraft now."

"It matters and you know perfectly well it does," Ruth snapped. "She's pregnant, isn't she?" she asked, and I held my breath. Again, Henry's response was hard to make out.

"Oh, dear Lord!" Ruth said, and I pictured her wringing her hands, her cheeks growing red. "Soon she'll be showing and everyone will know. How could you be so foolish, Hank? She trapped you. She's a gold digger. There were a thousand and one ways you could have taken care of that short of marrying her."

My stomach clenched at her words. I sat up quietly, needing to hear the conversation more clearly. I needed to know my enemy.

"I've married her," Henry said. "I've done the right thing. And keep your voice down."

"How do you know it's yours?" Ruth asked. If anything, her voice was louder now.

"It's mine." Henry sounded very calm. "And she's my wife. You can't change that. You'll make her feel at home here, Mama." It was a command. "You'll take her to your book club and so forth. You'll help her fit in."

"Violet's in the book club!"

"Violet will adjust."

"I don't know how you can treat Violet so cruelly!" Ruth nearly shouted. "She loves you so much, Hank. I nearly died seeing my mother's ring on that girl's finger! I gave you that ring for Violet, no one else."

I glanced down at the diamond on my hand. What little light there was in the room seemed to collect in its facets. I felt guiltier than ever for wearing it.

Ruth wasn't finished. "Violet knew I always intended the ring to go to her," she said.

"You never should have told her that."

"She's loved you since you were children."

Henry made a derisive sound. "She's loved me from the day she realized I was wealthy, Mama. Not before."

"She helped you plan your new house! Why did you let her do that if you didn't intend to marry her?"

"I don't love her," he said.

"And you love this . . . this Italian Catholic gold digger?"

I winced.

"She trapped you and you fell for it," Ruth continued.

"I'm done talking to you about this," Henry said, "and I don't plan to discuss it with you again. She's my wife and I expect you to accept that and treat her with respect."

"You've humiliated me," Ruth said, and this time her voice was soft. Quivering. I heard a sob escape her. I thought of my last conversation with my own mother. Her words had not been exactly the same, but their meaning certainly had been. I bit my lip. I suddenly felt sympathy for Ruth. Her plans for her son, for her family's future, no matter how misguided, had been upended. I understood how that felt.

In a moment, Henry walked into the room. It was dim enough that he didn't see me sitting up in the bed, and he started when I spoke.

"I overheard some of your conversation with your mother," I said.

He'd been walking toward the dresser and I saw him turn to face me. "I wish you hadn't." He picked up his pipe from the dresser and lit it.

"She's very angry," I said.

"My mother always overreacts," he said, turning toward me. He took a puff from his pipe and the comforting sweet scent of his tobacco filled the room. "She'll be fine." He glanced at his watch and reached for the doorknob. "It's nearly time for dinner," he said. "I'm going downstairs. Why don't you get up and join me down there and we'll see what Hattie's managed to pull together from this week's rations?"

20

January 26, 1944

Dear Gina,

I've been a married woman living in Hickory for only four days and it already feels like a lifetime. It's not going well, dear friend. I hardly know where to start to tell you about it.

To begin with, my new husband didn't touch me on our wedding night, or on any night since, for that matter. I'm both relieved and mystified. Relieved because I don't love him (yet) and feel very little attraction to him—my heart still belongs to Vincent—but mystified because he was so ardent in that hotel room in Washington and now seems utterly passionless around me. Perhaps it's the baby? I don't know, and I don't feel comfortable enough with him to ask him outright.

Henry is very generous, however. He gave me money to spend on new clothing, since I'd brought so little with me, and yesterday he directed me to the most exclusive shop in Hickory's cute little downtown. The sort of shop where I feel like an imposter. I turned myself over to the saleslady and let her select outfit after outfit for me. Soon I will have to break down and buy maternity clothing, but for now, my girdle still hides my condition and no one is any the wiser. I had fun shopping, actually, but I would have had much more fun if you had been with me.

I'm living in a darling town, in a rather posh neighborhood of hilly, winding roads and beautiful homes. Henry's family home is among the prettiest and I still get lost in its many rooms. My favorite rooms are the library, which is filled with books on all subjects, and the upstairs parlor, where I feel snug and comfortable. It snowed yesterday and I spent much of the day nestled in that room, studying for the RN exam. I'm not sure how I will be able to get to Winston-Salem for the three-day exam in March, since Henry doesn't want me to take it and I will be five months along then. Travel might be challenging. But I'm determined! I've come this far and once my baby is old enough to leave with a sitter (Henry wants us to have an actual nanny!), I will be a nurse, by hook or crook!

Oh, Gina, I don't want to tell you how truly difficult these past few days have been! You will worry and I don't want you to. I know I'm very fortunate that my baby's father is taking responsibility for my child and myself, and certainly I'm living in paradise. But there is so much wrong. To begin with, his mother and sister already dislike me intensely. His mother, who is a lovely, sophisticated-looking woman, is kind to my face, but I know she wanted Henry to marry a girl named Violet who she thinks is a far more suitable match. Which she probably is. Henry denies they were engaged, but clearly there was some sort of relationship there that I have disrupted, and although I haven't met this Violet, I feel terrible for hurting her. Henry's mother has also figured out that I am expecting (though she's said nothing to me about it), and I know she thinks I'm very loose and unworthy of her son and the family name. I don't know how to win her over but I'm determined to try. Henry's younger sister, Lucy, is cold to me, and has perfected a sneer each time she looks at me. She is bitter because she had no debutante ball due to the war. Can you imagine the sort of girl she is? How will I ever relate to her? I remind myself it's only been a few days and we are all trying to make the best of things.

They have a maid named Hattie. I guess that means I also have a maid now! That's another adjustment, turning over my laundry to someone else to do. Not bothering to make my bed or dust the dresser because she's expected to do it. She's a wonderful cook, working magic with the little bit of rationed food we can get, and I like her. As a matter of fact, she is the kindest person in the house. She's the only person around whom I don't feel uncomfortable.

And dear Gina, they want to turn me into a Baptist! Henry has informed me in no uncertain terms that I am no longer Catholic. I've never met a Baptist in my life till now, and I know nothing about the Baptist religion, but I guess I will find out this Sunday when we go to church. Maybe I won't be able to go to mass any longer, but I will always be Catholic in my heart.

I'm so sorry to go on and on this way. Don't worry about me. This is all new and temporary—a period of adjustment. Henry is building a house for us nearby. I haven't seen it yet, but I don't care if it's a shack— as long as it puts some distance between us and his mother and sister.

Now tell me all about you. Any news from Mac? How is your mother? Treasure her before it's too late! And please, please keep in touch. I miss you, Gina. I miss my dear mother. And I miss Vincent more than I can say—I try not to think about him or I won't be able to function at all. If you should hear from him or learn anything about him, please don't tell me. I need to put him out of my mind as best I can. I know I can trust you to never reveal my whereabouts—or my condition—to him.

Oh, Gina, there is so much I've done that I wish I could undo! With love, Tess

21

The Krafts had their own pew in the Baptist church. Whether it was theirs in a formal sense or people simply knew to leave it vacant for the family, I didn't know. Either way, the third pew on the left side was empty when we arrived, while most others were filled. Lucy went into the pew first, followed by Ruth, then Henry and myself. Henry had tried to usher me in to sit next to Ruth, but I'd held back long enough to let him know I'd prefer he sit next to his mother. Although she was treating me civilly, I couldn't get those things she'd said about me out of my head.

Sitting in the church, waiting for the service to begin, I was very aware of my "differentness." My so-called foreign looks. The fact that I'd never before been to a religious service outside the Catholic church. The loneliness that came with knowing not a soul in the church other than the three people I was sitting with—and those three people were near strangers to me as well.

There was quiet chatter around us as we waited. I kept my gaze straight ahead. I was certain people were looking at me. Certain that the whispering I heard was about me. The church felt all wrong. It was too brightly lit, to begin with. There was no altar, only a lectern standing empty in front of us. No communion rail or crucifix or tabernacle or candles. There were none of St. Leo's extraordinary frescoes or stained glass or murals. No stations of the cross, no statues. No kneelers! I would have given anything at that moment to be back in my own church. I didn't belong here and I had the feeling that everyone around me knew it.

The man who appeared at the lectern wore a suit, like every other man in the church, and it took me a while to realize that he was the minister or preacher or whatever he would be called in a Baptist church. No vestments. Nothing to set him apart from anyone else. He welcomed everyone and then called for announcements. People stood up here and there throughout the church, asking for prayers for a sick aunt, announcing a birth, calling for donations for a youth mission trip. It was like being at a community meeting, not a church service, and I was extraordinarily relieved that the Kraft family refrained from announcing Henry's brand-new marriage. It was nothing to be proud of, I supposed. I was glad to keep the focus off myself as much as possible.

After the announcements, Henry handed me a hymnal and we sang a couple of hymns I'd never heard before but that everyone else seemed to know by heart. I stumbled through the words and melodies. Then the minister delivered a sermon about sin, which I tried hard to imagine had not been penned specifically for me. My mind began to drift as he spoke. Where was Vincent going to church this morning? Was he praying for me or had he given up on me altogether? How had he reacted to my letter? Was he angry or was he grieving? Most likely I'd left him utterly confused. He wouldn't understand that I'd saved him from myself.

When the service was over and we left the church and congregated outside on the sidewalk, people began to approach us. Henry rested his hand on my elbow in a manner that felt both protective and comforting and I was grateful.

"So you're the young lady who swept Hank off his feet," one woman said, her smile overly curious.

"What lovely hair you have!" said another. "I don't believe I've ever seen hair quite that thick before."

I greeted everyone with a warm smile, trying to imagine them as part of my new church family, but their curiosity didn't feel like friendliness to me.

An older man and woman approached us and Hank let go of my elbow to shake the man's hand. "This is my wife, Tess," he introduced me. "Tess, this is Hickory's mayor, Arthur Finley, and his wife, Marjorie."

"How do you do?" I smiled at them.

"Welcome, dear," Marjorie said. "We're happy to have you with us." It felt like the first sincere greeting of the morning.

"Our Hank is full of surprises," said the mayor. "How long have you two known each other?"

"Quite a while," Henry answered quickly, and I nodded.

"Well, I hope you'll be very happy in our beautiful city." The mayor touched my shoulder and then he and his wife moved on to speak with someone else. I wished they had stayed with us. I wanted to hold on to their kindness.

I kept a smile on my face, and as I continued to meet people and respond to their comments and questions, I became aware of a girl standing nearby. She was chatting with a group of young women, one of them Jeanetta Gill from the justice of the peace's office, but her eyes kept darting in my direction and I knew in my bones who she was: Violet Dare. She was a stunner, her white-blond hair in a silky pageboy, her eyes so blue I could see the sky reflected in them from where I stood. Her legs were slender and long, and beneath her charcoal-gray princess coat, I could see that her figure was shapely, the coat nipped in at her tiny waist. I saw Henry nod to her, and watched her turn away from him with a haughty shake of her head.

"That's Violet, isn't it," I whispered to him.

Before he could answer, the minister broke through the throng of people and came to stand in front of us. "Mr. and Mrs. Hank Kraft!" he boomed. "Congratulations!"

Henry smiled at the man, reaching out to shake his hand. "Pastor Smith," he said, "I'd like you to meet my wife, Tess."

"I'm pleased to meet you, Tess." The man lightly touched my arm. "Your reputation precedes you."

"Thank you," I said, feeling more awkward than ever. I doubted he'd meant that comment as a compliment.

"You're from Maryland, is that right?" he asked.

"Yes," I said. "Baltimore."

"Some wonderful Baptist churches up there. Which one did you attend?"

"I . . . actually, I attended a Catholic church." I glanced at Henry to see the muscles in his jaw contract.

"Ah, I see," the pastor said. Then he chuckled. "Well," he said, "we should get you into a Bible-study class pronto! If you call my office, we can let you know the schedule."

"Thank you," I said, knowing I would never call. From the corner of my eye, I noticed Lucy had walked over to Violet's cluster of girlfriends. She embraced Violet, who shot me one more glance, then gave Lucy a mournful look. I turned away. I hated being the cause of another girl's pain.

I leaned close to Henry, my lips nearly touching his ear. "Can we go, please?" I asked, and he nodded.

I stood still and alone on the sidewalk as he collected his mother and sister, and it seemed as though an invisible wall formed around me, letting the good people of Hickory keep their distance. I was the interloper. The stranger. No one dared get too close.

22

Monday morning hit me hard. I woke up from a dream about my mother, shaken, although I couldn't remember much of what had happened. It had felt so real, though, and as Henry and I walked downstairs and into the dining room for breakfast, I couldn't shake the feeling of having my mother with me, inside me somehow. Lucy had spent the night at a friend's house—I was quite certain the friend was Violet—so it was only Ruth, Henry, and myself eating the eggs, ham, and grits Hattie had made for us. Ruth was dressed to the nines, ready to go to a Kraft Fine Furniture board meeting, and Henry was dressed for the office. The two of them talked factory business while I nibbled my breakfast and held the dream-like memory of my mother close.

When Henry and Ruth left, I went upstairs and sat in the parlor to read, but I was unable to get my mother out of my mind, and before I knew it, I was crying hard. It was as though the reality of her being gone was only now hitting me. I would never again be able to call her. Talk to her. Hug her. I buried my head in my hands and let out the grief I'd been holding in for the past couple of weeks.

"Miss Tess?"

I jerked up straight to see Hattie standing in the doorway of the parlor, a pile of folded sheets in her arms. Embarrassed, I brushed the tears from my face.

"Excuse me, Hattie," I said, even though *she* was the one interrupting *me*. I tried to smile. "I'm just having myself a good cry."

Hattie walked into the room and crossed over to one of the upholstered armchairs. With her tall, reedlike build and long legs, she had a way of covering a good distance in very few steps. There was nothing hesitant about Hattie. Not in the confident way she cooked our meals, or mopped the floor, or crossed a room.

Now she sat down, the neatly folded sheets on her lap, and leaned toward me. "Mr. Hank told me your mama passed," she said. "That's what got you in the doldrums?"

"Yes," I admitted.

"He say she fell out and smacked her head on somethin'."

I nodded. "She probably had a seizure from diabetes." Would Hattie know what diabetes was?

"She had the sugar," she said.

"Yes," I said. "The sugar."

"And you missin' her. Wish you could talk to her one more time?"

"Exactly," I said.

"I can help you," she said, "but you got to promise you ain't gonna tell Mr. Hank or Miss Ruth what I say. Right?"

I stared at her. "Hattie," I said, "I think this is one of those problems that's beyond help."

"No, Miss Tess, you wrong. You got to talk to Reverend Sam."

"Who's Reverend Sam?"

Hattie looked toward the door as though someone might overhear us, even though no one else was home.

"He talk to the spirits."

I had to laugh. "I'm afraid I don't believe in that sort of thing," I said.

"That's because you ain't never talked to the likes of Reverend Sam," she said, smoothing her hand over the pile of sheets. "I see him whenever I'm in the mood to have a visit with my brother Conway."

"Conway?"

"He passed when I was ten year old. Reverend Sam found him for me some years back and we been visitin' ever since. Sam don't ask for money or nothin'. He just do it out of a kindly heart."

I kept my smile in check as I wondered how to respond. If she got some comfort from this Reverend Sam I didn't want to take it away from her.

"That's wonderful," I said. "But I don't think it would work for me."

"Oh, honey, it works for everbody," she said. "I can give you a wrote-down-on-paper guarantee. My man see him too, from time to time. He likes to have a chat with his daddy that passed."

"You have a man, Hattie?" I asked, surprised. How quickly I'd come to think of her as "ours," with no life outside the Kraft house.

"Yes, ma'am, I sure do. Oscar. He's a fine man. Works over at that textile mill by Mr. Hank's factory." She grinned at me. "But that's between me and you, now, hear?"

"Of course," I said. "I'm so pleased to hear you have someone." I really was, and I was touched she would confide it in me when she'd known me such a short time.

"And like I say, he thinks the world of Reverend Sam too."

"Well," I said, thinking it was time to bring this "Reverend Sam" conversation to a close. At least she'd gotten me out of my "doldrums." "Thank you for telling me about him."

We both turned at the sound of a door opening and closing downstairs, and Hattie immediately jumped to her feet, sheets in her arms. She didn't want to be caught taking a break. Or perhaps she didn't want to be caught talking to *me*. She walked toward the door, then turned back to look at me.

"You gonna go see him?"

"I don't think—"

"He lives in Ridgeview," she said, glancing toward the hallway and the stairs. "You know where that's at—Colored Town? Big blue house on Second Avenue. Diffent from all them other houses. Can't miss it."

"Thank you," I said again. "And I'm sorry you lost your brother, Hattie."

"Oh, he's still around, Miss Tess," she said from the doorway. "Jest like your mama."

23

I kept to myself my first few weeks in the Kraft house. Around Ruth and Lucy, I feigned ignorance as though I had no idea they knew I was carrying a child. But I discovered that Henry rather liked talking with me about the baby. At night, we'd lie on our mismatched twin beds and have long conversations about names—he liked Andrew after his grandfather while I favored Philip after my father. If it was a girl, I wanted to name her after my mother—Maria—but Henry refused to even consider it. "Mary" was as close as he was willing to come. I was so certain my baby was a boy that I didn't make an issue out of it. It was clear that Henry thought his claim on naming our male child was stronger than mine. It would be a Kraft, after all. We ultimately decided on Andrew Philip Kraft.

"Not Andy," Henry said. "Never Andy."

Secretly, though, I thought of the little charmer inside me as "Andy" all the time. I loved the cuteness of the name. I loved imagining what he would look like. My dark hair and Henry's blue eyes? What a handsome combination that would be. And I loved Henry's excitement. He was dreaming of the future with our child, just as I was. Finally we had something in common. It was thoughts about my baby that got me through those early days in the Kraft house. He—or she—kept me going.

When Henry and I weren't talking about the baby, though, our marriage felt empty and false. Henry touched me only in front of others, as though he wanted people to think we were a close and loving couple when we were anything but. In his bedroom, there wasn't even the pretense of us being husband and wife. He was not unkind to me, but rather . . . businesslike. Our marriage had been a business arrangement right from the start, I realized. I shouldn't have expected anything else. Might I someday fall in love with him? Would he someday fall in love with me? I prayed that would happen, yet how could I ever give my heart to a man when it still, deep down, belonged to another?

When Ruth and Lucy were out and I felt free to poke around, I explored the house. I read some of the books in the well-stocked library, and I felt some warmth toward Ruth when I paged through the family scrapbook she kept on the small table by the library window. The scrapbook was filled with photographs and newspaper clippings that obviously had meaning to her. Her wedding announcement was in there. Henry's and Lucy's birth announcements. The whole history of the Kraft family told through newspaper articles, starting with the building of the factory in the late nineteenth century. I couldn't believe I was now a part of that family, although I imagined there wouldn't be a mention of me in the book until baby Andrew—or Mary—was born.

Outside the Kraft house, I felt conspicuous. Once I took a cab into town while Henry was at work, wanting to get to know Hickory better. I walked past the shops and restaurants, learning my way around, and I felt as though the gaze of everyone I encountered was on the middle of my body. Everyone suspected, yet no one said a word—to me, at least. My girdle had become unbearable and I knew that soon I would need to buy maternity clothes and people would then know what they'd already guessed. Although she never spoke to me about my condition, Ruth stared at my stomach every time I walked into the room, and she spoke to me with a politeness that I knew masked her disdain.

Lucy, on the other hand, didn't bother to hide her feelings. She was downright derisive of me. She criticized my hair, which I always struggled to tuck neatly into a bun and victory roll.

"You need to cut it," she told me over the breakfast table one morning when it was just the two of us. "And you should really have it thinned. It's too much hair to do anything with. Plus, you need to tweeze those eyebrows."

I'd been tweezing my eyebrows since I was fifteen. I was confident they were well shaped, but even so they were thick and dark. They'd always been my curse. My dark looks had fit in perfectly in Little Italy, but here they set me apart, as though I needed anything else to make me feel like a stranger in Hickory.

I struggled to find a way to respond to Lucy's insults. I put up with a great deal, not wanting to alienate her. I usually smiled and agreed with her about my terrible eyebrows, my ornery hair, my unstylish clothing, laughing at myself along with her while inside I seethed. I couldn't say what I truly thought or felt in this house. I was losing myself here. Losing Tess, day by day.

I was stir-crazy toward the end of my second week in Hickory and decided to visit the public library. Wearing one of my new skirts, new blue cardigan, and new cream-colored coat, I took a cab into town and was contentedly exploring the library's fiction shelves when I came across *A Tree Grows in Brooklyn*. I'd found that book on my mother's night table a few days after her death, a bookmark close to the end, and I'd donated it to St. Leo's along with all her other belongings. Now, I pulled the book from the stack and cradled it in my hands. My mother must have enjoyed it to make it nearly to the end. She had a habit of starting books and not finishing them.

At the front desk, I filled out a form to get a library card. The middle-aged woman looked at my information, but didn't seem at all interested in the fact that I was a Kraft and I was relieved. She gave me my card and the book and sent me on my way.

Outside the library, I hugged the book close to me, not only because the day was cold. I couldn't wait to start reading. I wanted to feel close to my mother.

I was walking toward the main street where I hoped I could find a cab, when one of the city buses pulled to a stop on the other side of the street. Across the front of the bus, above the broad window, the sign read RIDGEVIEW. *Big blue house,* Hattie had said. *Can't miss it.* Maybe it was because I was holding the book my mother had been reading and she was much on my mind and in my heart, or maybe it was because I was bored and in need of an interesting way to spend the afternoon, but something made me run across the street and hop on the bus. Only as it pulled away from the curb and I turned to search for a seat did I realize mine was the only white face among the passengers.

Crazy crazy crazy, I thought to myself as the bus traveled from the familiar streets of Hickory to a neighborhood I didn't recognize. Ridgeview was a world apart from the rest of town. The bus passed coffee shops and a launderette, beauty shops and a little movie theater. I spotted a funeral home, two doctor's offices, a pool room, and several churches. Passengers—mostly women in housekeeping uniforms—got off the bus at each corner. I watched the street signs, looking for Second Avenue. Finally, I spotted the lopsided street sign and realized that Second Avenue was nothing more than a narrow dirt road. I stood up and walked to the front of the bus. Two women, obviously maids or nannies, got off the bus with me, and they glanced at me curiously before they headed briskly up the road.

My own pace was slow as I began walking along the narrow dirt road in search of the blue house Hattie had told me about. The afternoon was clear, the air sharp and cold, and the sky a vivid blue. Children playing in the yards stared at me as I passed and I smiled and waved. They waved back at me uncertainly, giggling. I didn't think I'd ever felt so out of place in my life. What on earth was I doing here? I didn't see a single car other than a couple of old trucks parked in dusty driveways. On either side of the street stood tiny houses, barely more than shacks. Some of them *were* shacks, I thought, made of unpainted wood, the siding cracked and warped. Most of the yards had trees but no lawns, just dirt swept smooth, brooms leaning against sagging porches. I saw a few victory gardens, idle for the winter.

I spotted a house that stood out from the others, but it wasn't blue as Hattie had said. No, this little house was pale yellow with white trim and the roof appeared to be newly shingled. Someone had taken good care of this particular house and I admired it as I walked by.

A Tree Grows in Brooklyn was still clutched to my chest and my cheeks were beginning to burn from the cold when I finally spotted the blue house a short distance ahead of me on the left. I knew it right away. It was far larger than the others on the street—two stories tall with a broad front porch—and it was painted the color of the sky.

Before I had a chance to change my mind, I walked across the bare yard and up the five porch steps. I pulled off my gloves and knocked on the heavy wooden door. No answer. I put my ear close to the door and listened, but there wasn't a sound from inside. *This is a sign*, I thought. I should simply turn around and go home. I wondered when the next bus would come through the neighborhood. I was about to leave when the door abruptly opened and I was face-to-face with a man about my height but many years older.

"Oh," I said. "I didn't think anyone was home. I'm looking for Reverend Sam."

"You've found him," he said. "Can I help you, miss?" His skin was several shades darker than my own and he had a smattering of freckles across his nose and cheeks. His short cropped hair had the wiry texture of most Negro hair but it was reddish brown in color and turning gray at the temples. He wore a knowing smile, as though he'd been expecting me. As though he already knew me. For a moment I couldn't speak and he raised his eyebrows in an invitation. "What can I do for you?" he prompted.

My own smile was sheepish. "My name is Tess Kraft," I said. "Our family's maid—Hattie . . ." I realized I didn't know Hattie's last name, but he nodded. He knew who I was talking about. "She told me about you," I said. "And I wondered . . . I recently had a loss and I—"

"Come in," he said, stepping back to let me pass him.

I hesitated only a moment before walking inside. The house was dark and it took my eyes a few minutes to adjust after being in the sunlight for so long. We were in a cool, dusky living room cluttered with furniture. Two sofas and several overstuffed chairs. Tables and overflowing bookshelves. There was a scent in the house that was strong and peculiar, though not unpleasant, like firewood that had burned for a long time before being extinguished. I glanced toward the brick fireplace. There was no fire burning now.

"May I take your coat?" He sounded almost courtly.

I took off my coat and hat, and he hung them from hooks near the front door. I held on to the library book, though. I didn't want to forget it.

"Follow me to my office," he said.

I wasn't sure why I trusted him enough to follow him down a long dark tunnel of a hallway, but I felt certain I had nothing to fear. I was comforted by the thought that Hattie, whom I'd quickly come to like very much, had spent time with him and trusted him. Yet when he opened the door to his office, I gasped. In front of me stood a life-sized skeleton, the bones almost aglow in the dim light. I stopped in the doorway.

"What . . . ?"

He chuckled. "This is my anteroom," he said. "Don't be afraid. Those old bones can't hurt you. That fella's been dead for hundreds of years, if not thousands."

I stepped into the room, my eyes warily on the skeleton on my left. It stood on some sort of stand so that it was upright, a few inches taller than me. "This is real?" I asked.

"If you mean was it once a man, yes indeed." He swept an arm through the air, taking in the shelves and tabletops covered with other objects. "All of these are real," he said. "Indian funerary relics."

I turned in a circle, beginning to make out the objects around me. Ceramic bowls. A headdress dripping with feathers. A framed collection of painted arrowheads. A couple of skulls.

"My." I heard the shiver in my voice and was acutely aware of the door behind me. The way out of this strange little museum. I tightened my grip on the book where I held it against my chest.

"Relax, child," he said, seeing my trepidation. "These treasures were my great-uncle's. He was a free black man and an adventurer. And now they're mine." He chuckled. "I don't know where Uncle Porter got them. All I know is that I can only connect well with spirit when I'm in their presence, so they stay." He must have seen the uncertain look on my face because he quickly continued. "But this isn't where you and I will talk, so nothing to fear."

He opened a door I had not even noticed until that moment and stepped into another room, but I hung back, not sure I wanted to see what other "treasures" he had hidden away.

"Come along, now. Nothing to fear," he said again.

I'd come this far and, despite being unnerved by the "anteroom," I was intrigued. I followed him into the smaller room. There was barely enough space for an enormous desk, nearly twice the size of Henry's desk in our library. A tall, ladder-back chair stood behind the desk and two smaller wooden chairs were in front of it. Reverend Sam sat down behind the desk and motioned to the chairs. I lowered myself into the one closest to the door, my damp hands folded on top of the book.

I took in a deep breath. "I'm here because I—"

"Hush." He leaned toward me, his arms outstretched on his desk, his hands motioning for me to put mine in them.

In for a penny, in for a pound, I thought. I set the book on my lap and leaned forward to rest my hands in his warm, dry palms. He closed his fingers lightly around mine and shut his eyes.

"Dear Lord," he said, "with your protection and if it's your will, help us open the door between two worlds today. Bring us only peace, and lift our hearts and souls." Then he let go of my hands and sat back in his chair.

"How old are you?" he asked.

"Twenty-three."

"Ah," he said with a slow nod, as if my answer revealed far more than my age.

"I don't want to know the future," I said quickly. I hadn't thought of that. That he might tell me something I didn't want to hear. What if he said my future would be even worse than my present? Not that I believed anyone truly had the ability to predict the future. Still, I didn't want to know.

He chuckled again. "That's very fortunate," he said, "because I don't know how to see into the future, although spirit will sometimes give me a glimpse into what's coming. But I personally have one gift and one gift only: I can connect with the spirit world. As far as gifts go, that seems like more than enough for one man to be able to manage, wouldn't you say?"

"Yes," I said, "though I'm not sure I believe that you—or anyone—can do even that."

"And yet, you came here." He hadn't lost his smile. "You're hopeful."

"I guess I am," I said. "Although . . ."

"Although?"

"The person I want to . . . to talk to was angry with me when—"

"Hush," he said gently, and he closed his eyes again. "Let's just see who will come. It's better that way."

He mumbled another short prayer, then raised his head, eyes still closed. "Ah, yes." He spoke very calmly to the air. "I hear you. I hear you."

I thought he was putting on quite a performance and felt foolish once again for being there. I was glad I wasn't expected to pay for this.

He opened his eyes to half-mast. "I'm not sure yet who's coming through," he said. "Do you pray?"

"Yes," I said. "Of course."

"Beseeching prayers?"

"I . . . yes." Every night I prayed for my baby's health and safety. I prayed for Mimi and Pop and Vincent and Gina. I didn't pray for Henry. Odd. It hadn't occurred to me to do so.

"Prayers of gratitude as well?" he asked.

"Yes," I said, though I realized I hadn't offered prayers of gratitude in a while. I was not feeling very thankful these days.

He suddenly shut his eyes and sat up straighter, eyebrows raised. "What?" he said into the air. "Yes, I hear you." Eyes still closed he leaned a few inches toward me. "Someone is here," he said. "I see spirit . . . I see . . . Maria?"

My heart gave a thud. I sat forward, holding my breath. "Who?" I whispered, wondering if I'd misheard.

"Maria," he said again, then added, "Spirit is beautiful. Very peaceful."

Tears stung my eyes and my body began to tremble. This couldn't be real. Yet I felt myself getting roped into his game in spite of myself. I *wanted* to be roped in.

"Maria was my mother," I said.

He didn't answer. He seemed far away from me. Could he truly be connecting to my mother? If so, I needed to talk to her. "Please tell her I love her," I said. I heard the intensity in my voice. "Please tell her I'm sorry I disappointed her."

"Maria," he said, "your daughter loves you very—" He stopped, tilting his head as if listening. Then he nodded, his eyes still closed. "Yes, of course." He leaned toward me again, his closed eyelids fluttering slightly. "She says she loves you. And she asks you to finish the book for her."

"Finish the . . . ?"

"Do you know what she means?" he asked me. "Was she a writer?"

"No, she . . . Oh!" I looked down at the book in my lap. "Tell her I will." I laughed, pressing my hand to my mouth. I felt a ridiculous surge of joy. "Tell her I'll let her know how it ends."

Reverend Sam opened his eyes then. "She's gone, dear," he said. He looked a bit drained. "What was that about the book?"

I lifted *A Tree Grows in Brooklyn* from my lap. "I just got this from the library," I said, speaking quickly in my excitement. "When she died, I found the same book on her night table. She hadn't finished it yet. I can't believe this just happened. How did you . . . how is this even possible? It's *not* possible," I said, suddenly deflated. Surely this was some sort of trick. "Did Hattie tell you about me? About my mother?" Though Hattie didn't know my mother's name, did she? And she certainly didn't know I'd picked up *A Tree Grows in Brooklyn* at the library.

"No, child," he said patiently. "I haven't spoken to Hattie in a couple of months."

"Were you really talking to my mother?"

"To the best of my knowledge, I was. She knew you very well. And loves you deeply."

"How do you do it?" I asked. "And who *are* you? Are you really a reverend? A minister?"

He smiled at my rush of questions. "I grew up in the next town over," he said calmly, and I had the feeling he was accustomed to responding to doubters. "Newton. My mother was born a slave in a family that lived not far from there. They gave her a paid job after emancipation, most likely because she was a favorite of the man of the house, if you understand my meaning." He gave me a questioning look, and I nodded. "He was almost certainly my father," he continued, "and he sent me to a Negro boarding school and then Bennett College in Greensboro. My degree's in philosophy, and no, I'm not a minister, but the folks around here have called me 'reverend' for as long as I can remember."

"But how do you . . ." My voice drifted off as he nodded, knowing what I was about to ask.

"I'm not sure, is the truthful answer. When I was a little boy, I had an older sister. I was very close to her. She died of scarlet fever when I was seven or eight. One night, I was lying in bed thinking very deeply about her and I suddenly felt her spirit with me. She told me she'd been trying to contact me to let me know she was fine. I told my mother, who gave me a whippin' for talking nonsense." He chuckled. "So I kept my visits with my sister to myself, but I knew I'd found a way to reach her. I learned that I had to concentrate hard on her, and most of all, I had to believe she was there for me to reach out to."

"Do you still talk to her?"

"Oh, all the time," he said. "She's still only nine years old, but she's very wise."

I nodded, disbelieving. Yet hadn't he just talked with my mother? I couldn't explain it.

"How did you end up here? In Hickory?"

"My father left me money and I bought this house. Mama lived here with me until she died. I married a lovely girl and we have three sons, all of whom think I'm off my rocker." He winked at me, and I smiled. "I have five grandchildren. Two of them are fighting in the Pacific right now."

"You must worry about them," I said.

"Indeed." He nodded.

"I'm glad you have a family," I said. I didn't want to think of him alone.

He smiled. "You're a sweet girl," he said. Then he sighed. "I've had a . . . shall we say, a difficult life, in some ways because of my gift. I've been sued. Once I was even put in a colored hospital for the insane and I would still be there if my father hadn't fought to get me out." He leaned back in his chair. "It's wonderful to be old now," he said. "I'm enjoying it. Everyone simply thinks of me as the crazy but harmless old man in Ridgeview. I suppose every neighborhood needs one of those."

I laughed, and he looked at me intently. "But returning to you, Tess. How do you feel?"

I thought about the question, taking inventory of my emotions. "Good," I said simply. "I feel good. And I feel grateful." I looked at him warmly. I'd nearly forgotten that outside this house I had a life that worried and distressed me. A life that challenged me at every turn. I didn't want to leave, but Reverend Sam got to his feet and I did the same, still clutching the library book in my hands. I felt slightly disoriented. When we walked into the anteroom, though, I was jarred back to reality by the skeleton. It seemed like hours since I'd first seen it and I moved past it quickly.

We walked quietly through the hallway and the living room. I put on my coat and hat, then turned to face him. "Can I come back again sometime?"

"Of course, child," he said. "I'll be waiting for you."

24

The day after my visit to Reverend Sam, Ruth hosted one of her Ladies of the Homefront meetings at the house and Henry suggested I attend to please his mother. I would have liked to spend the entire day reading *A Tree Grows in Brooklyn,* feeling close to my own mother and holding tight to the feeling of comfort I'd taken away with me from Reverend Sam's, but I knew I needed to participate in this household and it would be a chance to get to know some of the women in Hickory. I needed to make some friends.

Hattie baked oatmeal cookies for the meeting, using molasses in place of our rationed sugar, and the delicious aroma wafted up the stairs to the bedroom as I was getting dressed for the meeting. I went down to the kitchen, glad to find her alone as she pulled a tray of the cookies from the oven.

"Thank you for telling me about Reverend Sam," I said quietly.

She glanced quickly behind me as she set the tray on a couple of trivets and I knew "Reverend Sam" was a topic we had to keep between us.

"You seed him?" she asked, straightening up from the counter, her voice as soft as mine.

I nodded. "He talked to my mother."

A broad smile creased her thin face. "How 'bout that," she said, hands on her hips. Again, she glanced toward the doorway.

"It was amazing," I said.

She opened the oven door again to pull out a second tray of cookies.

"You best git on now," she said, reaching into the oven. "Best git ready for them Homefront ladies."

In the living room, I saw that a few rows of chairs had been set up for the meeting and Ruth was fidgeting with them, trying to make them arrow straight. I began to help, wanting something to do.

"I'm sure you'll fit right in today," Ruth said, and I thought she was expressing a hope rather than a belief.

"I'm looking forward to meeting everyone," I said, nudging a chair into place.

"There." She stood up straight and admired our handiwork. "Perfection," she said with a smile. "Now"—she patted the lapels of the blue jacket she was wearing and looked across the chairs at me—"would you tell Hattie I want to serve tea this morning?" she asked. "I'm sure we're very low on coffee from the rationing."

"Of course," I said, and headed down the hall toward the kitchen again. This time, though, I found the kitchen empty, the fragrant cookies now arranged on a platter. The window over the sink was open a few inches and I spotted Hattie standing at the clothesline near the back door, hanging laundry, Lucy and a young colored woman by her side. The three of them were laughing. I wasn't sure I'd heard Lucy laugh in my nearly two weeks in Hickory, and I leaned close to the window to try to hear what they were talking about.

"It wasn't funny!" Lucy was saying, though her smile suggested otherwise. "You and the boys were so mean."

"You were just so much younger than us," the young woman said as she handed a clothespin to Hattie from the fabric sack in her hands. She was tall and slender and wore a red wool jacket. Her skin was very dark, her teeth very white, and even from where I stood, I could see that her wide smile was dazzling. "You were just a good target," she said.

Was this Zeke's sister? I wondered. The one who'd grown up in the cottage where Hattie now lived? I tried unsuccessfully to remember her name. Henry had said she worked part-time at the factory. That was about all I remembered.

"But you were a girl, too." Lucy bent over to lift a pillowcase from the wicker laundry basket and handed it to Hattie. "You should have stuck up for me."

"Sorry, Luce." The woman tapped Lucy on the nose with a clothespin. "I wanted to be one of the boys."

"Them boys made you tough, Miss Lucy," Hattie said as she pinned the pillowcase to the clothesline. "You ought to thank 'em."

"You weren't there, Hattie." Lucy grinned with a good nature I hadn't known she possessed. "You have no idea how I suffered."

"Remember the day we put the mattresses at the top of the stairs and slid down to the pile of blankets?" the woman asked.

Lucy gave her arm a fake slap. "Y'all wouldn't let me do it!" she said.

"You would've broken your scrawny little neck."

"Nobody worried about my scrawny little neck the day y'all threw water balloons at me."

"We didn't *throw* them," the woman said.

"Oh, you was so evil," Hattie said to her as she lifted another pillowcase from the basket.

I heard Ruth moving around in the dining room and thought I'd better give Hattie her message. I reached for the doorknob.

"Miss Ruth was so mad," the younger woman said, "and Mama gave Zeke a whippin' but—"

She stopped talking when I opened the door, and all three of them turned their heads in my direction.

"Hello." I smiled, walking onto the back steps. I crossed my arms against the chill air. "I have a message for Hattie from Miss Ruth," I said. "She'd like tea for her group today."

"Sure, Miss Tess," Hattie said. She motioned toward the other woman. "This is my cousin Honor," she said. "She took the bus out here to help me set up them chairs for the meetin'."

"That was nice of you," I said to Honor. "You and your brother and mother used to live in Hattie's little cottage, right?"

"Yes, ma'am," Honor said, sounding very formal, the joviality I'd heard in her voice moments ago completely gone. I felt guilty for putting an end to the lighthearted mood.

"What was that about water balloons?" I asked, striving for a friendly tone.

None of them spoke for a second and I stood there feeling intrusive. It took me a moment to realize I was staring at Honor. She was almost regal looking, the way she held her tall, slender frame. Her eyelashes were thick and unusually long like her brother's and her eyes were startling, as green as jade.

"The boys and Honor put them water balloons atop the back door," Hattie said, "so when Lucy, who was but four years old—"

"Five," Lucy corrected her.

"When she give the door a little push," Hattie said, "them balloons dropped down on her."

"Oh." I gave Lucy a sympathetic look. "It must have been hard to be the youngest."

She shrugged, looking away from me. "It wasn't bad," she said.

"I'll take care of that tea, Miss Tess," Hattie said. "You git inside before you catch your death."

"Will you be at the meeting today, Lucy?" I asked.

"Can't," she said, lifting her hand to study her pink fingernails. "I'm meeting some friends at the country club."

"And I need to get back to my babies, Hattie," Honor said, handing the sack of clothespins to her cousin.

"Nice meeting you, Honor," I said, reaching for the door.

"You, too, ma'am," she said.

I shut the door behind me and walked toward the kitchen window, listening, wondering if they were going to talk about me, but now the three of them spoke only in whispers. I felt ever so slightly betrayed by Hattie. Maybe, though, whatever she was saying was in my defense.

I expected the Ladies of the Homefront members to be around Ruth's age, so I was shocked when I opened the front door to find Violet and several of her girlfriends standing on the landing. Violet looked equally surprised to see me. We simply stared at one another for a moment. I was first to recover.

"Please come in," I said, stepping back with a smile. Although I'd seen Violet the two times I'd attended church, these were the first words I'd spoken to her. I felt bad for her and wanted to treat her kindly. "Miss Ruth and the others are in the living room."

They walked past me without a word and I followed them into the living room. I doubted they realized how close I was behind them, because I heard Violet whisper to one of her friends, "I didn't think she'd be here." Her friend squeezed Violet's shoulder in sympathy. "Just ignore her, dear," she said. "Pretend she's not even here."

I wished I hadn't agreed to come to the meeting, but it was too late now. I walked into the living room and sat down on the edge of one of the folding chairs that Hattie and Honor had set up. I sat there alone, my own false smile plastered on my face.

When all sixteen of the women were seated, Ruth took her place at the front of the room. Her navy blue skirt and jacket fit her slender body perfectly. Her white hair was freshly coiffed and she wore a pearl necklace as well as a small gold brooch that formed the initials *LHF*. Ladies of the Home Front. All of the women had one of those brooches, I noticed. All of them except me.

Ruth gave the women a welcoming smile as she stood in front of them, her hands folded together at her waist.

"As always," she began, "it does my heart good to see young women at a Ladies of the Homefront meeting." She smiled directly at Violet, who sat in the row in front of me and to my right. "Congratulations for recognizing the importance of maintaining our femininity in the face of the many modern forces trying to turn us into men," she said. "We are the fortunate ones, of course. The ones who don't have to put on trousers and do men's work. But we all know that many other women are not so lucky. They've had to go to work in the factories and offices, taking over jobs our brave men cannot do right now. Through Ladies of the Home Front, we're doing our part to prevent these girls from becoming hardened, chain-smoking women who've turned away from their Christian values and who will have forgotten their gentle natures by the time their poor husbands come home." She prattled on and on about how we "Ladies of the Homefront" needed to help the hardened women hold on to their feminine values even as society seduced them to become more masculine.

I kept glancing at Violet. I couldn't help myself. She seemed enraptured by every word from Ruth's mouth. With that pale, silky hair and delicate features and ivory skin, she was simply one of the most stunning creatures I'd ever seen. Despite Henry's denials to Ruth about caring for Violet, how could he not be captivated by her? I thought of how easily he had fallen into bed with me. Had he also slept with her, perhaps many times over the years? She'd probably been much smarter than me, finding a way to protect herself from getting pregnant.

One of Violet's friends raised her hand and Ruth acknowledged her with a nod.

"I saw a girl I used to pal around with the other day," the girl said. "She used to be so lovely, but she had to go to work in one of the hosiery mills and I barely recognized her. She was wearing *dungarees* on the street and smoking. Her fingernails were actually *yellow*. I talked to her for a while and she said she *likes* her job, that she has no intention of quitting when her husband comes home. Isn't that worrisome? Sometimes I think this is a flood we can't stop, Miss Ruth."

"Well," Ruth said, "I don't pretend to think we can stop it in every case, but we can let women know we're here for them and they're not alone."

Another woman, this one middle-aged with short salt-and-pepper hair, raised her hand. "My niece is a nurse," she said, and my ears instantly pricked up. "Now, the truth of the matter is, we need nurses, don't we? We need nurses and teachers and librarians and other female occupations. So I think our challenge is helping those women—the ones who do the jobs we desperately need—we need to help them resist the pressures that come along with being a working woman as well as a wife and mother."

I didn't hear the conversation that followed because I wasn't really listening. I was caught up in the fact that this woman had a niece who was a nurse. Did she live nearby? I would love to meet her, someone who would probably be more like me than anyone I'd met so far.

Everyone gathered in the dining room after the meeting, pouring themselves cups of tea and nibbling cookies from china plates.

I approached the woman with the salt-and-pepper hair. "Excuse me," I said to her. "I was curious about your niece. Is she an RN? A registered nurse?"

"Oh yes," she said. "I believe she is."

"I wonder if I could meet her," I said. "I have my nursing degree, though I still need to take the licensing exam to become an RN. I'd enjoy getting to know—"

"Tess, dear." Ruth was suddenly at my side, her perfume at war with the scent of tea and cookies. "Could you come into the kitchen with me for a moment, please?"

I smiled at the woman. "I'll be back," I said, and I followed Ruth down the hall.

I was still smiling when we walked into the kitchen, but as soon as Ruth turned to face me, I knew I had nothing to smile about.

"Tess," she began, "you need to get the idea of being a nurse . . . of working at all . . . out of your head." Her voice dripped with false kindness. "You'll be too busy being a wonderful wife to your husband and a devoted mother to your children. In time, perhaps we can find a role for you on the board of the factory, if you want to be involved. That will be plenty for a good Christian woman. All right, dear?" She smiled, resting a hand on my arm.

"I liked nursing," I said. "I think I'm good at it."

"Listen to me, Tess." Her voice was tighter now. "You don't know this new social landscape you're in and it's up to me to help you negotiate it, so that's what I'm trying my best to do. The *last* thing you want to do is let Mrs. Wilding out there think you're anything like her niece Grace," she said. "Grace is a very selfish, wild party girl who refuses to settle down and everyone in town knows it. She drinks, for heaven's sake. So now they're all in there talking about how Ruth Kraft's daughter-in-law is a party girl. Surely that's not what you want, is it?"

How ridiculous, I wanted to say. I felt as though she was waiting for me to agree with her. Maybe to apologize. But I wasn't going to kowtow to this woman. "I don't see the harm in meeting another nurse," I said. "I'm just going to ask Mrs. Wilding how I can get in touch with her niece. That's all."

"Don't you dare," Ruth threatened, but I walked past her, through the hallway and into the dining room, only to discover that the meeting had disbanded in my absence and Mrs. Wilding was nowhere to be found. The only people who remained were a few of Ruth's close friends and Violet and her entourage. As soon as they saw me, they headed for the front door. Already riled up from my conversation with Ruth, I followed after them. It was time to put an end to this chill between Violet and myself.

"Violet, wait," I called. "Please."

She had reached the open door, but she stopped as her friends continued out onto the front steps. She turned to face me. "Yes?" she asked.

I smiled at her and spoke quietly. "I just wanted to say that I'm sorry if my marrying Henry hurt you in any way," I said. "We both have to live here, and we'll be seeing each other all the time. I'd really like it if we could at least be friendly with one another."

She tilted her head to one side. Her pale blond hair spilled to her shoulder and the blue of her eyes was translucent and arresting.

"You are in way over your head," she said.

I'm sure I looked puzzled. I had no idea what she was talking about. Did she mean I was a girl from modest means trying to fit into a wealthy family? In that case, she was right. "I don't understand," I said.

"Henry told me everything."

"What do you mean?" I asked.

"Just what I said." She put one hand on her hip. "He told me how you seduced him. How you trapped him into marrying you."

I was too dumbfounded to speak. I was sure I was gawking at her, my mouth agape.

"I guess my mistake was not letting him have his way with me," she said, tipping her head to the other side now. "I thought he'd like a girl who valued herself enough to save herself for marriage," she added. "Apparently I was wrong."

She flounced her skirt as she turned to walk down the steps, and she didn't look back. Her friends surrounded her as they sailed down the brick walkway toward the road. If she had turned around, she would have seen me standing immobilized on the top step, stunned, humiliated . . . and very, very angry with my husband.

25

Henry actually laughed that night when I told him what Violet had said. "She's angry," he said. "She's trying to hurt you. Ignore her."

"Did you really talk to her about us?" We were in our bedroom and I was sitting on the pineapple bed in my robe.

"Briefly." He stood at the dresser lighting his pipe, enjoying his last smoke of the evening. "But I never put the onus on you," he added. "What happened was a mutual decision. A mutual mistake. And that's what I told her."

"It really isn't any of her business," I said.

"She thought we—Violet and I—would end up married," he said. "I suppose I expected that as well, not that I had any deep feelings for her or anything of that sort. We never discussed it, which I know made her a bit batty, but I wasn't ready to make any sort of commitment. Still, when I suddenly married you, I felt I owed her an explanation." He tapped his pipe on the edge of the ashtray and headed toward his bed.

"I can't help but feel that I derailed your well-planned-out life, but really, Henry, it's a noble thing you're doing. Giving our child a name."

"Nonsense," he said, getting into bed. "I don't deserve any medals." He sounded annoyed and I knew he wanted to be finished with this conversation. I wasn't quite done, though. In spite of Violet's attitude toward me, I felt sympathy for her. She'd wasted years on a man who didn't love her and suddenly lost him to a stranger. No wonder she seemed to detest me.

"I wish you hadn't told her I was pregnant."

"Folks are going to know soon enough, Tess," he said, lifting his book from the night table. "And on another subject, you should never have walked out on Mama when she was talking to you."

Ruth was furious with me. She was so angry, in fact, that she hadn't spoken to me since the meeting that morning. I saw that as a bit of a blessing.

"She told you, I guess," I said.

"Yes, she told me," Henry said. "I know she can be a challenge, but you've got to endure it until we move out. Speaking of which, let's go see how the house is coming along tomorrow morning before I go to the factory, all right?"

I nodded. I'd been to the property only once since arriving in Hickory. All there had been to see at that time was the foundation, and it had been impossible to envision the finished house. I'd been disappointed, knowing it would be a long, long time before we were able to have a place of our own.

He raised his book a couple of inches in the air. "Ready to read?" he asked.

I nodded, slipping under the covers, and lifting *A Tree Grows in Brooklyn* from my side of the night table. *Finish it,* my mother had told me. Tonight, I would.

26

February 17, 1944

Dear Gina,

I was so happy to hear from you and to learn that Mac is well and safe, even if he's not writing you the newsy letters you'd prefer. He's wise. I doubt any news he has from over there is news you would really want to hear. Yes, your life does sound a tad routine, but you are fortunate. Mine is anything but.

Thank you for asking about my little one. No, he hasn't yet moved, but I think that's normal, and he's definitely growing. When I take my girdle off at night, it's a great relief! I do love him. He and I are in this crazy mess of a life together.

Yesterday, Henry and I went once again to see the house he's having built for us. Oh, Gina, I do hope you get to visit us there. It's going to be truly lovely. It's going up so quickly now! The exterior walls are in place and I can see how enormous it's going to be. Plenty of room for Auntie Gina! It's set far back from the street and surrounded by trees on three sides. Although right now the front yard is nothing more than a sea of dirt and mud, I can picture how it will look covered in grass. A perfect place for my little one to play.

We walked around inside. Right now there are only beams and posts and the wonderful scent of wood, but with a little imagination I could see what it will be like. We went through room after room. The second story is not yet up, but Henry pointed out where the rooms would be and we figured out which one will be the nursery.

No, we are still not "close," as you put it. Quite honestly, that's all right with me for now. I'm certain it must be the baby and once he or she is born, Henry will again become the passionate man he was in the hotel in Washington. I hope so, because I don't want my son or daughter to be an only child as I was.

I think Henry is a good man but he definitely thinks he's the boss in our household. He even bosses his mother around, and that is not an easy thing to do! He doesn't want me to be a nurse (or have any sort of occupation at all, actually), but without him knowing, I've applied to take the licensing exam. I'm not going to tell him until I receive the no-tification that I can take it (I hope I'm the one to get the mail that day!). I've worked hard for this and I'm going to get that license!

And now, dear friend, I hesitate to tell you something I did, but if I can't tell you, who can I tell? You are going to think I've lost my mind, but I've been in touch with my mother! I visited a medium. Now, I don't believe in mediums or psychics or spiritualists any more than you do . . . or at least I didn't. But on a whim, I went to see him and, Gina, I can't explain how, but he knew my mother's name. He spoke to her and told me she's fine. I know this sounds crazy, but whether he is a charlatan or not, he made me feel better. He's the nicest person I've met since mov-ing to Hickory. I'd forgotten how wonderful it feels to be treated with kindness. Are you ready to send the men in the white coats for me? Some days I DO wonder if I'm losing my mind here. I am definitely losing the tough, self-confident girl I've always fancied myself to be. I hope that girl comes back soon.

Here is the next thing that will have you sending the men in the white coats after me: I think I'm being followed. I realized that I had no stamps for this letter, so I went downstairs to the library to see if Henry might have some in his desk. I've never looked in his desk before and I felt a little devilish peering in the various drawers, but none of them was locked, so fair game. I hadn't realized what an orderly man I married! All his files are neatly labeled. Unpaid bills are carefully clipped together. Busi-ness cards are neatly stacked. The wide middle drawer held several large empty manila envelopes, each of them bearing a blank white address la-bel perfectly centered, as if he'd taken careful measurements before gluing the label in place. But no stamps anywhere and I knew I would have to go into town to the post office.

Henry usually insists I take a cab wherever I go, but today was very warm here for February and I decided to walk into town. It's not terribly far. I'd barely left the house when I became aware of a police car slowly passing me on the street, driving in the same direction I was walking. I didn't think much of it. Oakwood is a wealthy neighborhood and I supposed the police keep a careful eye on it. But two blocks later, the car passed me again at a snail's pace. For a while, it actually seemed to drive at the same pace I was walking. I was nearly to town when it crept by me for a third time. This time, I got a good look at the policeman behind the wheel. He was young, probably about my age, with short, sandy-colored hair beneath his police hat. When our eyes met, he sped up. It was quite disconcerting! I'd reached the post office by then and went inside to buy stamps for both Henry and myself.

Walking home, I found myself watching for the police car, but the officer must have moved on to another part of town and I had a good laugh over my paranoia. Why would a police car be following me? Still, I can't shake the feeling that it was.

I know you're thinking that Hickory is making me lose my mind. I wonder that myself sometimes. You are right, though. I am lucky to have married Henry. When I feel sad or lonely in this marriage, I will remind myself that I'm married to an excellent provider. Our child will grow up in a beautiful house and he or she will want for nothing. My sweet baby will have a happy life and that's what's most important.

I pray for you and Mac every night, Gina. I follow the news each day and hope the Allies are planning something big. Maybe something that will finally put an end to this terrible war. I pray that Mac remains safe through it all and comes home to you very soon.

With love,

Tess

27

The night after I wrote the letter to Gina, Henry didn't come home. I had gone to bed while he remained reading in the upstairs parlor, a pattern we'd quickly fallen into. When I woke up at three in the morning, I could see that his bed hadn't been slept in. Concerned, I put on my robe and slippers and quietly walked to the parlor, expecting to find him asleep in his reading chair, but the room was dark and empty. I padded downstairs and peered into the library, but it too was dark, and when I flipped on the light, I saw that the ashes in the fireplace looked gray and cold. I wandered through the living room, the dining room, the hallway, moving quietly past Ruth's bedroom so I wouldn't wake her. The house was ghostly quiet. From the window in the kitchen, I looked into the backyard, silvery with moonlight. Hattie's little cottage was dark, as was the garage. Wrapping my robe more tightly around my body, I slipped out the back door and down the steps, making my way carefully along the walk as I headed toward the garage. When I reached the building, I peered through the side window. The Buick was there, the one with the worn tires, but Henry's Cadillac was gone. I saw my frown reflected in the window. Where was he? Where would he go in the middle of the night? Should I be worried?

I shivered as I walked back to the house. Once inside, I stood in the kitchen hugging myself to warm up. Back upstairs, I hesitated in the hall outside Lucy's room before knocking lightly on her door. I waited a moment, unsure if I should knock again.

"Who is it?" She sounded as though she were speaking into her pillow.

"It's me. Tess. May I come in?"

There was the rustle of sheets and in a moment she opened the door, a pink tulle hairnet covering her blond pincurls.

"What's going on?" she asked.

"Henry's gone," I said. "I mean, he never came to bed and now his car is gone." I glanced down the hallway toward the window that overlooked the backyard. "Should I be concerned?" I asked.

She turned her head away from me, an odd smile on her face. "That's just Hank," she said. "He doesn't need much sleep. He goes to the factory at night sometimes." She looked at me squarely now. "He likes to work there when there's no one around. He says he gets a lot done then."

"But it's three A.M.," I said. "He'll be exhausted in the morning."

"That's his problem," she said, already backing into her room. "He lives his life and I live mine." She closed the door without saying good night. I stood there a moment, staring at her door, before walking back to the bedroom I still thought of as "Henry's" rather than "ours."

It took me a while to fall asleep. When I awakened at six, Henry was sound asleep in his bed, his breathing soft and even. I got up quietly. He could sleep another hour before he absolutely needed to get up, but as I headed for the closet, I heard the creak of bedsprings.

"Good morning," he said.

I turned to face him, holding my robe tight around my body. "I woke up in the middle of the night and you were gone," I said. "I didn't know where you were."

"At the factory," he said. "Working on the books."

"Well, the next time, could you tell me you're going, please? So I don't worry?"

He smiled. "I'm not used to having anyone worry about me," he said.

"You'll tell me then?"

"The problem is, I don't usually know I'm going until I make the decision. And by the time I did last night, you were asleep. I didn't want to wake—"

"You could leave me a note."

He looked at me blankly for a moment, then nodded. "Fair enough," he said. "Next time I'll leave a note."

I sat down on the edge of the pineapple bed. "Isn't it spooky there at night, that big empty building?" I shuddered. I'd seen the factory at night from the road. The long two-story brick building was ominous looking, all its many windows like dark eyes staring out into the night.

He laughed. "I've been in that building all times of day and night my whole life," he said. "I know every inch of it. And Zeke lives there, so it's never completely empty."

"Zeke actually lives at the factory? How come?"

Henry shrugged. "He's part maintenance man, part guard, I guess you'd call him. I like having someone there all the time to keep an eye on things. He could get an apartment somewhere, but this works out well for us both."

"Could I see the factory?" I asked. "I'd like to see where you work."

"You've seen it," he said. "You've been to my office."

"I mean the whole place. It must be fascinating."

"Fascinating?" He chuckled. "Sure, I'll take you around this Sunday. Better to do it when the building is empty."

"Wonderful," I said, getting to my feet. I headed toward the closet for my clothes.

"You don't need to worry, Tess," he said, and I turned to look at him. "I don't want you to have to worry about anything. I want you to be happy here. Happy and content."

For some reason, his words choked me up. There was so much I wanted to say. *Are you ever going to make love to me? Will you at least kiss me? Your mother and sister—can you change their attitude toward me?* I remembered the new house where we would soon be living together with our child. Things would be different then. Things would be good.

"I *am* happy," I lied. "Everything is fine."

28

After church that Sunday, I met Violet's father, Byron Dare, the district attorney prosecuting Henry's friend Gaston. He was a pompous, handsome man with a full head of white hair and a syrupy Southern accent that set my teeth on edge.

He approached us on the sidewalk in front of the church as we were heading toward the car. He stepped directly in front of us, blocking our path.

"I've been too riled up to speak to you before now, Hank," he said to Henry. "You broke my little girl's heart. You toyed with her all these years. You—"

"Now is not the time, sir," Henry said, his hand reliably at my elbow. "You haven't met my wife, Tess. Tess, this is Hickory's fine district attorney, Byron Dare."

The man didn't so much as glance in my direction. "Is it the Joyner case?" he asked. "Was that why you cooled toward my Violet?"

"Of course not," Henry said.

"I know Gaston Joyner is a longtime buddy of yours, but I'm just doing my job," Byron Dare continued. "You shouldn't hold that against Violet."

"It has nothing to do with your job," Henry said, "and Violet will be fine. Now, if you'll excuse us. Mama and Lucy are waiting for us in the car." He tugged me away before the man could say anything else.

"I'm sorry about that," he said to me as we walked away. There were red blotches high on his cheeks and I knew he was angry.

"It was like I was invisible," I said, as we neared the Cadillac.

"He's a monumental jackass," Henry said, opening the car's rear door for me. I always insisted Ruth ride in the front seat when she was with us. "He thinks he's more important than everyone else."

"What took you so long?" Lucy asked. "We've been waiting ages."

"Mr. Dare wanted to talk to Henry," I answered, as Henry slid into the driver's seat.

Lucy laughed. "Oh, I bet he did," she said.

"I'm going to give Tess a tour of the factory this afternoon," Henry said, most likely to change the subject.

"How thrilling," Lucy said sarcastically.

"I'm looking forward to it," I said.

"And well you should," Ruth said. "That factory's been the Kraft family's bread and butter for many years."

I barely heard her. Coming toward us on the other side of the street was a police car and I leaned forward to try to make out the driver's face. Henry gave a little toot of the car horn and waved, and as we passed the car I got a clear look at the driver. It was definitely the same young officer I'd suspected of following me on my way to town the other day.

"Do you know that policeman?" I asked Henry. "When I walked to town the other day, he kept driving past me, over and over again."

"It's Teddy Wright," Lucy said. "I've known him forever. Everybody knows everybody in Hickory."

"I felt like he was following me," I said. "It was the strangest thing."

I saw Lucy and Henry exchange a look in the rearview mirror. I was certain it wasn't my imagination.

"He was probably just on patrol," Henry said. "Keeping an eye on things."

"On another subject, girls." Ruth turned to look over the seat at us as Henry started the car. "The box supper is Saturday night at the Presbyterian church. Hank, can you bring us three of your small boxes to fill and decorate?"

"Sure," he said.

"What's a box supper?" I asked.

"It's an event to sell war bonds," Henry said.

"We decorate and fill our boxes with enough food for two people and then they get auctioned off," Lucy said. "The highest bidder for each box gets that amount in war bonds and stamps plus our box of food."

"*Home-cooked* food," Ruth added. "A full meal for two people."

"So, we actually get to cook something ourselves?" I asked, pleased by the thought. Since my arrival in Hickory, I hadn't so much as boiled an egg. Hattie took care of everything.

"Yes, indeed we do," Ruth said. "So put your thinking cap on and decide what you'd like to make. I'll go into town tomorrow and purchase ribbons and sequins and whatever else we might need to decorate our boxes."

"Could I do that shopping for you, Miss Ruth?" I asked. I relished any opportunity to get out of the house.

"If you'd like to, of course you may." Ruth seemed pleased by my enthusiastic response. She very nearly smiled at me over the top of the seat and I wondered if there might be hope for our relationship after all.

29

Like most people I'd met in Hickory, Zeke Johnson didn't seem to think much of me. I knew it from the moment Henry and I reached the second story of the factory and spotted him there, opening the door to the room next to Henry's office. He was dressed in a suit and tie and he looked from Henry to me and back again, his face registering surprise. I had a clear view past him into the room. A double bed was against one wall. It was the same pineapple style as my twin bed in Henry's room at home. There was a dresser topped by a huge framed mirror, a black and tan oriental rug on the floor and a sofa and coffee table. There were even pictures on the wall. Was this Zeke's room? When Henry had told me Zeke lived in the factory, I'd pictured him sleeping on a cot. Not living in such luxury. But it was a furniture factory, after all. No wonder his room was filled with lovely things.

"Here on a Sunday?" Zeke asked Henry.

"I thought it was time I gave Tess a tour of the place," Henry said. "Are you just coming from church?"

Zeke nodded. "And dinner at Mama's." He was speaking to Henry, but his gaze was on me. "Glad you're here, Hank," he said. "I was going to call you. We got a problem with the boiler again. One of the valves is failing, plus I'm not sure how long the igniter's going to last."

I was surprised he called him Hank instead of Mr. Henry or Mr. Hank. It seemed overly familiar for a maintenance man, but I remembered they'd grown up together. I pictured them as kids, sliding down the stairs on a mattress with Zeke's sister Honor. Getting a whipping for it, in Zeke's case, at least.

"You'd better show me," Henry said. "Come on, Tess." He rested his hand softly on my back and the three of us headed down the stairs again. "We'll start your tour with the most glamorous part of the factory." He laughed as we walked down a dark corridor, Zeke a few steps ahead of us. "The boiler room."

At the end of the corridor, Zeke pushed open a thick, heavy metal door.

"The boiler room has to be separated from the rest of the building by a fire wall," Henry explained. "Fire in a furniture factory is not something you ever want to see."

We stepped into a small room filled with a huge furnace. Pipes and ducts in all shapes and sizes crisscrossed below the ceiling and down one wall. The air was warm and damp and the smell of oil and metal stung my nostrils.

"See this here?" Zeke said, pointing toward a valve on one of the many pipes jutting from the boiler.

"Let me do it." Henry moved past him, taking off his tweed coat and handing it to him. "Don't want to mess up your Sunday clothes."

Zeke stepped aside and Henry fiddled with the valve while I hung back. I was beginning to perspire inside my own coat while they talked about the type of bolt they needed and a few other boiler-related topics that went over my head. There was a familiar ease between the two of them, and Zeke said something I couldn't hear but that made Henry laugh out loud. I thought it was the first time I'd heard Henry truly laugh.

When the two of them had finished their conversation, Henry opened the door to the boiler to reveal a cauldron of yellow flame. He looked over at me. "This old boiler heats the entire building," he said. "Impressive, isn't it?"

I nodded, though I realized I'd taken two steps back, away from the heat and flames.

Henry closed the boiler door, then smiled at me. "You look like you're melting," he said. "Come on. Let's see the rest of the factory."

We left Zeke in the boiler room and headed back down the corridor. We stopped in many of the large workrooms along the way, Henry switching on the overhead lights to show me the worktables and machinery. The factory was eerily silent, but nothing could mask the smells of chemicals and wood, and sawdust seemed to be everywhere. By the time we were back in front of Henry's office, my lungs and eyes were burning and I had to brush the sawdust from my coat.

"Just want to let Zeke know we're going and he can lock up," he said, knocking on Zeke's door near the top of the stairs. He went into the room without waiting for a response. I stood in front of Henry's office door, waiting for his return. I heard the quiet rumble of their conversation, and then I heard Zeke say, in a voice almost too low to make out, "I don't understand. You had it all planned perfect. Why are you doing this?"

I couldn't hear Henry's response at all, but I had the feeling that whatever they were talking about had to do with me.

"Zeke seems very close to you," I said, once we were back in the car. What I really wanted to ask him was what Zeke had meant about Henry's perfect plans. I knew better than to question him though. If there was one thing I'd learned about Henry, it was that he didn't like me to probe.

"Remember I told you he used to live with his mother, Adora, in the cottage where Hattie lives now?"

"Yes, I know. When you were kids."

"We palled around together till high school, when . . ." He shrugged. "We had to be in different worlds," he said.

"I don't think he likes me," I said.

"You don't think anyone likes you." He sounded annoyed and I decided to drop the subject. I wondered if he was right. Was I misinterpreting the way people behaved toward me? Whatever Zeke had been talking about, maybe it had nothing to do with me at all.

30

It was too cold to walk into town the following day, so I took a cab to the fabric store, where I spent over an hour picking out an abundance of beads and ribbons and lace and buttons that we could use to decorate our boxes for the box supper. Then I bought a pattern for a baby sweater and some yellow yarn. I hadn't knitted a thing since I was a teenager and Mimi taught me how, but with my baby coming, it seemed like the perfect time to dust off that skill.

Then, almost without thinking, I walked across the street to the bus stop, and I waited in the cold with an old man and his wife for the bus to Ridgeview.

Reverend Sam smiled broadly when he found me shivering on his front porch.

"Come in," he said in greeting. "I've been expecting you."

I didn't bother to ask him how he knew I was coming when I hadn't known it myself until half an hour ago. It didn't matter. What mattered was that I was there with him, the person who seemed interested in the real me when no one else in Hickory cared to find out who I was deep inside.

Wordlessly, I followed him down the dark hall to the anteroom. Despite the fact that I knew the skeleton was there, my heart still threw an extra beat when I saw it. Those hollow bony eyes seemed to follow me as I crossed the room to Reverend Sam's inner office.

I sat down across from him and he immediately reached for my hands. I put my chilled fingers in his warm ones. After a moment, he let go of me and sat back.

"Did you finish the book?" he asked.

I had to smile because that was exactly the subject on my mind. I nodded.

"How did it end?"

I thought about how to answer the question. "The character, Francie, grows up during the story. Many things happen to her and she's strong and tough and ultimately changes for the better."

"How does the tree fit in?"

"The tree is . . . well, it's sort of like her. Like Francie. It gets chopped down and battered and bruised, but it keeps on growing."

"The tree is a metaphor," Reverend Sam said.

"Exactly."

"Would your mother have liked that ending?"

I thought about my mother. I had no idea how she would have felt about the ending as far as Francie was concerned, but I knew she would have loved that the tree remained standing. "My mother loved trees," I said. "There was a park not far from our house and she would go there sometimes just to look up at the tall trees. Our yard was very tiny and had only a few scrubby old trees in it. So . . ." I had a sudden idea.

"Your face just lit up," Reverend Sam said.

"My husband is building a house for us," I said. "There are a lot of trees on the property already, but maybe we could plant another. A special one. For my mother."

He smiled. "Lovely," he said.

I thought of the property, trying to remember it well enough to figure out the best place to plant a tree.

"Your marriage is good?" Reverend Sam interrupted my thoughts.

I looked him in the eye. "No," I said. "It's not good, actually. It's not good at all."

And then, in the safety of that quiet little office, the skeleton standing guard outside the door, I told him everything. How I'd been engaged to the man I loved and foolishly cheated on him with Henry. I told him about the pregnancy and how Henry had asked me to marry him. How no one in Hickory seemed to like me. And although he didn't conjure up my mother on this visit, or offer advice, or say much of anything other than murmurs of sympathy and understanding, I left feeling far stronger and freer than when I'd arrived.

31

When I arrived home from seeing Reverend Sam, I found the mail scattered on the floor beneath the slot in the front door. In the scattering of envelopes, I spotted the one I'd been waiting for: a response from the North Carolina State Board of Nurse Examiners. I tore it open and grinned to myself. *Your application to sit for the North Carolina state board examination for graduate nurses has been accepted.* The letter suggested some hotels near the exam site for the three days in March when I would need to be in Winston-Salem, and my heart began to skitter with excitement. I'd be five months along by then. Would it be all right for me to take a train at five months? I thought so. I knew my pregnancy wouldn't be the biggest obstacle to my taking the exam, but I was going to take that exam, by hook or crook.

That evening, Ruth, Lucy, and I sat at the dining room table to decorate the shoebox-sized boxes Henry had brought us from the factory. He'd also brought a much larger box, this one sealed and seemingly heavy, which he'd carried upstairs to Lucy's room.

"Just some things for Lucy," he'd said when I expressed curiosity about the box, and Lucy had given me a look that told me whatever was inside it was none of my business.

The next hour or so had to be the most congenial I'd spent with my new in-laws since my arrival and I wondered how much of it was due to the sense of calm I'd carried with me since seeing Reverend Sam that afternoon, as well as my happiness over the upcoming nursing exam.

Ruth, Lucy, and I complimented one another's designs as we glued the lace and beads to the cardboard boxes and we chatted endlessly about what we'd cook to put inside.

"We should all make fried chicken," Ruth suggested, "and deviled eggs. That would make it easy on us rather than coming up with three different dishes."

"Everyone's going to be making fried chicken, Mama," Lucy complained. "I'm terrible at it, anyway. I think we should each do our own individual specialty." She patted a ribbon into place on the lid of her box. "I can make meat loaf, though I guess I'd have to really stretch the meat because of rationing. And I can make my famous red velvet cake for dessert."

"Well, darling daughter," Ruth said, "where will you find the sugar and food coloring for your famous red velvet cake?"

Lucy shook her head in annoyance. "Rationing gets in the way of everything!" she said.

My specialty had always been chicken parmesan, but I thought I'd best stay away from Italian food for this event . . . and every other event as well. "I can make stuffed ham," I said. I knew we could get a ham from one of the local farmers.

"Stuffed ham?" Lucy scoffed. "How on earth do you stuff a ham?"

"Everyone in Baltimore makes stuffed ham," I said. "They don't make it here?"

"Never heard of such a thing." Ruth cut a length of lace to fit the sides of her box. "How is it done?"

"Well," I said mysteriously, "first I need an old pillowcase. Do we have one?"

They laughed. "You're pulling our legs," Lucy said.

"Not at all. You cut the bone from a ham and make deep slits through the meat, then stuff the slits with greens and tie the whole thing up tight in a pillowcase. You boil it for about half an hour in water that's been seasoned with loads of spices, and then chill it. It has to be served cold or it won't look pretty."

"All the food has to be cold," Lucy said. "Or it will be anyway, by the time the bidding is over on the boxes."

"When you cut the slices, each one has streaks of stuffing in it," I added.

"Oh, that must be delicious," Ruth said when I'd finished reciting the recipe. She actually sounded sincere, but I was beginning to learn that

Ruth could sound like she adored you at the same time she was slipping a knife between your ribs. "And yes, certainly we can find you an old pillowcase or perhaps a sheet you can cut up. That should do the job."

We worked for a few minutes in silence, until Ruth said, out of the blue, "So, tell me, Tess, dear"—her fingers sifted through the small pile of beads on the table in front of her—"exactly how far along are you?"

My hands froze on my box. I was taken aback, though I probably shouldn't have been. I wasn't wearing my girdle this evening. I'd taken it off when I got home from Reverend Sam's and I simply couldn't bear to put it on again before coming downstairs. I knew I was showing without it. I didn't think it was noticeable unless someone was truly examining my figure, but I guessed Ruth was doing exactly that. She knew I hadn't gotten pregnant on our wedding night. I'd told Reverend Sam about the baby, of course, but here in Ruth Kraft's kitchen, saying out loud that I was four months pregnant seemed so . . . obscene, somehow. I stared down at my fingers, white and stiff against the blue ribbons and lace on the box. The silence in the room felt electric and I had to break it.

"Four months," I admitted. "I'm due in late July."

"Well," she said, avoiding my eyes as steadfastly as I was avoiding hers, "I suppose we'll have to do some creative fudging when the baby's born then. We'll say it came quite early. And we'll keep visitors at bay for a while. We don't want anyone to think the worst, do we?"

"People aren't idiots, Mother," Lucy said.

"Well, Lucille," Ruth said to her daughter, "let's not help them jump to the wrong conclusion, all right?"

"They already know. Everyone's talking about it."

"And who is everyone?" Ruth's voice was tight.

"Violet and her friends, to begin with."

"Well, yes. But who can blame her? She adores him."

I bristled as they talked about me as if I weren't there.

"Oh," Ruth said suddenly. "Late July? I just realized you and Henry may be in the new house by then." She furrowed her brow. "I'll come over in the beginning to turn any visitors away," she said, "and we'll have to instruct the nanny to do the same. I'll begin asking around for nanny referrals. You don't want to wait too long to pin someone down."

"I'd really rather not have a nanny," I said. I couldn't wait to take care of my own child. I wanted so badly to hold my baby in my arms.

"You'll feel differently once that baby is actually here," Ruth said. She tipped her head to the side in an attempt to look at my stomach, hidden behind the table. "We need to find some clothing that masks . . . you know. Your condition," she said. "I'll get one of those Lane Bryant catalogs for you to shop from. And it's time we set up an appointment for you with Dr. Poole."

"An obstetrician?" I asked.

"He's our longtime family doctor and he delivers the babies of everyone in Hickory," she said. "All the white babies, anyway. And he knows when to keep his lips sealed. As soon as you start to show a bit more," she added, "you mustn't leave the house."

I didn't respond. I knew women of Ruth's generation hid themselves away during their pregnancy, but this was 1944 and I hoped to have at least another couple of months of freedom. The thought of being trapped in this house was overwhelming. Plus, I wanted to be able to visit Reverend Sam whenever I chose.

"Maybe church this Sunday should be your last outing," Ruth said.

That would be one bonus of not leaving the house, I thought. The fewer church services I needed to attend, the better. "Maybe," I said, hoping that answer would be enough to satisfy her for now.

We fell quiet again, and I wondered if all three of us were thinking about how we would get through the next few months. I wished it was already July. I wanted to meet this little person nestled inside me. The one person in Hickory I knew I would love. The one person in Hickory who was going to love me back.

In bed that night, I asked Henry if we could plant a tree for my mother at our new house. At first he laughed. "There are more than forty trees on that land already," he said.

"This one would be special," I said. "It would have meaning for me."

He looked at me across the empty space between our beds then, the humor leaving his face. "Sure, Tess," he said. "You can do whatever you want with the house and the land. It will be yours. All right?"

I thanked him, thinking as I always did how many girls would love that invitation. If only a big house and beautiful land was what I wanted.

32

My ham came out perfectly that Friday evening, the best I'd ever made. It had been almost like a dream come true, cooking with my sister- and mother-in-law. We even laughed a bit. We put my ham, Lucy's meat loaf, and Ruth's fried chicken in the refrigerator to chill for Saturday's box supper. Lucy had scraped together enough sugar to bake her red velvet cake, and Hattie had shown her how to create its vibrant color using beets instead of food coloring.

"We can take the leftovers to Adora and Honor and the kids," Lucy said to her mother as we straightened the kitchen after our cooking project. "Adora's birthday is Sunday, remember?"

"Oh yes," Ruth said. "Taking them the leftovers is an excellent idea."

All three of us turned at the sound of Henry's car in the driveway.

"Maybe Henry can drive us to Adora's on the way to church Sunday morning so we don't have to take one of those blasted stinky old cabs," Lucy said.

"Watch your language," Ruth scolded as she took off her apron.

Henry walked in the back door and I knew right away he was in a sour mood. It emanated from him like something tangible. I stood awkwardly by the table, never knowing how to greet him when we were in front of his family. Certainly there would be no welcome-home kiss. We didn't even kiss in private.

"What's the matter with you?" Lucy asked.

He took off his coat and tossed it over the back of one of the kitchen chairs, then stood in front of us, hands crammed into his pants pockets. "Gaston's trial ended," he said. "He lost."

"I'm sorry," I said. I still hadn't met Gaston Joyner, although I'd seen a picture of him and his wife, Loretta, in the paper that morning. They stood side by side outside the courtroom and I felt a stab of sympathy for them. The wife, Loretta, had a hand to her cheek as though wiping a tear away, and Gaston was speaking to someone outside the photograph, exhaustion in his face. I knew Henry had been hoping—unrealistically so—that the state would recognize their interracial marriage as valid and his friend could stay out of prison.

"Well, of course he lost." Ruth set her dirty apron on the table near the back door where Hattie would be sure to see it. "He was a fool to think he could come back here with a colored so-called wife and get away with it. It's the law, pure and simple."

"A backward law," Henry muttered. He sounded like an angry little boy who hadn't gotten his way.

"Oh, you're just being obstinate," Ruth said.

"It may be backward, Hank," Lucy said, "but it's the reality. Even if the law went away, Gaston and Loretta couldn't live here in peace. People are already up in arms about them. You know that. It's just the way it is."

"Frankly, it makes me sick to think of them married." Ruth shuddered. "Just horrible. And Gaston was such a nice young man."

"He's *still* a nice young man," Henry countered his mother. "Only now he'll be a nice young man in prison unless they can get out of Hickory right quick. The judge will suspend the sentence if they leave the state." He turned toward the door that led to the hallway. "I'm going up to my room," he said.

"Don't you want to see what we cooked for the box supper?" I asked, knowing even as I spoke that my timing was poor, and I wasn't surprised when he walked right past me as if he hadn't heard.

The following evening, still in a foul mood, Henry drove us to the Presbyterian church. I spotted Violet the instant I entered the huge, smoky hall that had been set up for the event. She and Henry exchanged a look, and I thought there was an unmistakable message in that exchange, one I couldn't read. Then she glanced at me with an amused sort of smile, and I turned away quickly, shaken. *You're being paranoid,* I told myself.

Ruth, Lucy, and I delivered our boxes to a long table at the front of the room where a few dozen other gaily decorated boxes were already on display. On the wall above them, someone had hung several war bond posters of soldiers and their weapons caught in the act of fighting an unseen enemy. AIM TO WIN!, one of the posters proclaimed. ATTACK! ATTACK! ATTACK! read another.

As he often did in public, Henry took my elbow and guided me to a table where I sat with him and Ruth and Lucy and a few of Ruth's friends whom I didn't recognize. Henry lit his pipe and I wished I could have a cigarette, but I never smoked in front of Ruth. I didn't want to give her one more thing to criticize about me.

Violet sat on the other side of the room with a few of her friends. She was dressed in royal-blue taffeta, and the light from the overhead fixtures pooled in her pale blond hair. People gathered around her table and she seemed to be in control of them all, laughing one moment at something one of them said, giving instructions to someone else the next. She was the magnet in the room. The white-hot center. I spotted her father, Byron Dare, and his wife at a separate table. They were hard to miss because people kept clapping Mr. Dare on the back, loudly congratulating him on winning the Joyner case.

Mayor Finley, whom I remembered meeting the first time I attended the Baptist church, stood at a podium at the front of the room, gavel in hand, and I guessed he would be presiding over the bidding. He slammed the gavel on the podium a few times to stop the chatter in the room and sent a warm smile into the crowd. I recalled liking both him and his wife in our brief meeting at the church.

"As with last year," he said, once he had everyone's attention, "we'll dispense with the usual rules that govern the traditional box supper, given that so many of our young men are fighting for our freedom rather than being here to bid on these beautiful boxes and consume their contents with the ladies who made them. In other words, high bidders, both men and women, will simply enjoy the meals inside the boxes they win as they purchase war bonds and stamps, knowing their bids will support our boys and our country."

He spoke a while longer and then the bidding began. The first box was auctioned off for twenty-three dollars after some brisk bidding, and I suddenly realized that the name of the woman who cooked the meal and decorated the box would be announced. Of course. What had I expected? Given my unpopularity in town, I feared no one would bid on my box and I would be humiliated. Worse, I worried about humiliating my husband.

Lucy's box went to Teddy Wright for fourteen dollars. As he walked up to the front of the room to collect his box and war bond and stamps, it took me a moment to recognize him as the policeman I'd thought was following me the day I walked to the post office. Out of his uniform, he looked very young, no more than twenty, and he had a simple sort of handsomeness about him with his sandy hair and blue eyes. When he turned around to walk back to his seat, he winked at Lucy with a grin. And then—I was sure of it—he glanced in my direction, and the smile left his face.

"And here we have this lovely box created by Hank Kraft's new bride, Tess Kraft," Mayor Finley announced, holding my lace-and-bead box in the air. "Who will start the bidding?"

I didn't have time to feel nervous before Byron Dare leaped to his feet. "You know, Arthur," he said to the mayor in his syrupy drawl, "I'm an old-fashioned kind of fella. I like a box supper where we get to dine with the gal who did the cookin'. So I'm goin' to just preempt any other bid and pledge one hundred dollars for that box . . . as long as I also get the honor of dining with the young lady who made it."

A hush fell over the room except for one small word uttered by Violet.

"Daddy?" She nearly whispered it, and her father pretended not to hear her. I kept my gaze on Mayor Finley, but I could have sworn that every head in the room turned to look at me. I plastered a false smile on my face. Next to me, I felt Henry stiffen.

"Well, good for you, Byron," Mayor Finley said. "One hundred dollars going once. Going twice." He slammed down the gavel. "Looks like the district attorney will be dining with Mrs. Henry Kraft tonight."

Mr. Dare looked toward us with a victorious smile. I thought his gaze was on Henry rather than me. There was a war going on between these two and I was not going to be a pawn in it.

When the bidding for boxes was over, Byron walked toward our table, my decorated box nestled in the crook of his elbow and a glass of some sort of liquor in his hand. He held out his free arm to me.

"Mrs. Kraft?" he said. "Let's find ourselves a nice quiet little spot to enjoy your fine cookin'."

Henry leaned close to whisper in my ear. "You don't have to do this," he said.

"I'm all right," I whispered back and got to my feet. I took Mr. Dare's arm and he led me to a nearly deserted corner of the room. I sat down across from him at a table already set with paper plates and silverware and studied his head of bushy white hair as he lifted the top of the box.

"Let's see what we have here," he said, removing one of the thick slices of ham and unwrapping it on a paper plate. "Well, ain't this pretty," he said, studying the ham. "What do you call it?"

"Stuffed ham," I said. "It's a specialty in Baltimore where I come from." Maybe I could win him over. He was a very different man tonight than the one who'd completely ignored me at church the day he went on and on to Henry about how he'd hurt his daughter. This evening, he was ingratiating, his eyes on mine, his smile unrelenting. Maybe I stood a chance with him. I'd spent my whole life being liked. I'd even been thought of as popular in high school and nursing school. Why did I allow myself to be so intimidated here? "It's fun to make," I added.

He spooned a couple of the small potatoes onto my plate. "Hank got himself a real looker, didn't he?" he said. "You look like you could be on stage or in the movies," he added. "Do you know who Dante Rossetti is?"

I shook my head. "No idea." I poured myself a glass of lemonade from the pitcher on the table.

"He's an English artist famous for his sensual paintings of beautiful women with exceptionally thick, long hair," he said, cutting a corner from his ham and lifting it to his mouth. "I'd wager that's how your hair looks when you let it down."

I squirmed ever so slightly in my seat, forgetting my idea about winning him over. He was too slick. "Shall we eat our supper?" I asked. I looked across the room to see Henry dining with the mayor and his wife. I'd completely lost track of Ruth and Lucy.

"Have I made you uncomfortable, Mrs. Kraft?"

"Not at all." I smiled.

"Please accept my apology if I have." He bowed his head slightly. "That wasn't my intention. In Baltimore, maybe gentlemen aren't as free with their compliments."

"I've never been compared to a painting before," I said awkwardly.

"Dante Rossetti," he repeated. "You must give him a gander sometime." He chewed a bite of ham, his gaze riveted on my face, and I feigned cutting my potato with great interest. "A booming town, Baltimore," he said. "Hickory must seem like a sleepy little backwater to you."

"Not at all," I said. "It's lovely."

He sipped his drink. "Tell me about your people," he said.

"My . . . family?"

"Yes. Your kin. Are they all in Baltimore?"

"I'm afraid I lost both my parents," I said. "And I was an only child." I wouldn't let myself think about the rest of my "kin"—Mimi and Pop and Vincent.

"Oh, now that breaks my heart to hear," he said. "The thought of my little girl growing up without a daddy or mama . . ." He shook his head. "I'm sorry you had to come up that way."

"Thank you," I said. "My father passed away when I was very young, but I lost my mother just recently. So I actually grew up with a lot of love and support." I didn't want him to see me as some pathetic little orphan.

"Good, that's good." He nodded, popping another bite of ham in his mouth. "Now how exactly did you meet our lucky Hank?" he asked, once he'd swallowed. "Where was it that you swept him off his feet?"

Oh, I didn't like this man! I had to find a way to take control of the conversation, sooner rather than later. He was fishing for something and I had no idea what.

"Washington, D.C.," I said.

"And when was that?"

I nibbled a piece of ham. "Quite a while ago," I said evasively.

"Well, well." He sat back from the table and observed me with a one-sided smile. "Who would have guessed that Hank Kraft had a little something like you on the side all this time."

Stunned, I set down my fork, bristling. "I think you have a mistaken idea of my relationship with my husband," I said. "We've been friends for a long time, and sometimes friendship can turn into something deeper. I believe that's all you need to know."

He looked surprised that I'd actually defended myself. I was finished playing his game. I was tempted to get up and march away from the table, but that was the coward's way out. Instead, I smiled prettily at him. "So,"

I said, "I think you've gotten in your hundred dollars' worth of insults," I said. "Now why don't you tell me a little about your work?" I asked. "It must be fascinating."

Slowly, I saw a look of respect replace the surprise on his face. "Very well," he said. "Where shall I begin?"

33

Before we left for church the following morning, Lucy and I piled the leftovers from our box supper meals into a hamper for Adora and her family. We planned to drop the food off at their house on our way. I was so glad this was to be my last church service. I always found the service lacking compared to what I was used to, and I ended up daydreaming about Vincent before I could stop myself, wondering as I always did how he'd reacted to my letter. He must truly hate me now.

Henry drove us to the Ridgeview neighborhood, which now felt familiar to me, although I would never let him or my in-laws know I'd been there before. What would they think of me taking the bus to "Colored Town," walking up the dirt road to Reverend Sam's house, mine the only white face for miles around? I smiled to myself at the thought. Reverend Sam was my sweet secret.

For the first time, Ruth insisted I sit in the Cadillac's front seat with Henry.

"In your condition," she'd said, "you really should get the roomier seat."

Now that my "condition" was being openly discussed in the house, I guessed I was going to be treated with deference.

We'd had a bit of a spat that morning, Henry and I. While I was fixing my hair at the dressing table, I told him about the licensing exam. When I explained that it would be given over three days in Winston-Salem, he simply stared at me in the mirror, his hands frozen on the tie he was knotting at his neck. I was not as apprehensive as I'd expected to be as I waited for his response. There was nothing he could say that would keep me from that exam. I still had a tiny bit of my own money left from my account in Baltimore. It would be enough for the trip, but just barely.

"You can't do it," he said, his hands working once again on the knot. "I thought we'd settled that already."

"It's so important to me, Henry," I said, tucking a stray lock of my hair behind my ear. "I've worked hard for this."

"No," he said simply. "No further discussion needed."

Yes, I thought to myself. *Further discussion is definitely needed.* But I knew it would have to wait.

Since it was a Sunday, downtown Ridgeview was quiet. Only the churches seemed alive with people. It was fairly warm for February, and the churchgoers crowded the sidewalks dressed in Sunday finery.

Henry turned onto the long dirt road that probably still bore my footprints from my second visit to Reverend Sam. We passed the tiny crumbling houses on either side of us until we reached the house that had stood out to me the first time I was in Ridgeview—the small yellow house with white trim and new-looking shingles on the roof. The house that looked so well cared for. Henry stopped the car in front of it, and I guessed this was where Adora lived.

"We'll stay in the car," he said to me as Ruth and Lucy started to get out. The front door opened and two children—a little girl about four years old and a boy slightly older—ran onto the porch and down the two steps toward Ruth and Lucy, the screen door slamming behind them. The children were dressed for church, the little boy in a miniature suit and bow tie, the girl in a pink dress that flounced around her legs as she ran.

"Miss Lucy, Miss Lucy!" they both shouted, and I was surprised when Lucy set down the basket and leaned over to hug them. I so rarely saw any warmth from her.

Honor, in a pink dress and matching hat, opened the screen door. She shouted something to the children I couldn't understand and the boy turned around and headed back toward the house while the girl took Lucy's hand and walked with her, happily swinging her arm. Honor looked past Lucy and Ruth toward the car, unsmiling. I waved, an automatic gesture of friendliness. She didn't wave back, but turned her attention to Lucy and Ruth as they walked into the house.

"The children are Honor's?" I asked.

"Yes," Henry said.

"They're so cute. What are their names?"

"Butchie and Jilly."

"Is Honor's husband overseas?"

He nodded. "Yes," he said. "Del. Though they're not technically married."

"Even though they have children?" I asked. That seemed appallingly wrong to me. But really, in my odd set of circumstances, who was I to judge?

"It's not our business," Henry said.

"He helps out though, I hope." I thought of how fortunate I was that Henry had stepped up to the plate when I got pregnant.

"Not our business," he said again.

"Their house is very cute," I said. "It looks like a brand-new roof."

Henry didn't say anything for a moment. "Zeke and I put the roof on," he said finally. "We look after Adora."

As if on cue, a heavyset woman stepped from the house onto the porch. She clutched the railing as she slowly descended the two steps to the ground. Wearing a broad smile, she walked toward us. She was dressed in a matching pale blue skirt and jacket trimmed with navy piping. An enormous blue hat laden with faux flowers sat on her head. She waved as she got close to the car.

"Roll down your window," Henry said, and I did. He leaned past me to smile at the woman as she neared the car. "Happy birthday, Adora," he said. He was so handsome when he smiled. It made me realize he didn't smile very often.

"Thank you, Mr. Hank," she said, but her eyes were on me. "I told Miss Ruth I wanted to meet your new wife."

"Hi." I smiled. "I'm Tess."

"Oh, she's a pretty thing, Mr. Hank!" Adora said. She wore thick glasses and I could see myself reflected in them. "He taking good care of you, honey?"

"Yes," I said, "he is."

"You lucky you done landed with this family," she said. "Kindest folk there is."

I managed to hold on to my smile. "Yes," I said.

"I seen that ham you made," she said. "Ain't that somethin'? I never seen nothin' like it."

"Get in the house, Adora, before you freeze," Henry said, even though the day was hardly cold.

"He's the boss." Adora gave me a wink. "You take care of him for me, hear? I knowed him since he was nothin' but a little tadpole. He tell you that?"

"He said you worked for his family for a long time," I said. I remembered that she'd saved his life somehow, but this didn't seem like the time to bring that up. I knew it wasn't Henry's favorite topic.

Honor opened the front door. "Mama, get in here!" she shouted. "We need to get ready to go."

"Looks like I got two bosses," Adora said with a shrug.

"Have a good birthday, Adora," Henry said.

"Nice meeting you," I said.

I watched her walk slowly back to the house as I rolled up the window.

"She's sweet," I said.

Henry glanced at his watch. He seemed suddenly impatient, his gaze on the porch of the house as we waited for Lucy and Ruth to return to the car.

"You're going to need new clothes," he said suddenly, out of the blue. "Given your condition," he added, nodding toward my stomach, and I wondered if I was showing now more than I thought. I had on my panty girdle today in an attempt to mask my bulging middle for the church crowd, but maybe it wasn't up to the job.

"Yes," I said.

"I'll leave you money tomorrow morning," he said. "Get whatever you need."

"All right," I said. "Thank you."

We were quiet for a moment. Then suddenly, he spoke again.

"I'm going out tonight," he said. "Gaston Joyner and his wife are leaving tomorrow. I want to spend some time with him before he goes."

"That's good news, right?" I asked. "Good that they're leaving? Will they go back to Pennsylvania where they got married?"

He shook his head. "They're driving all the way across the country to the state of Washington, so I don't know if I'll ever see him again."

Washington seemed like another planet to me. So far away. "Why there?" I asked.

"Gaston says they'll be more accepted in Washington State. Interracial marriage is legal there. I hope he's right. It's a dangerous journey for them to make. Loretta will have to hide in the backseat if they're someplace where they shouldn't be seen together, which I suppose will be most every-place."

"Do you really think it's okay for a colored person to marry a white person?" I asked. It was hard for me to imagine, and it bothered me that Henry seemed to think it was fine.

"Well, like Gaston says, it's hard to control who you fall in love with," he said. "You love somebody that deeply, you're willing to risk everything to be with them."

I wondered if he was thinking about us. How neither of us was in love, deeply or otherwise. Did that fact make him as sad as it made me?

34

I didn't know what time Henry got in that night after being with Gaston. When I awakened in the morning, he was gone yet again but it was obvious that his bed had been slept in, and there were ten ten-dollar bills on my night table. I'd taken to staying in my robe well into the morning, but today I dressed quickly, looking forward to my shopping trip. I was about to go downstairs to breakfast when there was a knock on the bedroom door. I opened the door to find Hattie with one of Henry's suits over her arm, most likely fresh from the cleaners.

"Can I hang this in the armoire?" she asked.

"Oh, I'll do it, Hattie," I said, reaching for the suit.

"You sure, Miss Tess?" She held it out of my reach. "Just as easy for me to hang it."

"I'm happy to do it," I told her with a smile. I'd never lost my discomfort over watching Hattie work while I did nothing. I might be sitting in the upstairs parlor reading while she ran the carpet sweeper around my feet. When I expressed my discomfort to Henry, he scoffed. "She's not a slave, Tess," he said. "She's well compensated for her work." I didn't bother explaining to him that it had nothing to do with her being colored. Black, white, purple, it made no difference. I just didn't like being waited on.

"Have you seen our mutual friend lately?" I asked her, referring, of course, to Reverend Sam.

She pressed a finger to her lips. "Miss Ruth don't want me talkin' to you so much," she said in a near whisper. "She don't think you understand how things is s'posed to be."

"Oh," I whispered back, feeling sad. I didn't want to lose my relationship with Hattie. "I don't want to cause you any trouble, Hattie," I said. "I'm just grateful you introduced me to him."

She gave a little nod, then left the room. I shut the door behind her and headed for the armoire with the suit. I turned the ornate key and opened the mirrored door carefully, respectful of its age and a fragility I might only have been imagining. I was still taken by that beautiful piece of furniture. The incredibly smooth finish of the exterior wood, the subtle scent of cedar when I opened the door, and that satin aquamarine lining. Even the floor of the armoire, which was about at the height of my knees, was lined with the satin. Looking down at that floor after hanging up the suit, I saw something—a piece of leather?—jutting up from between the floor and the wall of the armoire. Odd. It looked a bit like the tapered end of a belt. I reached for it, my fingers grasping it as I tried to pull it from the crevice between the wall and floor. I was surprised when the whole floor of the armoire came loose in my hand, and I realized the bit of leather was simply a tab used to pull up the false bottom. I lifted the satin-covered board completely out of the floor of the armoire and gasped when I saw what was below: money. The bottom of the armoire was two-thirds full of bills, all denominations, it seemed, banded together in stacks. How much was there? And why? I knew Henry did his banking at First National. He was hardly the type to sock money away beneath his mattress. I knelt down in front of the armoire and began to count the bundles. A little more than two thousand dollars. A fortune! What was it doing here? I fitted the false floor back in place, arranging the leather tab so it looked exactly as it had when I'd discovered it. I felt as though I'd snooped into Henry's private world. I would say nothing to him about this discovery. At least not yet.

Downstairs, I was glad to find that Ruth had already left for one of her many meetings. I never enjoyed trying to make conversation with her over a meal. I joined Lucy at the table where she was reading the newspaper and she didn't bother to look up at me as I took my seat. Hattie brought me a plate of eggs and grits and poured coffee into my cup, and I opened one of the sections of the paper next to my plate.

I looked across the table at Lucy, who seemed engrossed in whatever she was reading. I thought of asking her to join me on my shopping spree. How I missed Gina! We always had so much fun shopping together. If only I could have a similar relationship with my sister-in-law. Sitting there, eating together quietly, though not companionably, I felt intimidated about asking her to go with me. She had nearly finished her eggs and was sipping her coffee when I finally found the courage.

"I'm going shopping for clothes today," I said. "Would you like to come with me? It's so good to get someone else's opinion on what to buy."

She set down her cup and looked up from the paper. "No offense, Tess," she said, "but I don't really want to be seen with you in town."

My cheeks burned. "Why do you dislike me so much?" I asked.

She leaned back from the table. "Let me count the ways," she said. "First, you're a slut."

I knew I should stop the conversation right there, but maybe it would be good to finally get it all out in the open. "I'm not a slut," I said. "Henry is the only man I've ever slept with and it was only that once and I deeply regret it. Not that it's any of your business."

She rolled her eyes. "Do you really expect me to believe that? That he was the only man you ever slept with? And how well could you have possibly known him? He didn't go to Washington all that often. He had to have been a near stranger to you. It's appalling. Did he pay you?"

"Of course not," I snapped.

"And then you get pregnant and come here expecting him to marry you and—"

"I didn't expect him to marry me," I said. "I just wanted help. Financial help, so I could raise this child on my own."

She stared at me. "Everybody knew . . . *Everybody!* That he and Violet would get married. That house he's building? Violet practically designed it. They worked on it together with an architect. So I'm sorry that you, on your so-called first-time-sleeping-with-a-man got pregnant, but you should have found some other way to deal with it than to come here and ruin our lives."

"I don't think he was in love with her."

"Well, do you think he'd tell you that?"

"I didn't hold a gun to his head and tell him he needed to marry me," I said, my anger starting to boil. "He asked me of his own free will."

"Because he's a good man. Of course that's what he did." She lifted her coffee cup to her lips again, but set it down without taking a sip. "Everyone here hates you," she said bluntly. "They love Violet. And really," she said, shaking her head, "you don't know the half of it."

"The half of what?"

She looked at her empty plate and let out a great sigh. "Nothing," she said.

"What more is there, Lucy?" I asked. What more could there possibly be?

When she looked up at me, there were tears in her eyes. "Do you love him?" she asked.

I steadied myself, getting my anger in check. She was hurting, for a reason I didn't understand. "Not yet," I said. "But I hope in time . . ."

"This wasn't the plan," she said. "You weren't part of the plan."

"What are you talking about?" I recalled Zeke talking to Henry at the factory, almost out of my hearing. *You had it all planned perfect,* he'd said. I thought of the money I'd just discovered in the armoire. Was that part of the plan too?

"I can't go shopping with you." Lucy stood up, lifting her plate from the table. "People will think I approve of you, and I don't," she said. "I never will."

35

As I waited on the sidewalk for the cab that would take me downtown, a police car drove past at a snail's pace. Before I even saw the policeman's face, I knew he would be the same one who'd driven past me repeatedly the day I walked to the post office. He'd been the high bidder on Lucy's box supper. Teddy Wright. When he was close enough for me to see his face, I waved. He turned away from me abruptly and sped up, looking straight ahead, as if he hadn't noticed me at all. A strange young man, I thought.

The cab delivered me downtown where there were several small clothing shops I might have gone into, but I decided to try the Belk-Broome department store instead. I thought I might be more anonymous in a big store. I doubted it would have a maternity department, or if it did, it would be tucked away in some hidden corner and I wouldn't dare ask for it. After all, I'd only been married a little over a month and wasn't about to give myself away.

I hoped to get three or four loose-fitting dresses and something smart—a suit, perhaps, if I could find one roomy enough to accommodate my expanding figure. I wanted to wear it when I traveled to Winston-Salem to take the exam, now only two weeks away. I hadn't brought the subject up with Henry again because, frankly, I didn't want to hear him say I couldn't go. I was going to do this on my own, whether he approved or not.

I found the dress department easily and an auburn-haired salesgirl in her late twenties approached me, a green floral dress over her arm.

"You're Hank Kraft's wife, aren't you?" she asked.

So much for being anonymous. I smiled my most winning smile. "Yes," I said. "Do you know Henry?"

"Of course," she said. "Who doesn't? But I recognized you from the box supper when Violet Dare's daddy took quite a shine to you."

It had hardly been a "shine," I thought, but I managed to hold on to my smile. "That was a fun night, wasn't it?" I asked.

"Sure was." She smoothed the skirt of the dress she held in her arms. "And how can I help you today?"

"I'd like to buy a few dresses," I said. "And perhaps a suit."

Her gaze dropped instantly to the center of my body. Somehow she knew. How? Did all of Hickory know the truth about Henry and me?

"Well, bless your heart," she said, and I knew better than to think the words were spoken from kindness. She hung up the dress on a nearby rack, then turned back to me. "Let's see what we can find," she said, pulling a tape measure from the pocket of her skirt. "What's your usual size?" she asked. "Or do we need to go up one?" She raised her eyebrows, looking innocent.

My waist had been twenty-three inches since I was a teenager. I knew that wasn't what it measured now. I took a step away from her and her tape measure. "I think I'll know the right size when I see it," I said. A ridiculous statement, I thought, but I would have to live with it.

"Well, let's find you something darling that's also nice and loose," she said, and I gritted my teeth. What could I say? This had been a mistake. I should have traveled to another town for this shopping spree, and I wished Henry had thought to suggest it. I felt like leaving, but I'd only create more rumors if I fled. Instead, I would try to win the salesgirl over.

"Your hair is the most beautiful color," I said as I followed her through the racks of dresses. Her short, rich auburn bob really was attractive on her.

"Thank you," she said, smoothing her hair with her palm.

"Have you lived in Hickory all your life?" I asked, as she looked through the dresses for one that might fit.

"Now, how about this one?" she asked, as if I hadn't spoken. She pulled a yellow housedress from the rack, and I knew I wasn't going to be able to engage her. She already had her mind made up about me. She was probably one of Violet's friends.

I tried on two dresses. They fit well and neither the salesgirl nor I mentioned that they each had extra room at the waist. But they were both an inch or so too long.

"I'll have these taken up for you and delivered to your house in two or three days," she said.

"Wonderful," I said, ushering her out of the dressing room. I didn't want her to see me in my slip. I knew I was finished with this shopping trip. I would have to do without a suit.

I stewed over the experience quietly as I rode in the cab home. I would tell Henry about the salesgirl and ask him if there was another town nearby where I might have some anonymity.

And I would have asked him, if he'd ever come home that night.

36

A few mornings later, I was sitting at my dressing table in my slip when I heard the doorbell ring. I was studying the knitting pattern I'd bought for my baby's sweater, and when the bell rang a second time, I remembered that Hattie was at the market. I had no idea where Ruth or Lucy were. I quickly threw on a housedress and headed for the stairs.

In the foyer, I found Ruth closing the front door. She was holding the mail, and she looked in my direction.

"That was a delivery boy from Belk's," she said. Her white chin-length hair, rigid with hair spray, sat on her head like a helmet.

I looked at the table by the front door where we left packages and mail for one another. "Did he have a package for me?" I asked.

"He did," she said, not looking up as she sifted through the stack of mail in her hands. "But I told him to take it back."

"You sent it back?" I asked in disbelief, remembering the ordeal I'd endured as I tried on the dresses, the salesgirl hovering over me.

Ruth plucked a catalog from the stack of mail and held it in the air. "I guess you didn't recall our conversation where I told you to order clothing from the Lane Bryant catalog," she said. "There was no reason for you to trouble yourself with a trip into town."

"It was no trouble." I tried to keep my voice even, but I was seething inside. Was there some way to get those dresses back?

"I'm so curious to understand why you'd tell Mary Sue Lamb you're expecting." Ruth wore a puzzled smile, and her question knocked me momentarily off balance. I guessed Mary Sue Lamb was the salesgirl at Belk's and that Ruth somehow knew every detail about my visit to the store.

"Is that the salesgirl?" I asked. "I didn't tell her or anyone else that I was expecting. She already knew. Is she a friend of Lucy's? Maybe Lucy said something to her."

There was an almost visible crack in Ruth's false smile. "Let's not pass the blame on to Lucy, shall we?" She handed me the catalog. "It will be much simpler for you to find the appropriate clothing in here," she said.

"Ruth," I said, "I want that package back. I'm an adult. It took me a long time to find the right dresses. I purchased them on my own with my own money. I don't think—"

"With *whose* money?" she asked.

I might have continued defending myself if I hadn't noticed the small pink envelope in the remaining stack of mail she was holding. Gina's stationery. That envelope was my connection to the one person I knew loved me.

"Is that letter for me?" I asked, walking toward her, my hand outstretched.

She looked at the envelope and for a moment I thought she was going to taunt me with it, holding it out of my reach, but after a few charged seconds, she handed it to me.

"You won't go into town again," she said.

I ignored her, turning away and heading for the stairs. I was too busy tearing open the envelope to care what Ruth wanted.

37

The Catholic church was a small granite building on the corner of Tenth Street and McComb, and as soon as I walked inside I felt the embrace of the stained-glass-infused light. I dipped my fingertips into the holy water font and blessed myself, then walked to a pew halfway to the altar. A woman knelt in one of the pews near the front of the church, but otherwise I was alone. The heady, musky scent of the air filled my lungs. It filled all of me, actually, right to the tips of my fingers.

Vincent, I thought to myself. *I made so many mistakes. Forgive me. I love you. I miss you.*

Near the altar, a priest walked from one side of the church to the other, genuflecting as he passed the tabernacle. His pale blond hair was combed back from his forehead and he looked quite young from where I knelt. I wished I could talk to him, but I couldn't bear the thought of being berated again. I was tired of being made to feel small and guilty. I studied the priest, trying to glean if he might, by some miracle, be the first person who really understood who I was at my core. I was human. I made mistakes, like everyone else. The only problem was that my mistakes came with terrible consequences.

I pulled Gina's letter from my handbag and read the painful middle paragraphs one more time in the dim light of the church.

I know you told me not to give you any information about Vincent, and I've driven myself crazy trying to decide if I should tell you this or not. I know you feel as though you hurt him terribly and that he might never recover from the blow, so I decided I should tell you what I know. I hope it eases your worry about him and doesn't add any pain to your situation.

When you first left, he called me often and pleaded with me to tell him where you were and of course I said nothing. Then his calls stopped. Yesterday, I bumped into Rosemary Tomasulo and she told me that Vincent is now working at that Harriet Lane Hospital for Children at Johns Hopkins and he likes it. She also said he's seeing a nurse who works there and is really happy. I know how much you loved him, Tess, so I hope you can be happy for him. And I hope it isn't a mistake for me to tell you all this. Please forgive me if it is.

I sat still, my eyes closed. The pain I felt was intense, as though my heart were squeezing itself dry. I had to make myself be happy for Vincent. It was good he'd found someone so quickly, I told myself. Someone to take his mind off how I'd hurt him. Yet thinking of him in love with another girl tore me apart.

Clutching the letter in my hand, I suddenly felt the bubbly flutter of life in my belly. It made me gasp, the sound echoing in the still air of the church, and the woman kneeling in prayer turned around to look in my direction. I smiled, lowering my head but too awed by what I'd felt to be sincerely embarrassed. I pressed both my hands protectively over my belly.

"I'll take care of you, little one," I whispered. "I'm giving you a father. That's the important thing. You and I . . . No matter what happens, we're going to be all right."

38

March 9, 1944

Dear Gina,

You were right to tell me about Vincent. It hurts beyond belief to know he's with someone else, but I'm happy for him. I only hope she treats him better than I did. I want the best for him. I'm also delighted that he's working at a hospital for children. Pediatrics has always been his passion and he is so good with the little ones.

I still have no idea how I'm going to finagle this trip to Winston-Salem, and the exam is less than a week away. I'm apprehensive about mentioning it to Henry again. I think I will simply have to disappear for a few days. He disappears all the time, working at the factory all night long, so now it's my turn! Wish me luck.

Love,

Tess

39

I left very early the first morning of the exam. I dressed as quietly as I could and tiptoed out of the house after leaving a hastily scribbled note for Henry on the night table. I'd barely slept and only hoped I would be able to stay awake for the examination.

Dear Henry,

Imagine working for years on a beautiful design for a dining room suite, and it's finally perfected and ready to be taken to market. Before you can do that, the furniture must be inspected for craftsmanship, but you can't get an appointment with the inspector. All your hard work stands in the balance. No one can see this beautiful thing you've created because you can't accomplish this one final step.

All right, maybe this is an awkward analogy but it's the best I can do at this early hour. I have to take that exam, Henry. I've worked hard to get to this point and I am determined to take this final step and be able to call myself a registered nurse. I know that means nothing to you, but it means everything to me.

I'm taking the train to Winston-Salem and I have reservations at a hotel. I will try to call you at the factory when I arrive. I'll be perfectly safe and will return on Thursday.

Fondly,

Tess

Outside, the wind nearly knocked me off my feet and I was glad to find the cab already waiting for me in front of the house. The driver let me off at the train station and I joined a few men on the platform. They all appeared to be wearing business suits beneath their long black wool coats and I felt out of place—I was certainly the only person on the platform with knitting in her suitcase. I ignored their curious gazes as I shivered in my own coat, my handbag and the exam handbook cradled in my arms.

The train was late and that only made me more nervous. What if I didn't make it to the exam site on time? Would they still let me in?

"Tess!"

I turned to see Henry rushing toward me from the parking lot. *Oh no.* I had the feeling my fellow passengers were going to witness a scene. I stood my ground as though my shoes were encased in concrete.

Henry reached me and wrapped his good hand around my arm. He leaned close to my ear. "Why didn't you tell me you were doing this?" he asked, his voice low enough that only I could hear him.

"You would have tried to stop me," I said, attempting to wrench my arm from his grip without being too obvious about it. "Please, Henry. Let me go. I have to do this."

He shook his head. "You're not getting on a train," he said. "I won't allow it. Not in your condition." He bent over and picked up my suitcase, but I didn't budge. "I'll drive you," he said. "Come on."

I thought I must have misunderstood him. "You'll drive me? Where?"

"It's in Winston-Salem, right?"

"You'll . . ." I could hear the train whistle as it approached the station and wondered if I should snatch my suitcase away from him and run to board the train.

"I'll *take* you, Tess," he said earnestly. "I have the gas. We can cancel your hotel reservation and stay someplace very nice, all right? You'll take your exam, and you damn well better pass it after all this nonsense." He smiled at me, that smile I so rarely saw.

I didn't know whether to trust him, his change of heart was so unexpected. My scribbled note must have had more of an impact than I imagined. I watched the businessmen board the train without me, and Henry reached for my gloved hand.

"Come on," he said again. "What time do you need to be in Winston-Salem?"

"The exam starts at ten," I said, falling into step next to him.

"Then we'd better hustle, hadn't we?"

We walked quickly to his car and I fully expected him to drive out of the parking lot and head directly for home, but he turned in the opposite direction from Oakwood, and when he pulled onto Route 64, I put my hand to my mouth, stunned.

"You're really taking me to Winston-Salem?" I asked.

He kept his eyes on the road and it was a moment before he spoke again. "I want you to be happy, Tess," he said, his hands tight on the wheel. "I know you had other plans for your life. I know living . . . in this situation . . . has been challenging for you." He gave a little shrug. "I also know that I'm not the best husband in the world. I work all the time. I have enormous responsibility, running the business, and it leaves little time for you. So if this will make you happy, I'll help you. But"—he glanced at me—"it doesn't change the fact that I don't want you to work, as a nurse or anything else. You can have the satisfaction of your degree or license or whatever you—"

"License." I grinned. I felt ridiculously happy.

"You can have the satisfaction of having earned your license, but what I ask of you is that you devote yourself to our child. Our family. Not a job."

I nodded. I was so touched that he was taking me to Winston-Salem that I would agree to anything, at least for now. I smiled to myself. I had a good, kind, and forgiving husband.

I moved closer to him, leaned over and planted a kiss on his cheek. "Thank you so much for this," I said, and I opened my handbook to study.

The exam was hard, but I'd anticipated that. What I hadn't anticipated was the discomfort of sitting in one place hour after hour while pregnant. I prayed for the bathroom breaks.

Henry spent most of the daytime hours on the phone handling factory business long distance. At night, our relationship was the same as it always was, with each of us in our separate beds, reading. I'd wondered if, in a hotel room without his mother and sister nearby, he might be a bit more amorous, but no. I had to accept the fact that, at least while I was pregnant,

Henry was not interested in a physical relationship with me. Not that I was particularly longing for one with him.

By the end of the three days, I was both exhausted and euphoric, certain that I'd passed. Even Henry seemed to catch my mood and he took me to his favorite Winston-Salem restaurant to celebrate before we headed for home in the dark.

"We are going to lie to my mother and sister," he said, when we were about halfway to Hickory.

"About the last three days?"

"Yes. I told Mama this was a business trip and you decided to come with me at the last minute."

"That's fine," I said. I liked that we shared a secret from Ruth. "What did I do all day while you worked?"

"Shopped?" he suggested. "Isn't that what girls do?"

"I was never one of those girls, Henry," I said. "And I never will be."

He looked over at me and although there was little light in the car, I saw him smile. He reached across the seat to lightly touch my cheek.

"How did I ever get tangled up with the likes of you?" he asked.

40

I woke up in the darkness a week and a half after our return from Winston-Salem, a tight fist of pain in my belly. I'd been dreaming that a stomach bug had taken hold of me when one of the spasms finally jerked me awake. Gasping, I sat up and turned on my night table lamp. My alarm clock read 5:20 and the pain was passing. Maybe it really *had* been a dream. But even though the fist was gone, a vague discomfort lingered. *Please, God,* I thought to myself. *Let this be a stomach virus and not the baby.*

I got out of bed and tried to put on my robe and slippers calmly, as though there were nothing at all wrong. Once in the bathroom, though, I saw tne blood and began to tremble. *This can't be happening,* I thought. *Please, no.*

I was crying softly by the time I returned to the bedroom and shook Henry by the shoulder.

"Hm?" he said. Early morning sunlight now sifted through the sheer curtains at the windows, illuminating his face as he looked up at me from the bed. "What is it?"

"I'm spotting," I said, although that was a gentle term for what I was experiencing.

"Spotting?" He raised himself to his elbows. "What are you talking about?"

"Bleeding. Something's wrong." I heard the shiver in my voice. "I shouldn't be bleeding," I said. "I'm only five months along. And I have some pain too."

He was instantly on his feet, his arm around me. "Sit down," he said, and I lowered myself to the edge of his bed. "I'll call Dr. Poole."

He threw his robe over his pajamas and left the room. I heard his quick footsteps on the stairs as he headed down to the kitchen and the phone, and I closed my eyes and whispered *please please please.* I'd seen Dr. Poole for the first time only the week before. He was a kindly man of indeterminate age who was clearly accustomed to keeping Hickory's secrets, and he'd assured me that my baby and I were fine and healthy. He'd told me to order a special maternity girdle, but I'd seen no reason to bother with it, and now I wondered if that had been a mistake. Had my baby needed more support? I knew deep down that was crazy, but I *felt* crazy at that moment. Crazy and terrified.

I began to get dressed, moving very slowly as though I could keep my baby inside me if I was careful. I had put on my slip, dress, and mules by the time Henry returned to the room, ashen faced and grim.

"He'll meet us at the hospital," he said.

I didn't seem able to move from where I stood at the end of my bed. "What did he say?" I asked. "It's bad, isn't it."

He took my arm and guided me gently toward the door. "Let's pray for a miracle," he said.

41

The fetoscope jutted from Dr. Poole's forehead when he walked into my room at the hospital.

"Wasn't due to see you for another few weeks, was I," he said pleasantly, giving me a small smile as he leaned over to press the scope to my bare belly. He moved the scope from place to place, listening, and I supposed he was counting my baby's heartbeat. The tight fist of pain was back, making me cringe. It had started up again as Henry drove me to the hospital, a stony silence between us, and although the pain let up from time to time, it always returned. As soon as we reached the hospital, I'd been placed on a gurney, hooked up to a saline drip, and wheeled away from Henry down a long hallway. My head had been on a pillow and I could see Henry's face grow smaller and paler until the gurney turned a corner and he disappeared altogether from my view.

Now Dr. Poole listened to my baby's heartbeat for a few more seconds, then he straightened up, a grimace on his face as though the act of standing straight hurt his back. He covered my belly with the sheet, then left without another word to me. A moment later, two nurses came into the room. I gave them a worried smile and wondered briefly if the younger girl was a student nurse, as I had been. I was an RN now myself, having learned only two days ago that I passed my exam. Suddenly, that seemed very unimportant.

"We need to get you ready to deliver," the older, gray-haired nurse said as she hung another bottle of liquid from the pole above my bed.

"Deliver?" I thought they had me mixed up with some other patient. "It's too soon!"

"Sugar," she said, as she set up a basin of water along with a white towel and a razor on the table near my bed, "your baby has no heartbeat and you're having contractions."

I clamped my legs together beneath the sheet. "No heartbeat?" I asked. "Dr. Poole couldn't hear it?"

"I'm afraid there's no heartbeat to hear, sugar," she said.

I looked at the younger nurse, hoping she could give me a different answer, but she avoided my eyes altogether.

"I don't understand," I said. I would refuse to understand.

"This happens sometimes," the gray-haired nurse said. "But there's no reason you won't be able to have more babies."

"I don't want more babies," I said. "I want *this* one." My voice rose and I covered my belly protectively. "I *need* this one!"

"Something's gone wrong with this one," she said. "It happened to me when I was nearly as far along as you, but now I have four healthy children, so you—"

"No! You don't understand." I started to sit up, but she held my shoulders. Pressed me back against the pillow. "I want *this* baby," I pleaded. It wasn't just my child she was talking about taking from me. It was my companion. My ally. The only living soul I had in Hickory. "Where's Henry?" Everyone knew and liked Henry. They would listen to him.

Another man—another doctor?—wheeled something I couldn't see into the room. He nodded to the nurses, but ignored me even when he reached the side of my bed and began adjusting the equipment he'd brought with him.

"Your husband's in the fathers' waiting room," the older nurse said as she checked the bottles on the pole above my bed. "He's not allowed in here, of course, but Dr. Poole will tell him what's happening."

Her voice suddenly sounded as though it were a million miles away and when I opened my mouth again to speak, I forgot what I was about to say. Something—a mask?—came toward my face, and I turned my head away, resisting it. Fighting it. But against my will, my eyelids fell shut and I gave up the battle.

I awakened alone, cramping and sore, still tied to the IV. I knew all at once my baby was no longer inside me, and the loneliness I felt was overwhelming. I wanted to be home in Little Italy in my little row house. I wanted my mother. My Vincent.

A nurse I hadn't seen before, brown haired and wearing pale pink-framed glasses, padded into the room on her soft-soled shoes.

"There you are." She smiled. "It's all over now, honey," she said, as she rearranged my covers. "Dr. Poole will keep you here a few days while you heal and—"

"I want to see my baby," I said.

She reached for my wrist, checking her watch as she took my pulse. "You lost your baby, Mrs. Kraft," she said, her gaze never leaving her watch. "I'm so sorry."

"I know," I said. "But I want to see it."

"Oh no, dear, you don't." She let go of my wrist and poured a glass of water from the pitcher on my bedside table.

"Was it a boy or a girl?" I asked.

She hesitated. "A boy," she said.

My Andy. "I want to see him," I said firmly.

She stood next to the bed, shaking a pill into her hand from a small glass bottle. "He wasn't full term, you know, and—"

"I want to see him!" I shouted. I felt as though a different woman inhabited my body. One who shouted. One who demanded what was hers.

"It doesn't matter now," she said. "He's an angel in heaven. That's how you have to think of him. He's with Jesus now."

"Please." I started to cry. "Please let me see him."

"We don't do that," she said. "If he'd been full term and you really, truly wanted to see him, you could have, but not with a twenty-one-week-old fetus." She tried to hand me the pill, but I didn't take it from her. "Now you really must swallow this, honey," she said. "It will make you feel better."

"Where is my husband?" Maybe Henry could persuade them. Everyone listened to Henry Kraft. But what would I say to him? What would happen to us now that there was no baby to bind us together?

"He's gone to his job for a while," she said, "but he said he'd be back soon. And he's the one who arranged for you to have this room, away from the maternity ward. He doesn't want you to be with other mothers who . . ." Her voice trailed off. "He's a very thoughtful man, isn't he," she added.

I felt grateful to Henry for realizing it would be intolerable for me to be in a ward where I would hear crying babies and joyful women.

"I'm going to leave this pill right here," the nurse said, setting the pill and glass of water within my reach on the nightstand. Then she squeezed my shoulder. "Don't worry, Mrs. Kraft," she said. "You'll have more babies."

I wanted to slap her. Why did people keep saying that to me? Didn't they know how precious this baby was? How irreplaceable?

"I wanted *this* baby," I whispered, more to myself than to her, and I doubted she heard me.

"You get some rest now, dear," she said, and she left me alone with my grief.

Henry arrived later that afternoon carrying a vase overflowing with flowers. Silently, he set them on the nightstand next to my bed. I thought he was avoiding looking at me.

"I'm so sorry," I said. My throat felt dry and tight.

He sat down in the only chair in the room and let out a sigh. "Dr. Poole said it's nothing you did. That it's hard to explain why things like this happen. They just do."

I heard no blame in his voice. "I wanted to see him," I said. "They wouldn't let me."

"It would only make it harder."

"I don't think so."

"He said there's no reason you can't have more children."

I turned my face away. I couldn't respond to that sentiment one more time.

"Mama and Lucy send their best," he said.

I nodded, but I found that hard to believe.

I looked at Henry. Really looked at him. Those blue eyes were rimmed with red. It was not my imagination. It gave me courage to try to connect to him in a way we never had before.

"Our Andrew," I said in a near whisper. "Our precious Andrew."

His Adam's apple bobbed in his throat as he got to his feet. He didn't look at me.

"I need to get back to the factory," he said, "But I wanted to check on you. Make sure you're all right."

"I'm not all right," I said.

He didn't seem to know how to respond to that. "I know," he said after a moment. He rubbed his wounded left hand with his right. "I'm sorry things turned out this way." He walked toward the door and pulled it open, then looked over at me one last time. "Let's not name him," he said. "There really is no point." He left the room then. Left me lying in that bed by myself, aching and empty. I'd never felt so alone.

42

We were trapped, both of us.

In early May, six weeks after I lost Andrew, Ruth insisted I return to church with the family. I'd spent the past month and a half in a fog. Dr. Poole had prescribed something for my "melancholia," and it kept me numb. I welcomed that numbness. In the past, the nurse in me would have been curious to know the name of the medication and exactly how it worked in my body. Now I didn't care. I just wanted it to erase the emotional pain. Nothing else mattered.

For the first few weeks, Hattie'd brought my meals up to the bedroom. When she'd return a while later to pick up the tray, she'd scold me for leaving so much food behind.

"You need your strength, Miss Tess," she'd say. "I know you grievin' over that baby, but—"

"Andrew," I said. I was determined to make everyone see my baby as a person.

She nodded. "You grievin' over Andrew," she said, "but you gonna need your strength more than ever." She leaned close, nearly whispering although there was no one around. "You should visit our friend."

I knew she meant Reverend Sam, and I gave a slight nod to placate her. The truth was, even the thought of seeing that dear old man did nothing to comfort me. Nothing in the universe could possibly lift my grief.

"You two should get divorced," Lucy said a week or so later at the dinner table. "I know it's not easy, but it's not impossible either." It was the second or third dinner we'd all eaten together. I wasn't sure. My mind was too foggy to separate one meal from another.

"Completely against our faith," Ruth said. " 'What God has joined together, let no man put asunder.' " She cut a small piece from the ham steak on her plate. "And besides, there are no divorces in the Kraft family." She looked from me to Henry. "The two of you made your bed, now you have to lie in it."

"I have no intention of divorcing Tess." Henry rested his hand on mine on the table. As always, his displays of affection still occurred only when someone was watching. "She's my wife," he said.

"Oh for heaven's sake," Lucy said. "Drop the pretense. You got married because she was pregnant. That's the only reason. Modern people find a way to divorce. It's not a tragedy."

"The reason doesn't matter," Ruth said. "They're married. We make the best of things in this family."

I listened to them talk around me as if I weren't there. The conversation didn't bother me, though. It was almost as if they were talking about someone else, I felt so unmoved by their words. My mind was still on Andrew. The emptiness I felt was both physical and emotional. When I woke up each morning it took me a moment to remember what had happened and then the sorrow would wash over me again. I would have given anything for a time machine to take me back to my old life, where I had a mother and a home and where the most difficult thing I had to face was living without Vincent for a few months while he worked in Chicago. How foolish I'd been to make a fuss over that! If I could go back in time, I certainly wouldn't sleep with Henry. I wouldn't go to Washington with Gina at all. But that old life was gone and now I was trapped in this one. I couldn't stop myself from wondering if losing Andrew was my punishment for everything I'd done.

Henry and I never spoke of anything of consequence. He grew frustrated with me when I talked about Andrew, especially if I used his name. Henry was done with that chapter of his life. That chapter in our marriage. His nights out became more frequent and I never questioned him about them. I didn't care. I only wanted to find a way out of the trap I was in.

43

May 22, 1944

Dear Gina,

I miss you so much. It was kind of you to call me on Saturday. You knew I'd be in terrible straits that day, didn't you? May twentieth, the day I was to marry Vincent. If I hadn't derailed my life, we'd be on our Niagara Falls honeymoon right now. I wonder if he thought of me Saturday, or is he so happy with his new girlfriend that the date meant nothing to him? Sorry to go on like this! Really, I only wanted to thank you, not get caught up again in my sadness.

Well, the news here in this part of North Carolina is polio. Infantile paralysis. And it's not even summer yet, when it usually attacks. This morning I was sitting with Ruth and Lucy on the screened porch and Ruth read an article to us from the paper about there being a couple of cases in Charlotte, which is a bit too close for comfort. It's such a terrible, frightening, ominous disease! Are you seeing any of it in Baltimore? I can't imagine the terror of having a child diagnosed with it. Odd that they call it infantile, isn't it? President Roosevelt is so crippled from it and he was an adult when he contracted it. No one is really safe from polio.

I saw a few cases of it when I was a student nurse, and Vincent told me about some of his patients last summer when he was working in Chicago, but what has always stood out in my mind was his description of his cousin Tony's battle with the disease when they were children. One day Tony was fine. The next day he couldn't move a muscle. He recovered, at least partially, but so many children don't.

Anyhow, I couldn't help myself as I sat there with Ruth and Lucy. I said, "I have a friend whose cousin had polio." It just popped out of my mouth. It was as though I couldn't resist bringing Vincent onto the porch with us. I felt a thrill run up my arms just thinking about him. The two of them stared at me and I realized how little I'd spoken to anyone in the family, Henry included, since Andrew's death. I've become closed off from everyone (except you).

"It only happens to poor children though," Ruth said. "You know, with poor sanitation."

That gives you an idea of the sort of woman Ruth is!

"FDR wasn't poor or a child," Lucy pointed out. She loves to argue with her mother and I don't blame her.

"And my friend's cousin wasn't poor," I said. I truly have no idea if Tony was rich or poor. I just wanted to counter Ruth's silly argument.

"Well, generally it's poor living conditions," Ruth said firmly. "Rampant flies and unclean water. This is common knowledge." She gave me a look that shut me up and I let it go. I have to live with this woman. And honestly, I felt happier than I had in a long time because I was thinking of Vincent. That isn't good, is it, dear friend? I know I need to live in the real world, but my real world is too difficult for me right now.

Well, guess what I did this afternoon? I went to the library and researched divorce in North Carolina. The results were depressing. Gina, it's impossible! I grew more despondent the more I read, but I simply have to find a way out of this loveless, lifeless, stultifying marriage! Henry is dead set against a divorce. He's good to me, but he clearly doesn't love me so I don't understand why he's so against ending our marriage. It would be a stain on the Kraft name and I guess that's enough to make it unthinkable for him. Nevertheless, I feel a need to educate myself to the possibilities.

It took me nearly an hour to track down the book I needed at the library because I didn't dare ask the librarian where I might find it and have to answer any nosy questions. "The North Carolina Code of 1944." Yawn! I settled down at one of the tables to read and immediately found myself bogged down in pages and pages of tiny text. Anyway, here are the miserable facts: to get divorced, Henry and I would need to live sepa-

rately for two full years . . . unless I could prove that he'd committed adultery, or that he was impotent, or that he'd committed an "abominable and detestable crime against nature with mankind or beast." Oh my! I pondered the word "adultery" for a long time. I've told you he sometimes doesn't come home at night. Is he really working at the factory those nights like he says? Could he possibly be having an affair? He's so disinterested in having relations that it's hard to picture, although maybe he's only disinterested in having relations with me.

But as I continued reading, I began to get an idea. I read that a marriage can be voided if the man is impotent. Voided. Similar to an annulment. It would be as if we had never been married. Henry had certainly not been impotent the night we were together in Washington, but maybe something has happened to him since then. Some change, physical or psychological. What do you think? When I was pregnant, I thought he might be afraid to be intimate with me, and afterward, of course, the doctor told us not to have relations for six weeks. But now, eight weeks have passed, and Henry's no more interested in making love than he had been when I was pregnant. So could he possibly be impotent? And how on earth will I ever be able to ask him that question! He's such a private person that I can't imagine it. But it might be our answer—or at least my answer. I'm hoping the word "void" might be more palatable to him than "divorce." I doubt, though, that he'll embrace the word "impotence" very easily.

At any rate, I'm meeting him later today at the new house to see how it's coming along and I plan to broach the subject with him then. I have no idea how. We don't talk easily about anything, really, so this is going to be particularly delicate. Gina, if by some miracle he agrees to end our marriage, do you think I could live with you and your mother for a short time until I find a job and can get a place of my own?

As usual, I've gone on and on about myself. I'm so thrilled that you finally heard from Mac. Please let him know I'm thinking of him and I hope he's not in harm's way. Tell your mother I said hello. How I miss you and Little Italy and St. Leo's and everything! Have some pizza for me, Gina. They've never even heard of it down here, and I am ever so tired of grits!

Love,

Tess

44

I dropped the letter to Gina in the corner mailbox as I walked the short distance to Henry's new house. I still couldn't think of the house as ours. With Andrew gone, I didn't want to.

The day was beautiful, the blue sky dotted with cottony white clouds, and I began to dream about the future as I walked. If our marriage ended, was returning to Baltimore the best plan? I wasn't sure. I would be too close to Vincent if I were in Baltimore and that would be difficult, but moving in with Gina and her mother for a while would allow me to get on my feet again. The best part of ending my marriage to Henry would be leaving Hickory. Leaving Ruth and Lucy. I could leave the husband who treated me kindly but not warmly, the way you'd treat a stray cat you came across from time to time. I needed to get out of this marriage to find myself again. I wanted *Tess* back. I'd lost her these last few months. More than anything, I wanted my freedom.

Henry's new house had changed dramatically since I'd last seen it. It was no longer a simple wooden frame. Now encased in rich red brick and two stories tall, it had a warmth that had been lacking before. I stood on the curb, staring at it, trying to decide if it was imposing or inviting. A bit of both, I thought.

Henry's Cadillac was parked on the street so I knew he was already there. I picked my way carefully up the long dirt driveway and he met me at the side door.

"What do you think?" he asked, smiling.

"It looks beautiful." I returned his smile. "I love the brick."

"Come in." He held out his arm to guide me inside.

We walked through the main level where the space that had earlier been a network of posts and beams now boasted actual rooms with solid white walls and ceilings and hardwood floors, a clean canvas waiting to be filled with life and color. The stairs were finished and we climbed them carefully, since there was no banister yet in place. Upstairs, the hallway opened onto four bedrooms and a den. I bit my lip. I remembered him asking me which bedroom I would like for the nursery. He may have been recalling the same conversation, because as we explored each room, he lightly rested his hand on my back. He was being sweet this afternoon. Why was he picking today to be so loving when I was gearing up to suggest a way we could end our marriage?

"Now, finally," he said, as we stood in the middle of the largest bedroom, the one we would share, "it's your turn to make decisions about the house. You can pick out the wallpapers and paint colors. And we should shop for furniture." He smiled at me. "You can select a spot in the yard to plant that tree for your mother."

I'd almost forgotten about the tree, there were so many other things on my mind. I was touched that he remembered.

"It's going to be a very busy few months," he continued. "I've secured a professional designer to work with you. You're to give her a call and she'll meet you here. How about sometime next week?"

"Henry," I said, "can we talk for a minute?"

He raised his eyebrows. "About what?"

I looked around us, wishing there was a place to sit, but the bare rooms offered nothing more than floors scattered with sawdust. I leaned back against the wall.

"I know you don't want a divorce," I began, "and neither do I. Neither of our churches support it, and—"

"What do you mean, 'neither of our churches'?" He frowned at me, slipping his hands into his pants pockets. "Tess, when are you going to accept that you're no longer Catholic? I've wanted to talk to you about being baptized in the Baptist church, but I didn't think it was the right time yet, with everything that's gone on. But—"

"That's not what I'm talking about," I said quickly. I'd started this conversation the wrong way. "I'm not talking about our religions, really. I'm talking about a possible . . . annulment." There. I'd said it. "It might be possible to have our marriage voided," I said. "It would be like we'd never been married at—"

"I know what an annulment is," he said. "I'm not interested in it." He stared at me from beneath knitted brows. "I don't understand you," he said. "I just said you can have this house, for God's sake." He looked around us at the four walls of the room. "You can decorate it any way you like, to your heart's content. Most girls would leap at that chance."

"It's a beautiful house," I agreed, "but if we don't have a . . . true marriage, then . . . will we really be happy anyplace?"

"We're married, Tess," he said. "If you would just relax a little . . . try harder to fit in . . . then yes, we can be happy here."

I struggled to figure out what to say. He looked so mystified by my complaints, and those downcast eyes suddenly hurt to look at. I knew I couldn't say anything about impotence now. It was too personal. Far too insulting and emasculating.

"It's just that we haven't . . . if there's no . . . you know . . . consummation, then it's possible to get a marriage voided. Annulled. It's as if there's no real marriage."

He pulled his hands from his pockets and rubbed the fingers of his right hand over the knuckles of his left as though they ached. "I'll give you the number for the interior decorator," he said, heading for the door of the room. "You can call her at your leisure."

I shut my eyes, not budging from the spot where I stood leaning against the wall. I hadn't handled that well. I would give him time to think through what I said. Surely he had to acknowledge that what we had was not a real marriage. He couldn't possibly be happy with our relationship the way it was. Could he?

I fell into a troubled sleep that night, curled on my side. Sometime after midnight, I awakened to realize that Henry was lying behind me on the narrow bed. He touched my breasts through my negligee, his fingers light, the tips of them like feathers on my nipples. The touch was enough to arouse me and I rolled over to face him. In the dark, I couldn't make out his features. What would I see in his face? I wondered. What would he see in mine? He lifted the hem of my negligee and gently spread my thighs apart with his hands, and then, for the second time in my life, I felt a man inside me. I prayed we were not creating another child. Not yet. I was still grieving for Andrew. I always would be. I lay there, moving with him, feeling very little other than the automatic response of my body to his thrusts. I knew it wasn't desire motivating him, and it certainly wasn't love. I knew his true motivation as clearly as I knew my own name. Henry was locking me into this marriage for all time.

I knew what he was doing. I just didn't know why.

45

"Where on earth is Hattie?" Ruth asked the following morning. She and Lucy and I had come down to the dining room expecting breakfast to be ready. When there was no sign of food or even our table settings, the three of us walked into the kitchen to find it sparkling clean. It was clear Hattie hadn't yet arrived. I knew she occasionally spent the night away, with her boyfriend, Oscar, but she was always at the house early enough to make breakfast for Henry, who often left for work before the rest of us were up. I'd been glad to find Henry gone when I woke up that morning. I was both perplexed and irritated by his lovemaking last night.

Ruth peered out the window toward the cottage. "I hope she's not ill," she said.

"I'll go check on her," Lucy said, but before she could open the back door, a truck pulled up near the garage and Hattie stepped out of the cab in her gray uniform and white apron.

"That's Zeke's truck," Lucy said, as the truck began backing out of the driveway. "She must not have stayed in the cottage last night." She pulled open the door as Hattie rushed onto the back steps. Even from where I stood, I could see that her eyes were red.

"Sorry I'm late!" she said, hurrying breathlessly into the kitchen, a handkerchief wadded up in her fist. "I'll cook y'alls' breakfast right—"

"What's wrong, Hattie?" Lucy interrupted her.

Hattie stood in the middle of the kitchen, looking woefully at the three

of us before burying her face in her hands, her shoulders heaving. Ruth
pulled a chair from beneath the table.

"Sit down, dear," she said. "Tell us what's happened."

Hattie lowered herself onto the chair, her dark cheeks streaked with
tears. "Butchie has the polio!" she said.

"Oh no," I said, and Ruth took a step backward as though Hattie might
be a carrier of the dreaded disease.

"How horrible!" Lucy pressed a fist to her mouth.

"Zeke come get me last night and brung me over Adora's to help out
before they knowed what was wrong," Hattie continued. "Doctor says he's
the first case in Hickory. He's real sick. Can't move. Can't even swallow
and ain't breathin' right." She looked up at us, a mystified expression on
her face. "Why my baby cousin got to be the first one?" she asked.

"Poor Adora," Ruth said, genuine concern in her voice. "Did the doctor give him some medicine?"

Hattie shook her head. "They come in a ambulance and took him away
to Charlotte," she said. "Honor's all tore up. They wouldn't let her go with
him. They let me and Zeke leave the house, but Adora and Honor and Jilly
is all under that quarantine now."

"This is terrible." Lucy twisted her hands together in front of her. "He's
such a sweet little boy." Were there tears in her eyes? She ordinarily struck
me as so self-absorbed. This was a different side to her.

Ruth looked at Lucy. "We need to take them something," she said.
"What do they need, Hattie?"

"They need their baby boy back," she said, blotting her eyes with the
handkerchief. "That's about it."

I remembered little Butchie running out of Adora's house the day we
took them the leftovers from the box supper. His adorable little suit and
tie. The joy in his face at seeing Lucy. I hated to think of him so sick.

"I could make them one of those stuffed hams," I said, wondering if
my contribution would be welcome. Hattie had told me how much they'd
liked my ham, but my connection to Adora's family was peripheral at best.
I looked at Hattie. "You said they loved it."

"They did." Hattie sniffled. "That'd be right nice, Miss Tess."

I felt Ruth and Lucy studying me in silence. "They did like that," Ruth
acknowledged after a moment. "We can get a ham. What else do you need
for it, Tess? Hattie can go to the store."

I ticked off the ingredients on my fingers and Hattie nodded after each one, committing them to memory.

"If you make it, I'll take it over," Lucy said to me. "I'm not afraid of those germs."

"Can't go in the house, Miss Lucy," Hattie said. "Nobody 'lowed in now, not even me. The health people put a big sign on the door."

"Well, you can just leave it on the porch for them," Ruth said to Lucy.

Hattie got to her feet, smoothing the skirt of her uniform and sniffling. She reached into the cupboard where she kept the skillets. "Let me git some breakfast for y'all before I go to the—"

"Don't worry about it, Hattie," Ruth said. "We'll take care of ourselves this morning. You just get ready to go to the store."

Henry came home at noon for lunch—a rarity for him. His cheeks were pale and his expression grim when he walked in the back door, and he grew even paler when he found me sweating over a pot of boiling water in the kitchen. Lucy'd found some linen for me to wrap the ham in rather than using another pillowcase, and the scent of the meat and herbs and spices filled the kitchen.

"What are you doing?" he asked.

"I'm making stuffed ham for Adora's family," I said, putting the lid on the pot. "Her grandson—that little boy Butchie?—has polio, and—"

"I know," Henry interrupted. "Zeke told me. But you don't have anything to do with that family and I don't like to see you tiring yourself in the kitchen. Let Hattie take care of it."

"Nonsense." I smiled.

"She don't let me lift a finger, Mr. Hank," Hattie said. She was slicing tomatoes on the counter near the sink.

I knew my face was glistening, tendrils of my hair glued to my forehead and cheeks. It felt good to be doing something other than stewing about my suddenly consummated marriage. Hattie had complained that I was in her way in the kitchen, but I thought she was only teasing. I had the feeling she was touched that I was making something for her relatives.

"I'm enjoying it," I said to Henry.

He looked at me blankly, that worrisome pallor in his face, and I knew there was more on his mind than his distress at finding me in the kitchen. I touched his arm.

"What's wrong?" I asked.

He turned away from me, setting his briefcase on the seat of one of the kitchen chairs. "Just some problems with the factory," he said. "If it's not the boiler, it's the spray booth. If it's not the spray booth, it's the kiln. We had a near accident with the boring machine today because it malfunctioned." He sighed. "Always something that needs attention."

Lucy suddenly burst into the room. "You're home!" she said to Henry. "Did you hear about Butchie?"

He nodded. "I told Zeke he could take time off to drive Honor to the hospital in Charlotte so she could be with him," he said, "but she's under quarantine, and it looks like she wouldn't have been able to see him anyhow. Zeke drove all the way over there and they told him no one can visit Butchie for the first two weeks."

"First two weeks!" Lucy exclaimed. "He'll have to be there that long?"

I knew Butchie could be in the hospital much, much longer than two weeks, but didn't say anything. Everyone seemed too upset as it was.

"Could be a very long time," Henry said. "Polio doesn't generally go away quickly." He looked around the room at all three of us. "By the way," he said, "I told Zeke to give the hospital our phone number, since Adora doesn't have a phone. Just in case they need to get in touch with an update on his condition."

"Thank you, Mr. Hank," Hattie said. "I don't know what Honor's gonna do without her baby boy home to dote on."

"She'll have him back in no time," Lucy said, patting Hattie's arm.

"Should someone get in touch with . . ." I tried to remember the name of Butchie's father. "Del, is it?" I asked.

For a few seconds, no one said a word. Then finally, Hattie spoke up.

"Is there a way?" She looked hopefully at Henry.

He hesitated. "I doubt it," he said finally. "But I'll look into it." He shot me a look that told me I shouldn't meddle. I supposed the last thing Del needed was to worry about his son when he was overseas, fighting for his country, in danger every day.

———

I made the stuffed ham, wrapped it in waxed paper, and set it in the refrigerator to chill. I knew it would do little to ease that family's worries, but at least it would keep them fed. I tried to imagine what it was like for little Butchie to be without his mother, unable to move parts of his body, struggling to breathe. If it hurt *me* to imagine him scared and separated from his family, what must it be like for Honor? Being pregnant and losing my baby seemed to have made me more sensitive to anything having to do with motherhood.

When Henry came home from the factory in the early evening, he and Lucy took the ham over to Adora's.

"Shall I come too?" I asked. I felt as though I should go with them, since the ham was my contribution.

"No," they both answered at the same time.

"No point to it," Henry added, "since we can't even go inside. We'll let them know you made it though."

I packed the ham in a large paper bag and handed it to Lucy. As the two of them left by the back door, Henry stopped. He turned back to me, touched my shoulder.

"Thank you," he said. "It was kind of you to do this."

46

May 27, 1944

Dear Tess,

I felt very excited as I read your letter! I hope Henry agreed to your plan to have your marriage "voided," though frankly I can't imagine Mac ever willingly admitting to impotence! You left me with a cliff-hanger, so please fill me in as soon as you can. I want you to come home!

Speaking of home, though, I'm afraid there's a snag. You asked if you could live with Mom and me for a while, and up to a few days ago, that would have been possible. But I've decided to move out. I don't know if I ever told you about my coworker Sarah, but we are getting an apartment together. It's the second story of one of those row houses by St. Leo's. You know where I mean? It's really cute and already furnished, but it's very small. Sarah and I will each have a tiny bedroom. Then there's a little living room and a miniscule kitchen. It's all we can afford, but it will do until Mac and I get married, assuming this war ever ends. I'm so sorry, but there won't be room for you to stay with us. I can talk to Sarah to see if she'd agree to let you sleep on our couch for a few days until you find a place of your own. I feel terrible turning you away!

No, there isn't much polio here, as far as I know. It sounds dreadful. I hope it doesn't get too serious there.

Love,
Gina

47

Gina's letter distressed me. I was unfairly envious of her friendship with her coworker. I'd never met Sarah. Never even heard Gina mention her before, and although I had no right at all to my jealous feelings, I couldn't tamp them down. Her letter drove reality home to me: Gina had a good friend who wasn't me, and even if I could figure out a way to leave Hickory and my marriage, I didn't have anyplace to go.

I had no friends in Hickory. That was the sad truth. Lucy's friends viewed me as an old married woman and, of course, Lucy's dislike of me poisoned their feelings about me. The women in Ruth's social circle still seemed to view me as the hussy who had trapped Henry into marriage. So it was not unusual that I was home alone when the Charlotte hospital called a couple of days later. The hospital receptionist or whoever she was put a doctor on the line, and in a cool, clinical voice, he told me that Butchie Johnson was dead. Without even realizing it, I rested my hand on my empty belly. I asked for details and received few, only that the disease had spread too quickly through the boy's little body to save him.

I sat still for a long time after hanging up the phone, wishing I could miraculously change the last few minutes. Hattie was at the store and I was glad she wasn't home. I dreaded telling her. I dreaded telling *anyone* and thought Henry should be the one to deliver the news. When I gathered my thoughts, I picked up the phone again and called him. He answered a bit gruffly, and I knew this was a terrible time to give him bad news with all that was going wrong at the factory. He was so silent after I told him that I thought we'd been cut off.

"Someone has to tell them," I said, picturing Adora's little yellow house in Ridgeview. I remembered her cheerful round face as she spoke to Henry and me through the open window of the Cadillac. "Maybe you can tell Zeke and he can go over to tell them?"

"I'll take care of it," he said finally.

"It's so sad," I said.

"It doesn't concern you."

"I can relate though," I said. "I just lost a child."

I heard him scoff. "It's not the same thing in any way, shape, or form," he said, shutting me out. He hung up abruptly and I sat for a moment, staring at the phone in my hand. I was hurt by his continued unwillingness to acknowledge that our son had existed. But I supposed he was right that this loss didn't really concern me. I barely knew Honor. Still, for the rest of the day I was consumed by a deep sadness that felt like it might suck me down if I didn't fight it.

Hattie cried when I told her, and so did I. Only I did my crying in the bedroom where no one could tell me I had no right to the tears.

48

A few days later, I woke to the sound of someone pounding on the front door. I sat up in the narrow bed, groggy and disoriented. The pounding stopped and I supposed that either the person had gone away or Ruth had answered the door. I looked at my alarm clock. It was only a few minutes past six.

Henry rolled in my direction and opened his eyes. "Did I hear someone knocking?" he asked.

"I think so," I said. "I don't know if—"

Ruth suddenly flung our door open. "Get up, get up!" she commanded, breathless from the climb up the stairs. "The Allies attacked the French coast!" she shouted. "Teddy Wright just came over to tell us to turn on the radio." She was smiling broadly and I could see the pretty young girl she had once been in her face. "There are thousands of troops!" she said, clasping her hands together. "Thousands upon thousands! Hurry downstairs."

I didn't think I'd ever seen Henry move so quickly. He nearly leaped from his bed, reaching for his robe as he ran to the bedroom door. I was right behind him, grabbing my own robe and stepping into my slippers.

In minutes, all four of us plus Hattie, already dressed in her uniform, sat as close as we could get to the radio in the living room, awestruck by what we were hearing.

"The Allies stormed the northern coast of France," the excited announcer said. "A fleet of more than five thousand ships carrying one hundred and sixty thousand troops has invaded Hitler's Europe and are fighting their way up the beaches."

A hundred and sixty thousand troops! I tried to picture the scene as the commentator described it. Thousands of soldiers fighting their way ashore, a cloud of fighter planes above them in the air. All those young men. All that courage! I wanted to cheer and cry at the same time. I hugged myself, leaning over to get closer to the radio, listening to every word. *Please, God,* I thought. *Let this horrible war come to an end.*

"Casualties may reach a dreadful toll," the commentator said.

I thought of the boys from my Little Italy neighborhood who'd enlisted or been drafted, picturing them among the hundreds of men on that beach in France.

"Thousands are known to be dead or wounded," the announcer continued, and Lucy covered her mouth with her hand. She knew boys over there too. We all did, and in that moment I thought each one of us was filled with both fear and gratitude for those young men. Henry's jaw was set. He rubbed the thumb and forefinger of his left hand with his right, the way he did when he was upset or stressed. I imagined every house in Hickory was filled with the same mixture of emotions at that moment. Every house in the country.

"Teddy said the church is open." Ruth got to her feet. "Everyone's going. I'm getting dressed and calling a cab to take me there myself. Lucy and Tess, you come with me. And Hattie, you can go to your church too, if you want." As if on cue, church bells began ringing throughout the town and we all laughed giddily at the timing.

"I need to go to the factory," Henry said, standing up. "I should let everyone off today to go to church."

"Mr. Hank, can you stop by Adora's on your way to the factory and tell them what's goin' on?" Hattie asked as she got to her feet. "They ain't got no radio and you know they ain't allowed out." Adora, Honor, and little Jilly were still under quarantine. They hadn't even been allowed to attend Butchie's funeral, which seemed unbearably cruel to me. Henry had attended with Ruth and Lucy. They'd probably been the only white people in the church.

"Might Honor's husband be one of the troops?" I asked. I knew Henry hadn't been able to get word to Del that Butchie had died.

"You mean the father of her children," Ruth said, with clear disdain. "Certainly possible, I suppose."

"Oh, Mama." Lucy scowled. "You're so hard on Honor."

"That girl's a thorn in Adora's side." Ruth headed for the foyer. "Now get ready to go or I'll leave without you," she said.

I didn't miss the sorrowful look on Hattie's face as Ruth criticized her cousin Honor. I didn't think Henry missed it either. He rested his hand on Hattie's arm.

"Don't worry," he said to her. "I'll let them know."

The Baptist church was filled with excited, anxious parishioners by the time Ruth, Lucy, and I arrived. People kept coming, pouring through the doors, hugging one another as they crowded in. They brushed tears from their cheeks, and I knew that for those who had lost loved ones, the morning was bittersweet. I felt the joy and sorrow, fear and hope in every one of our hearts.

I pressed my hands together and bowed my head. Until today, my prayers had felt weak and empty in this sterile church, but today I lifted them up, one with my neighbors, as we all prayed for the same thing: victory.

49

In the days that followed D-day, a confusion of emotions reigned in the town. Excitement and cautious optimism were tempered by grief, since one local boy was among the casualties and the blue star that had hung in the window of his family home changed to gold. But the town was also gripped by fear that had nothing at all to do with the war. There was no way around it: Catawba County was in the middle of a polio epidemic that felt more immediate, more real, than anything that might be happening in Europe. New cases were reported every day and the hospital in Charlotte overflowed with sick children. People were frightened, many of them avoiding movie theaters or restaurants where they might come into contact with carriers of the virus. The county health officer, Dr. Whims, had become a household name. We constantly heard his voice on the radio and saw his picture in the paper as he struggled to be a calming influence.

"Community hysteria doesn't help at all," he said in a radio broadcast, right after he informed us that children twelve and under were now barred from public places. Parks and pools were closed, and although the cause of the epidemic was unknown, Dr. Whims warned parents not to let their children drink unprocessed milk or play in the creeks. "Repair your window screens," he said, "and do everything possible to control flies." Many of the women in Ruth's circles, those who had children or grandchildren and means, escaped to their mountain or lake homes. Hickory had a ghost-town feel to it without the laughter of children.

At church that Sunday, Ruth stood up to make an announcement.

"Most of you probably remember my former maid Adora Johnson," she said, and heads bobbed throughout the church in recognition. "Well, Adora's grandson was one of the first to succumb to this infantile paralysis that's affecting so many children of lesser means."

I was starting to detest Ruth for her holier-than-thou attitude, and I lowered my head so no one would see me roll my eyes. Surely by now Ruth had to know that the children of doctors and lawyers were falling victim to polio as quickly as the children of the poor.

"I'm taking up a collection to cover the cost of a headstone for her grandson," Ruth continued. "Please see me after church if you'd like to contribute."

"Thirty-eight dollars," Ruth said half an hour later when we'd piled into the Cadillac for the ride home. She sat in the front seat next to Henry, counting the bills and coins in her lap. "They can get a nice little headstone for that," she added. "Perhaps I can get the money to them this week, once the quarantine is lifted. They must be going stir-crazy over there."

"We could take it over now," Lucy suggested. "Drop it off on the porch with a note, like I did with the ham?"

"Nicer to do it in person," Ruth said.

I would run this conversation over in my mind repeatedly in the weeks that followed. If only we'd taken the money to Adora and her family then.

If only.

PART TWO

50

June 15, 1944

Dear Gina,

Lucy is dead. She's dead and it's my fault. My hand's shaking so much as I write this . . . I hope you can read it. I haven't been able to stop shaking since it happened. Lucy died right before my eyes and I'll never get over seeing the horrible terror in her face. That poor girl! Oh, God, Gina, how am I going to live with myself after this??

It was an accident. Henry told me never to use his Buick because the tires were bad, but I thought it would be all right for a short trip. So foolish of me! Lucy and I wound up in the river, water rushing through the windows. It rose so quickly, Gina! When I shut my eyes, I still feel it rising up my body. I was able to get out, but Lucy's legs were pinned. Maybe if I hadn't panicked, I could have saved her? I don't know. All I know is that I'll never be able to stop thinking about her face as the life left her eyes.

I hardly remember anything that happened after the accident. I was unconscious and when I came to, an ambulance had arrived and I heard the driver say I was in shock. I thought he'd take me to the hospital, but I ended up in the police station. I sat there wrapped in a blanket for what seemed like hours, but it was probably only minutes. I was shivering so hard, my teeth chattered and I bit my tongue. I kept asking if they'd managed to save Lucy. I knew in my heart she was gone, but I kept asking and hoping and . . . I think I lost my mind for a while, Gina. Even now, I know I'm not thinking straight. Anyway, no one would answer me. I felt as though I were speaking from inside a bubble, I was so numb and dazed. I could hear the policemen talking to each other, but not to me. One of them was that Teddy Wright, the policeman I thought was following me when I first moved to Hickory, remember? He was a friend of Lucy's and very upset. I felt so cut off from everyone. I didn't know how I was going to face Henry or Ruth.

When Henry got to the police station, I started sobbing and shaking even harder. He barely glanced at me, then turned away as if I were invisible. Teddy and two other policemen approached him. One of them put his arm around his shoulders, while I sat alone in my wet clothes, trembling and racked with guilt. Then Henry said we were leaving. He was so angry. He walked ahead of me and I followed him out to the car. I was sobbing. I don't think I've stopped crying for more than a few minutes since it happened.

Henry says he doesn't blame me, but how can he not? Although he hasn't yet let me talk to his mother, I'm certain she blames me. If it wouldn't harm the family name, I'm sure she'd find a way for Henry to divorce me. I wish she would. I haven't been able to find a way myself.

You asked about my plan to void our marriage. Right now, that seems very unimportant. But anyway, my plan failed. Henry made love to me that very night. It was just that once and I have the feeling he never will again, especially not now. But he won't let me go, Gina. He'll never let me go, despite everything. Despite the fact that I'm responsible for his sister's death. I think my only choice now is to try to apply for a job somewhere, quietly, on the sly. Then I'll move to wherever that job is and begin the two years of living apart that will allow us to get a divorce. The job will have to be far enough from Hickory that word of my location can't get back to him. I don't think I should return to Baltimore, so please don't worry about not having space for me in your new apartment. I can't bear the thought of bumping into Vincent and his girlfriend, and if he and I were both working in the medical community in Baltimore . . . I would always be looking for him. Hoping to see him. I don't know where I'll go but wherever it is, I'll have to keep it a secret or Henry will come after me and try to drag me back. Once those two years of separation are up, I'll try to force him to agree to a divorce. But truth be told, I don't have the gumption to make this happen right now. Even though I wasn't hurt physically in the accident, my heart and soul feel dead. I keep seeing Lucy's face as she died. She was right in front of me and I could do nothing to save her. When I walk around this house, I sense her near me and feel as though I'm losing my mind. She haunts me, Gina. And she hates me.

Yes, I'm speaking metaphorically. (At least about the haunting part. She surely did hate me). She was just a very naïve girl who hadn't experienced much of life. She'd been raised like a princess, and maybe in time, with more experiences behind her, she would have become a wonderful person. I'm terribly sad that she'll never have that chance.
Love,
Tess

51

The morning of Lucy's funeral, Henry told me that Ruth didn't want me to go. I still hadn't seen Ruth to tell her how sorry I was. I'd asked Henry several times if I could speak to her—or rather, if she would speak to me—but he seemed determined to keep us apart. Maybe that was for the best. Of course she blamed me for the accident, though probably not as much as I blamed myself.

"You can come downstairs afterward when people are back here at the house," Henry said as he buttoned his shirt. "I'll insist she agree to that."

It would be awkward seeing Ruth for the first time with other people around, but maybe it would be all right. Maybe that would soften her reaction to me.

I was glad that Henry no longer seemed quite so upset with me. When he'd driven me home from the police station, he'd barely been able to contain his anger at me.

"I told you not to use the Buick," he'd said.

"I know." I'd run my palms over my damp skirt. "Lucy pleaded with me and I thought it would be all right. She wanted to take the money for the headstone to Adora. She didn't want to have to take a cab."

He kept his eyes on the road. "Then why were you near the river?" he asked.

"She had some . . . I don't know exactly what it was . . . a business document she said you wanted her to take to someone on the other side of the river."

I thought his face paled a bit. I didn't want him to blame himself.

"It's my fault." I reached over to touch the back of his hand on the steering wheel. "I should have just told her no."

When we got to the house, he told me to go straight upstairs and I did. I sat on the edge of my bed, still in my clammy clothes, and I knew the exact moment Henry told Ruth what happened. I heard her agonized wail and the sobs that followed. Her cries were loud enough to rise up the stairs and through the bedroom door. I held my hands over my ears, choking on my own tears as the reality of the accident washed over me. Lucy was dead, gone forever, her future stolen from her. Nausea came over me and I raced from the bedroom to the bathroom. I was sicker than I'd ever been in my life, and I welcomed the misery. I thought I deserved far worse.

Once Henry and Ruth left for the funeral, I lay on my bed in my black skirt and white blouse, staring at the ceiling as I imagined the scene at the church. Lucy's girlfriends would be there, weeping, feeling vulnerable, unable to believe that one of their own could so easily die at the age of twenty. The Ladies of the Homefront would certainly be there as well, and all of the women from Ruth's various book clubs and the bridge club. Members of the country club would come, I was sure, and many of the townspeople too, despite their anxiety about gathering together while a polio epidemic raged through the area. They would come anyway, loving the Kraft family. Wanting to show their support.

The house felt spooky to me with everyone gone. It was rare for me to be there entirely alone. Even if the family was out, I was always aware of Hattie's presence, but Hattie was at the church with everyone else after spending the early hours of the morning in the kitchen preparing food for when people came back to the house.

I got up from the bed and left the room, then stood in the eerie silence of the upstairs hall. The door to Lucy's room was directly in front of me and I stared at it for a moment before crossing the hall and pushing it open. Instantly, I smelled her. I didn't think it was the scent of her perfume as much as the hair spray she used to hold her dark blond bob in place. The scent was so distinctively Lucy that I let out a little *"Oh."* I stood inside the door, looking around the room. The crisply made bed. The lavender wallpaper. The assortment of cosmetics and perfume bottles on the doily that topped her vanity. There were photographs tucked into corners of her vanity mirror and I walked closer to look at them. Most were high school graduation pictures of her girlfriends and I recognized a couple of them. There were two pictures of young men in uniform. But the photograph that grabbed my attention was of Henry standing on the front porch of the house. He stood in the middle of two girls, an arm around each of them. Lucy and Violet. All three of them smiled at the camera. They looked so comfortable with each other. So happy together, and I wondered, as I often had in the last few months, what alliances I had disturbed when I came on the scene.

Staring at that photograph, I had a sudden feeling that someone was standing behind me, watching me. I turned quickly, but no one was there. Yet the feeling was still strong. I felt dizzy and held on to the corner of the vanity.

"Lucy?" I said out loud, feeling crazy. There was no response, of course, yet I still had a strong, almost suffocating, sense of her presence. I quickly left the room, slamming the door hard behind me, and hurried across the hall to Henry's bedroom. I was shaking by the time I reached the haven of my bed. *So silly,* I chided myself. My guilt was wreaking havoc on my imagination.

I must have drifted off because the next thing I knew, car doors were slamming outside. I lay still, barely breathing, listening. Voices downstairs, first two or three, then many, until they formed a sea of sound that hummed in the walls of the bedroom. I got up from the bed and smoothed my white blouse and black skirt. At the dresser, I stared at my pale face. The skin beneath my eyes was purplish and baggy. The little sleep I'd had since the accident had been marred by dreams about Lucy. Dreams about drowning. I looked at my compact and rouge on the top of the dresser. I wouldn't bother with them. Nothing was going to save my face today. Instead, I tried to run a comb through my tangled hair. I hadn't styled it since the accident and I had to admit that Ruth had been right when she said I looked like a Gypsy. Today I truly did. I gathered my hair into my hands and twisted it into a bun at the nape of my neck. It was the best I could do for now.

Palms sweating, I made my way down the stairs. The first person I saw as I neared the foyer was Violet, and it wasn't until I reached the bottom step that I realized she was speaking to Henry, her hand on his arm. Both of them looked in my direction at the same moment. Violet dropped her hand quickly and, with a last glance at Henry, moved away. Henry, his face unreadable, walked toward me.

"Are you sure you want to be down here?" he asked when he reached my side.

"I think I should be."

He looked reluctant. "Avoid my mother," he said. "I thought it would be all right, but . . ." He shook his head. "You can talk to her later, when the guests have gone, but now is not the time to try to speak to her."

I nodded. "All right."

Someone called to Henry and he left me standing there alone feeling awkward and vulnerable. I took a deep breath and stepped into the entrance to the living room. I spotted Honor Johnson passing a tray of food from one group of people to another and guessed she was helping Hattie in the kitchen. I saw some of the women from the Ladies of the Homefront, including Mrs. Wilding—who had never gotten back to me about her niece the nurse. I approached them, hoping to find a small circle to fit into.

"Thank you for coming," I said, as they turned toward me.

Absolute silence greeted me. Each of them stared at me as though I were a stranger. Mrs. Wilding finally spoke.

"Do you think you should be down here, Tess?" she asked.

I straightened my spine. "I cared about Lucy," I said.

"You weren't supposed to use that car," scolded one of the women—I couldn't recall her name.

I could think of no response, my mind a miserable blank canvas.

"Whatever possessed you to drive a car with rundown old tires?" asked a third woman.

"Excuse me," I said, stepping away from them. I couldn't face their coldness any longer, and yet where could I go? I saw many people I knew, however vaguely. Lucy's girlfriends. Byron Dare and his blond wife, stunning in black. Mayor Finley and his wife, Marjorie. So many of Ruth's friends. I felt their furtive glances in my direction. Where was Henry? If I was to be down here, I needed him by my side. I happened to glance through the window toward the backyard and spotted him crossing the lawn, moving away from the house.

I walked into the dining room and over to window for a better view of my husband. He'd reached Hattie's cottage, where Zeke was pointing toward the eaves. Henry stood next to him, looking up, pointing toward the eaves himself, and I guessed they were talking about something that needed repair. Zeke suddenly reached toward Henry, resting his hand on Henry's shoulder in what looked like a gesture of comfort over Lucy's death. I felt a bit like a voyeur, witnessing the true nature of their friendship in that moment. It was a friendship that went way, way back and I was both touched by it and envious of it.

I stepped away from the window and saw the faces of the people in the dining room turn from me. I couldn't stay down here any longer without Henry. I headed toward the foyer, but when I reached the stairs I felt a tug on my skirt and looked down to see Honor's little girl standing next to me. She carried a good-sized doll in her arms.

"Hi," she said.

"Hi." I smiled at her, then sat down on the next-to-the-bottom step so I was at her level. "What's your name?" Her name was Jill, I knew, but I would let her tell me.

"Jilly," she said. "What's yours?"

"Tess," I said. "How old are you, Jilly?"

"Four," she said, holding up four fingers. Her hair was smoothed back into two short thick braids that grazed her shoulders and she wore a little green pinafore over a white blouse.

"That's a pretty doll," I said, and Jilly held it in front of her to show me. The doll had eyes that opened and closed, pursed pink lips, and molded blond hair. I wondered what it was like for a colored child to have a white doll. Jilly was not as dark-skinned as her mother, but the doll's pearly skin was pale in the little girl's toffee-colored hands. I knew they made colored dolls. I remembered seeing one in a little toy shop in Baltimore when I'd been shopping with Gina sometime before Christmas. That felt like a lifetime ago.

"Does she have a name?" I asked.

Jilly sat down on the step next to me. I could feel her warmth and her wired little-girl energy.

"She don't have a name," she said.

"Oh my goodness," I said. "She needs one, don't you think? Everybody needs a name."

Jilly studied the doll, which was almost too big for her to hold on her lap. "This baby don't need one," she said.

"Was she a present?"

"Miss Lucy gave her to me."

I felt my heart contract. For all Lucy's self-absorption, she'd cared about this family. Sometimes I felt like I'd misunderstood my sister-in-law the same way she'd misunderstood me.

"That was sweet of her," I said. "I guess Miss Lucy and Mr. Hank grew up with your mama and your uncle Zeke, hmm?"

Jilly looked at me blankly as though she didn't understand what I was saying. "Miss Lucy's in heaven now," she explained. "She's with Butchie."

"Oh," I said. "Yes, she is. I'm sorry Butchie got so sick. I'm sure you miss him."

To my surprise, she leaned against me, her little head resting on my arm. "I'll see him again someday," she said, "but not till I'm a old lady."

"That's right." I freed my arm and put it around her shoulders. At that very moment, Honor walked through the foyer carrying a tray of pimento-cheese-stuffed celery. She did a double take when she saw me sitting next to her daughter.

"Jilly!" She stood in the middle of the foyer, the tray balanced in her hands. "Go in the kitchen with Nana 'Dora. You shouldn't be out here."

"Oh, she's fine," I said.

Honor didn't seem to hear me. "Go on now," she said to her daughter. "Git!"

Jilly got to her feet and, without looking back at me, took off at a run for the kitchen.

"Sorry if she disturbed you, Miss Tess," Honor said.

"She was fine," I repeated, getting to my feet. I dusted off the back of my skirt. "She's very sweet."

Honor didn't respond, but she looked away from me toward the rear of the foyer. I'd only seen her up close once before, that day in February when she and Lucy were talking with Hattie at the clothesline. I was mesmerized by her green eyes. There was so much sadness in them today.

"I was so sorry about Butchie," I said. "And I hope your hus—your son's father—Del? I hope he can come home soon, safe and sound."

She looked back at me, at first mutely as though she didn't understand what I'd said. Then she smiled. There was pain in that smile. She was apart from the man she loved. I knew exactly how that felt.

"I hope so too," she said. "I miss him." She hiked the tray a little higher. "Can I get you anything, Miss Tess?" she asked. "Would you like one of these celery sticks?"

"No, thank you," I said. "I was just about to go upstairs when Jilly—" I stopped speaking as my eyes lit on Jilly's doll. She'd set it on the step and forgotten it when she ran to the kitchen. "She forgot her doll," I said, picking it up.

"Just leave it there. I'll come get it when I put this tray down."

"I'll take it to her," I said. The last few minutes of civil conversation with Jilly and Honor had given me courage, and I left the foyer and walked with my head held high through the dining room, ignoring everyone I passed.

In the kitchen I found Adora and Jilly sitting at the table, eating ham biscuits, while Hattie arranged more of them on a tray. All three of them looked up at me.

"What you need, Miss Tess?" Hattie asked.

I'd been holding the doll behind my back, but now I produced it and Jilly sucked in her breath.

"My dolly!" she said, hopping off her chair and running over to me. I handed the doll to her and she cuddled it before carrying it back to the table.

I thought Hattie looked overwhelmed, surrounded by half a dozen plates of hors d'oeuvres. She'd been kind to me since the accident. *It weren't your fault, honey,* she'd said to me that horrible first night. *That girl could make anybody do what she want. You was just tryin' to please her.*

I moved deeper into the big kitchen. "How can I help?" I asked. "How about I take that tray out for you?" I pointed to the tray of ham biscuits. It would give me something to do. A reason to approach the unwelcoming circles of people. I reached for the tray, but Hattie gave my hand a little swat.

"No, Miss Tess," she said, "that ain't your job."

"Honor'll pass it 'round," Adora said.

"Let me," I said to Hattie. "Please."

Hattie shook her head like I was the stupidest woman in the world, but she raised her hands in the air in surrender. I carried the tray to the swinging door that led to the dining room, feeling Hattie's and Adora's eyes on me.

In the dining room, I carried the tray from person to person, relieved to have something concrete to do other than struggle to make conversation. People treated me as if I were invisible, which was fine with me.

"Tess!"

I turned to see Ruth hurrying toward me, pushing her way through the crowd that had congregated around the table. *Avoid my mother,* Henry had warned me. I wasn't going to be able to avoid her now.

"Ruth, I—"

"Come with me," she said, walking past me until she'd reached the corner of the dining room. She stood next to the buffet, away from the people gathered near the table. I followed her, tray in my hands, and she turned to face me.

"You don't want to do this," she said quietly, motioning to the tray. Her cheeks were pale and drawn as though she hadn't eaten or slept in days. "Set the tray down and come into the living room with the guests."

"I'm fine," I said. "Really. I'd like to help. And I wanted to tell you—"

"No." Her smile was tight and I was aware that some of the people in the room were glancing in our direction. "You need to set it down, dear," she said quietly. "Let Honor or Hattie pass the hors d'oeuvres. That's their job, not yours."

I didn't want to let go of the tray. It felt like a lifeline, the only way I'd found to be comfortable in the room.

"I wanted to be useful," I said.

"You're not a servant, Tess," she said. "Put it down."

Reluctantly, I set the tray on the buffet. Then I dared to reach out to touch her arm. "I'm so sorr—"

"Don't touch me!" she said, jerking her arm away from my hand. Her voice, suddenly loud—*too* loud—held such disdain that I took a step away from her. Behind me, all conversation stopped, leaving a silence as big as death in the room.

Ruth leaned forward, closing the distance between us, her lips next to my ear. "You are so common," she said, only loud enough for me to hear. "I rue the day you ever set foot in this house."

So do I, I thought, but I steeled myself. Tightened my jaw. I would take whatever she dished out to me. "I'm sorry, Ruth," I whispered again. My eyes burned. "I wish there was something I could—"

"You ruined my son's life and destroyed my daughter's," Ruth said, her breath sour against my ear. "You're a low-class tramp with no right to be here in my beautiful home and if there was a way to cut you out of the Kraft family without bringing shame to us, I would do it in a heartbeat."

"*Mama.*" Henry broke through the crowd and was instantly at my side. With one look at our faces, he seemed to intuit our disintegrating exchange. He took my arm and turned me in the direction of the foyer. "Go upstairs," he said quietly. My body felt wooden and he had to give me a push to start me moving. "Just go."

I felt everyone looking at me as I walked through the dining room toward the foyer. I stared straight ahead, but from the corner of my eye I could see Adora and Zeke in the doorway of the kitchen and Violet and her parents near the arched entrance to the foyer. A couple of Lucy's girl-friends stood near the foot of the stairs. They couldn't have heard all of the conversation with Ruth, but surely they could guess the heart of it. They would be talking about me for the rest of the day. Perhaps the rest of the month.

I didn't go downstairs for dinner that evening, and when Hattie brought me one of the ham biscuits, I thanked her but told her I had no appetite. Henry was quiet when he came upstairs and it wasn't until we were in bed that I broke the silence.

"Do you think of me as a tramp?" I asked him. We were both lying on our backs looking up at the dark ceiling.

"Of course not," he said. "Don't listen to Mama. She's wounded, Tess. She lost her only daughter."

"She hated me before that and she hates me even more now."

"We'll be out of this house in a month," he said. "That is, if you'll ever sit down with that interior designer. Things will be different then."

I suddenly wondered if Henry's lack of interest in lovemaking had something to do with living in Ruth's house. Maybe he was concerned about making noise? But no, I thought. Henry was simply one of those rare men who had little interest in sex. I had to accept that. If we stayed locked in this marriage, we would never have a truly intimate relationship.

Not physically. Not emotionally. Vincent's face flashed into my memory and I blocked it out. Thinking about Vincent would do me no good at all.

"I *did* sleep with you when I barely knew you," I said. "That was a terrible thing to do. A trampy thing."

"And I slept with you when I barely knew you," he said. "We're both culpable."

"It's kind of you to say that," I said. "Not many men would, I don't think."

He sighed. "This is a very rough patch, Tess," he said. "We just have to get through it."

"Henry, please . . ." My voice broke. "Please can we find a way to end this marriage?"

I felt rather than heard his annoyance, and it was a moment before he spoke again. "We're not talking about this now," he said, and he rolled onto his side away from me.

He fell asleep quickly, while I lay awake for hours, torturing myself with memories of that afternoon. I should never have gone downstairs. There had been nothing to be gained by it. I wasn't thinking clearly these days. I played Ruth's insults over and over in my mind.

If only I could talk to Lucy to tell her how sorry I was. I'd tell her I wished I'd gotten to know her better. I thought of her giving that baby doll to little Jilly. How good she'd been to care for that family. I would withdraw forty dollars from my bank account and take it to them for the headstone. I'd bring them extra groceries when we could spare them, as Lucy would have done. The least I could do was take over that caring role for her. And there was one more thing I wanted to do for that family.

I got out of bed and wrote a quick note to Gina.

52

_____

June 19, 1944

Dear Gina,

    I have a favor to ask. There's a little toy shop near Hutzler's department store. They used to have a colored doll in the window. Could you see if they still carry that doll, and if so, buy it and send it to me, please? I'll repay you, of course. It's for a little girl I know here. She's the granddaughter of the Krafts' former maid and she recently lost her brother to polio. Thank you in advance, dear friend.
Love,
Tess

53

In the morning, I waited upstairs for Henry and Ruth to leave the house. I knew Ruth had a meeting with her estate attorney and I was glad she was going out. When I was certain they were both gone, I put on my robe and left the room, intending to go downstairs to breakfast. But when I walked into the hallway, I stopped short. There it was again, that eerie feeling that Lucy was nearby. I looked at the closed door to her bedroom. I felt as though, if I pushed that door open, she would be there. She'd be sitting at her vanity, looking up at me with hollow eyes.

I shuddered. I was being ridiculous. Shaking off the feeling, I walked resolutely down the stairs and sat at the dining room table. Henry had left the newspaper on the table as he did most mornings, and I pulled it close to read the front page.

Hattie opened the swinging door between the dining room and kitchen and walked in with the coffeepot. "You got some appetite for eggs and grits this morning, Miss Tess?" she asked as she poured.

I suddenly remembered Adora and Zeke standing in the doorway of the kitchen after Ruth had raked me over the coals. Surely Hattie and Adora, Honor and Zeke, had talked about me every bit as much as the guests had. I wondered what they'd said. What they thought of me now.

"That would be lovely," I said, smiling gamely. I couldn't quite look her in the eye and I turned my attention back to the paper.

The top half of the front page was filled with war and polio. Seven more cases of infantile paralysis from the area had been sent to Charlotte

Memorial Hospital and another Catawba County child had died. The situation in the county was worsening, the article said, and Dr. Whims was meeting today with two physicians from the National Foundation for Infantile Paralysis to plan a course of action. The hospital in Charlotte was calling for more nurses. And what was I doing? Sitting here being waited on hand and foot. Could I go to Charlotte? Maybe I could get a room there. I could do some good and escape Hickory, at least for a while. I'd feel closer to Vincent, emotionally at least, doing the sort of work he'd been involved with in Chicago last summer. Henry would say no, of course. If I left, I'd have to be able to support myself on whatever the Charlotte hospital was paying its nurses. I would no longer be able to count on Henry's money to support me.

Hattie came into the room again and set a plate of scrambled eggs, sausage patties, and grits in front of me, the coffeepot in her other hand. I made myself look up at her.

"Thanks, Hattie," I said.

"Sure, Miss Tess," she said, refilling my cup.

I spread the paper open in front of me as I ate. A young man from Hickory had been seriously wounded in New Guinea and another was being sent home from Italy with a broken leg. I read the article on what this week's rationing coupons would buy, which was not much. There was a small article about federal agents cracking down on counterfeit gasoline rationing coupons. Apparently that was becoming big business throughout the country.

At the bottom of the page was a large ad for Kraft Fine Furniture. Instead of advertising furniture, though, it encouraged people to buy war bonds and asked them to contribute to the scrap-metal pile Henry maintained in the parking lot by the side of the factory. Henry's signature—*Hank Kraft*—was in large bold script at the bottom of the page, turning the ad into a personal plea.

I nibbled my breakfast as I read, unable to eat more than a few bites of egg and sausage. I was taking my time, uncomfortable about going back upstairs where Lucy's ghost was waiting for me. When Hattie came into the room to pick up my plate, she shook her head and tsk-tsked.

"I always know when you upset, Miss Tess," she said. "You don't eat nothin'."

I looked up at her. If there was anyone who'd understand how I was feeling about Lucy's ghost or spirit or whatever it was, it would be Hattie.

"Do you feel Lucy in the house, Hattie?"

She cocked her head at me as if she didn't understand. Then she let out a laugh. "Lordy, you need Reverend Sam bad, honey," she said.

"I don't truly believe in ghosts or spirits or any of that," I said. "But upstairs . . ."

"Oh, she's up there, all right."

"You feel her presence too?"

"Yes, ma'am. She's there."

"Maybe I *should* go see Reverend Sam," I said, more to myself than to her. "I want to ask Lucy to forgive me."

"It was jest an accident, Miss Tess," she said. "But he put your mind to rest. You oughta go."

I pictured myself taking the bus to Ridgeview. Walking down that dirt road past the little houses. Past Adora's yellow house. I could take her the money for the headstone at the same time. "I'll go," I said to Hattie. I glanced toward the foyer and the stairs. "But first I have to get dressed, and I feel like she's waiting for me up there." I laughed at myself and she chuckled.

"Want me to go up with you?" She grinned. "Keep her away from you while you put your clothes on?"

I laughed, getting to my feet. "You're not good for me, Hattie," I said. "You humor me too much."

"Well, you good for me, Miss Tess," she said, her voice suddenly serious. "Don't let Miss Ruth run you off, ya hear?"

54

I took a cab to the bank and asked the driver to wait for me while I withdrew forty dollars from my personal account, leaving very little left for a move to Charlotte or anywhere else, for that matter. I slipped the envelope with the money into my red handbag, the one I ordinarily saved for dressy occasions and the only one I had now that I'd lost my everyday handbag in the accident. When I got back into the cab and told the driver to take me to Ridgeview, he asked me if I was sure that's where I wanted to go.

"I'm sure," I said.

He shrugged and put the cab into gear.

I had him let me off in front of Adora's house. The day was hot and I was perspiring by the time I got out of the cab. The short sleeves of my dress stuck to my arms, and I knew that unruly black tendrils were curling over my forehead. I walked up to the door, dodging a rusting tricycle on the crumbling sidewalk. In the front window, I spotted one of the red-bordered blue star flags and guessed it was for Del.

Although only the screened door was closed, it was too dark to see inside the house. I knocked on the door frame.

Honor pushed open the screened door and there was no warmth at all in her jade-green eyes, only a look of surprise. She peered behind me, and I guessed she was looking for a car or perhaps for Ruth or Henry.

"What are you doing here?" she asked.

Jilly spotted me from the living room and ran onto the porch. Gripping her doll in one arm, she wrapped the other around my thighs. I felt touched by her reaction to seeing me. She acted as though we were old friends instead of two strangers who'd shared a five-minute conversation at Ruth's house. I welcomed her innocence and trust.

"Jilly!" Honor chided her, but I rested my hand on the back of the little girl's head.

"Hi, little one," I bent over to say. "How's your dolly today?"

She let go of me and hugged her doll with both arms, rocking it back and forth. "She's happy," she said.

"Oh, that's wonderful." I smiled at her, then looked at Honor who stood holding the screened door open with her hip, her arms now crossed at her chest. "May I come in?" I asked. "Just for a moment."

"Who is it?" Adora asked as she hobbled up behind Honor and peered around her shoulder. "Why, Miss Tess!" She smiled and I felt relieved. "What can we do for you?"

"When Lucy and I had the accident," I said, more to Adora than Honor, "we were on our way here."

"Here?" Adora frowned.

"Yes." I looked from her to Honor. "Lucy and Ruth had collected some money at church to help you get a headstone for Butchie and we were bringing it over. Or at least we *planned* to bring it over, but Lucy wanted to . . . run an errand on the other side of the river, and . . ." My voice trailed off as I pulled the envelope from my handbag. "Anyway, I brought you the money." I held out the envelope. "I'm sorry it's taken a while to get it to you."

"We don't want your money," Honor said. I was taken aback by the hostility in her voice. She'd treated me politely at the house after the funeral. I supposed that, at the house, she'd had no choice. Now I was on her turf. I felt a bead of sweat trickle down my cheek and brushed it away with damp fingers.

Adora gave Honor a light swat on her arm. "Act like a good Christian for once in your life," she said to her daughter.

"No, it's all right," I said hastily, not wanting to be the cause of animosity between mother and daughter. "I'll just leave the envelope with you, Adora, and go."

Adora looked past me toward the street. "No car?" she asked. "You took the bus?"

"A cab."

"Oh, that's better," she said. "Why don't you set down here before you go back?" She pointed to the two white rocking chairs on the porch. "Mite bit cooler in the shade."

Honor gave her mother a look of daggers. "I need to go out," she said, and without so much as a glance in my direction, she walked past me and down the porch steps.

"Where you going, Mama?" Jilly called after her.

Honor didn't answer and Adora held the door open with one hand while leaning over to draw her granddaughter to her by the shoulder. "She be back soon, Jilly, don't fret," she said.

"I didn't mean to stir things up," I said softly.

Adora waved away my comment and limped heavily across the porch to one of the rockers, motioning me to follow her. Jilly sat down on the wood floor of the porch and began talking to her doll, making it dance through the air.

"Honor thought of Miss Lucy as a friend," Adora said as she sat down. "She don't feel too kindly toward you, I'm afraid."

"I'm sure she's still grieving her son too," I said, sitting on the second rocker. "She's had two losses in a row, plus she's apart from her . . ." I searched a bit desperately for the right word. Boyfriend? Lover?

"From Del, yes." Adora saved me. "It's all been hard on her and you're right. There's an empty spot in this house with no Butchie, that's for sure," she said. "Like I imagine there is at your house with no Lucy."

I nodded.

Adora leaned forward in her chair, nearly close enough to reach out and touch me. "I want to tell you somethin'," she said. "I'm glad Mr. Hank chose you."

I was surprised. "You are?"

"Uh-huh." She nodded. "That Violet, she a real pretty thing but she ain't no good. She don't feel for other people," she said. "You do, don't you? You feel things in your bones."

"You barely know me," I said, though she was certainly right about me. My bones ached with all I was feeling these days.

"Oh, I know enough." Adora brushed a droplet of perspiration from her temple. "Jilly took to you right off. Honor told me how she sat with you at the house after Miss Lucy's funeral. She only four but she got one of them sixth senses about people, you know what I mean?"

I nodded uncertainly. I looked at Jilly who was trying to tie a little bonnet over her doll's molded blond hair.

"You can tell a lot about a person by the way a child takes to them," Adora said. "You don't hold yourself above nobody, not even a little bit of a thing like Jilly. Miss Violet, though—" She shook her head. "She hold herself above everybody. Above Jesus." She chuckled. "I hated when it looked like Mr. Hank was gonna marry her. 'Course I had no say. Miss Ruth was thrilled. Two big families comin' together. That kind of thing be important to Miss Ruth. Not so important to Hank though. He got a better head on his shoulders, thank the Lord."

She wasn't going to mention that I'd given Henry little choice but to marry me when I showed up carrying his child. I was sure she knew. Everyone else did.

"Henry told me you saved his life when he cut off his fingers," I said.

She leaned back in the rocker and set it moving with her feet on the porch floor.

"Just lucky I was there or I don't know what would of happened to that boy," she said, looking past me into the distance. "I'll never forget it, long as I live. Nineteen twenty-three, it was. I was coming from the cottage to the house when Hank come running out of the shed screamin' his fool head off, blood flyin' everywhere. So much blood it took me a minute to realize three of his fingers was gone."

I bit my lip at the picture taking shape in my head.

"I quick tore the rag off my head—I was younger, skinnier, and faster movin' in those days." She winked at me from behind her glasses. "And I made one of them tourniquets and yelled for Miss Ruth to call for help. They was one of the only families with a phone back then and old Dr. Poole—the new Dr. Poole's daddy?—had a phone too and he come right over. Meanstime, the blood done gone everywhere. All over Hank. All over me. All over the ground."

I tried to imagine what Adora had looked like all those years ago when she came to work for Ruth and her husband. Behind her round face and thick glasses, I could see a pretty young girl. She'd probably been slender then too, like Honor.

"I don't know if I could have done what you did," I said, "and I'm a nurse."

Her eyes lit up. "You a nurse, honey?"

"Yes, though obviously I'm not working as one. Henry doesn't want me to work."

"That's a fine job for a girl, but you being a Kraft, you got no cause to work now, do you?"

I sighed. "I have no cause, but I'd still like to," I said.

She didn't seem to hear me. She was staring into the distance. "My children was Mr. Hank's only playmates after he hurt his hand," she said. "Other children called him a monster and such."

"Really?" I supposed this was why Henry didn't like talking about the loss of his fingers.

"Oh yes. Nobody would play with him after that. He would of died from bein' lonely if Zeke and Honor didn't play with him. They loved him like a brother till they was old enough to know better."

Jilly had walked over to me and dumped her doll unceremoniously on my lap. "I can't make this hat go on," she said in frustration, handing me the bonnet.

"Would you like me to do it?" I asked.

Her head bobbed up and down and I began to tie the bonnet beneath the doll's chin. "I'm glad he had Zeke and Honor," I said to Adora.

"He needed them, for sure," Adora said. "That little Violet was the worst about Hank's hand. One of the ringleaders really. She didn't care nothin' for him until her mama and daddy put the idea of all Hank's money in her head. Then suddenly, she mad in love with him."

I thought of that picture in Lucy's room, the one of her and Violet standing with Henry. He hadn't looked all that miserable at finding himself with his arm around the pretty blond. I handed the doll back to Jilly.

"What you say?" Adora asked her.

"Thank you," Jilly muttered. Then with her eyes on my face, she added, "You're pretty."

I laughed. "So are you, sweetheart." I watched as she flopped down on the floor again with the nameless doll. I hoped Gina could find the colored doll for her. I wondered if she'd give that one a name.

"She's a pip, ain't she." Adora nodded in her granddaughter's direction.

"She's darling," I said.

"Hank give Zeke that job at the furniture company when he got sent home from the Marines," Adora said, continuing our earlier conversation.

"Nobody wanted to hire a colored man with a gimp leg, but Mr. Hank never forgot who his true and honest friends was."

I thought of Zeke's surprisingly lovely room at the factory. Lovely, but lonely, perhaps, living in that huge factory day and night. "Does Zeke have a family?" I asked.

"No, that boy ain't never met a girl he liked well enough." Adora sounded a bit annoyed by that fact. "He a good man, but tough to please."

"How about you, Adora?" I asked. "You lived in that little cottage for twenty years, right? What about your husband?"

"When I started working for Mr. and Mrs. Kraft, I was twenty-four with two little ones and my husband worked for a farmer over to Newton," she said. "We lived with his parents not far from here." She pointed south of where we sat. "He got pneumonia one winter and . . ." She shook her head. "He went right quick."

"I'm sorry," I said. I did the math in my head and was shocked to realize Adora was not even fifty. Arthritis and hard work had really taken their toll.

"That's when Hank's daddy built that little house for me and the children. They was good to us, the Kraft family."

"I think they were lucky to have you." I motioned toward her current house. "This little house is darling," I said. "Prettiest house on the street."

She smiled. "Zeke and Hank keep it up for us," she said. "They paint it. Fix the roof. Hank got us these rocking chairs."

"I'm glad they look after you," I said. For a moment, I loved my husband. "Well, I'd better get going." With a sigh, I got slowly to my feet, smoothing my skirt.

Adora suddenly looked worried. "How you gonna get home?" she asked. "We ain't got no phone to call the cab."

"Oh, I'll take the bus," I said. "It's not a problem." I hoped she didn't watch me as I left, since I'd be walking in the wrong direction for the bus as I headed toward Reverend Sam's house. "Thank you for the shade and conversation," I added. "I enjoyed it."

She winced as she stood up, then shuffled with me across the porch.

"Everybody always 'spected Hank'd marry Violet and that would of been a terrible thing," she said. "Maybe you saved him from something terrible, Miss Tess. You think of it that way, all right?"

55

I was clammy with perspiration by the time I climbed the steps to Reverend Sam's big sky-blue house and knocked on his door. On my second knock, he pulled the door open and his face lit up in surprise.

"Tess!" he said, his smile warm. "I've missed seeing you. How have you been?"

I opened my mouth but couldn't find my voice. My eyes filled and I shook my head. "A lot has happened," I managed to say.

He lost his smile. "Come in, child," he said softly, stepping back to let me pass, and I walked into his dark, cool living room and breathed in that suddenly familiar scent of old burned-out firewood. "Let's go to my office." He motioned toward the hallway.

I followed him down the dark hall and through the anteroom, barely noticing the tall white skeleton and other artifacts lining the walls. In his office, we took our places, Sam behind his desk, me in one of the wooden chairs opposite him. He immediately reached across the desk, and I rested my hands in his. He shut his eyes.

"Dear Lord," he said. "With your protection and if it's your will, open the doors between worlds today so this child can find peace."

I swallowed against the lump in my throat and said nothing. I was certain he didn't want me to tell him why I was there. I doubted I could get the words out, anyway.

"Yes?" he asked the air, turning his head slightly and opening his eyes to half-mast. "Ah," he said. "Walter is here with us."

"Walter?" I whispered, puzzled.

"I see spirit running down the street." He smiled at me. "Bouncing a ball."

I shook my head, disappointed. Maybe I'd imagined that he had a gift. Maybe I'd believed what I wanted to believe about him.

"I don't think you know him very well, Tess." Reverend Sam frowned, his eyes tightly shut again.

"I don't know any Walter at all," I said quietly. "At least not any who have passed away."

Reverend Sam wore a slight frown above his closed eyes. "Yes. Yes," he said, and I could tell again that he wasn't speaking to me. Then he opened his eyes and looked directly at me. "You're definitely connected to this Walter in some way," he said. "Some way outside our knowing."

"All right," I said. I would just accept it.

"There are many connections in this room today," he said, still frowning. "I feel them pummeling me. Vying for my attention. It's hard to separate them."

I nodded, feeling dubious. *Walter?*

He shut his eyes again, muttering a few words that I guessed were a prayer.

"Ah," he said suddenly. "I see spirit . . . I see . . . Lucy? Lucy, is it?"

"Oh." I clutched the arms of the chair.

"Spirit is beautiful," he said. "Surrounded by a healing blue light."

"Lucy is?" I asked.

He didn't answer. He seemed far away from me. If he truly was connecting to Lucy, I needed her to know how sorry I was.

"Please tell her I'm sorry," I said. I heard the intensity in my voice. "Please tell her I'd do anything if I could bring her back." My eyes stung. "Tell her how sorry I am that I couldn't save her."

"Shh." He frowned again, his eyes closed. After a moment, he shook his head. Opened his eyes. "She's gone," he said.

"Oh no. I'm sorry. I shouldn't have spoken. I—"

"She died in a terrible way?" he asked.

"Yes. I wasn't supposed to use the car, but I did and we blew a tire and landed in the river and I couldn't get her out." The words rushed out of me and I began to cry in earnest. My hands were in fists on his desk and he leaned forward and covered them with his own.

"No, child," he said softly. "Lucy is beautiful. Lucy is fine. I told you, she's wrapped in a healing blue light."

I looked into his kind bronze-colored eyes, longing to believe him.

"Never think about the way someone died," he said. "Never stew on that. Think about the way they are in spirit, my dear. You tried your best to save her, didn't you?"

I nodded, gulping my tears.

"Your Lucy is fine," he said again. Then he shut his eyes and said another prayer and I suddenly felt distrustful of him. Was I a sucker? The cynic in me wondered if he might be a charlatan after all. He knew my name. Tess Kraft. Everyone knew the Kraft family, even here in the Ridgeview neighborhood. Everyone knew about the accident that killed Lucy Kraft. Maybe Reverend Sam read the newspaper with a magnifying glass, memorizing the names of people who'd passed away in case their loved ones showed up at his door. He'd started with the name Walter. I didn't think I'd known a Walter in my entire life. How had he known my mother's name, Maria, the first time I saw him though? That I couldn't explain.

"Someone else is here," he said, interrupting my thoughts.

I hesitated. "Who?" I asked, and I imagined he was going to say my mother's name again.

He frowned, turning his head slowly left then right, his brow furrowed in concentration. "Andrew," he said.

Oh my God. I let out my breath, and with it my doubts about Reverend Sam's honesty.

"Andrew doesn't speak," he said, "but I feel him with us in this room."

My tears were back, burning my eyes. "He was my baby," I whispered, and Reverend Sam's eyes flew open.

"Born too early?" he asked.

I nodded, my voice failing me.

He closed his eyes again. He didn't speak but appeared to be listening. "He feels his mother's love," he said finally. "Your love. That's all he needs. He loves you very much."

I wept then, my face buried in my hands. *My baby.* I felt him in the room with us. I truly did. *I'm so sorry I didn't fight harder to hold you, Andy.*

I cried a long time while Reverend Sam waited quietly on his side of the desk. When I finally pulled myself together, he was looking at me, clear-eyed sympathy in his face.

"No one understands," I said. "They act as though he never existed."

"He exists in spirit now, child. Peaceful spirit."

"Is he in a healing blue light?"

"I didn't see the light," he admitted, "but I felt the peace. You can let go of any guilt or worry about Lucy or Andrew, Tess. Let go of it all."

We talked a while longer and I began to sense his weariness. I was overstaying my welcome, yet I hated to leave.

"I want to give you something back," I said finally. "Please, can't I pay you for your time?"

He looked surprised. "I don't take money," he said, then smiled. "I don't *need* money."

"But this tires you, doesn't it?" I asked, suddenly worried about him. "It takes a lot out of you."

He nodded. "I believe you're the first person ever to ask me that. To *realize* that," he said, then he folded his hands neatly in front of him on the desk. "Understand, Tess, that I enjoy helping people," he said. "Comforting people. But yes, I often nap for two or three hours after I connect with the spirit world."

"But who comforts *you*?" I probed. "I think you give and give and give, but who gives back to you?"

"You are an inquisitive girl," he said, looking amused. "And a very kind girl as well. My sons look in on me. They live in Charlotte and they take turns making sure I'm still alive. And my wife visits me quite often."

"Your wife?" I said, surprised. "I thought she was . . ." I stopped, then laughed as I understood his meaning. "Well, good," I said. "I'm glad she comes to see you."

I got to my feet, not really wanting to go but knowing he needed to rest. He walked me out, through the anteroom, past the skeleton and down the dark hallway. We said good-bye, and when I stepped into the bright sunlight and began walking down the street toward the bus stop, I knew without a doubt Lucy would no longer bother me in the house. I knew it like I knew my own name. But more important to me at that moment, I'd been able to talk safely and openly about Andy. Someone else had honored his existence. If only Henry had, just one time, acknowledged that our baby had been a real person. A real baby boy. With a name. With a future stolen from him. But now I knew Andy existed someplace safe and serene. I would never get to hold him. Touch his sweet cheek. See him smile his first smile, bright-eyed and gurgling. But he was at peace. I could ask for no more than that.

56

I came home after my visit with Reverend Sam to find Ruth sitting at the desk in the library working on her scrapbook. I needed to clear the air between us and I took a deep breath as I stood in the doorway.

"Ruth," I said, "I want to apologize for upsetting you after Lucy's funeral yesterday."

She didn't lift her head from her work as she pasted a small news article into the scrapbook. "I shouldn't have made a scene in front of everyone," she admitted, surprising me. "That sort of discussion should be private. Now let's close the subject." She whisked me away with her hand.

I stood there another moment before leaving the doorway, then I crossed the foyer and climbed the steps to my room. I was surprised by her near apology. It had been more than I'd expected.

At dinner that night, though, she insisted on having a place set for Lucy across the table from me. Henry acted as though nothing were amiss, but Hattie and I exchanged a look. Either Ruth wanted to keep a place open for Lucy because she couldn't bear the loss, or this was her way of reminding me of my role in her death. We could close the subject, as Ruth had said, but I had the feeling the empty chair at the table was going to keep it open for all time.

Two days later, I was reading in the upstairs parlor when Henry came home from the factory. I heard him on the stairs and it sounded as if he were taking them two at a time. He was nearly breathless when he walked into the room.

"Have you listened to the radio today?" he asked, and I closed my book, instantly on edge.

"Is there news from Europe?" I asked. Every day, the Allied forces were advancing on one town or another, and I only hoped that whatever news Henry had was good. I couldn't tell from his expression.

"No, no," he said, sitting down on the arm of one of the upholstered chairs. "Nothing about the war. It's about the polio epidemic. There's going to be a meeting tonight at the high school. Everyone in town is supposed to be there. The Lake Hickory Fresh Air Camp's being turned into a hospital for polio patients."

"Really?" I frowned. I'd seen the Fresh Air Camp where underprivileged children played and swam during the summer. The only building I recalled being on that property was a small stone structure that could hardly be turned into a hospital. "That building is tiny," I said. "How can it be a hospital?"

"They're adding on to it," he said. "Do you know who H. C. Whims is?"

"The public health doctor for the county?"

"Right. He met with some men from the National Polio Foundation this morning. Charlotte won't take any more patients and since most of the sick kids are from this area, they decided to look in Hickory for a building they could convert into a hospital. But it's going to have to happen fast." I didn't think I'd ever seen him look so excited. "Lumber's already on its way for a second structure," he said. "I've been working at the camp this afternoon. Zeke too. And I've let some of my men take off to help. They're over there, working." He sounded like a man with a purpose. "It's going to take all of Hickory to make this happen,"

I'd clearly missed a lot by not listening to the radio. "Are you going to the meeting?" I asked.

"Yes, and you are too." He stood up. "My mother as well. Everyone's supposed to be there. I'm sure Adora will go, so I can give her the money for the headstone if I see her."

"Oh," I said. "I actually took care of that."

He looked down at me, confusion on his face. "What are you talking about?"

"I withdrew forty dollars from my bank account—that's about the amount that was lost in the accident—and I took it to her."

"You went to Ridgeview?" He frowned. "How did you get there?"

"I took a cab there and the bus back," I said. I could tell he wasn't pleased.

"You didn't need to do that," he said. "I would have gotten the money to them eventually."

"I wanted to do it for Lucy," I said. "And I know you've been busy, so I—"

"You shouldn't go to that neighborhood," he said.

"I don't mind at all," I said. "Lucy said your family takes care of Adora, so I can take them food sometimes, and—"

"It's not for you to do," he said. "You don't even know them."

"Well, I'm *getting* to know them," I said, annoyed. "Jilly's so adorable. She has that white doll and I know of a place in Baltimore where I may be able to get her a colored doll. Gina can buy it for me. Don't you think that would be—"

"I think you need to stay out of their lives." His cheeks were suddenly blotchy with color. "Maybe y'all mixed like that where you're from but we don't do that here. All right?"

I bristled. "No, we didn't 'mix' where I'm from," I said. "But Lucy—"

"Lucy's dead," he said bluntly as he walked toward the door.

"Adora told me about the day she saved your life," I said, just as bluntly. I wanted to bring him down off his high horse. "And she told me how other kids picked on you and how Zeke and Honor were your only friends."

He glared at me. "Adora isn't the official historian of my life, all right?" he said. "And I don't want you going there again."

I thought it was a good thing that he left the room before I had a chance to answer. I felt like an oppositional child. The more he told me not to do something the more I wanted to do it. I hoped Gina could find that doll. I couldn't wait for it to arrive. I couldn't wait to take it to Jilly.

57

Henry, Ruth, and I arrived at the high-school auditorium that evening to find it already packed with people from the town, colored in the balcony, white in the floor seats. Ruth sat on the other side of Henry from me, her hands rigidly clasped over her handbag on her lap. She'd been horrified when Henry told her about the plans for the hospital.

"That's a terrible idea!" she'd said as we talked about it over dinner. "Why can't they do it in some other town? Why Hickory?"

"Why not Hickory?" Henry had argued. "It's central to the all the polio cases that have turned up."

"So now Hickory will be known as the town full of polio germs." Ruth had pouted. "I can think of a hundred more suitable locations for a hospital, and none of them are in Hickory!"

I looked around the packed auditorium and wondered how many other people in the audience shared her worries about bringing polio patients to Hickory.

Henry, though, seemed unconcerned. He pointed toward the stage, where three men were sitting, waiting for everyone to take their seats. "The man on the left is Whims," Henry said. "The fella next to him is Hahn and the third is Crabtree."

"Three shortsighted men," Ruth muttered.

We watched as Dr. Whims stood up and walked to the podium. He thanked everyone for coming and laid out the problem—the ever-increasing number of polio cases in the area surrounding Hickory.

"We need a solution and we need it now," he said. "Dr. Hahn and Dr. Crabtree and I talked about using one of the buildings that already exist in town, but we crossed each of them off our list for one reason or another. So our focus is now on the Fresh Air Camp. I contacted the director there this afternoon and within forty-five minutes the camp's children were evacuated and driven home by volunteers." He smiled. "And that's the word of the day: volunteers. It's going to take all of us to pull together to make this hospital a reality, which is why we're meeting with y'all here tonight. I'm in charge of upgrading the existing building at the camp and coming up with the new construction we'll need. On very short notice, local architects Mr. and Mrs. Q. E. Herman, whom I'm sure many of you know, are at this moment drawing up plans for the new buildings and lumber has already arrived. Tomorrow the fire department will install hydrants. Governor Broughton is sending prisoners from the state prison to dig trenches for sewer lines." There was an audible buzz from the audience before he added, "Under supervision, of course." He checked his notes. "The telephone company is donating and installing a switchboard, and the National Guard arrives tomorrow to begin clearing trees for the new buildings."

I was stunned. All this had been set in motion in half a day?

"Now, how can y'all help?" Dr. Whims asked. "We need all of you—every single one of you—to think of ways you can contribute. Dr. Hahn"—he motioned toward one of the men seated on the stage—"is in charge of getting the supplies for the hospital. In the community, we'll need some of you ladies to make gowns, caps, and masks for the doctors and nurses—we must remember this is an extremely contagious and serious disease. We need donations: washing machines, wringers, hot plates, blankets, linens, beds, mattresses, and sundry other items. Keep an eye on the *Hickory Daily Record* and listen to WHKY to find out what items we're looking for. We also need people to go door to door to collect those items, and until we get the kitchen up and running we'll need you housewives to cook meals in your homes for the patients. We need volunteers to help with the phones and to greet people in the hospital's reception area. And of course we'll need nurses and doctors and physical therapists. Dr. Crabtree"—he turned to nod at the third man on stage—"is responsible for securing the medical staff, and most of them will be recruited by the Red Cross or the National Polio Foundation and will be coming from other parts of the country. I understand some of them are boarding trains even as we speak."

I thought of Vincent and the work he'd done with polio patients in Chicago. If he didn't now have a paying job at the Harriet Lane Hospital in Baltimore, he would probably still be volunteering somewhere. Maybe even here. My heart shivered. I forced the thought from my mind and replaced it with another: I wanted to be a nurse in this new hospital. I couldn't simply sit at home while the need was so great. I sat up straighter. I was going to volunteer.

"Hotel Hickory can put up the nurses from outside the area," Whims continued, "but please consider opening your homes to the other medical staff. The physicians and physical therapists and epidemiologists. We can do this. We can help our children. And speaking of the children"—he paused momentarily—"we won't have the space to separate colored from white right away, so until we do, the facility will be integrated." He held up his hands as if to stop any complaints before they began. "That can't be helped," he said. "We need to remember that polio knows no socioeconomic or racial lines. It affects all of our community and it will take all of us to fight it."

I sat in the backseat of the car on our way home and for the first few minutes of the drive, the three of us were quiet. The meeting had given us a lot to take in.

Henry finally broke the silence. "After I drop you two off at the house," he said, "I'm going back to the camp to help out."

"At night?" Ruth queried. "What can you do at night?"

"They're setting up floodlights," he said. "We'll be able to continue working even at night."

"You were there all day," Ruth said. "I think you need to get a good night's sleep."

"I wasn't there all day," Henry argued. "I was at the factory half the time. And we need to get this done, Mama. I can sleep once it's up and running."

I felt proud of him, and it was time for me to speak up myself.

"They need nurses," I said. "I'm going to volunteer."

Ruth scoffed. "No, you most certainly are not going to volunteer."

"But I should," I said. "I have the skills. It feels wrong for me not to—"

"You may not work there," Ruth said firmly. "Did you hear what that man said? Extremely contagious? Colored children right next to white children? You'd get covered with polio germs and bring them home. If you absolutely must do something for that hospital, collect donations," she said. "Did you know that Violet is collecting records and record players to send overseas for our servicemen? You can do something like that if you want to do something charitable."

"Violet doesn't have the skills I have," I said before I could stop myself, and my words were greeted with a silence so heavy I felt it pressing down on my shoulders. What was going on with me today? I seemed unable to bite my tongue.

"Mama." Henry finally spoke up, and by his tone I knew he was going to shift the topic, if only a bit. "How about offering our spare bedrooms to a couple of the doctors who'll be coming?"

"I don't want strangers in the house," she said.

"I think we're all going to need to make some sacrifices," he said. "It won't be forever."

Ruth was quiet. "I'll donate money," she said finally. "I'll write a check for a thousand dollars, all right? That's the best I can do."

Henry turned his head to glance back at me. "Mama's right, Tess," he said. "I don't want you working in the hospital either. You can be one of those people who collects donations. They're desperate for any help they can get."

In bed that night I lay awake thinking about my life as it was right now. My secretive, money-hiding husband stayed out many more nights than it would take for him to work on the factory's books. I had to face Lucy's place setting at the table every night. I was hated by my mother-in-law and disliked by many people in town. I was unable to do the work I loved and I still longed for a man I couldn't have.

I prickled at the memory of the car ride home. My nursing skills disparaged. Ruth and Henry telling me what I could and could not do. And then I remembered my last visit with Reverend Sam, how I'd felt listened to and comforted in his presence. I needed to see him again, I thought. Sooner rather than later.

58

Reverend Sam's bronze eyes crinkled with amusement at finding me on his porch the next morning so soon after my last visit. I was soaked to the skin, my blouse, skirt, and nylons sticking uncomfortably to my body after running through a pouring rain from the taxi to his house.

"Are you too tired for a visit?" I asked, then rushed on. "I won't make you work today, I promise. I just need a friend to talk to and I'm afraid you're the only option."

He laughed. "I'd never be too tired to talk to you," he said, stepping back to let me in.

I walked inside and the ashy scent of the fireplace wrapped around me like a comfortable old robe.

"Since you're not going to make me work," he said, "why don't we sit in the living room and I'll pour us some sweet tea?"

"Thank you," I said. "That would be wonderful."

He left the room for the kitchen and I sat down on one of his two big sofas, sinking into the deep cushions that puffed up around my damp skin. I'd never had the chance to look around this room before, and I saw now that it was filled with a woman's touch. Doilies on the tabletops. Elaborately framed photographs on the walls, crocheted afghans folded over the arms of the sofas. Reverend Sam's wife was still alive in this room.

He returned to the living room with two tall glasses of sweet tea and took a seat on the other sofa.

"I can feel your wife here," I said.

He raised his eyebrows, then smiled, looking around. "Yes, she's here. My sons tell me I should redecorate the whole house, or better yet, sell it and move to Charlotte to be closer to them, but . . ." He shook his head. "This is where I belong and this is the way I like my house." He chuckled. "Could you imagine me and my skeleton in a house in the big city?"

I smiled and shook my head.

"This is home," he said. "So what, my dear girl, is on your mind today?"

"Have you heard about the polio hospital they're building at the Fresh Air Camp?" I asked.

"Of course," he said. "Hard to live in Hickory the past twenty-four hours and not hear about it. I know there was a big meeting last night, but . . ." He shook his head. "I preferred to stay home. Were you there?"

"Yes," I said, "and really, it's quite amazing—and maybe impossible—what these three doctors have managed to dream up in just a few hours. I don't know how they're ever going to be able to do what they're proposing." I held up my hands in wonder. "But to make it possible—to turn the camp into a hospital—it's going to take a lot of volunteers. And one of the things they need desperately are nurses. And I'm a nurse."

"Ah," he said, his eyes lighting up. "I'd forgotten that about you. How fitting."

"I am," I said. "And I want to volunteer there, but both my mother-in-law and my husband say no. They expect me to sit around all day doing nothing useful." My voice broke, surprising me. "I've made so many mistakes, Reverend Sam." I folded my hands together tightly in my lap. "I used to be proud of who I was. Now I've lost myself. I really need to do this."

Reverend Sam looked at the ceiling for a long moment. Finally, he returned his gaze to me. "Your mother-in-law, I assume, is Lucy's mother," he said. There was sympathy in his voice. Sympathy for Ruth, not for me, and suddenly, I felt some of that sympathy myself. Ruth had lost her daughter. She was a cold and difficult woman—that was her nature—but she had to be suffering terribly over that loss. I lowered my eyes, feeling guilty for my negative feelings about her.

"Yes," I said quietly. "Lucy's mother. She believes nursing is beneath me and that I'll bring home germs and disease."

"She's a fearful person."

I started to contradict him. Ruth never struck me as fearful, and yet . . . maybe it *was* fear that drove her. Fear of losing her status in Hickory. Fear of losing her friends. Her place in the world.

"Maybe," I said.

He didn't respond. He suddenly seemed removed from me, from the room, his eyes closed, head bowed, as he beseeched the Lord and the universe to open the doors between two worlds. I sat still, listening to him talk to God. Suddenly, his voice changed.

"Yes, I see," he said to the air, his eyes still shut. "Yes. Yes."

I sat still, wondering what he was seeing behind those closed eyelids.

Finally he opened his eyes. "Walter says you must help," he said.

Walter again? "I don't know a Walter," I said. "You mentioned him the other day, but I don't—"

"Doesn't matter," he said. "He knows you. Possibly he's your spirit guide? Many of us . . . those of us who are very fortunate, anyway . . . we have spirit guides. Walter may be yours. We may never know his exact connection to you, but he has a definite sense of what it is you need to do. You must help at the polio hospital, not only to save the children. You have to help there to save yourself."

I stared at him. *Yes*, I thought. *Yes.*

"All right," I said, and I smiled. "I will."

59

It was one thing to say I would become a nurse at the new hospital. Another thing to make it happen.

Reverend Sam had loaned me a huge black umbrella for the walk to the bus stop and once I arrived home, I called a taxi to take me out to the camp, four miles away. The driver was an older man with thinning gray hair and a prominent nose.

"Lots of activity out there today, Miz Kraft, even with this rain," he said. "Gonna hurt my business though."

"Why will it hurt your business?" I asked.

"No one's gonna want to come to Hickory with them polio germs here. It's already bad, since there's so many cases 'round about."

"I think people are overreacting," I said.

"I told my daughter to get my grandkids out of town for the summer," he went on as though I hadn't spoken. "They're heading out to Myrtle Beach. They'll stay there till this blows over."

He reminded me of Ruth with his talk about the polio germs, and he kept it up the whole way to the camp.

I could hear the pounding of hammers and the growl of chain saws as soon as we turned onto the muddy red dirt road that led to the stone building. Cars and trucks were parked everywhere on the weedy grass and among the trees. The rain had let up, but the day was still dark and threatening. The taxi driver was correct though: the weather hadn't deterred the work and the camp was alive with activity. A long wooden structure had already gone up near the original stone building and men were working on the roof, hammering and sawing. I could see that Zeke was one of them, his wet shirt stuck to his back. A line of men, all of them dressed in khaki pants and blue shirts, were digging a trench under the watchful eye of a man with a shotgun. They had to be the prisoners Dr. Whims had mentioned at the meeting the night before. A truck from the phone company was parked near the stone building, and behind me, men cut down trees and cleared brush.

I felt overwhelmed, standing there gawking in wonder, clutching the closed umbrella at my side. I needed to find the person in charge of hiring and wasn't sure who to ask. I didn't know where Henry was working, but he must have spotted me because the next thing I knew, I saw him walking toward me. His shirt was soaked, and his hair, darkened by the rain, was plastered to his head.

"What are you doing here?" he asked as he neared me.

"I have to work here, Henry," I said. "As a nurse." I held my chin up, daring him to tell me I couldn't. "I can't sit home with all this going on, and while I'm happy to gather donations or whatever, I want to help in a more direct way."

He stared at me as though he couldn't believe I was defying him.

"You're helping the way *you* can." I filled the silence. "I want to help the way *I* can."

I saw the muscles in his jaw tense. "The best way you can help is by getting our house up and running so we can move the hell out of my mother's home," he said, his words measured and slow as if he wanted to be certain I understood them. He rarely cursed—it was an indication of how angry he was—but I wasn't going to back down.

"I need more than that," I said flatly.

"Why can't you be satisfied fixing up a house? Making it beautiful? Making it your dream house, for pity's sake? Most girls would be thrilled."

Violet, I thought. Violet would love every minute of it.

"I'll work on the house," I said. "I promise I will. But this is a more pressing need."

"You'll create problems with my mother, Tess," he said, wiping his hands on the rag hanging from his belt. "I'm sorry, but I can't allow it. I have enough to deal with as it is without adding the bickering between you and Mama."

Two men carrying huge coils of black cable over their shoulders walked past us, and we had to take a few steps out of the way to make room for them. I waited until they passed to speak again.

"I'm going to work here." I spoke quietly to avoid making a scene.

"You sound like a disobedient child." His cheeks were growing red and I had the feeling I was testing him to see exactly how far his anger could go. "Where's this sudden willfulness coming from?" he asked.

"I've been talking to someone about it," I admitted. "He's . . . a sort of adviser. He knows I'm a nurse and want to help, and he encouraged me. He said I really *have* to do it. Work here." *To save myself,* I thought. *Yes.*

Henry narrowed his eyes at me. "Who is this 'adviser'?" he asked.

"He's a minister," I said, though I recalled Reverend Sam telling me he was no such thing.

"What church?"

I thought it best to dodge the question. "His name is Reverend Samuel Sparks, and I—"

"That charlatan in Ridgeview?" Henry's eyes widened. "Have you lost your mind?"

"He's for real," I said. "I know that sounds crazy, but I really do think he is." I felt a pulse of joy shoot through me at the mere memory of sitting with Reverend Sam. "I can't explain it." I knew I wore a giddy smile. "You wouldn't be able to explain it either. I've never experienced anything like it before, Henry. I thought it was impossible too, until—"

"What the hell is wrong with you?" he said, and I knew I shouldn't have mentioned Reverend Sam at all. It was simply that the man seemed like such a part of my life all of a sudden. An important part of my life.

"There's nothing wrong with me," I said. "I—"

"You are *not* working here and you are never to see that quack again, understand?"

"I can't promise that," I said stubbornly.

Henry pulled the rag from his belt and dropped it on the ground. Taking me by the elbow, he began leading me away from the new building. "We're going to go see your 'adviser' right now," he said. "I need to give him a piece of my mind and tell him to stay out of our business. And out of your head!" His grip tightened on my elbow.

"Henry, no!" I said. "He's an old man. I don't want you—"

"I think everything that's happened has left you more vulnerable than

I realized," he said, walking fast across the muddy clearing while I struggled to keep up. "I didn't think you were the type to fall for something like this," he added. "I'm worried about you."

I tried unsuccessfully to yank my arm from his grasp. "I won't go to him again," I said. "All right? We don't have to go see him. Please, Henry." I didn't want Reverend Sam to have to deal with my angry husband.

"We're going," Henry said. He'd parked the car a good distance from the activity at the camp and I stopped arguing as we picked our way along the muddy road, avoiding the rain-filled ruts as best we could. I felt powerless. I dreaded what lay ahead for us in Ridgeview.

I finally spotted the Cadillac, its yellow paint splattered with mud. Henry opened my door for me and I got in.

"Please don't make a scene," I begged as we drove down the rutted lane. "He's a gentle man. He's elderly. And he's very kind. You don't need to argue with him. Please." I felt terribly protective of my friend. Henry had never struck me as the violent type, but the way he was talking and behaving right now, his anger filling the car, I worried he might actually try to harm the old man.

Henry said nothing as he pulled onto the main road leading away from the camp. The skies opened up then and rain battered the windshield.

"You know, Tess," he said, as we headed toward Ridgeview. "I knew all along you were different," he said, his eyes on the road. "I knew you had ideas that wouldn't let you fit in very well with my family." He glanced at me quickly. "But I never realized until now that you're crazy."

60

Reverend Sam opened the front door as we climbed the steps to his porch, rain thrumming onto the umbrella Henry held over both our heads. Sam must have seen us coming. I only hoped he could also see the apology on my face. I held Henry's arm as much to keep him from charging at the man as to maintain my balance on the slick stairs.

Reverend Sam smiled at us and I felt affection for him. He was coming to feel like a father to me. At the very least, a dear friend.

"This must be your husband," he said.

"Yes. Henry, this is Reverend Samuel Sparks. And Reverend, this is Henry Kraft."

"Kraft Fine Furniture," Reverend Sam said, and he held out his hand to Henry, who ignored it.

"I want you to stay away from my wife," Henry said, closing the umbrella with an angry snap.

"Henry," I said, my fingers digging into his arm more forcefully than I'd intended. "*I* approached *him*. He didn't—"

"Please come inside, Mr. and Mrs. Kraft," Reverend Sam said, stepping back to make room for us to pass.

Henry hesitated and I gave a little tug on his arm. Reluctantly, he leaned the umbrella against the house. Then we walked inside and I tried to see the dimly lit living room through his eyes. The mélange of furniture. The ashy scent of the fireplace.

"Let's go to my office where we can chat." Reverend Sam began leading us down the hall.

"There's nothing to chat about," Henry said, but he followed close on Reverend Sam's heels with me still clutching his arm. "You have no right interfering in our family's business," he said. "It's not your place to—"

He stopped mid-sentence. Reverend Sam had opened the door to the anteroom and the skeleton looked out at us in all its bony glory. I was torn between laughter and terror, unsure what Henry's reaction would be.

"What the hell?" he said, his voice much softer than I'd anticipated. "What is wrong with you, old man?"

"Come in, come in." Reverend Sam ignored the question as he motioned to us to enter.

"It's all right," I said, tugging Henry's arm again. "This is the anteroom. His office is on the other side."

Henry glanced dubiously at me as we walked past the skeleton and the skulls and the artifacts that had probably been stolen decades earlier from old Indian burial sites. He had nothing to say until we were seated in the inner office. Then, suddenly, he had plenty.

"I don't want you to talk to my wife again," he said, once he had gathered his composure. "She's vulnerable. She's been through a difficult time these past few months, and—"

"All right, sir," Reverend Sam said.

"Don't fill her head with nonsense and don't tell her she should do things I've told her she can't do."

The old man nodded. "I understand, sir," he said. He listened to Henry go on and on about how Reverend Sam had overstepped his bounds and how he was a trickster and how he—Henry—wouldn't allow him to take advantage of me. Reverend Sam kept nodding and yes-sirring. I hadn't seen this subservient side of him before and I found it both sad and distressing. I liked the Reverend Sam who seemed to have all the answers, not the colored man who could be cowed by the white furniture magnate.

"You see, Mr. Kraft," Reverend Sam said, once Henry finally stopped for breath, and I thought I saw a spark of mischief in the old man's eyes. "It's hard for me not to help someone when I feel an instant kinship to that person, as I did with your wife," he said. "Especially when the contacts from the spirit world begin flooding me."

Henry made a sound of disgust. "That's enough," he said, getting to his feet and holding his hand out to me. I took his hand reluctantly and stood up.

"Particularly when her spirit guide, Walter, appeared to me." Reverend Sam continued without budging from his seat behind the desk.

Henry suddenly let go of my hand as if it burned him. "What?" he asked.

"We discovered your wife has a spirit guide named Walter," Reverend Sam said calmly. "And Walter was quite insistent that your wife follow her heart and become a nurse at the polio hospital."

The color had drained from Henry's face. I'd only seen him that pale once before: the day he came to pick me up at the police station after the accident. He leaned his hands heavily on the reverend's desk as though holding himself up.

"Henry?" I touched his shoulder, alarmed by the change in him. He looked quite ill.

Henry narrowed his eyes at the man. "Who the hell are you?" he said slowly, enunciating every word. He sounded both suspicious and shaken, and he turned to me. "We're leaving," he said, not waiting for an answer as he stood up straight again. He gave me a tug toward the door. "We'll let ourselves out," he said, without looking back at Reverend Sam. We walked through the anteroom and into the hallway, where he let go of my hand and marched resolutely ahead of me toward the front door as if he couldn't wait to get out of that house.

Once on the porch with the door closed behind us, he seemed to gather his strength again.

"That," he said, pointing toward the house, "was ridiculous. I can't believe you fell for his nonsense. What a colossal waste of time. You're not to talk with him again, do you understand?"

Now that I knew he wasn't about to keel over from a heart attack or worse, I felt annoyed by the way he was talking to me. I wasn't his child. "I can't promise that," I said.

He looked at me as if he couldn't believe my obstinacy. "Just get in the car," he said. "I'm taking you home before I go back to the camp." He plowed down the steps and onto the front walk.

The rain had once again stopped and we were quiet in the car. I stared out the side window, sitting as far from Henry as I could get. I would see Reverend Sam again if I wanted to. I wasn't Henry's prisoner. I simply wouldn't tell him. I never should have told him in the first place.

When we parked in front of the house, I reached for the door handle.

"Wait," he said, and I turned toward him. "I don't understand this, Tess," he said. "I don't understand why you'd go to Ridgeview, of all places, to talk to an old man who is completely off his rocker."

"Who is Walter?" I asked. "It obviously meant something to you when he—"

"He just caught me by surprise," he said, waving away the thought with his two-fingered hand. "Don't try to throw this back on me. Tell me why you went to see him."

I didn't want to get Hattie in trouble. "I heard someone in town talking about him," I said, "and it made me think about Lucy. I wanted to ask her to forgive me. I know it's crazy sounding. I know that. I don't even believe in a . . . a spirit world. At least I didn't. But now, after talking to Reverend—"

"He's a quack, Tess. You were taken in. I'm sorry."

To my horror, I began to cry. "He knew who Andrew was, Henry," I said. "He communicated with Andrew. He—"

"Stop it!" He held up a hand to cut me off. "That's really enough. Do you hear yourself? Do you hear how crazy you sound?"

"He . . . acknowledged our son," I said. "He acknowledged that we *had* a son. That I had a baby. He understands my grief. I lost our child and *you* don't even acknowledge that he existed!" I let out a sob. "I'm so *lonely*, Henry," I said. "You don't touch me. You don't love me. I don't love you! I don't want to live this way for the rest of my life. I want you to let me out of this marriage. *Please.*"

To my surprise, he reached toward me. Pulled me to him. I melted into him, too weak and weepy at that moment to do anything else.

"I'm sorry," he said after a moment, and I knew that I had gotten through to him. "I'm so sorry, Tess." He stroked my back. I wept against his shoulder, the scent of his aftershave fighting to come through the sweaty smell of his shirt. My own body shuddered with the end of my tears. It felt good to be held. I sank deeper into his arms.

"It will get better when we're in our own house," he said finally, "but I can't be more to you than I am right now."

"Why not?" I asked.

"Many marriages survive this way," he said, not answering my question. "Quite honestly, I think my own parents' marriage was rather . . . loveless."

"Don't you want more than that?"

His smile was sad. "I want us to be happy together. Or at least, content. I know you want to be a nurse at the hospital, but that's not in the cards. It's not worth the battle with my mother, Tess, for either of us. This afternoon, you can use my car to gather donations, all right? Let's go in the house and have some lunch. Then you can drive me back to the camp. They have a list of people who are donating all sorts of items and they need drivers to pick them up. You can help that way."

I sighed, not wanting to fight any longer. "All right," I said, though I wasn't finished with this argument. Today I'd be an obedient wife and help with the donations. Tomorrow, I'd pick up this battle where we left it off.

61

I spent the afternoon dodging rain showers as I collected donations. I drove to the houses on the list I was given and gathered sheets and blankets, towels and hot plates, dishes and glasses and any other sundry items that would fit in the Cadillac—which I drove with great care. Then I brought the donations to the fledgling hospital and stored them in the freshly built cupboards of the two new pine wards. Each time I arrived at the hospital, I was astonished by the progress. The new switchboard was in. Therapy tubs were being set up. The sewer lines were functional. Fire hydrants had been installed on the grounds. Men carried in dozens of donated beds and cribs, lining the walls of the wards with them. Businessmen and carpenters, lawyers and plumbers—so many volunteers!—mucked through the mud, carried wood, cut down green trees as the donated lumber ran out, and hammered on the roof of the building that would eventually become the kitchen. All of them were working toward one end: getting the Emergency Infantile Paralysis Hospital up and running as quickly as possible.

I was amazed by the generosity of my Hickory neighbors as I drove from house to house. People scoured their homes for items they could share. They helped me load things into the car and thanked me for volunteering. Even people who were obviously struggling to make ends meet gave what they could, as well as those households with blue stars—and in one case, a gold star—hanging in their windows. Surely their minds were on their own families and not Catawba County's sick children, but still they gave. Nearly everyone shared a story of a friend or acquaintance from another part of the country who had been touched in some way by polio. In one afternoon, I discovered something I hadn't learned in my five difficult months in Hickory: the town was full of generous, compassionate people. My experience of Hickory had been limited to the Kraft family's small circle of judgmental friends who'd seen me as a manipulative interloper. The majority of the townspeople were nothing like that at all.

It was possible, I discovered, to perspire even in the rain, and I was both sweaty, rain-soaked, and exhausted by four o'clock when I pulled the Cadillac up to one of the new wards and began unloading a batch of donations. I carried an armful of linens into the building and headed for the cupboards, where I found Ruth's friend Mrs. Wilding, the woman whose niece was a nurse. I almost didn't recognize her in capris and a sleeveless yellow blouse. She was checking the plug on one of the donated hot plates.

"Hello, Tess." She smiled at me. "I heard you were collecting donations today too."

"Yes." I returned her smile as I set the linens on one of the cupboard shelves and brushed the sweat from my eyes. "Who knew it would be such hot, wet work?"

"That's why I'm dressed this way," she said. "I don't ordinarily go out of the house like this, but really! You must be stifling in those nylons."

"I am," I admitted. A dozen times that afternoon, I'd thought about stopping home to change into something more comfortable, but I hadn't wanted to take the time.

"But you're Ruth Kraft's daughter-in-law, aren't you." She gave me a knowing smile, then chuckled. "You have an image to uphold."

I tried to determine what was behind her teasing tone. Sympathy? Understanding? Whatever it was, at that moment I felt she was on my side.

"I try." I smiled back. Wanting to get the conversation off myself, I motioned behind us toward the two long rows of beds and cribs. "This is amazing, isn't it?"

She nodded. "This is Hickory," she said. "The real Hickory. I'm glad you're finally getting a chance to see it."

I was heading back to the Cadillac for yet another load of linens when a truck pulled—way too fast—into the clearing. Everyone looked up from his or her work, including Henry, who was hammering molding around one of the windows. I gasped, afraid the truck was going to plow straight through Henry and the window, but it stopped short of the building with a squeal of brakes.

A man and woman jumped from the cab, wild-eyed, wild-haired. Both of them were dressed in dungarees, and the man grabbed Henry's arm.

"We need a doctor!" he shouted.

"Our boy!" the woman said, lowering the tailgate and climbing into the truck bed. "He woke up with the polio!"

"The hospital's not up and running yet," Henry said to them, gently extricating himself from the man's grasp. He looked toward the rear of the truck, and I walked toward the truck myself, trying to see inside the bed. A crowd of workers was beginning to gather around it. "You'll have to take him to Charlotte," Henry said. "There's no medical staff here yet."

"Charlotte!" the woman said, kneeling down in the truck bed. "That's too far. He could die!"

I moved close enough to see the boy she knelt over. He lay motionless on a folded blanket in the truck's bed and his mother clung to his hand.

"I'm a nurse," I said, walking even closer to the truck. I didn't dare look at Henry. "May I see your son?"

"Tess, no," Henry said, but there wasn't much heart behind the words and they were drowned out by the man's response.

"Yes!" he shouted. "Please!" He helped me climb into the truck bed and I felt one of my nylons run in the process. This was foolish of me, I thought. I had no mask or gloves or anything to protect me from this boy's illness, whatever it was.

I knelt next to the boy, across from his mother. The little guy was seven or eight with hair the color and texture of hay. His blue eyes were open. He was pale for a farm boy, but he smiled up at me and I returned the smile.

"Hi, sweetheart," I said. "Can you tell me your name?"

His father started to answer from where he stood outside the truck, but I held up my hand to stop him. I wanted to see how alert and aware this child was.

The boy licked his paper-dry lips. "Frankie," he said.

"He had a bellyache and was sick on his stomach all night," his mother said. "That's the infantile polio, ain't it?"

"It could be one of many things," I said. "Did he also have diarrhea?"

"Yes, ma'am," Frankie answered for himself. "My belly near exploded."

"Has he been around anyone who was diagnosed with polio?" I asked his mother, pressing my palm to his forehead. He was no warmer than I was on this clammy day.

"No, ma'am," his mother said.

"He's been keepin' to hisself, helpin' us with the crops," his father said. When I raised my head to look at the man, I saw that a crowd of curious volunteers had gathered around the truck. I returned my attention to Frankie.

"Do you have a sore throat, Frankie?" I asked.

"No, ma'am."

"Any other illnesses in the last few weeks?"

"Nothin'," said his mother. "He's the healthiest boy there is."

I examined him as best I could without any instruments. I checked his reflexes—all normal. I lifted his shoulders from the truck bed to see if he could support his head. He could. I bent his legs and asked him to push them against my hands. He quickly knocked me off balance and I fell from my kneeling position to my bottom, laughing. I was not a doctor, but I didn't need to be one to feel quite certain this boy didn't have polio. I knew the definitive test was a spinal tap, but I doubted Frankie was going to have to endure that painful procedure.

"What did you eat yesterday?" I asked him. "Starting with breakfast."

"He had the same thing for breakfast he always has," his mother said, and again I stopped her.

"Please let Frankie tell me," I said.

He told me about his breakfast of eggs and ham, the three ham sandwiches he ate for lunch, and the fried chicken and okra he had for dinner.

"Did everyone else"—I looked at his mother—"did you and your husband eat the same things?"

"We did, exceptin' for I only had one sandwich," she said.

"I had the three too," Frankie's father said.

"How about snacks?" I asked Frankie.

"Nothin'," he said. "Ain't no time for a snack on account of they got me workin' in the field every darn minute."

"Frankie!" his mother said. "Watch your tongue!" She looked at me. "We've got to get the crops in," she said.

"What were you harvesting yesterday?" I asked.

"Pole beans," Frankie and his mother said at the same time.

"Ah," I said. "Did you snack on any of them?"

His mother laughed. "They're his favorite," she said. "He can't get enough of them."

"How many would you say you ate while you were working yesterday, Frankie?" I asked.

He shrugged, and I had the feeling he was afraid of getting in trouble.

"A lot?" I asked, and he gave a guilty nod.

"A *whole* lot?" I smiled at him with a wink.

"Maybe," he said, not making eye contact with any of us. "I don't rightly recall."

I was quite certain I knew what was wrong with this boy, and it was nothing that a day away from raw green beans wouldn't fix. But if I was wrong?

I peered over the side of the truck bed and saw that Mrs. Wilding was one of the onlookers. "Could you call Dr. Poole and see if he'd be able to take a look at this boy if his parents bring him over?" I asked her.

Mrs. Wilding nodded, then left to give the hospital's new switchboard its first call.

I told his parents why I didn't think he had polio and that it was possible he'd simply eaten far too many raw beans the day before.

"You're sure?" the man asked.

I shook my head. "I can't be one hundred percent sure," I said, "which is why I want you to see Dr. Poole. But his symptoms really don't seem to fit polio."

A few minutes passed and Mrs. Wilding ran—yes, she *ran*, and I felt proud of her—back to the truck. "He says to bring him right over," she said.

I gave the husband directions to Dr. Poole's office. His wife hugged me and thanked me, and Henry helped me climb from the truck bed. We watched as the truck pulled out of the clearing, and the workers who'd observed the whole exchange gave a little round of applause. I blushed, feeling like the sole performer in a drama. I turned to Mrs. Wilding, ready to escape the attention.

"Can you help me get another armload of donations from the car?" I asked her, and together we headed across the muddy clearing toward the Cadillac.

Henry walked into the building as I was placing a stack of folded blankets in the cupboard.

"Tess?" he said.

I looked up from my work. "Yes?" I stiffened, expecting him to be angry. He would tell me I'd overstepped my bounds by having anything to do with that young boy.

"You were different out there." He stood in front of me, hands in his pockets. "It was a side to you I haven't seen before. Self-confident and . . . I don't know. Capable, I guess is the word."

"Thank you," I said.

"I was proud of you."

I felt myself blush yet again. "Thank you," I repeated.

He drew in a long breath and let it out in a sigh. "The hospital is going to need you," he said, "and you need it. I can see that. You can work here if you want."

"As a nurse." I made it a statement rather than a question.

"As a nurse," he agreed.

"What about your mother?"

"I'll deal with my mother," he said. "Just let me be the one to tell her."

"Thank you, Henry," I said again, and as he walked away and I folded another blanket and put it on the shelf, I grinned to myself. "Well, Walter," I whispered to the air, "what do you think of that?"

62

I was one of twelve nurses who arrived at the hospital the following morning. Ten of us were volunteers, most of us local. Two were from the State Board of Health. We were young and old, married and single. I was the only one whose uniform was at least a size too large. I hadn't realized how much weight I'd lost over the last few months. I didn't care. I'd put on my cap, my white shoes, my white nylons, then buttoned my uniform and smiled at myself in the mirror. "You're an RN," I whispered to my reflection. I hoped I would remember all my training.

At least twenty more nurses were on their way from other parts of the country, due to arrive in a few days by train or bus. It felt strange that morning to have a hospital filled with nurses and no patients, but there was no doubt in anyone's mind that the ratio would soon change. And there was so much preparatory work to be done.

Ruth was angry and not talking to either Henry or myself.

"It will pass," Henry said to me, though I knew he was bothered by his mother's disapproval. She'd actually suggested that I share Hattie's cottage with her instead of sullying the house with all the germs I'd be bringing home, but Henry silenced her with a stern "enough, Mama!" I was touched by how he was sticking up for me, as well as how hard he was working day and night as he split his time between the factory and the hospital. He had to be exhausted.

One of the nurses was Grace Wilding, Mrs. Wilding's niece. She wore her hair, as dark as mine, in a victory roll, as I did, and I felt an instant bond with her.

"Isn't this simply staggering?" she said, sweeping her arm around the ward we were preparing for patients. "I can't believe what's been accomplished here in two days."

"I know," I said. "It's amazing." The idea for the emergency hospital had been conceived on Thursday, and here we were on Saturday morning, standing in the middle of a hospital ward with the scent of sawn wood still strong in the air. All the bed frames had been fitted with mattresses and they lined the walls, waiting for us to make them with our donated linens. We needed to get to it quickly: the first patients were due to arrive that afternoon.

We spent the morning getting acclimated to the hospital's two sun-filled wards, the second of which was still under construction. With their pine walls and bare floors, they felt more like wide-open mountain cabins than a hospital. Volunteers, including Henry, hung screens in the windows as we worked, and someone delivered a raft of fly swatters to us, just in case those screens didn't do the job. We hammered nails into the walls and hung the swatters. Women from the community—including several I recognized from Ruth's book clubs and the Ladies of the Homefront—scrubbed fifty-five bed frames from top to bottom. I knew that other Hickory women were preparing food for the hospital in their homes, since the kitchen wouldn't be functional for a few days yet. I doubted there was a man or woman in Hickory untouched by the goings-on at the former Fresh Air Camp.

We made all the beds, filled jars with alcohol for the thermometers, and prepared a giant vat of disinfectant where we would empty all patient waste to prevent the spread of disease. And then we began what turned out to be the most arduous task of the morning: cutting lengths of wool from donated blankets to be used in something called the Sister Kenny Method. A volunteer physiotherapist explained the approach to us: when a patient with paralysis arrived, we would further cut the wool to precise measurements for his or her affected limbs. Then, at least a couple of times a day, we'd boil the pieces of wool, run them through a wringer, and wrap them around those paralyzed arms or legs. Once the hot packs were removed, we'd exercise the limbs to keep the muscles from atrophying. In the three polio cases I'd seen as a student nurse, we'd immobilized the affected limbs with splints and in one case a cast. Suddenly that approach was viewed with disfavor and this new, incredibly labor-intensive treatment was what we'd be using. It made sense in theory to me, but after only thirty minutes of cutting lengths of wool, my hand was cramping up. I didn't really care. For the first time since nursing school, I felt myself a part of something important. No one treated me as an outsider here. No one treated me as Hank Kraft's wife. I was just a nurse. I was happily one of them.

One end of the ward now held several therapy tubs made by a Hickory metal worker, along with an iron lung that had been sent from Morganton. Fortunately, they also sent along a technician trained in the huge respirator's use. The machine was long and green and simply overwhelming to behold with all its ports and knobs and giant pump. I knew the iron lung could be a lifesaver, but I also knew that caring for an iron-lung patient was tricky. I felt intimidated by the respirator's presence and hoped we never had a patient that sick.

In the clearing outside the two wards stood a small admissions tent where one of the nurses and a local physician, a Dr. Matthews, were preparing for our first patients. In another tent, an epidemiologist set up his tables and microscopes, getting ready to research the cause of the disease, and more researchers were on their way. I remembered Vincent wanting to stay longer in Chicago to help with the research and I was angry at myself now for being impatient to get him home. I'd been selfish and so shortsighted.

The patients seemed to arrive all at once that afternoon. A few came by ambulance. Two others were delivered to us by hearse, since ambulances were in short supply. It gave me a jolt to see those hearses pull up in front of the admissions tent, but I had the feeling I would need to get used to the sight. The ward was suddenly a flurry of activity and I was assigned my first patient, a little girl named Carol Ann. Five years old, she'd awakened the day before in pain from head to toe. When she tried to get out of bed, she fell, and within hours, her legs were paralyzed. One of the men carried her into the ward and I, dressed in my mask and protective gown, tried to settle her in a bed. She screamed and sobbed, asking over and over again for her mama, who was not allowed in the ward. My heart broke for her. This would be one of the hardest parts of my job, I thought: dealing with my patients' absolute terror over being separated from their parents—from everyone they knew—when they were so sick and helpless. The quarantine would have to last ten days, and the parents who watched their children being carried or wheeled away from them were as terrified as the patients.

By late afternoon, the ward buzzed with activity. My fellow nurses and I were exhausted from stumbling our way into some sort of routine, learning care techniques that were new to many of us, and treating a disease some of us had never seen before. We knew this was only the beginning. More patients were on their way.

I was a little bit in love with Carol Ann by the end of that day. She was a very sick girl, but not so sick that she couldn't respond to the funny stories I told her as I wrapped her legs in the hot wool packs and exercised her stiff limbs, trying to keep her mind off her pain and fear. But her giggling could give way to tears in an instant. How was I going to leave her at the end of the day when she'd finally gotten attached to me?

The night nurse who came in to take over for me scared her. I doubted the little girl had ever met a colored person before and she screamed and clung to me as I tried to leave. So the nurse, Betty, and I sat together with her, singing songs from behind our masks for nearly an hour while Carol Ann grew more comfortable with Betty, and I knew the emotional component was going to be as important, as critical, as the physical in our patients' recovery.

A volunteer drove me home that evening. Ruth was already in bed—or at least in her room—by the time I arrived, and Henry was still working, either at the hospital or the factory. I didn't know where he was. I'd lost track of him sometime during the day.

A letter from Gina was propped up on the small table in the foyer and I carried it upstairs. I was a sweaty, grimy mess and more tired than I could ever remember being, so I took a much needed bath before settling into bed to read the letter. It was short, full of how much she missed Mac. She was worried about him. In his last letter, she told me, he'd written that he would never be the same after all he'd seen and done.

And I found the doll you asked for, she wrote. *It's very cute and I've already mailed it, so you should have it soon.*

I smiled to myself. It would be a while before I'd be able to take the doll to Jilly. My life was too full right now. *My life was too full.* I could barely believe it.

By Sunday evening, the Hickory Emergency Infantile Paralysis Hospital had sixteen very sick and frightened young patients, two doctors, twelve nurses, one epidemiologist, two physiotherapists, and dozens of meals provided by women in the community. When I left that Sunday night, as Betty and the other colored—and a few white—nurses came in for their night shift, I was exhausted to the point of tears and I had not felt so happy, so simply in love with my life, in a very long time.

63

July 1, 1944

Dear Gina,

I'm amazed that news of our fledgling hospital has reached Baltimore! I guess Hickory is really on the map now. Down here, the papers are saying that the building and staffing of the hospital in fifty-four hours was "miraculous." We're still getting donations of money and goods every day from the people in town and from business owners. Henry donated countless tables and chairs from his factory. The hospital kitchen is finally functional and filled with cooks from the area (along with some female prisoners), to the relief of the all the ladies in the community who've been making meals in their homes day and night for the patients. We need more wards, and military hospital tents are on their way to serve that purpose. Yesterday, the men, including Henry and Zeke, the custodian at the factory, built walls and floors to support them. And the patients keep coming. And coming and coming.

You said you feel dumb, but please don't. Unless someone's had personal experience with polio, they're not going to know much about it. Most cases are minor and seem a bit like influenza, with nausea, sore throat, fever, and pain. Those children usually get better in a week or two. But the children with polio you often hear about are the more dramatic—and fortunately rarer—cases with central nervous system involvement. That's where the paralysis comes in and it usually takes many months for those patients to recover. Some of them never do. We have quite a few of those cases at the hospital.

I love my work, Gina! I spend the mornings taking care of this darling little girl, Carol Ann, and a second patient I was just assigned, a thirteen-year-old boy named Barry. They both have paralyzed legs, so I spend a lot of time applying hot wool to their useless limbs. My hands will be red and raw for the rest of my life! In the afternoons, I work in the admissions tent, and I'm also being trained to work with the iron lung. That machine terrifies me, and between you and me, having the responsibility for a patient who needs the respirator (iron lung) frightens me. Why they selected me for that training, I have no idea, but I think it's good for me to learn something new and challenging.

You asked how the iron lung works. Have you ever seen a picture of one? It's a long steel airtight tube. Only the patient's head sticks out, and a rubber diaphragm prevents air from leaking out of the machine around his neck. A pump changes the pressure inside the tube so that the patient's lungs are forced to expand or contract. In other words, it makes the patient breathe. Yesterday, a twenty-seven-year-old man, by far our oldest patient, was brought in with chest paralysis and he is now in the iron lung. The thought of being locked in that airtight tube makes me feel panicky, but our patient is frankly too ill to care. The sound of the lung, the rhythmic whooshing, has quickly become the background noise of the ward.

I'm proud of my husband, Gina. He's working so hard, at both the factory and the hospital. When I see him working on one of the buildings—not for money, but out of dedication to his town—I'm touched. He's exhausted and so am I. But right now, I can honestly say I'm happy and I believe he is too.

I must get to the hospital. I hope this dreaded disease is nowhere near you in Baltimore!

Love,

Tess

64

I was working in the admissions tent that Thursday when I looked up to see Honor yank open the screen door and Zeke rush inside, Jilly limp in his arms. I'd been cleaning our thermometers and I got immediately to my feet, thinking, *This is impossible.* It had been weeks since Butchie died. Could the virus still be in their house?

I rushed over to them. I wasn't sure they knew it was me, since I was covered in a long protective gown, surgical cap, and mask. I pulled the mask down so they could recognize me. "What are her symptoms?" I asked, slipping the mask back in place.

"She woke up this morning burning up and hurting all over," Honor said. Her hair was tucked under a yellow kerchief and the skin around her jade-colored eyes was swollen. I could tell it was a struggle for her to get the words out. "It's like it was with Butchie," she said, her voice breaking.

"Put her on this cot, Zeke," I said, stepping over to one of the cots we used for intake. "Dr. Matthews is behind that curtain with another patient"—I pointed to the small curtained area in the rear of the tent—"but he'll be out very soon."

Zeke laid Jilly down on the cot. Her eyes were closed but she whimpered, her little face contorted in pain.

"It's not *exactly* like it was with Butchie," he said. "Butchie couldn't breathe. She's breathing all right, at least so far."

"I can't lose another baby," Honor said, more to the air than to either

Zeke or myself. She stood at the end of the cot in a brown and gold dress, rubbing her hands together, her gaze on her daughter. Zeke went to her side and put his arm around her.

"She's gonna be all right," he promised her, as though he could somehow make that a reality.

I pulled a chair across the room for Honor. She looked like she needed to get off her feet and indeed she sank into the chair almost before I had it behind her. I began a preliminary examination of Jilly, taking her temperature, which was very high, and checking her reflexes, which were normal, at least so far. I knew how quickly polio could worsen. I'd seen too much of it in the past few days. I jotted my findings down on a chart.

A few minutes later, Dr. Matthews came out of the curtained area and walked immediately over to us.

"This is Honor Johnson and her brother, Zeke, and Honor's little girl, Jilly," I said. "Honor's son, Butchie, passed away from polio four weeks ago."

"Five weeks," Honor corrected me.

"Unlikely it was the same virus after all this time," Dr. Matthews said gruffly as he checked my preliminary findings on Jilly's chart. "Just bad luck."

I'd come to think Dr. Matthews was a good doctor who dealt well with his young patients, but he didn't have the best bedside manner when it came to the parents. He was also very tired. We all were.

He examined Jilly, whose eyes were now open and who submitted to his poking and prodding with little more than a whimper, while I jotted his findings down on her chart.

"I believe it's polio," he said after a few minutes, "but her reflexes are very good. It appears to be a minor case."

"Minor?" Honor asked. "She'll get better?"

"It's encouraging, Honor," I said. "Hopefully it will be very mild."

Dr. Matthews looked at me. "We'll admit her," he said. "Call someone to take her to the ward."

"Can I go with her?" Honor asked. There was so much hope in her eyes, but I could tell she knew better, having been through this once before.

I shook my head. "I'm sorry," I said.

"She's just a baby." Honor choked on the word, and I rested my hand on her shoulder. I ached for every parent who had to leave his or her child with us, a group of strangers, but knowing what Honor had gone through with Butchie made her pain even more palpable to me.

"I'll get assigned to her," I promised. "I'll be the one to take care of her."

She turned her face away from me to look at her brother as though he might be able to change what was happening.

"I'm working here," he said to her. "I can go into the ward. I'll watch her."

I nodded. "That's right. That's good," I said. Zeke was doing much of the maintenance in the hospital, and there was plenty to do. "You can carry her into the ward, if you like, Zeke," I said.

I settled Jilly in the ward. It saddened me to see her so lethargic, too tired even to cry when her uncle Zeke had to leave her alone in that crowded ward filled with bustling nurses, sleeping—and often weeping—children, and the ever-present whooshing of the iron lung. Once she had fallen asleep, I carried my egg salad sandwich outside to eat it on one of the rudimentary benches that had been constructed in the shade. Through the trees, I could see men, my husband included, working on the military tents that would become our new wards.

I spotted Honor sitting alone on a nearby bench. I had no idea she was still on the hospital grounds. I walked over and sat down next to her.

"Are you waiting for a ride home?" I asked.

She shook her head. "I'm not going home," she said, wearing a determined expression. "I'm staying right here. As close to Jilly as they'll let me."

"You need some rest, Honor," I said. "It won't do Jilly any good if you get sick too." How many times had I said those words to how many mothers in the past few days?

"I'm fine," she said, but then she began to cry, her head buried in her hands.

I rested my palm on her shoulder. "Dr. Matthews doesn't think it will be like it was with Butchie," I said. "Most cases of polio don't result in paralysis. Most children recover completely." I prayed he was right. I didn't want to give her false hope.

She finally lifted her head, tears dangling like jewels from those long black eyelashes. "We got rid of all Butchie's things," she said. "We did everything we were told to do. How could she get it? How? It's just not fair."

"You're right, it's not," I said. "I guess there's still a lot we don't know about polio, but I do know she's in the right place. The doctors here are good and we have plenty of nurses now. We have people doing research to try to figure out what causes the disease and . . ." I stopped myself. She didn't need to hear all of that. She was only thinking about her little baby girl.

"Jilly's father," I said. "Del, right? I know you couldn't reach him after Butchie . . . passed away, but I wonder if there's a way to get him home now? They have compassionate leave in the service. I know it's hard to get, but maybe under these circumstances—"

"I don't want him to know," she said. "He'll be worried. He doesn't need more to worry about."

"I understand," I said. I thought of getting her mind off Jilly. "How did you two meet?" I asked.

She looked into the distance, toward the woods. "I've known him all my life," she said. "We came up in the same church. Our mamas were friends." A small smile played on her lips at the thought of him. I wished I could tell her about Vincent. I wished I could tell her that I understood how it felt to love someone you'd known all your life.

"I'm sorry he's so far away," I said instead, and her look darkened again.

"All my baby girl's toys and dolls have to be destroyed," she said.

"Yes," I said, thinking of the doll Jilly loved so much. "And I'm so sorry you and your mother will be under quarantine again. It must be—"

"No," she said with a shake of her head. "The public health man came out to talk to me and said we don't need to be quarantined this time. We're most likely immune, he said. But he still said I can't go in the ward. I don't understand why not."

I didn't really understand either. I thought the rules were being applied haphazardly these days. Why could Zeke come and go in the hospital but Honor could not? Why, for that matter, could I come and go as I pleased? But the rules were the rules and none of us seemed to have the time or energy to buck them.

"I know it doesn't seem to make sense," I said, "but—"

"I'm not going home," she said. "I have to stay close to Jilly." She looked at me. "I let them take Butchie away and I never saw him again. He died without me there. At least out here I feel like I'm closer, even if I can't see her."

"Honor," I said softly, "you can't just stay out here on this bench. You can't sleep here."

"I'll stay at the factory with Zeke," she said. "I can sleep on his couch and ride with him when he comes here to work in the mornings." She looked at me. "Maybe there's some work I can do here?" she asked. "Something useful I could do?"

"They might need help in the kitchen," I said hesitantly. Everyone I knew who was working in the kitchen was white. I wasn't sure what they'd say to Honor if she offered to help.

"I could do that," she said. "I'll do anything to stay close."

I looked toward the ward. The screened windows were a bit high off the ground, but there was a wooden crate nearby and I had a sudden idea. "Come with me," I said, getting to my feet. I picked up the bag with my sandwich in it. I would have no time to eat it now, but I wasn't going to leave it for the ants either. We walked over to the side of the building. I reached for the crate and shoved it beneath one of the windows. I tested its stability with my foot, then climbed on top of it. I had a perfect view of Jilly, asleep in her bed.

Smiling, I stepped down and motioned to Honor to climb onto the box. She held my arm for balance and peered in the window.

"Over on the right," I told her. "Third bed down."

I saw her smile. Bite her lower lip. "My baby," she said, almost in a whisper. She rested one hand against the screen. "I love you, baby." Then she looked down at me. "A nurse just did this to me." She whisked her hand through the air in a "scat" motion.

I laughed. "Ignore her," I said, helping her down from the box. "You're not doing any harm." I would have a word with the other nurses. I could see no problem with allowing parents to see their children through the windows.

"Thank you," she said, looking directly into my eyes, and I thought it was the first time she'd truly made eye contact with me. She was always so chilly when I was around. I knew why, of course.

"Honor," I said, needing to clear the air, "I know you were Lucy's friend. I wish there was something I could do to bring her back."

A shadow passed over her eyes again. "You just take care of my Jilly for me, all right?" she asked.

"I will," I said. "I promise."

65

Henry drove me home from the hospital that evening. I couldn't have said which of us was more grimy and tired. In the car, I told him about Jilly's admission, but he'd already heard about it from Zeke. He just shook his head wordlessly as I described her condition.

"Hard to believe in God sometimes," he muttered finally.

"I know," I agreed. This past year, I sometimes felt as though God had fallen asleep on the job.

When we arrived home, Ruth was in the kitchen making herself a cup of tea.

"Hattie's chicken and dumplings is in the refrigerator for you," she said to us, "but first, you both get upstairs and wash that blasted hospital off yourselves before you sit at my table."

"Nice to see you too, Mama," Henry said sarcastically, clearly annoyed as he walked past his mother toward the hallway. "Do you want the tub first, Tess, or can I take a quick shower?" Neither of us seemed inclined to use Lucy's old bathroom yet.

"Go ahead," I said, following close behind him.

"There's a box for you in the foyer, Tess," Ruth called after me.

The doll! What perfect timing.

The box was on the table by the front door. I sat down on the stairs and tore off the brown paper wrapping and then lifted the lid of the white box. There she was, an adorable doll a bit over a foot tall dressed in a ruffly blue gingham dress, white anklets, and black Mary Janes. She looked exactly like Jilly's beloved doll—obviously made by the same manufacturer—with the exception of her cocoa-colored skin. Her features were decidedly Caucasian. Even the molded hair had a golden glow to it, but it was as close as we were going to get to a Negro doll.

I carried the box upstairs, wondering if I should hide the doll from Henry. He'd been adamant that I stay out of Adora's family's lives, but having Jilly as my patient changed everything, at least in my opinion. Of course, I'd asked Gina to get the doll long before Jilly had been diagnosed with polio. I set the open box on the dresser in full view, and when Henry walked into the room, his hair wet and his navy blue robe tied around his waist, he stopped short.

"What the hell is that?" He pointed toward the doll.

"I ordered it for Jilly," I said, then rushed on. "Don't be angry. I know you said you don't want me to do anything for that family, but I couldn't resist this, Henry. And now Jilly's losing that doll she loves—she's losing all her toys—and this is just perfect, don't you think?"

I expected him to chew me out. Instead, a smile slowly spread across his face. "She'll like it," he said, crossing the room to the armoire. He opened the door. Searched through his shirts. "And the bathroom is now yours."

"I've never seen anything like it," Honor said the next morning when I sat next to her on the bench to show her the doll. I thought it was as close as she had come to smiling since bringing Jilly into the hospital. She fingered the hem of the gingham dress, then looked at me. "I can't believe you did this for her," she said. "Thank you."

True to her word, Honor seemed determined to spend all her time at the hospital. She rode in with Zeke early that morning and she'd talked someone in the kitchen into letting her work there in the afternoons. Jilly was still very tired, but her fever was slowly coming down and Dr. Matthews seemed even more certain that she had a mild case of the disease. Still, he was watching her carefully. Sometimes mild cases of polio improved for a few days, then suddenly turned deadly serious. He didn't expect that to happen with Jilly, but he didn't want to let her go home prematurely.

Honor touched the doll's little white sock and gave me a worried look. "Won't the doll have to be destroyed when Jilly gets better?" she asked.

I'd thought of that myself. The doll would need to be disinfected before it went home with Jilly. "Don't worry," I said. "I'll take care of it." I placed the lid back on the box. "Would you like to watch through the window when I give it to her?" I asked.

She nodded. "I would."

I stood up and she grabbed my free hand.

"You're a kind person," she said.

I squeezed her hand. "I'll let you know when I have a break to give her the doll," I said. Then I left her on her bench to stay as close as she was able to get to her baby girl.

The hospital was bursting with new patients that morning, and the nurses, myself included, were overwhelmed with work. The Sister Kenny method, which we were all committed to now, was so time-consuming. How much easier it would be to have our patients' legs and arms splinted and immobile than to wrap them in wool and exercise them several times each day. But I was determined to give my young patients the best chance at recovery they could have.

We received a second iron lung late that morning. Everyone had been nervous with only the one respirator, since that was still in use by our twenty-seven-year-old patient. What if we urgently needed another one? I helped the technician set it up. The other nurses were only too happy to let the respirators be my bailiwick.

Jilly was my least needy patient. I kept popping over to her bed to give her a little time and attention in between caring for my patients with paralysis. She knew who I was, despite my mask and cap, and I could tell that she liked me, but she still cried for her mother. It wasn't until nearly noon that I had a few free minutes. I went out to the yard and motioned to Honor to go to the window. When I saw her appear at the screen, I propped Jilly up and handed her the doll. She stared at it with openmouthed wonder, then hugged it to her chest.

"Let's give this one a name," I said. "All right?"

"Nursie," Jilly said.

"Nursie? Is that her name?"

"Yes. She got a little hat like a nurse hat."

"You're right," I said, realizing that the doll's hat did look a little like my own white cap. "Nursie it is. And Jilly. Look who's at the window." I pointed toward the window and Jilly followed my fingers to where Honor was waving at us.

"Mama!" she shouted, and I was delighted to see her energy.

"Shh." I laughed. "Some people are trying to sleep, Jilly."

"Mama! I got a doll!" She held the doll in the air. "Her name's Nursie!"

Honor nodded and smiled but said nothing. She was not about to shout across the entire ward. She gave a final wave and disappeared from the window.

"Where's she at?" Jilly asked.

"She's going to work in the kitchen here, honey," I said. "She'll be one of the people who makes your dinner."

"Will she bring it to me?"

"She can't do that, but she'll be in the kitchen, cooking it with love."

I had to spend a bit more time in the admissions tent that afternoon, and when I returned to the ward, I was surprised to see Henry sitting on the edge of Jilly's bed. Since he was working at the hospital, he—like Zeke—could go anywhere he pleased, but I was dismayed to see he was wearing no protective clothing whatsoever. Ruth would have a fit if she could see him at that moment. I walked toward Jilly's bed, and as I drew close, I could hear her giggling over something Henry said to her.

She spotted me walking toward them. "Mr. Hank brung me a color book," she said, and I saw the coloring book and small box of crayons next to her new doll on her lap.

Henry got quickly to his feet as though he knew I was going to chew him out for not wearing a gown and mask. He gave me a sheepish smile.

"That was nice of him," I said to Jilly. I was wearing a mask, but I hoped Henry could see my own smile in my eyes. I was so touched that he'd reached out to Jilly this way.

"I need to get back to work, Jilly," he said to the little girl. "Next time I stop by, maybe you'll have a picture colored for me, huh?"

"Okay," she said, already turning her attention from him to the coloring book. She dumped the crayons out of the box and onto her sheet.

I walked with Henry toward the exit.

"Next time," I said, "you need to put on a gown and a mask."

"Yes, nurse," he said with a small salute, and I laughed.

He left the building and I watched him through the screened door as he walked toward the tent wards, still under construction. His attention to Jilly had been a side to him I hadn't seen before and I felt nearly overcome with sadness that our baby hadn't lived. Henry would have been a good father.

Later that afternoon, I soaked lengths of wool in boiling water for little Carol Ann's paralyzed legs. I used sticks to feed the too-hot-to-touch wool through the wringer, then set it on a cart and wheeled it over to her bed. She whimpered as I began laying the fabric on top of her right leg. "Too hot, sweetheart?" I asked.

"Yeah," she said.

I knew the wool wasn't technically too hot now—not hot enough to burn—but I could imagine how, on a stifling summer day, the weight and heat and stench of the wool could be suffocating.

Two new doctors had arrived that afternoon and one of them was making his way down the row of children, examining each one. He reached Carol Ann as I was still applying the wool. Like me, he was gowned and masked.

"I won't leave it on too long, honey," I said as I picked up another length of wool from the cart. "She's a bit tired of all this wool," I said to the doctor, who hadn't said a word to either Carol Ann or myself. I looked at his eyes, the only part of him visible between his cap and his mask, and I gasped, my hands frozen in the air above Carol Ann's legs. His eyes were a soft, rich brown and oh so familiar.

Vincent.

66

He was as stunned to see me as I was to see him. We stood there speech-less, seemingly paralyzed ourselves, until Carol Ann whimpered again and I shook myself from my stupor.

"Yes, honey," I said, tucking the ends of the wool around her thin legs. My hands trembled. "We're finally done. And this is Dr. Russo," I said. The name felt so good in my mouth. If I hadn't turned my life upside down, that would be my name now. "Dr. Russo, this is Carol Ann."

Vincent seemed to have trouble shifting his gaze from me to the little girl, but he collected himself and began examining her. "How are you feel-ing today, Carol Ann?" he asked.

"Hurt," she said.

"Tell me where."

"My back hurts," she said.

"She's a brave girl," I said. "An excellent patient." I looked down at Carol Ann. "We'll let the wool warm up your muscles," I said. "And I'll be back in a little bit to do your exercises with you."

I started to roll the cart toward the rear of the ward, anxious to get away from Vincent. I needed to be alone. I needed to collect my thoughts and settle my nerves.

"I want to talk with you later, nurse," Vincent said. His voice was busi-nesslike. Abrupt. It was not a voice I'd ever heard before.

I looked at him. Looked directly into those eyes that I'd loved all my life. "All right," I said, my own voice coming out hoarse and weak. How could I ever explain to him what I'd done and who I'd become?

There was no time for me to stew over what I would say to Vincent for the rest of the day, and that was good. Mayor Finley's twenty-two-year-old married daughter, Amy Pryor, was brought by hearse to the hospital late that afternoon, and she was in such dire straits with rapidly progressing paralysis that Dr. Matthews told us to move her immediately into our second iron lung. Her arms and chest and abdomen were already paralyzed by the disease and she struggled to breathe. She could only moan rather than speak. Although she could still move her legs somewhat, they thrashed wildly as Grace Wilding and I transferred her to the bed of the respirator. Along with Grace, I was put in charge of her care since I'd been trained in using the iron lung. I didn't know which of us was more nervous, Grace or myself. Not only was the iron lung still new to us, but this was the mayor of Hickory's beloved daughter and she was desperately ill. Her husband was overseas and her mother was taking care of her two-year-old son. To complicate matters even further, she was seven and a half months pregnant. The blessing in disguise was that she seemed to have no idea at all what was going on. She was in that blurry mental state we often saw in our most severely ill patients, confusion and delirium born of pain and fever and fear. If someone ever wheeled me into that long tube, forcing my breath in and out of my lungs, I thought I would panic, but Amy seemed oblivious, and it was a relief to Grace and myself when we saw her color quickly improve and the thrashing of her legs cease. I wrapped her neck in a cloth saturated with lanoline to prevent the diaphragm from chafing her skin, and we examined the seals on all the ports to be sure the lung was airtight. Nervously, I checked the power supply. The hospital hadn't lost power yet, but it would be disastrous for our iron-lung patients if we did. Once everything was in order, Grace and I looked at each other and let out our breath with exhausted smiles.

I was relieved when it was Dr. Matthews and not Vincent who came to examine Amy. I saw Vincent several times over the remainder of the day, but he was always on the other side of the ward from where I was working. If he was looking at me, I didn't know. I kept my face turned away from him, afraid of what he could read in my eyes. The guilt. The love I still had for him. Those emotions went hand in hand and I knew I'd be fighting both of them for the rest of my life.

The night shift arrived and I filled Betty in on my patients, most particularly Amy Finley Pryor. I could tell Betty was unnerved at the prospect of taking care of the mayor's daughter. She was more than competent and had worked with polio patients before—she had more experience working with an iron lung than I had—"but I've never taken care of a mayor's kin before," she said with a shaky laugh.

"You'll be fine," I told her. I imagined that in the hours to come, she was going to be in better shape than I was. I was still unsure when I'd be able to talk with Vincent and even less sure what I would say.

He was waiting for me outside the door of the ward when I left. I saw Henry in the distance, standing by the Cadillac, chatting with Zeke, and I knew he expected to give me a ride home. I panicked, having both men in my vision at the same time.

"I can't talk now," I said to Vincent. "I'm getting a ride home." I nodded toward the clearing and the Cadillac and he followed my gaze in that direction.

"I have my car here and I can give you a ride home," he said, "wherever *home* is." I heard anger in his voice. "I'll drive you home *after* we've talked," he added.

"I . . ." I glanced in Henry's direction again. I didn't think he'd seen me. I held my chin a little higher. "That's my husband," I said. "I have to go."

I started to walk past him, but he put an arm out to stop me.

"You owe me a conversation, Tess," he said.

I dropped my chin, giving in. My knees were shivering. "All right," I said. "Let me tell him I have to stay."

He looked reluctant to let me go and I thought he didn't believe that I would return. He thought I was a liar, and I made up my mind right then that I would tell him the truth. All of it.

"I'll wait for you at the entrance to the stone building," he said. "My car is on the other side."

67

We were quiet as we circled the stone building, heading toward the area where cars were parked haphazardly among the trees. I recognized his old Ford and the sight of it nearly put tears in my eyes. How many hours I'd spent in that car!

He opened the door for me and I got in and rolled down the window. He did the same on his side and the evening breeze and sound of cicadas filled the car. He didn't say a word and I knew he was waiting for me to begin.

I leaned my back against the door and looked at him. Really looked. He wore a blue short-sleeved shirt I'd never seen before, but everything else about him was familiar. Familiar and beautiful.

"Did you know I was here?" I asked. "In Hickory?"

"I had no idea where you were," he said. "Gina refused to tell me anything."

"I made her promise."

"That letter you left me . . ." He shook his head. "My Tess? Marrying someone else? Cutting me out of her life without a word of explanation? I thought it was impossible. And of course, you left me no way to get in touch with you. I felt like I'd been punched in the gut." He looked out his side window into the woods. "When I finally got to Baltimore after your mother died, and I walked into your house and saw your engagement ring on that letter . . . I couldn't believe it. Neither could my parents. It was such a shock. Such a slap in the face to all three of us."

I winced. "I know," I murmured. "I hated hurting all of you."

"I was sure Gina knew who the man was and where you were, but she told me to forget you. Just move on. And once my mother accepted the fact that you were gone, she said the same thing. 'Tess isn't the girl we all thought she was,' she told me. But how was I supposed to forget about you?" he asked. "It was impossible. Then Gina stopped returning my calls, and I finally realized you'd shut me out of your life for good and I had no choice but to accept it and move on."

"I'm so sorry, Vincent." My heart skittered in my chest as I listened to him, imagining how he'd felt.

"I was worried about you at first," he said. "That behavior . . . it just wasn't like you. And then I got angry." He gripped the bottom of the steering wheel. He looked at me. "I'm still angry," he said.

"Of course you are. Probably not nearly as angry as I am at myself."

"I thought our relationship was strong enough to survive me being gone for those few months. I was so busy and maybe I took you for granted when I became a lazy letter writer."

"That wasn't it," I said. "It wasn't your fault in any way."

"Was it my talk about possibly moving to Chicago someday? I knew you didn't want that, and—"

"No, of course not." I reached over to touch his hand, but quickly pulled my fingers away. I had no right to touch him. "And anyhow, you ended up back in Baltimore," I said. "Gina told me."

"I like Chicago, but my mother got sick and I knew I had to stay close to home."

"Mimi was sick?"

"She still is. It's her heart. It's slowly giving out on her. She's a little weaker every day."

"Oh, Vincent." I wished I could wrap my arms around him. Comfort him. I kept my hands locked in my lap. "What about Pop?" I asked. "How is he?"

"Afraid of losing Mom," he said, shaking his head. "They've become little old people. Seems like it happened overnight." He turned to face me. "So, are you going to tell me what happened, Tess?" he asked. "Why are you here? Who did you marry?"

I bit my lip to stop its trembling. "I'm so ashamed," I said. He reached out his hand. Touched my lip with the tip of his finger. He might as well have been touching my breasts for the current of electricity it sent through me. He drew his hand away as though he suddenly remembered his anger, not his love.

"Tell me," he demanded.

I knotted my hands again in my lap. "I was upset with you being gone so long," I said. "I realize now I was being childish, but I was so used to having you close by and you seemed much more interested in your work than in me, and I was . . . I was being a big baby." I twisted my rings around and around on my finger. "Gina suggested we go to Washington one weekend and we did. We stayed in her aunt's tourist home. Two men were staying there and we all went out to dinner together." I watched his face. His expression was impassive and unreadable. "It wasn't like a date," I said. "We went out as acquaintances. I didn't feel as though I was cheating on you, doing that. But at dinner, I drank too much."

"You? When have you ever had too much to drink?"

"That night I did. Martinis. Too many. And when we got back to the tourist home . . ." I pressed my hands together so hard they hurt. "I don't even remember how it happened, actually," I said, "but Henry—that's his name—ended up in my room."

Vincent frowned. "Did he rape you?"

I shook my head. "I'm so ashamed," I said again.

"You willingly had relations with this man? This Henry?"

"Yes."

"Good Lord, Tess. I thought you were going to tell me he was so charming that you instantly fell in love with him. Not that you slept with him within hours of meeting him."

"I know. It was as though some other girl had taken over my mind and body."

"Gina was a terrible influence on you."

"Don't blame Gina. She slept alone. I made my own poor decisions that night."

"So you started seeing him and he swept you off your feet and—"

I shook my head. "No. I didn't see him again," I said. "I was mortified by what happened and felt so undeserving of you. So guilty. And then . . . here's the terrible part, Vincent. I discovered I was pregnant."

He caught his breath. "You have a child?"

I shook my head. I felt overwhelmed by the whole story. "When I realized I was pregnant by another man, I knew you and I were finished. I decided the only thing I could do would be to move away. I'd tell people I had a husband overseas. I'd start fresh. I didn't know where I was going to go but I knew I needed money. And I knew Henry had money—he owns a furniture factory here in Hickory. So I came down here to ask him for money. Instead, he asked me to marry him. I know it sounds crazy. We didn't know each other, but he wanted to take responsibility for the baby. To give him a name. And so I felt like saying yes was the best thing I could do for the baby. But a few months later . . ." I pressed my fists against my belly, feeling the loss all over again. "The baby came too early," I said. My voice broke. "It was terrible." I wouldn't tell him about the accident. About Lucy. It was too much to go into just then. This was enough. "I loved my baby," I said. "He was all I had, and then he was gone and I was trapped, married to a man I don't love. I'm *still* trapped."

We were both quiet for a moment, and when he spoke again, his voice was soft. "You made one mistake," he said. "You slept with someone else. I can hardly believe the Tess I knew would do that, but you did. But then you compounded it with a thousand other mistakes instead of just coming to me. Telling me what you did. Why didn't you do that, Tess? Didn't you trust me to forgive you?"

"How could you forgive me when I couldn't forgive myself?" I asked. "I ruined myself that night in Washington. I ruined myself for you. I knew you didn't believe in premarital sex and—"

"I think you had me on a pedestal," he interrupted me. "I'm nearly twenty-eight years old, and I decided long ago that I didn't want the life of a priest," he said. "Do you think I've been celibate all my adult life?"

I was shocked. "You . . . while we were together?"

He shook his head. "No, of course not. But there were a couple of girls before you and I were serious. And one since you and I . . . since you left." His new girlfriend. The nurse Gina had told me about.

"But," I said, "you and I never . . ." I let my sentence trail off.

"I knew your feelings about sex before marriage and respected them," he said. "I was willing to wait because it was so important to you. Or so I thought."

"I wish I'd known that about you," I said. "Maybe I wouldn't have felt so . . . dirty." I thought we'd known everything there was to know about each other but obviously that wasn't the case. "Gina said you're involved with someone now," I said, fighting the jealousy rising up in my chest. "Is it very serious?" The thought of him being with someone else, loving someone else, was excruciating.

"I'm not seeing her any longer," he said. "It was . . . casual."

"If I had come to you last fall," I said. "If I'd confessed what I'd done . . . how would you have reacted?"

"I would have been very upset, that's true," he said. "Though probably not as upset as I am right now. I'm angry at you for"—he shook his head—"for everything. For leaving the way you did, without a word. For not trusting me and our relationship."

"I didn't want you to know. I felt like I didn't deserve you."

"You're human. You made a human mistake. I would have forgiven you. I loved you."

I noticed the past tense. *I still love you,* I thought.

"So," he said. "This Henry. What is he like?"

Images flashed through my mind: Henry, early that afternoon, sitting on Jilly's bed, making her giggle. Henry, staying out all night with flimsy excuses as to where he'd been and what he'd been doing. Henry, holding me in his arms as I cried over our lost son. Hiding money in the armoire. Berating Reverend Sam for no good reason. "For the most part," I said, "he's a good man, but I don't think I can ever love him. We . . . there's no closeness there. No emotional closeness. No physical closeness."

He raised his eyebrows, and I shook my head.

"It's strange, Vincent. There was that one time in Washington, when we'd both had too much to drink. And when we got married, he never seemed attracted to me and I realized he only married me for the sake of the baby. And when I lost the baby, I thought we could get divorced, but he refused. Then I thought we could have our marriage voided, since we'd . . . there'd been no consummation, at least not since we'd been married. I asked him and he got angry about it. And that night he . . . suddenly there was. Consummation. As though he wanted to lock me into our marriage. But there's been no . . . no closeness since." My cheeks burned. "It's as though he both wants and doesn't want to be married to me."

"And what do *you* want?" His jaw was tight. I knew that tense, angry look. I'd missed every one of his expressions, even this one.

294 | Diane Chamberlain

"I want my old life back," I said. "I'd give anything to turn back the calendar. To be back with you the way we were. Looking forward to our wedding and our future together. I know I ruined it all. I'm so sorry."

He sighed. "Are we going to be able to work together?" he asked. "Will our past get in the way?"

"We can't let it," I said. "The work here is too important."

"I don't ever want to meet your husband," he said with a flare to his nostrils. "I'd knock his block off. He took advantage of you. What kind of scum picks up a girl in Washington and sleeps with her that same night?"

"What kind of girl does the same thing?" I gave my head a weary shake. "He's no more to blame for that night than I am," I said. "He did the honorable thing by marrying me, though I know he doesn't love me."

"Do you love him?

I shook my head. "I love *you*," I said, before I could stop myself.

He looked away from me. "A little too late for that, isn't it," he said, and I winced, wishing I'd kept my feelings to myself.

"Can you take me home now?" I asked. If I didn't get home soon, Henry would be full of questions.

He turned the key in the ignition without another word. It had grown dark and I guided him out of the site, through the woods and onto the main road. I hated for him to see where I lived. I didn't want him to think that I'd been attracted to Henry for his money.

"Where are you staying?" I asked as we neared my neighborhood.

"The Hotel Hickory," he said. "Strange environment," he added. "Eighty nurses, an epidemiologist, and me."

I nodded, trying to imagine how different the hotel must feel right now from when I'd stayed there with Henry.

I told him where to turn, and when he pulled up in front of the house in all its grandeur, the front porch lights warm and welcoming, he simply looked at me with a shake of his head.

"I'm sorry you're not happy, Tess," he said. "Truly, I am."

68

July 8, 1944

Oh Gina,

He's here. Vincent. I was in shock when I first saw him. We have to wear masks and gowns in the hospital and it wasn't until he was right in front of me that I recognized him. Those beautiful eyes. How I've missed them! How I've missed him!

I told him everything. He's angry with me for the way I handled what happened and I'm angry with myself. I told him I still love him. I didn't mean to say it, but the words slipped out. I don't think he loves me though. He's too angry and disappointed in me. He knows I'm not happy with Henry and that Henry won't give me a divorce. Even if he would, I don't think Vincent wants a future with me any longer.

I still think of leaving Henry to start living the two years apart that will be necessary for me to have a chance of getting a divorce, but even if I could figure out where to go, I can't possibly leave right now. The hospital needs me and, frankly, I need it. I love being a nurse so much, Gina. That's the one good thing in my life.

I'm so torn. On the one hand, I'm thrilled Vincent is here and that we're working together (which is what we always wanted to do!) and I don't ever want him to leave. Every time I see him across one of the wards or walking around on the grounds, my stomach does a flip. On the other hand, it's painful to know he could have been my husband and now I can't have him.

Thank you for getting that doll for the little girl I told you about. She adores it! And thank you for keeping my secret all these months, Gina. Vincent told me you did a good job of it!

Love,

Tess

69

"You're so quiet lately," Henry said as he drove me to the hospital the third morning after Vincent's arrival. "Are you all right?"

"Tired," I said. "The work is exhausting. But I love it," I added quickly, not wanting him to suggest I stop. "It's a good kind of tired."

To be honest, if I wasn't completely absorbed by a task I was doing, my mind was on Vincent. Whether by coincidence or design, he and I never seemed to be in the same place at the same time since our conversation in his car. Oh, we were often in the same *ward*—that was unavoidable. But I would be at one end, usually caring for Jilly or Carol Ann or behind the curtain with Amy Pryor, still in the iron lung, and he would be at the other. I had to fight with myself not to look at him. My greatest fear was that I would arrive at the hospital and he would have left. Gone home to Baltimore. I wouldn't be able to bear it, even though I couldn't have him or touch him or talk to him or even look into his eyes. I needed his presence. I needed him close by. I would be bereft if he left.

I thought we were both doing our best to avoid contact at the hospital. On his part, there was anger. I felt certain of that and I didn't blame him. On my part, there was shame and regret. My regret was strong enough to consume me, and outside of the hospital, I grew quiet and introspective, so much so that Henry was beginning to notice. I passed it off as fatigue every time he mentioned my strange mood.

The one good thing in my life was that my patients were doing well. Carol Ann's polio seemed to have stabilized and now it was just a matter of keeping her limbs from atrophying. And Jilly Johnson's fever was gone and, with it, most of her aches and pains. She was still very tired, though, sleeping for hours each day, but she waved to Honor through the window with more energy, and one morning I was able to help her walk over to the window, where I lifted her up to say hello to her overjoyed mother.

I was getting more comfortable working with the iron lung. Amy couldn't breathe for more than a few minutes on her own when I slid her out of the steel tube to bathe her and give her an enema, so it was often a three-person task. Grace would operate the handheld inflator to keep Amy breathing, while one of the other nurses rolled her onto her side and I washed her and got her bowels moving the only way possible. When I'd slip her back inside the lung, I'd rub moisturizer over her face and drop oil in her eyes because the tiny air leaks from the lung made them dry and scratchy. Amy could say a few whispered words and they were often "thank you." She was so sweet. Sometimes, caring for her, I wanted to cry. That would do no one any good. Instead, when I moved away from her to care for someone else, I'd say a prayer for her recovery. A prayer for her and her unborn baby.

On the fifth day after Vincent's arrival, I knew that something was different the moment I walked into the ward. The shift was changing and things were always a little chaotic during that time, but the charged atmosphere seemed like more than that. I glanced quickly at Carol Ann and Jilly and they looked fine. Jilly sat up in bed, coloring, and one of the Hickory volunteers was reading to Carol Ann. But I could see at a glance that we didn't have enough nurses.

"Sophie and Lillian are sick and we're swamped!" Grace said as she passed me with a bedpan. "Sophie just has a cold, but they think Lillian has polio."

"Oh no," I said, my hand to my chest. It was a risk we all took. I knew the odds. One out of every ten nurses in a polio ward was likely to contract the disease. We'd been lucky so far.

I tucked the news about Lillian into the back of my mind and joined in the fray, planning to help with Sophie's and Lillian's patients as well as my own. First, though, I needed to check on Amy Pryor. I approached her curtained cubicle just as Amy's night nurse, a very young woman I'd met only briefly the day before and whose name I couldn't remember, was coming out.

"She's been crying and complaining all night long," she griped loudly enough for Amy to hear. I honestly felt like hitting her, I was so angry at her attitude. All our nurses were dedicated and kind. She was the only sour apple in the bunch.

I spoke quietly. "You'd cry and complain too if you were stuck in an iron lung, away from your family and your soldier husband and your little boy, not knowing if you're going to survive," I said.

She was wise enough to look guilty. "It's just been a hard night." She brushed a strand of auburn hair under her cap. "I need to get back to the hotel and sleep."

"Did you give her her morning enema yet?" I asked, because I was beginning to doubt that Amy had been well cared for by this woman.

"No, she wouldn't eat so I figured nothing would be moving—"

"She wouldn't eat?" That was worrisome. Although swallowing could be challenging for her, Amy had so far been able to get down small amounts of soft food.

"She just shook her head when I tried. Very obstinate today."

I was going to hit her if I didn't get away from her, so I walked past her, slipping behind the curtain that surrounded Amy and the iron lung.

"Good morning, Amy," I said. I knew right away something was wrong. She was pale and perspiring. Her eyes were closed, her face in a frown, and she didn't react to my voice the way she usually did. I opened the side port and reached into the iron lung to take her pulse. It was rapid. Too rapid. I closed the port and moved to her head, bending over so that she'd be able to see me in the small mirror that was tilted at an angle above her face.

"Amy?" I said. "Can you hear me?"

She opened her eyes and moved her lips, trying to speak. I leaned my ear close.

"Stomachache," she whispered.

"You need that enema, don't you," I said. "I'll get it ready for you and then you'll feel a whole lot better."

I saw Grace applying lengths of wool to a little boy in the bed next to Jilly. I'd get everything ready and then have her come help me. Somehow the two of us would have to do what was usually a three-woman job.

I prepared the warm soapy water, filled the enema bag, and had the treatment tray ready to go before I opened the iron lung. I rolled out the bed, then poked my head through the opening in the curtain, trying to hurry Grace along. Grace held up a finger to let me know she'd be with me in a moment. I wasn't sure how long Amy would be able to breathe on her own today, since she seemed so agitated. I was beginning to roll her onto her side when I saw the bloody liquid on the sheet beneath her body. I caught my breath. Was she losing the baby? I quickly pushed away the blanket covering her legs and to my shock and horror, I saw that the baby was crowning. Amy wasn't losing her baby. Her baby was being born.

"Grace!" I shouted, not daring to move away from Amy long enough to open the curtain. "Get a doctor! Hurry!"

I had no sooner gotten the words out of my mouth than the little head slipped from Amy's body. My hands barely had time to move into place before the tiny infant turned to the side and slid into my palms, where it lay gray and lifeless. I could barely breathe myself.

Grace burst into the curtained enclosure. "Dr. Russo's coming," she said. "What's . . . Oh my God!"

"Get the inflator for Amy!" I said, knowing Amy wouldn't be able to breathe on her own much longer.

Grace grabbed the inflator from the bottom of the cart and raced to the head of the bed.

"He's not breathing." I tried to keep my voice calm for Amy's sake. I didn't know how much she understood of what was happening. Her body was completely still now that the baby had been born. I cleaned him with a towel, trying to rub life into him. I couldn't bear the limpness of him. I put him on his back next to Amy's legs, pulled off my mask, and bent over him, lifting his chin and covering his tiny nose and mouth with my mouth. I remembered from my training that I should only use the air from my cheeks, and I blew gently. I saw his pale chest rise and fall.

I was only vaguely aware of Vincent stepping into the cubicle as I continued trying to resuscitate the infant.

"He's not breathing," Grace said to him.

I felt both of them watch me for several seconds as I continued breathing for the baby, then Vincent spoke. "Stop for a moment, Tess," he said. "I think he's breathing on his own now."

I lifted my head and saw the baby's chest rise and fall without my help. Already, his skin was turning pink. I looked up at Vincent and let out my breath. I hadn't realized I'd been holding it. I felt overwhelmed by the miracle taking place in front of me.

Vincent took the baby from my hands, checking him over quickly. He cut the umbilical cord, examined Amy, delivered the placenta. I supposed it was all done with my help, but my tears were in the way and I moved on autopilot.

"Take this baby out of the ward," Vincent said to me. "Keep him warm and get him some oxygen and an ambulance to the nursery at the local hospital."

I nodded, wrapping the baby in a towel, my hands shaking with adrenaline. Then I carried the tiny bundle through the ward, stopping only long enough to let Amy see her little son before heading outside. In the stone building, I sat down next to one of the oxygen tanks and told the switchboard operator to call an ambulance. We had no masks tiny enough for a baby, so I held the cannula close to his nose. He could not have been more than five pounds but he was beautiful, with pale fuzz on his head and perfect features. I held him in my arms still swaddled in the towel. I held him the way I wished I could have held my own son. Held him and whispered to him and wondered how I was going to let go of him when the ambulance finally arrived.

70

The ambulance took Amy's baby away, and I sat down on the bench in front of the stone building. I was needed in the ward, but I needed time to myself even more. I heard the ward's screen door slam, and in a moment, I saw Vincent walking toward me. He pulled off his mask as he walked, then sat down next to me. For a few seconds, neither of us said a word. His presence felt like such a gift.

"Do you remember," he said finally, "when I was about sixteen and you were about twelve, and we were sitting on my stoop eating watermelon and seeing who could spit the seeds the farthest, and that little girl from down the street rode by on her rollerskates?"

I nodded. "Beatrice, her name was," I said. I knew where he was going with this.

"Beatrice. That's right. How old was she? Five?"

"I think so."

"And she fell right in front of us."

"Probably caught her skate on a watermelon seed." I smiled.

"Probably," he said. "I used to think about that day. Whenever you and I would talk about eventually working together in our medical office, I'd think about that little girl and how it felt to help someone side by side with you. I remember looking down at your twelve-year-old hands. You were calmly pressing my handkerchief against that bloody cut on her forehead, while I was trying to hold her broken arm in place."

"I remember," I said. He'd been more of a big brother to me then than someone I would eventually fall in love with.

"Those few minutes with Amy and the baby brought that all back to me." His voice was quiet and calm. His hands rested on his thighs. "That was our dream, wasn't it?" he asked, though it wasn't really a question. "Working together someday?"

Among other dreams, I thought. My throat felt too tight to speak.

"You saved that baby's life, Tess," he said. "You performed like a nurse with twenty years' experience."

My eyes burned. I tried to say "thank you," but again, the words caught in my throat. They came out in a whisper I wasn't sure he heard.

"I just wanted to tell you that," he said, getting to his feet.

I grabbed his hand, not wanting him to leave, then instantly let go, afraid someone might see us. I looked up at him.

"Every day, I come to work terrified you won't be here," I confessed.

He sat down again and took my hand, holding it between both of his. I savored the warmth of his palms. His fingers. Their shape. The smooth skin. So familiar to me. I pressed my palm against his.

"I keep thinking I should leave," he admitted. "There are other doctors who could take my place, and it frankly hurts like hell to be this close to you and know you're married to someone else." He squeezed my hand. "I don't want to leave though. Now that I've finally found you . . . and I can see you're not happy. You got yourself in a bind. I'm angry you didn't tell me. Didn't trust me enough to come to me."

"How could I?" I said. "How could I admit to you that I'd slept with a stranger? That I was carrying his baby? What would you have done? Would you still have married me?"

"I would have had to do some soul-searching," he admitted. "But I know you, Tess. Or at least, I knew you then. I knew what a good person you were. I knew that one mistake didn't define you. Of course I still would have married you."

A truck drove into the clearing not far from where we sat. I pulled my hand from between his at the same moment he rose to his feet again. He looked down at me.

"Are you ready to come back in?" he asked. "Things are crazy in there today."

He would have married me, in spite of my infidelity, in spite of the fact that I was carrying another man's child. I threw it all away. I lost the chance to be his wife. I lost the chance at happiness. I wondered if it was possible to find it again.

"Yes," I said, standing up. "I'm ready."

71

When our shifts ended that evening, Grace and I walked outside to see a small crowd of people in the clearing. A car bearing the radio station logo WHKY was parked in the scrubby grass nearby.

"What's that all about?" Grace asked, pointing.

As we walked closer, we could see that the group stood in a semicircle around a man holding a microphone. Henry was there, and he smiled when he spotted me and waved us over. When we reached the outskirts of the circle of people, I realized that the man with the microphone—a reporter?—was interviewing Vincent. Next to him stood Mayor Finley and his wife, Marjorie.

Marjorie spotted us and let out a squeal. She grabbed me, pulling me into a hug. "Thank you!" she said, then turned to Grace. "Thank you both so much!"

"These must be the nurses," the reporter said, grinning at us, and only then did I realize WHKY was there because of what had happened that morning with Amy Pryor and her baby.

Vincent smiled. "Yes, these are the nurses," he said. "Tess DeMello."

"Kraft," I corrected him.

"Tess Kraft," he said. "And Grace Wilding. All the nurses here are excellent," he added, "but Amy Pryor and her son are alive today because of these two women. Grace operated a handheld inflator to help Amy breathe while outside of the iron lung, and Tess delivered the baby on her own. The baby wasn't breathing and Tess performed artificial respiration—what we call mouth-to-mouth insufflation—on him, which required a great deal of care and skill."

"Mrs. Kraft," the reporter said to me, "can you tell us more about what happened?"

I explained what had taken place the best I could without making the whole event sound too frightening for Amy's parents to hear. The man next to Henry threw a question my way and I noticed he was jotting my answer down on a notepad. A newspaper reporter, I guessed, and then I realized he was not the only one. A couple of men and one woman were taking notes. Another man was snapping pictures. The story was bigger than I'd imagined.

"Did you have special training to know how to save the baby?" one of the reporters called out.

"Only in theory," I said. "Frankly, I never thought I'd have to put what I learned into practice."

"How does it feel to save a life?" the female reporter asked.

I was surprised when I teared up at the question. I'd saved a life. No doubt about it. "I'm just glad Grace and I were there at the right moment," I said, my voice thick.

I felt Vincent's hand on my back. "She's being modest," he said. "I've known Tess all my life, and I always knew she'd be an exceptional nurse. What she did took a clear head, quick action, and a lot of courage. She and Grace really saved the day today."

Henry and I were quiet as we walked toward the Cadillac after the meeting with the reporters. He had his hand on my elbow, and I felt affection in the touch. He smiled at me as we got into the car. "I'm really proud of you," he said.

I thought it might have been the kindest thing he'd ever said to me.

"Thank you."

He started the car and began driving out of the clearing and we opened our windows to let in the evening air.

Neither of us spoke for a few minutes. Then he glanced at me. "So, what did that doctor mean when he said he'd known you all his life?" he asked. "He called you Tess DeMello before you corrected him."

I hesitated, unsure how much to say. "It's a coincidence that he's here," I said finally. "His family lived next door to my family in Baltimore."

"Did he know you were here? In Hickory?"

"He had no idea," I said. "We were shocked to see each other when he arrived at the hospital last week."

The air felt heavy between us. I licked my lips, unsure whether to tell him more. Finally, he spoke.

"He looked at you like he cares about you." He glanced at me.

"He's the man I was engaged to," I said, as simply as if I'd said the weather was balmy.

Henry didn't respond right away and I bit my lip, waiting. After a moment, he pressed on the brake and gradually steered the car to the side of the road. He turned off the engine, then shifted in the seat until he was looking at me.

"Why didn't you tell me this as soon as he showed up?"

"I saw no reason to," I said.

"And he didn't know you were here?"

I shook my head. "He didn't come looking for me, if that's what you mean," I said. "He had no idea where I was. I wanted it that way."

I felt Henry's gaze on me. I couldn't meet his eyes.

"Why didn't you marry him, Tess?" he asked.

"Why do you think?" I asked. "I got pregnant with your baby. I didn't think he would still accept me if I told him I cheated on him with you and that I was pregnant, so I never told him. I just left. And then you asked me to marry you, and . . ."

"He knows you're married to me?"

"Yes. Of course. I explained everything to him."

"And . . . ?"

"There is no 'and.' I'm married to you, not to him. He and I both understand that, so you have nothing to be concerned about."

Henry looked through the windshield at the darkening sky, his right hand rubbing his left. "I thought I was doing something good, asking you to marry me."

"You were," I said. "And if Andrew had lived, everything would be so different."

"Are you still in love with him? The doctor?"

There seemed to be no point in lying. "I love him with all my heart," I admitted, my voice again growing thick.

Henry shut his eyes. Leaned back in the seat. I couldn't tell if he was angry or sad or indifferent. I waited. Finally, he opened his eyes and looked at me.

"This is a painful story, Tess," he said. "I'm very sorry. Your tragedy was my salvation."

"*How?*" I asked, utterly perplexed. "How is our marriage your salvation? I don't understand."

He reached his hand out to run his fingers down my cheek. His smile was sad. "You're very dear to me," he said, and then he started the car and I knew that was all the explanation I would get from him tonight.

72

Ruth was already at the dining-room table when Henry and I came down to breakfast the following morning. The front page of the *Hickory Daily Record* was spread flat on the table in front of her, and next to the articles about the war, I could read the headline: NURSES SAVE THE LIVES OF MAYOR FINLEY'S DAUGHTER AND GRANDSON.

"So," Henry said to his mother as he placed his napkin in his lap, "what do you think of your daughter-in-law now?"

I wanted to hush him—he was baiting her terribly—but I couldn't help but smile. All last evening, Henry had treated me kindly. Even tenderly, rubbing my shoulders, stiff from my day's work. Of course he didn't make love to me or even kiss me, but he told me repeatedly how proud he was of me. How grateful he was that I'd agreed to marry him. I would never understand my husband.

Ruth looked up from the paper. "You actually put your mouth on that baby's mouth?" she asked. "Wasn't it covered in all sorts of . . ." She shuddered.

"I cleaned him off quickly," I said. "And I blew into his nose, not his mouth. I held his mouth closed."

Ruth tapped the article with her fingertip. "How did you know what to do?" she asked. "How did you know how to deliver a baby?"

I shrugged. "I'm a nurse," I said, a bit of pride creeping into my voice. "That's what nurses do. Though to be perfectly honest, this baby really delivered himself."

Ruth let out a worried sigh. "So now you have the polio germs inside you, don't you?" she asked.

"It doesn't work that way," I said. "The baby doesn't have polio and probably won't get it. The virus doesn't cross the placenta."

"*Hush.*" Ruth shuddered. "This is *not* a conversation for the breakfast table."

Hattie brought us plates of eggs and grits and bowls of blackberries. "You famous now," she said to me. "Can I touch you?" She poked my shoulder with her finger and I laughed. "How's my little Jilly doin'?" she asked.

"She's doing very well, Hattie," I said. "I wouldn't be surprised if she could go home today or tomorrow."

"Praise Jesus," Hattie said as she headed back toward the kitchen. "Adora don't know what to do with herself without her baby girl in the house."

"Well," Ruth said to me as Henry and I began to eat, "I received a phone call this morning from Madge Pilcher. She wants you to join us at our book club meeting tonight."

"I wish I could," I said, "but I know I'll be too tired after working all day. Please thank her for the invitation." I kept my smile to myself. Was I finally to be accepted by Ruth's social group? I was not a bad person. I could still hold my head high. How was it that I'd forgotten that about myself?

"I'll drop you off at the hospital," Henry said between sips of his coffee, "but then I need to get to the factory. The phone isn't working for some reason and I have to get that taken care of, but I'll try to get back to the hospital later today."

"Oh *my*," Ruth said suddenly, her finger marking an article on the front page. She looked up at us. "*Life* magazine is coming to the polio hospital tomorrow! Did you know?"

Henry and I shook our heads. "They'll probably want to interview my marvelous wife," Henry said.

"Oh my gosh, I hope not," I said, overwhelmed by the thought.

"It says here people are calling Hickory 'polio city' now," Ruth said, looking at the article. "It says people roll up their car windows and cover their noses with handkerchiefs when they drive through town."

"What nonsense." Henry got to his feet. "You ready, Tess?"

There was excitement at the hospital when Henry dropped me off that morning. People were still talking about the mayor's grandson, who was by all reports doing very well in the hospital. Even more exciting to everyone, though, was the upcoming visit from *Life* magazine. Sometimes in the throes of our work, we forgot what Hickory had accomplished: the creation of a fully functioning hospital in fifty-four hours. We now had ninety-two patients, an exhausted but determined staff of nurses and doctors, and dozens of cooks, custodians, maintenance men, and community volunteers. And we were saving lives every single day.

Amy Pryor was far more comfortable now that she was no longer pregnant, and although the compressions of the iron lung made it hard for her to talk, she was able to ask me about her baby. As I washed her face and combed her hair, I told her every detail I could recall about him, choking up a little, remembering how I felt as I held him in my arms while waiting for the ambulance.

"He's perfection," I said. "I can't wait until you can hold him yourself."

"Neither can I," she whispered.

Jilly was able to go home that afternoon, and I was relieved by the timing. A damp, dark ward was to be opened in the basement of the stone building the following day, and our colored patients were going to be moved into it. I would have hated to see Jilly leave my ward and my care. I had to pry her doll away from her that morning. Toys could not go home with the children from the hospital, but as I'd promised Honor, I scrubbed the doll clean with disinfectant and dressed it in a new jumper and blouse I'd found at a toy store. I gave it back to Jilly once she left the building. She was still a bit weak, but she walked out of the hospital on her own two healthy legs into Honor's embrace. Honor lifted her up and covered her face with kisses until Jilly protested, pleading to be let down.

One of the volunteers scrubbed Jilly's bed and it was quickly filled by another patient. The epidemic showed no signs of abating.

My path crossed with Vincent's only a few times that day, and each time I felt that pull, that longing that was never going to leave me. Just being able to glimpse him occasionally over the course of the day fed my soul. Of course I wanted the polio epidemic to end. It *needed* to end and it *would* end, but then Vincent would be gone. I dreaded the day he would leave and I would have to face the rest of my life without him.

Henry sent a note to me, delivered from the factory by that same young man, Mickey, who had given me a ride to the train station so long ago. The one who'd told me about Violet's connection to Henry. He hadn't given me as much of a warning as I'd needed, I thought. *Things have gone to the dogs in my absence here,* Henry wrote in the note. *The phone still isn't working. I need to stay late tonight. Let Mama know.*

I got a ride home from one of the other nurses that evening. The house was dark and I remembered that Ruth was at a book club meeting. Hattie had left some chicken and collards for me in the refrigerator, and I was eating at the kitchen table when the doorbell rang.

The sun was beginning to set when I opened the door, the sky a dewy pink through the trees. A policeman stood on the step, hat in his hand, and it took me a moment to recognize him as Teddy Wright. I didn't like Teddy. I'd never forget how coolly he'd treated me at the police station after the accident or how he'd seemed to follow me in his police car when I walked into town. Seeing him gave me a sour taste in my mouth.

"Good evening, Mrs. Kraft," he said.

"Hello, Teddy." I heard the chill in my voice.

"Is Hank home?"

"No, he's not."

"Is he at the factory?"

"I don't know where he is tonight," I said. I knew he was at the factory, but I felt obstinate. I didn't feel like helping Teddy out. "Can I take a message for him?"

He looked past me as though he thought I might be lying. "You got a pen and paper? I can write it for him. And an envelope."

I hesitated before asking him in. "Follow me," I said as I headed toward the library.

He hung back in the doorway of the library, taking in the walls of books as I opened the desk drawer where Henry kept his stationery. I pulled out a sheet of paper and an envelope and invited him to sit at the desk.

I waited as he perched on the edge of the chair and jotted a note. He sealed it in the envelope and wrote "Hank Kraft" on the front, underlining the name several times to drive the point home that the note was for Henry and no one else.

"You got some of that sealing wax?" he asked.

"Sealing wax?" I repeated. "No. Sorry."

"This is for his eyes only," he said, handing the envelope to me.

"Of course," I said, then added, "You still don't think much of me, do you?"

"I know you saved that baby," he said. "That's one point in your favor."

I didn't know what to say to that.

"Just be sure you give that envelope to Hank right quick," he said, and he let himself out of the house. From the library, I watched him get into his police car. He turned the car around in our driveway and took off toward town.

I looked at the envelope in my hand. What was so important? I wondered. And why couldn't Teddy just tell me his message and let me pass it along to Henry myself? My curiosity got the better of me and I knew I was going to read the note. I could steam the envelope open over a tea-kettle, although I wondered if that worked in real life as well as in fiction. I was certain to ruin the envelope, at the very least. So I would open the note the usual way and then put it in a new envelope. Simple. I used the letter opener on Henry's blotter to slice the envelope, then pulled out the sheet of paper, flattening it on the desk. I lit a cigarette, then sat down to read the note.

> *Hank, the chief got some questions about you from the OPA today. The chief was in the dark, I could tell. I don't think they know anything about Lucy helping. I didn't let on, just listened and acted like I don't know anything. They might have been talking about getting a search warrant. The chief told them they were barking up the wrong tree. Just wanted to let you know. I'll keep my ears open. Teddy*

I must have stared at the note for five full minutes as I tried to make sense of it. What was the OPA? Did it have something to do with the factory? And what had Lucy been helping with?

I put the note in a new envelope and simply left Henry's name off the front. Suddenly exhausted, I climbed the stairs, quickly washed and changed into my nightgown, then fell into bed, leaving the note on the nightstand. I heard the front door open a while later and listened to the footsteps downstairs long enough to know it was Ruth and not Henry. I rolled onto my side and the moonlight reflected off the mirror of the armoire. I sat up with a gasp. Did the money in the armoire have something to do with Teddy's note?

I got out of bed quietly, not wanting Ruth to hear the creaking of the floorboards, and turned on the night table lamp. I opened the beautiful carved mirrored door of the armoire and was greeted by the soap-and-pipe scent of Henry's clothes. I spotted the leather tab on one side of the false bottom and lifted it gingerly. The bundled money was still there. As a matter of fact, I was certain there was quite a bit more of it than there had been. On top of the bundles lay three large manila envelopes, identical to the envelope Lucy had wanted to deliver to someone across the river and the empty envelopes I'd seen in his desk drawer.

Each of the envelopes had a white label affixed to the front, and each label had two or three letters on it. Initials? I lifted the top envelope and sat down on the edge of the bed, listening for Henry's car in the driveway. This label bore the initials R.T.D., written in Henry's hand. I turned it over and saw that it was only closed with a clasp. I pinched the two sides of the clasp together, lifted the flap, and slipped my hand inside to withdraw the contents. Gasoline rationing coupons, three booklets of them. Class C. And a red Class C sticker for a car. I knew what Class C stickers were. Most people had A stickers, allowing them three gallons of gasoline a week. Some people, traveling salesmen for instance, had B stickers entitling them to eight gallons a week. Class C was reserved for doctors, the police, and anyone else who shouldn't have their gasoline limited. I stared at the coupons. Where had Henry gotten these and what was he doing with them? He'd told me something about factory truck drivers being entitled to more gas. Maybe that was it? Maybe R.T.D. was one of Kraft Fine Furniture's truck drivers? And what exactly was Teddy warning Henry about? My head hurt from trying to figure it out. There was only one person who could explain it all to me, and I was married to him.

It must have been close to three in the morning by the time I finally fell asleep and Henry still wasn't home. I'd lain awake, feeling alternately angry at him and worried about him. When I woke at six-thirty, he was getting out of his bed, running his fingers through his hair. I was instantly awake and I sat up in bed and reached for the envelope from Teddy on the nightstand.

"Teddy dropped this off for you last night," I said, holding it out to him.

Henry frowned as he took the envelope from me. "Teddy Wright?" he asked. "From the police?"

"Yes."

I watched him tear open the envelope. His frown deepened as he read the note. He folded it up again and put it back in the envelope.

"What is it?" I asked innocently.

He shook his head, getting to his feet. "Nothing important," he said. "I can drop you off at the hospital this morning, but then I'd better get back to the factory."

"Is it something personal in the note or police business?" I prompted. "Teddy seemed pretty anxious for you to get it."

"I told you, it's nothing." He folded the envelope and slipped it in the pocket of his pajama top as he walked toward the door. "I'll use the shower first, if you don't mind."

"I know about the armoire." I blurted the words out and he turned to me.

"What are you talking about? What about the armoire?"

"The money. I saw it weeks ago. I saw that leather tab and thought something had gotten stuck in the crevice between the floor and the back of the armoire. I pulled on the tab and the bottom came up and I saw the money." I stopped briefly for breath. "Why do you have it stashed away like that?"

He said nothing for so long that I was sure he was going to simply turn away from me without an explanation. That was so like Henry whenever I asked a question he didn't want to answer. Instead, he sighed and sat down on the bed again. Our beds were so close together that our knees nearly touched.

"Look," he said. "I believe in having a nest egg. You know what happened in '29, when the stock market crashed? That affected my father and a million men like him. I just feel better having some of my money in cash here at home."

"What's in those manila envelopes on top of the cash?" I asked.

He gave me a tired look. "This is business, Tess," he said. "It doesn't concern you and please don't worry about it. It has nothing to do with the police or the note from Teddy and you're just going to work yourself into a tizzy. Trust me, all right?" He gave me a completely sincere look, so sincere that I nearly believed him. But I was utterly perplexed. He was a wealthy man. He had no need I could think of for this extra cash. Our new house was already paid for and there was plenty of money for furnishings and décor.

He leaned toward me and touched my cheek tenderly. "I'm sorry you've been worrying about this," he said. "There's no need to. Everything is fine."

73

Henry and I ate dinner with Ruth that night and she was full of questions about *Life* magazine's visit to the hospital, which had taken place that day. It was one of the more animated meals the three of us had had together. I might have enjoyed it if not for the fact that I was so filled with longing for Vincent I could barely eat.

The reporter and the photographers from *Life* had been low-key and respectful, although it seemed as though every time I turned around, one of them was standing behind me. They took pictures in the wards and on the grounds, the reporter marveling over what had been accomplished in such a short time. After the first couple of hours of having them around, the staff began to relax and we barely noticed the click of the camera and the pop of the flashbulbs. I knew I was in a few pictures, although whether any of them would be used in the article was anyone's guess. I did wonder about the photographs taken in the admissions tent in the afternoon, when Vincent and I had been working together. I wore my surgical cap, mask, and gown, and even though my eyes were the only part of me that was visible, did they give me away? Was it obvious how in love I was with the doctor by my side?

After dinner, I wasn't surprised when Henry said he was going back to the factory. "I've spent too much time at the hospital," he said. "Everything at the factory is going to seed. The phone's still not working properly. The boiler's giving Zeke fits and he ordered a new igniter for it. We're so short staffed, we're way behind on our orders."

I went to bed around nine, which was early for me. I wanted time alone to remember how it felt to work with Vincent in the admissions tent. When I was near him, his presence felt like something tangible, something I could put in a little box and carry around with me. A few times during the day, I caught him looking at me and each time our eyes met, he would smile. A couple of times, he touched my arm. My shoulder. This was all I could ever have of him, these stolen touches. Was he thinking about me right now? Was he too aching with the knowledge that we could never be together?

I'd drifted off to sleep when I was awakened by the ringing of the telephone. I got out of bed, pulled on my robe, and headed downstairs, wondering who would be calling us this late. The hallway was dark as I walked toward the kitchen, and I heard no sound from Ruth's room as I passed her door.

In the kitchen, I picked up the receiver. "Hello?"

"Tess? This is Susannah Bowman."

"Hello, Susannah," I said, perplexed by the hour of the call. Susannah was the nighttime nursing supervisor at the hospital.

"We're in a bind," she said. "Three night nurses are out sick, and five new patients are checking in. I know you worked a full day today, but is there a chance you could come back for a few hours?"

"Of course," I said, without hesitating. I was worried about those sick nurses though. I hoped none of them had polio symptoms. "I'll get there as soon as I can," I told her.

"Hurry, honey," Susannah said. "We're desperate."

I got off the phone with Susannah, then dialed the number for the factory to see if Henry could give me a ride to the hospital, but there was no ringing on the other end of the line. Just dead air. I remembered: the phone at the factory still wasn't working. I'd call a taxi to take me to the hospital. I could ask the driver to stop for a moment at the factory so I could let Henry know where I was going.

Upstairs, I quickly pulled on my uniform and stockings, taking only a few seconds to run a comb through my wild hair and pin it up in a bun. The taxi honked its horn out front as I made my way downstairs, and by the time I settled myself into the backseat I was winded.

"I need to go out to the polio hospital," I said, "but first we have to stop at the Kraft Furniture factory."

"The factory at this hour?" The driver looked at me in his rearview mirror. I couldn't make out his face well in the darkness, but the tone of his voice told me he thought I was a bit crazy.

"Yes," I said. "My husband is working there late tonight."

Neither of us spoke on the drive to the factory and I used the time to catch my breath after racing around to get ready.

"Don't look like nobody's home, ma'am," the driver said as we pulled up in front of the factory.

He was right. From where I sat, the enormous factory looked completely dark, but the small parking lot was illuminated by a street lamp, and I could see Henry's car parked next to Zeke's truck.

"He's here," I said, reaching for the door handle. "I'll just be a few minutes."

The front door was unlocked, as I expected it to be, and I walked into the foyer. The darkness felt overwhelming to me and I had to feel my way to the door that led to the stairwell. At the top of the stairs, I walked into the hall. There was no light coming through the crack at the bottom of Henry's office door, and I guessed he was somewhere else in the factory. How would I find him? Zeke's room was on my right, and a faint light came from beneath his door. He would probably know where Henry was.

I knocked on Zeke's door. At first there was no response and I worried I was waking him up. I knocked a bit more assertively.

"Yes?" It was Henry's voice, and I imagined Zeke was letting him nap on his sofa.

"It's me, Henry," I said, pushing open the door. The light from a lamp on the dresser illuminated the room with a soft glow and it took my eyes half a second to understand what I was seeing. They were covered only by a sheet in Zeke's bed, white and brown skin, arms wrapped around each other. Henry and Honor.

74

Honor sat up quickly, gasping. Turning away from me, she held the sheet to her chest, her free hand over her cheek as she tried to hide her face. As though I might possibly not recognize her. Henry stared at me, speechless, his face a pale blank slate. I shut my eyes, willing the scene in front of me to go away. Backing out of the room, I shut the door quietly. I stood in the hall, my heart pounding and my fists clenched at my sides. My fury was matched only by my humiliation. All those nights Henry came home late—or didn't come home at all. His inability—or unwillingness—to make love to me. To kiss me or even touch me. When all the while he'd been sleeping with Honor? I felt so foolish for how I'd helped her see Jilly in the hospital. How kind I'd been to her, when all the while, she must have been laughing at me behind my back.

I turned and ran to the stairwell and pounded down the steps to the foyer. Pushing open the exterior door, I ran out into the dark night heading toward the taxi, my steps fueled by my anger. I had to get away from the scene in Zeke's room.

"Tess!" Henry called from behind me.

I ignored him and kept running. I heard his footsteps, rapid, growing closer. In a moment, he grabbed my arm.

"Wait!" he said as I twisted away from him. He caught my arm again and this time I turned to face him. I tried to hit him, stupidly, ineffectually, both my arms flailing at him, my handbag jerking through the air. He grabbed my wrists, holding them at my sides.

"I hate you!" I shouted, not caring if the taxi driver could hear me. Not caring if *anyone* could hear. "I hate everything about you!"

"Tess, please," he said, his voice annoyingly calm. "Please come back inside. We need to talk. We—"

"I'm not going back in there!" I pulled my wrists free of his grasp. "I'm going to the hospital," I said, reaching for the door of the taxi. "They're down three nurses." I tried to yank the door open, but Henry leaned his weight against it.

"I'll take you," he said, then repeated, "We need to talk, Tess."

I hesitated, my heart still pounding with fury. There was only one thing we needed to talk about as far as I was concerned: divorce.

"Pay the driver," I said, turning around, and I headed for the parking lot and his car.

He caught up with me in the parking lot as I reached the passenger side door of his car. Leaning past me, he opened the door for me, and without a word, I slid onto the seat.

He got in on the driver's side and put the key in the ignition, but before he turned it, he looked over at me. The overhead light in the parking lot caught his pallor. The skin around his sad eyes looked bruised. "I'm sorry," he said.

"Just drive," I said.

He turned the key and headed for the exit of the parking lot.

"I sometimes thought you might be having an affair," I said, as he pulled onto the empty street, "but *Honor*?"

"I know it must be a shock," he said, "but—"

"You've been using me." I tightened my fists around the strap of my handbag. "No one would suspect you of a relationship with Honor if you were married."

He looked through the windshield into the darkness ahead of us. "I also wanted to give your baby . . . our baby . . . a name," he said. "I admit it though. When you walked into my office that day, I felt like my prayers had been answered."

"How does Violet fit into the picture?" I asked.

He concentrated on turning the corner and I thought he was glad to be able to put off answering the question for a moment. "I would have married her if you hadn't come along," he admitted finally. "I was getting up the nerve to propose to her, although I was frankly dreading it. I knew she'd want a big wedding. All the hoopla that went with getting married. It would have been such a charade."

"She would have been your cover then instead of me."

He drew in a breath. Let it out. "Yes," he said finally.

"That was always your intention," I snapped. "To marry someone— *anyone*—to prevent people from knowing about you and Honor."

"I suppose." He turned another corner. "But also, I needed a wife," he said. "It's hard to get by in this town as a single man. It looks . . . odd. And the woman I love, I could never marry."

"I'm a *human being*, Henry," I said. "You can't use someone this way because you happen to need a wife. It's just wrong."

He didn't respond. His eyes were fixed on the road.

"How long have you and Honor . . . ?" I let the sentence trail off.

"Nearly my whole life," he said. "I told you that she and Zeke and I were good friends when we were children, and then when we got to be teenagers, I started seeing her differently. I thought she was so beautiful." He looked ahead of us into the dark night again and his voice had taken on an almost dreamy quality. "We always knew we were playing with fire, but . . . I love her, Tess." He glanced at me. "The way you love that doctor. I love her and I can't have her."

His comparison to my relationship with Vincent made my heart contract. "What about the man who fathered her children? Del?" I asked.

He seemed to focus hard on the street ahead of us. "Del is *Honor's* cover," he said finally. "And she's his. Del is not interested in women."

"You mean, women other than Honor? Or do you mean . . ." I began to understand. "Is he a homosexual?"

He nodded.

"But he had children with her!"

"No," he said. "He didn't."

I frowned, then suddenly remembered Henry sitting with Jilly in the hospital. I thought it was so kind of him, his tender interaction with Honor's daughter. I pressed my hands to my cheeks, stunned. "Jilly is yours?" I whispered.

He nodded. "Yes," he said softly.

"Both of them? Butchie too?"

He nodded slowly. "Yes. He was my son," he said, his voice breaking on the word "son." "Though of course I could never acknowledge him as such."

For a moment, I forgot my own pain, his was so palpable. I felt the depth of his dilemma. To love someone you couldn't possibly marry. To have children you could never acknowledge. Children you could never safely love except in private. To lose one of those children and be unable to publicly grieve for him. I touched his shoulder.

"I'm sorry," I said. In the soft light from a street lamp, I saw the glistening of tears on his cheeks.

"Butchie's real name was Walter," he said.

A chill ran up my spine. "My God," I said.

"It has to be a coincidence."

"Not a coincidence," I said. "Reverend Sam has a gift. I don't understand it, but you can't deny it."

"It was such a shock when he said his name."

"Who knows about you and Honor?" I asked. "I assume Zeke knows. Where was he tonight?"

"Asleep on the couch in my office." He turned onto the dark, rutted road that would take us through the woods to the hospital. "And yes, he knows," he said. "Lucy knew, and Del, of course."

I thought of how loving Lucy had been to that whole family. The children were her niece and nephew.

"Gaston." Henry sighed. "He knew. And Adora. Poor Adora."

We bounced over something—a rut or a tree root—and I put my hand on the dashboard to steady myself. "What about your mother?" I asked.

"Good Lord, no," he said, as he pulled into the clearing near the ever-expanding hospital. He parked between a couple of other cars, but didn't turn off the engine. "My mother thinks I'm queer, Tess," he said, turning toward me. "Haven't you figured that out? That's why she insists we stay married. She can prove to all her friends that I'm some sort of he-man if I'm married. Of course, she was hoping I'd marry Violet, but I'm twenty-eight years old. She'd accept anyone as my wife at this point."

"My God," I said. This was all too much to take in.

Henry nodded toward the hospital. "Go on in," he said. "I need to get back to the factory. I just ran out on Honor. She's got to be terrified."

And well she should be, I thought, as I got out of the car. For the first time in my miserable marriage, I had the upper hand. I had the power to ruin Henry's life. Honor's life. And Ruth's. I would do whatever it took to get out of this marriage. Would Vincent still want me once I was a divorcee? I wasn't sure. Right then, all I knew was that I wanted my life back.

75

The new patients at the hospital absorbed all my time and attention for the next few hours, and I was glad of the distraction from my own life. I spent most of the night in the damp and musty basement ward that had been opened for the colored patients, and I was glad once again that Jilly had been able to go home. *Jilly.* Henry's daughter. She would probably never be able to know who her real father was. I put the thought out of my mind and focused on my work.

I didn't get home until dawn. Henry's bed was still neatly made and I knew he hadn't come home at all during the night. Exhausted, I climbed into my own bed and fell into a deep sleep. I woke up around noon, glad to discover that Ruth was out and I wouldn't have to make conversation with her over lunch. I had no appetite, but forced myself to eat the grilled cheese sandwich Hattie made for me before I called a taxi to take me back to the hospital.

When the taxi dropped me off near one of the new wards that were under construction, I spotted Henry installing a screen in one of the windows. He walked quickly toward the taxi, pulling his wallet from his pants pocket, and he paid for the taxi before I even had my handbag open. I had the feeling he was going to do all he could to keep me happy and my mouth shut.

"Are you all right?" he asked quietly. I saw the anxiety in his face. The tight muscles around his jaw. The plea in his eyes.

"We can talk later," I said, walking past him toward the main building.

In spite of my anger, I felt sorry for him, yet I wanted to make him worry. Make him stew over what I might do. I liked my new power. I only had to decide how to use it.

That night, we lay in our separate beds staring at the moonlight on the ceiling, talking. He told me what it had been like, falling in love with Honor when he was a teenager, and the terror that came with emotions that should have been joyful and pure.

"We weren't lovers back then, of course," he said. "We were just two kids who couldn't wait to see each other when we got home from our schools. Even though she lived in the cottage with Adora and Zeke, right here on our property, my mother kept an eagle eye on us once I was thirteen or fourteen. Back then, the woods over by the church hadn't been developed yet, so we'd go there. We'd walk over separately, of course, being careful no one could see us. She'd bring some of Adora's cookies." I heard the smile in his voice as he reminisced. "It didn't matter what time of year it was, we'd meet. And all we did for years, it seemed, was talk. We imagined a future that could never be." His voice had grown wistful.

"When did you finally . . . ?" I let my voice trail off.

"Not till I was in college. I lived at home . . . I intentionally went to Lenoir-Rhyne so I could stay home. My parents thought it was so I could help out at the factory. Learn the business. But it was about Honor. It was always about Honor." He stopped speaking for a moment, sounding choked up, and I wondered what he was seeing in his imagination. I was surprised that I didn't feel anger toward him as I listened. I thought I should. I *wanted* to. But instead, I felt sympathy for him.

"She was still in high school," he continued. "Her senior year. Still living in the cottage with Adora. My father had built that room at the factory for nights when he needed to work late. It wasn't as nice as it is now. Just a bed and a couch back then. But I had a key to the factory and Honor would tell Adora she was going to a friend's, and we'd meet there. It was fine until Butchie was conceived. That's when reality hit us hard and we knew we had to find a way to explain her having a baby. She'd known Del since they were kids and he was only too happy to act like the baby was his." Henry laughed softly. "Shocked everybody who knew him, that's for sure. Everyone suspected Del was queer from the time he was a little boy." He was quiet for a long moment, and I waited. "It's been hard, Tess," he said finally. "Hard and bittersweet. I know you don't approve of colored and white together. I know Gaston and Loretta's situation bothered you, but I can't help how I feel about her. And I love our children. The money in the armoire? It's for them. I had to sneak around to visit my own son and daughter, not to mention the woman I love. You know what would have happened to us if we'd ever been found out. What would *still* happen. Prison for who knows how long. I would lose the factory. I'd lose everything. Butchie and Jilly—Jilly, now—would be ostracized." He shifted on the bed. "I know you think you're trapped, Tess," he said. "But I've been trapped my whole adult life."

I was quiet. For the first time, I had a real window into my husband's world. I tried to imagine what it had been like for him and Honor all those years. What it was still like.

"What did she say when you told her you'd gotten another woman pregnant?" I asked.

He groaned. "She was furious, of course," he said. "I'd never done anything like that before. Never had relations with another woman. I'm not much of a drinker—you know that by now. And that fellow Roger kept the alcohol coming. It's no excuse . . ." He rubbed his chin with his good right hand. "I was so disgusted with myself about it—so hard on myself— that eventually Honor forgave me." He looked over at me. I could just make out his eyes in the darkness. "She was grateful to you for the way you helped her when Jilly was sick," he said. "And she felt guilty about it, but her need to be close to Jilly trumped her guilt about keeping you in the dark. I hope you can understand that."

"Yes," I said. I really could. I'd seen her as a mother, nothing more or less than that. The sort of devoted mother I would have been if only I'd been given the chance.

"She's frightened right now, not knowing what you'll do," he said. "Frankly, so am I."

I hesitated, once again feeling Honor and Henry's future in my hands. I could so easily hurt them. Devastate them. But I knew I never would. "Tell her she's safe," I said finally. "I wouldn't hurt you that way. I wouldn't hurt either of you."

He let out his breath. "Thank you."

"Did you think about doing what Gaston did?" I asked. "Moving to Washington State or someplace where you could legally marry?"

"Yes, I've thought of it," he said, "but Adora is here, and Zeke and my mother. And our friends and my family's factory." He sighed. "It's not fair."

I'd thought his friend Gaston had been foolish for falling in love with a colored girl in the first place. Hearing about Henry and Honor though . . . They couldn't put a stop to those feelings any more than Vincent and I could.

"Your story reminds me of mine with Vincent," I said. "We started out as kids together. Just friends. Then it turned into something more. Much more. Only we never had to hide our feelings. I can't imagine what that was like."

"Until now," he said softly. "You never had to hide your feelings for Vincent until now."

"Yes," I agreed. "Until now." I thought about the conversation we were having. One of those deep conversations that touched those places we kept hidden from other people. Even from ourselves. For the first time, Henry and I were vulnerable with each other. For the first time, listening and sharing, I felt something close to love for him.

"You can see him," Henry said. "Your Vincent. You can have an affair with him. I won't try to stop you."

"That's not what I want, Henry," I said. "I want a full life with a husband who loves me. I want children. I want a *divorce*. And I don't want to have to separate for two years before we get it. I want it *now*." My voice was calm but firm. "Which means we divorce on the basis of your adultery. We can fabricate a woman you've been seeing. You don't have to admit to it being Honor. But unless you want to admit to impotence or homosexuality or bestiality, it has to be adultery. They're the only grounds we can use to get a divorce."

He went very still. I'd spoken softly, but there was power behind my words and he knew it.

"I know I owe you a great deal, Tess," he said finally. "But can you give me some time to figure this out? There's so much going on right now, with things at the factory falling apart and Jilly being sick and me trying to help out at the polio hospital. It's just a difficult time to suddenly . . . split up and have to answer questions and . . . Can you give me some time?"

I took in a deep breath, studying the pattern of moonlight on the ceiling. For me, divorce meant freedom. Shame would come along with it, true, but I would be free. Henry never would be.

"How long?" I asked. "How long are you asking me to wait?"

"A month? Can you give me that?" he asked. "I have a lot of thinking to do."

"All right," I said. I could wait a while longer. Knowing I would eventually be set free—that knowledge would keep me going.

"Can you hold off on telling Vincent?" he asked. "He might . . . I don't know. Do something. Turn us in, or . . . He already hates me. I can tell by the way he looks at me at the hospital."

"He doesn't hate you," I said. "And he wouldn't 'turn you in.' And no, I'm sorry, but I have to tell him. He has to know I'm going to be free. I don't know if he'll still want me, but I need to tell him. I deserve that."

He sighed. "Yes," he said, "I suppose you're right."

I rolled onto my side to look at him. "What will you do?" I asked.

He studied the ceiling as if he could see his future there. "After we're divorced, and after an appropriate amount of time, I suppose I'll ask Violet to marry me."

"Henry, it's so wrong," I said.

"Violet isn't you," he said. "All she wants in a marriage is riches and a comfortable life. I can give her that." He suddenly laughed. "Actually," he said, "here's a crazy idea. I could start an affair with Violet during the next month. That would be my adultery."

I had to laugh at the brilliance of the plan. If I'd cared a whit for Violet, I might have thought to warn her. As it was, I found myself worrying that she would not be as easy to manipulate as Henry was thinking. I doubted Violet would surrender as easily as I had to Henry's lack of ardor and intimacy.

"I think she's going to be a more difficult wife than I've been," I said.

He chuckled, then rolled onto his side to face me. He stretched his arm across the space between our beds and I did the same to take his hand.

"Tonight," he said, "you are the most wonderful wife I could imagine."

76

The following day at the hospital seemed to drag on forever despite the fact that we were frightfully busy admitting new patients, a couple of whom were very seriously ill. Even though Vincent and I worked together in the admissions tent, I was afraid I wouldn't get a chance to ask him if we could talk after our shifts were over. Finally I gave him the message the only way I could manage: I wrote it on a slip of paper and attached it to the patient chart I handed him.

I need to talk to you. After work?

He looked up from the chart in surprise. He wore no mask—he almost never did—and the sunlight caught the perfect angles of his face, the thick-lashed dark eyes, the lips I hadn't kissed in far too long. I wanted that face back. I wanted all of him back.

He nodded, then returned his attention to his patient while I stood there with my heart pounding from both anxiety and desire.

I was undeniably nervous about talking to him. Telling him everything. I was unsure if he would still want me once I was divorced. I was no longer the sweet, innocent, untouched Little Italy girl he'd spent half his life hoping to marry. And how would he feel about Henry and Honor's relationship? If I didn't know the two of them as well as I did, if Henry had not shared his heart and soul with me as he had the last couple of days, I would still be shocked by their relationship myself. Vincent had been raised with the same values I had: colored and white should keep to their own kind when it came to romance. But he was a softhearted man. He would understand. I was counting on it.

We met in his car at the end of the day. The windows were rolled down to fight the heat and we had to bat away mosquitos, but they were a tiny concern compared to the things I needed to tell him.

"We should probably be talking in public," he said, before I even opened my mouth to speak.

"Why do you say that?" I asked.

"It's hard for me to be with you alone," he said. "It's hard for me not to touch you. I tend to forget you're no longer mine to touch."

I couldn't help but smile, my trust in him and our history returning. "Henry's going to give me a divorce," I said.

"*Tess,*" he said, his eyes lighting up. "Really? How did you change his mind?"

"I have a bargaining chip," I said, and then I told him about walking in on Henry and Honor. I told him everything I knew about their relationship. Everything Henry had told me. When I saw Vincent's expression finally shift from shock to compassion, I knew I'd given him a fair account.

He shook his head. "Well, I feel sad for them," he said, "but I'd frankly like to knock Henry's block off. How could he do this to you? He took advantage of you. He made you part of his illicit scheme."

"I was pregnant, remember?" I said. "I needed a husband."

"You could have had a husband who loved you, instead of this . . . con artist." There was bitterness in his voice and I knew he still had some anger at me for how I'd handled everything.

"You're still mad at me," I said.

He looked toward the woods, silent a moment, and then shook his head. "Only a little," he said with a small smile.

"I wish we were at St. Leo's right now instead of batting mosquitos away in your car." I looked at him. "I miss our old life so much, Vincent."

He took my hand. Held it on his knee. I felt my whole body melt.

"Let's get it back," he said.

"Can we?"

"As far as I'm concerned, yes," he said. "We can and we should."

"I'll be a divorcee," I reminded him. "The church won't—"

"I don't care," he interrupted. "And anyway, didn't you say you were married by a justice of the peace?"

I nodded.

"Then as far as the church is concerned, you're not married."

I gasped. I hadn't thought of that and it was as if a weight had suddenly been lifted off my shoulders. I hadn't realized how much the church—my Catholic faith—still mattered to me.

"I don't know how long the divorce will take," I said.

"I'll wait."

"I never wanted Henry."

"Shh." He squeezed my hand. "Let's not think about him."

"But I do care about him, Vincent," I said. "I don't love him. I don't want him. But I do care."

"You have a good heart, Theresa De Mello." He smiled at me. "That's the thing I love best about you."

"You'll still have me?"

"I frankly can't wait to have you."

"Oh, Vincent, I'm so sorry for everything!" I wished I could pull him into my arms. I suddenly thought of Mimi and Pop. I longed to see them, but would they ever want to see me again? "What about your parents?" I asked. "How much do they know? Will they ever forgive me for leaving the way I did?"

He moved my hand until it was nestled between both of his. "I told them why you left," he said. "I told them where you've been. And I told them what you've been doing."

I made a face. "They must think I'm a terrible person," I said.

He smiled. "They think you need their prayers," he said. He leaned forward and kissed me lightly on the cheek. "And now they'll think their prayers have been answered."

77

Over the next week, Henry and I settled into the most placid period of our marriage. It was amazing what our heart-to-heart talks could do, I thought, as I ate dinner with him and Ruth that Friday evening. Ruth still had Hattie set a place for Lucy, but I'd learned to ignore it. If this was the way she needed to grieve—or to express her anger at me—so be it. Over dinner, Henry and I would catch each other's eye and share a secret smile. He knew I'd told Vincent everything and he said he was happy I would have the future I wanted with him. He hadn't told me if he'd decided to start an affair with Violet or not, but he assured me the divorce would come, one way or another. I trusted him to keep his word on that. He knew the consequence of not following through could be dire. I only needed to be patient.

Now that Jilly was nearly well, Honor stayed home with her rather than work in the hospital kitchen, so I didn't see her every day as I had been. I thought that was probably best for both of us. I occasionally spotted Zeke at the hospital—Henry was still giving him time off from the factory to volunteer as one of our maintenance men—but unless it was my imagination, Zeke was avoiding contact with me. A couple of times, when he was repairing a broken bed or a window screen in the ward where I was working, I'd catch him looking at me, but he'd turn away quickly before I could read his expression.

I spent a lot of time with Amy Pryor, who was still in the iron lung. I had caring for her down to a routine now. She was well enough to look at pictures of her baby sent over by the mayor and his wife, and she told me about her little two-year-old son, even though she was only able to speak with each exhalation the machine allowed her. We talked as I brushed her hair or washed her face, and she was well enough to be bored, so one of the volunteers read to her off and on during the day.

The *Life* article came out and issues of the magazine flew off the news-stands. Ruth cut out the pictures and added them to her scrapbook, right next to the newspaper photograph of Vincent, Grace, and myself as we stood with the mayor and his wife after the birth of their grandson. I'd been touched beyond words when she showed me that picture in her scrap-book. She had no idea, of course, that the handsome doctor standing next to me in the photograph was the man I dreamed about day and night. I felt not only moved that she'd finally accepted me into the family, but guilty that I knew what she didn't: I would not be a part of her family for much longer. She'd get over it, I thought. Oh, she'd be upset, since there were "no divorces in the Kraft family," and angry with Henry for bringing shame to the Kraft name. But she'd be so delighted once she had Violet Dare as her daughter-in-law that I doubted her unhappiness would last for long.

That Monday evening, Henry told us that he had a community meeting to attend and left the house right after dinner. I was certain there was no community meeting. Most likely, he'd be with Honor at the factory. I knew in the long run his relationship with her was impossible, yet I envied him his ability to be with the person he loved when I was with Vincent only in my dreams.

Ruth and I were reading in the library around eight o'clock when the doorbell rang.

"Who on earth could that be?" Ruth asked.

Through the library window, I saw an unfamiliar black car in the drive-way. Hattie had left for the day, so I walked through the foyer and opened the front door. Two men stood on the step, one tall and lanky and very young, the other in his fifties with gray hair and mustache. They both wore suits, despite the muggy evening heat.

"Good evening, ma'am," the older man said. "We're from the federal Office of Price Administration, and we're here to speak to Mr. Henry Kraft."

Ruth appeared at my side. "What on earth is the Office of Price Administration?" she asked.

"Mr. Kraft isn't home." I felt perspiration break out across my back, recalling Teddy's cryptic note to Henry about the OPA. Now I knew what that acronym stood for, though I wasn't sure what they wanted with Henry.

"Where is he?" the man asked.

"He's at a meeting," Ruth said. "What do you want to talk to him about?"

"We're investigating counterfeit rationing coupons," he said.

"Counterfeit rationing coupons!" Ruth laughed. "Here? My Henry? That's ridiculous."

"We have a warrant to search the premises, but we really need to speak to Mr. Kraft," the older man said.

"Search the premises!" Ruth said. "This is nonsense."

My heart gave a thud as I thought of the money and gasoline coupons in the bottom of the armoire. Surely the coupons weren't counterfeit. Henry was wealthy. He had no need to involve himself in something so foolish. I realized though that I'd never asked him where all that cash had come from.

The skinny younger man produced a document from inside his suit jacket and the older man snatched it from him, unfolding it to hold out to us. "You need to let us in, ma'am," he said to both Ruth and myself.

"Oh, this is so silly!" Ruth said. "I don't want you tearing up my house." But she stepped back to let them pass. I had a helpless feeling, wondering if there were other caches of money or coupons hidden around the house for them to find.

"We won't do any damage," the mustached man said as he stood in the foyer, looking left and right.

They began their search in the basement, insisting that Ruth and I stay with them. I supposed they were afraid we would try to hide contraband goods if they gave us free rein while they searched. Ruth hobbled down the stairs behind the three of us. I knew her knee bothered her on steps, but I thought she was really milking the infirmity to show these men how put out she was by their visit. My palms were sweaty. I thought of slipping upstairs to call the factory in the hope Henry would pick up the recently repaired phone, but I didn't dare.

They finished in the basement and we led them back to the first story. They went room by room, including Ruth's bedroom, an intrusion over which she huffed and puffed indignantly. Quite honestly, I didn't think they were doing a very thorough job and that gave me hope they wouldn't look in the armoire. They peeked in closets and even removed the grill-work that covered the radiator in the living room, but they didn't bother with drawers or small cupboards and I guessed they were looking for something large—a printing press?—rather than the coupons themselves. I was certain Henry wasn't printing counterfeit coupons. The thought was ludicrous.

When they'd covered the first floor, they headed toward the stairs and I had an idea. "My mother-in-law can't manage another set of stairs," I said, thinking I could whisper to her to call the factory and alert Henry . . . although she'd probably try to argue with me that he wasn't there, since she thought he was at a meeting. But my plan quickly fell apart.

"You stay down here with her," the older man said to the skinny one, who still had not said a word. I thought the younger man must be a trainee of sorts.

"I don't need a babysitter," Ruth complained, but she walked with an indignant limp into the library, the young agent or whatever he was close on her heels.

I led the man upstairs. "Which is Henry Kraft's bedroom?" he asked, when we reached the top of the stairs.

I led him into our bedroom, averting my eyes from the armoire. He walked directly over to it almost as if he knew by my behavior that he should begin his search there. He pulled open the mirrored door, but he didn't bother to touch Henry's clothing or move it aside and he didn't seem to notice the leather tab protruding from the false floor. I was relieved when he shut the door. So relieved, I felt a bit cocky.

"You're really wasting your time, suspecting my husband of anything," I said. "He's a wealthy man. He has no need to make extra money, espe-cially not illegally."

He glanced at me, then returned to his search, opening the closet and peering inside. "With all due respect, ma'am," he said, "you don't know your husband very well."

His words sent a shiver through me. They were so close to those Lucy had spoken just before the accident when she told me I didn't really know her brother. Back then, I hadn't known Henry at all, that was true.

Now, though, I was certain Lucy had been referring to his relationship with Honor. But what was this federal agent referring to?

I followed the man all through the upstairs, then back down to the library.

"We need to search the garage and that little cottage out back," he said, smoothing his fingers over his mustache.

"My maid lives in the cottage," Ruth said. "I will not have her disturbed."

"Check the search warrant," the man said to her. "It says we can search all the buildings on the property."

"And we have a warrant forthcoming to search the factory too." The younger man finally spoke up, and I knew he'd made a tactical error when the mustached agent shot him an angry look. So, they didn't yet have a warrant to search the factory. Good, I thought. If Henry *was* hiding something there, this would give him time to get rid of it. I wished I knew what was really going on.

We left Ruth in the house with the green younger man, while I rousted poor Hattie out of her cottage in her nightclothes. The agent made short work of searching her three small rooms, then led me into the empty garage and shed. I was a bit nervous in those two unfamiliar spaces, especially the shed with its woodworking equipment. I probably wouldn't know a printing press from a table saw, but the man seemed interested in none of it, and we finally returned to the house, the agent guiding our way by flashlight because it was now dark. Both my feet and my nerves were exhausted.

As they left, the senior agent handed me a card. "Have Mr. Kraft call this number in the morning," he said. "It's very important. If he's innocent, I'm sure he'll want to clear his good name."

"Of course," Ruth said as she ushered them out the door. "Now don't go spreading any silly rumors about my son!" she called after them as they walked toward their car.

We watched their taillights travel down the road, then Ruth turned to me. "What a humiliating nuisance," she said. "I wonder why on earth they think Hank could have anything to do with something illegal?"

I shrugged. "I have no idea," I said. "They probably have him mixed up with someone else."

"Well, I'm going to bed," she said. "This was *not* how I planned to spend my evening!"

I waited until I was certain Ruth was in bed before I called the factory. The phone rang and rang, and I pictured Henry in Zeke's room with Honor, trying to decide whether or not to bother going into his office to answer. I didn't hang up though, and on the fifteenth ring, he picked up.

"It's me." I spoke quietly, not wanting Ruth to know I was on the phone. "Two men were just here from the . . ." I couldn't remember the exact name of the agency. "Someplace to do with price administration? They suspect you of printing counterfeit rationing coupons. They had a warrant to search the house, but I don't think they have one for the factory. Not yet, at least."

I'd spoken quickly, breathlessly, and I was sure I'd taken him by surprise. It was a moment before he responded.

"They searched the house?" he asked.

"Yes. But they . . . whatever they were looking for, they didn't find it." I lowered my voice even more. "They didn't notice anything amiss about the armoire," I said. "What's going on, Henry? Are the coupons in the armoire counterfeit?"

"Listen," he said softly. "I don't want to drag you into anything. Just . . . you don't know anything, all right?"

"I *don't* know anything," I said.

"Let's keep it that way," he said. "You said they don't have a warrant for the factory?"

"They . . . alluded to the fact one was coming though."

"All right. Thank you for calling me. I . . . uh . . . I need to take care of some things and I'll be home late tonight. Just . . ." He sounded distracted. Maybe anxious, I couldn't really tell. "Thank you for calling," he said again, and then he was gone from the line.

78

I barely saw Henry the following morning before he left for the factory. I'd been asleep when he got home the night before and he was already dressed by the time I woke up. He sat on the edge of my bed while I stretched and yawned myself awake.

"Thanks again for that call last night," he said. "Everything's fine. You don't need to worry."

"All right," I said. I decided not to ask him any more questions about the coupons. He was right: the less I knew the better. He looked haggard this morning. I propped myself up on my elbows to get a better look at him. "Did you get any sleep at all last night?" I asked.

"Not much." He gave me a tired smile, then stood up. "I've got to get to the factory early this morning and I expect I'll be there late again tonight. The replacement parts are arriving for the boiler sometime today, at last."

"What about breakfast?" I asked.

"I'll grab one of Hattie's biscuits to take with me." He leaned over and kissed my forehead. "Thank you for everything, Tess," he said. He left the room and I settled back down in the bed again, thinking that I had the strangest marriage in the world.

I had a wonderful day at the hospital, working side by side with Vincent a good part of the time. I spent most of the morning taking care of Amy

Pryor, but I was back with Vincent in the admissions tent for the afternoon. I loved watching him with the patients. Although I wore all of my protective coverings and my hair was tucked under a cap, Vincent wore only his white coat. No mask, as usual, and I thought that made him less frightening to the patients. He had such an easy, earnest style about him. Frantic parents grew calmer when he spoke to them, and he touched the children so gently as he examined them. I watched him with the littlest ones, saying a silent prayer that someday he and I would have children of our own. I knew I wasn't alone with my feelings. The way he looked at me, sometimes with a smile. Sometimes a wink. The way he touched my arm, my hand, when we moved past each other in the confines of the tent. Touches that were not completely necessary. I was hungry for that divorce! I would give Henry three more weeks. That would make a month since we'd put everything out in the open. If he didn't agree to start the divorce process by that time, I would have to apply pressure. I didn't want it to come to that. I was already looking in the paper for rooms to rent in case I was still working at the hospital at that time. Once the epidemic was over, I would return to Baltimore. With any luck, Vincent would be by my side.

Ruth was frustrated that night over dinner. "My husband never worked late like this at the factory, night after night after night," she said. "Hank's not getting well-rounded meals, and he's tired every morning. It's just not right. He's trying to do too much, working at the hospital as well as the factory."

I didn't tell her Henry's late nights had nothing to do with work of any sort. Instead, I changed the subject.

"Are you looking forward to your bridge game tonight?" I asked. Mrs. Wilding was to pick her up at seven for a bridge evening at one of the country club ladies' homes.

"Of course," she said. "Are you sure you won't join us?" Ever since the people of Hickory had warmed to me, Ruth seemed to view me in a new light.

"I'm sure," I said. "I'm going to read for a while and turn in early."

Mrs. Wilding picked Ruth up shortly after dinner and I changed into my shorts and sleeveless blouse, an outfit I only wore when Ruth wasn't around. I settled into the upstairs parlor with *The Fountainhead*. In the distance, I heard the sound of sirens. From my work in the hospital, I'd grown accustomed to the constant bleating of ambulances, but this shrill, relentless wailing seemed different. More than one vehicle was creating that racket. Maybe more than two or even three. I turned my book upside down in my lap and listened, reassuring myself that the sirens were not close. They were far enough away that I could put them out of my mind almost completely and concentrate on the book.

I'd read a chapter and a half when I heard pounding on the front door. Setting down the book, I headed for the stairs. The pounding was ceaseless and loud and I remembered the agents who'd searched the house the night before. Were they back with the police?

I pulled open the door to find Byron Dare on the porch, the pink sunset sky behind him.

"There's a fire at the plant!" he said. "I see Hank's car's not here. Do you and Ruth want a ride over there?"

For a moment, I wasn't sure what he was talking about. I never referred to the factory as a "plant." Then it sank in. *The sirens*. Henry was there, most likely with Honor, and I felt suddenly panicky.

"Ruth is out, but yes!" I said, grabbing my handbag from the table near the door. "Please take me!"

We raced down the walkway and across the street to his car, and he started driving off before I'd even shut the door.

"How do you know there's a fire?" I asked.

"I heard the sirens and called the police to find out what was happening," he said. "Where's Hank?"

"He's at the factory, as far as I know," I said. I twisted my rings around nervously on my finger.

"He probably got out just fine." Mr. Dare glanced at me. "Don't worry."

We drove in silence for another block or so, and the sky darkened. Both of us seemed to realize at the same moment that it was not sundown creating the darkness but smoke, and bits of ash began to settle on the windshield. I swallowed hard and saw Mr. Dare's fists tighten on the steering wheel.

"A furniture factory would go up like tinder," he said, more to himself than to me, and I braced myself for what we would find ahead of us.

When we turned the corner, we could see the blaze a couple of blocks ahead of us. The sight was shocking, flame and smoke licking from every window of the massive two-story brick building.

"Oh my God," I said, my hand to my mouth. I shut my eyes momentarily, thinking, *Please let them have gotten out okay.*

We drove a short distance farther and saw a crowd of people congregating in the street. They stood en masse, pointing toward the building, lit up by the flames a block away. A policeman stepped in front of the car, holding up his hand to stop us. He walked around to the driver's side.

"Mr. Dare," he said, obviously recognizing him. "You can't get any closer. We have to keep people back."

I leaned forward so the policeman could see me. "I'm Tess Kraft," I said. "Hank's wife. Did he get out okay?"

A muscle in the man's cheek twitched as he looked toward the building and the flames lit up his eyes. "We don't know," he said. "His car is in the parking lot, but we don't know if he's inside or out. The fire ain't under control enough for anyone to go in to look for folks."

"I want to get closer," I said, opening the car door.

"No, ma'am, you can't," the officer said.

"She's his wife," Mr. Dare said, surprising me with his support. "Let her do what she wants."

I got out of the car and started running toward the factory before anyone could stop me. The sky was black and filled with bulbous clouds of smoke, and the smell in the air was part flame, part chemical. Before I'd gone half a block, I had to stop. It was hard to breathe and my eyes watered and stung. Fire trucks and police cars were parked at crazy angles in the street, and ahead of me I saw the firemen aiming their hoses at flames that licked from the windows. The sound of breaking glass joined the sirens and the whoosh of water and the shouts of the men.

"Tess!"

The voice came from somewhere to my right, and I turned to see Zeke walking quickly toward me across a vacant lot.

"Zeke!" I rushed toward him. Grabbed his arm. "Did Henry get out?" I lowered my voice, although there was no way anyone could hear me over the chaotic sounds of the scene. "Was Honor in there too?"

"Honor's home," he said. "I was just coming back from taking her home when I heard the sirens. The place was already up in flames when I got here and I was gone no more than twenty minutes."

"Did he get *out!*" I shook his arm, panicky.

He didn't answer right away but looked toward the flames, squinting against the caustic air. "I don't know," he said finally. "I pray to the Lord he did, but I just don't know."

79

The fire burned for five more hours, finally coming under control around two in the morning. By that time, Ruth and I were both back at the house, sitting rigidly next to each other on the living room sofa, waiting for news. Hattie and Zeke were with us, Hattie wringing her hands as she sat on the ottoman. Zeke stood by the front windows, watching the dark street as though he hoped Henry might come strolling up to the house at any moment. I thought we all knew the truth by then. If Henry were alive, surely he would have gotten in touch with us.

Teddy Wright stopped by to tell us the firemen were finally inside the factory, searching for "anyone who might have been in there." He stood nervously in the doorway between the foyer and the living room, his cap in his hands. "It looks like it started in the boiler room," he said. "They think a spark from the boiler ignited some sawdust."

"Damn." Zeke shook his head. "Sawdust is like gasoline," he said. "Touch it with a spark and it explodes."

"I thought the boiler room was protected from the rest of the building," I said.

"Looks like the windows were open and the fire spread," Teddy said.

"We got a new igniter for the boiler today," Zeke said to Teddy. "I was at the polio hospital so I didn't get to install it. Hank might've tried to do it himself."

"Oh dear God in heaven." Ruth lowered her head to her hands and I rested my palm on her back. I was afraid of the images running through my own mind. I could only imagine what this was like for her.

"I'm going back over there," Teddy said. "I just wanted to tell y'all the fire was out."

"You let us know anything you find out, hear?" Zeke walked him to the door almost like it was his house and he was in charge, and I thought Ruth and I were happy to let him take on that role. We were too numb and frightened to do much more than sit on the sofa, our hands knotted in our laps.

At three, I insisted Ruth go to bed and Hattie return to her cottage. Zeke offered to stay with me, but I sent him to Adora's . . . once I realized that his home, that lovely room at the factory, was now in ashes.

"Honor must be going out of her mind, not knowing," I whispered as I walked him to the door.

"Yes, ma'am," he said rather formally. He seemed uncomfortable to be acknowledging Henry and Honor's relationship so openly. "I should go be with her."

"Thanks for staying with us, Zeke," I said.

He looked like he wanted to say something more, but gave his head a shake. "There's still hope," he said finally. "Until we know different, we got to hold on to that."

I was sitting alone in the living room an hour later, nursing a cooled cup of tea, when Teddy returned. I let him into the foyer.

"Please sit down, ma'am," he said quietly, and if I hadn't already known the nature of his visit, I knew it then. I walked stiffly into the living room with him close on my heels and lowered myself again onto the sofa. I looked up at him. He'd taken off his hat once more and held it between his hands.

"They found him?" I asked.

He nodded. "They weren't sure it was him at first," he said. "He was in the boiler room and everything was . . ." He turned his hat around and around in his hands. He was so young. He wasn't used to delivering this sort of news. "The fire burned real hot and long in there," he said. "The firemen said it was like one of them crematoriums. There wasn't too much left. Just . . ."

"Just what?" I prompted.

"Just mostly down to the bones," he said.

"Oh my God." I was horrified, glad Ruth wasn't in the room to hear this. The only comfort I could take from the scenario he described was that the end had probably been fast.

"I shouldn't of said that," Teddy said quickly, his voice a bit frantic. "I'm sorry, ma'am. I shouldn't of put it that way."

"How do they know for sure it was Henry, then?" I asked, although really, who else could it have been?

"The um . . ." Teddy looked like he was searching for the right thing to say. "The remains was charred real good," he said, "but the left hand? It only had the thumb and forefinger on it."

For some reason, that crushed me. His words felt like a sledgehammer to my chest, and I began to sob, my head bowed nearly to my knees. I thought of how Henry and I had finally connected over the past couple of weeks. How he'd shared the real Henry with me. How he'd loved Honor for most of his life and treasured the son and daughter he could never acknowledge as his. He'd had a sad life and now this tragic end. I hugged myself as I sobbed, ignoring Teddy who stood wordlessly nearby, unsure what to say. The depth of my pain surprised me. The realness of it.

"And there was this," Teddy said finally.

I looked up as he pulled something from his shirt pocket. He reached toward me. I held out my hand and he dropped the object into it. Henry's wedding ring.

I clutched the ring in my fist. "Thank you," I whispered.

He nodded. "I'll let myself out," he said.

I didn't watch him go. Instead I stared at the ring in my hand. It was all that was left of my husband. "I'm so sorry, Henry," I whispered to the air. "So, so sorry."

I'd wanted to be free of this marriage, I thought. But I'd never wanted my freedom at such a cost.

80

It seemed like all of Hickory turned out for Henry's funeral. At the time of Lucy's death, I hadn't truly realized the depth of respect the town had for the Kraft family. I hadn't known who all these people were. After Lucy's funeral, I'd viewed the guests who came to the house simply as towns-people who distrusted and disliked me. Now I saw most of them as generous people who'd helped create a hospital that was saving lives, and I could tell by the sympathy they showed me, by the way they took my hands in theirs, that they saw me as a part of that effort. I knew they'd finally come to accept me as a genuine part of Hickory.

At Ruth's invitation, Adora, Honor, Zeke, and Hattie had walked into the church with us and sat in our pew as if they were part of the family. People knew the linked histories of the Johnson and Kraft families—how Adora had worked for the Krafts for decades and how her children had grown up with Henry and Lucy—and I was unaware of any sideways glances at seeing us all come in together. I hadn't been at Lucy's funeral, but I supposed the same scenario had played out there as well. I wondered if anyone other than Honor, Zeke, Adora, and myself knew that Honor's connection to the family went far deeper than mine. All that was missing was the marriage certificate Honor could never hope to see and the rings on my finger that, in a different world, would be on hers.

This was the first time I'd seen Honor since the night I'd surprised her and Henry at the factory and I was sure she felt embarrassed and possibly ashamed for betraying me. She'd avoided my eyes before we walked into the church and now she sat at one end of the pew while I sat at the other. I wanted to clear the air between us. I wanted to tell her that Henry had helped me understand. I wanted her to know that the tears I cried while the minister spoke were more for her than for myself.

After the funeral, many of the attendees returned to the house to mingle and chat and eat the food Hattie had gotten up before dawn to prepare. I was certain I wasn't the only person feeling a strong sense of déjà vu, having been through this same affair for Lucy so recently. Much had changed since then, and today I felt able to greet people with my head held high. I was able to accept their sympathy. Lucy's close friends still gave me wide berth, and Violet most definitely avoided me, cutting me the occasional hateful look as though I'd been the person to strike the match. Her eyes were red rimmed and I wondered again if Henry had tried to start an affair with her. She didn't know that she was being spared a lifetime in a sham marriage.

As it was with Lucy's post-funeral gathering at the house, Honor passed trays of food, and I wondered how she was managing to hold her emotions together. It was so wrong, I thought, for her to be working when she was actually a grieving widow—or as close to a grieving widow as she could be. Like Violet, she avoided my eyes—avoided me altogether, actually—as she moved through the living room with her tray. It was up to me to make the first overture, and when I was finally able to catch her alone in the hall on her way back to the kitchen, I stopped her, my hand on her arm.

"I'm so sorry, Honor," I said, my voice a whisper. "I know how much he loved you."

She lifted her chin, a bead of tears on her lower eyelids. "Thank you," she said. She looked as though she wanted to say more, but people were beginning to fill the hall and she simply nodded. "Thank you," she said again, and walked back to the kitchen.

Early that evening, Hattie knocked on the open door to my bedroom, where I was organizing my uniform, shoes, and stockings for the following day. I needed to go back to the hospital. Back to work. I needed to be near Vincent.

"What is it, Hattie?" I asked.

"Mr. Dare here to see you and Miss Ruth," she said. "They down in the living room."

"Mr. Dare?" I asked as I hung my uniform in the closet. "What about?"

Hattie looked uncomfortable. "Mr. Hank's money, I think," she half whispered as though embarrassed to be talking about something so personal.

I'd given little thought to Henry's money or who would inherit it. I assumed the bulk of it would go to Ruth, and as long as I had enough to start my life over and surreptitiously give some of it to Honor for Jilly, that would be fine. I thanked Hattie and went downstairs.

"Good, there you are." Mr. Dare stood up from the chair near the empty fireplace as I entered the living room. He held a thin folder in his hand. "I wanted to speak to both you and your mother-in-law at the same time."

"All right," I said, sitting down on the sofa. Ruth was in the chair nearest the windows and she didn't look at me as I took my seat.

"I know you both must be exhausted after the last few days," he said, sitting down again and resting the folder on his knees. "Especially after today," he added. "It was a lovely service though."

"Thank you, Byron," Ruth said. The evening light from the window illuminated every line on her pale face and I was stunned to see the change in her. She'd aged dramatically in the few days since Henry's death. Her hands were folded together in her lap and they looked bony and white.

"I'm afraid I wasn't able to persuade Hank to write a will," Mr. Dare said. "I know he planned to do so back when he thought he'd marry Violet." He shrugged, then nodded in my direction. "And it seems he never got around to it after he married you, despite my encouragement."

I heard no animosity in his voice, although surely he still felt some toward me for stealing Henry away from his daughter.

"And you must know his estate will have to go through probate," he said, "so what that means, Tess . . . and Ruth, is that it will be a couple of years before you receive your inheritance. Tess, you'll receive a small sum to live on in the meantime."

I nodded. I wasn't exactly sure what "probate" meant except that it was a time-consuming process.

"So, the way the law's written makes it a bit complicated." Mr. Dare opened the folder and removed a single sheet of paper. "Since Hank didn't make his wishes known, the law says that the two of you will split his savings and any stocks and bonds he might have. As close as I can figure"—he glanced at the paper—"he has about five hundred thousand between his bank accounts and investments."

I thought my face must have gone as white as Ruth's. Half of five hundred thousand dollars? I felt too numb to respond, and Mr. Dare continued.

"Ruth, you'll get two thirds of the insurance money on the factory as well as two-thirds the value of that house Henry was building," he said. "Tess, as Hank's wife, you get a life interest in one third of that house."

"I don't think Henry would have wanted Tess to get anything from the factory." Ruth suddenly spoke up, her tone businesslike but I could tell there was anger behind the words. "It's been in our family for fifty years. There are Kraft relatives to consider."

"I don't need any of the insurance money," I said quickly. I wanted to keep peace between Ruth and myself. "Ruth is right. It belongs to the Kraft family."

"Of which, may I remind you, you are a part," Mr. Dare said.

"I don't need the insurance money," I repeated. My head still spun from the idea of inheriting two hundred and fifty thousand dollars. That alone seemed like far too much to me. We hadn't been married that long.

"Well, if Tess wants to relinquish her share of the insurance money, I'll have to look into the best way to do that," Mr. Dare said.

"And the house?" I queried. "I don't understand what that means, a 'lifetime interest' in the house."

"A life interest simply means that you can live in the house until your death," he said, "but you can't sell it or pass it down to any children you might have. Upon your death, the house will revert to Ruth's estate . . . or her next of kin if she predeceases you."

Again I fell quiet. I had no need for the house. I hoped that Vincent and I would be leaving Hickory as soon as the hospital closed its doors.

"That lovely house." Ruth shook her head sadly. "Hank was so looking forward to living there."

Mr. Dare looked down at the paper again. "Now I believe there's still about three hundred thousand dollars left in Henry's trust," he said, "so the two of you will each get half of that as well."

Overwhelmed, I slumped a little on the sofa. So much money! I supposed a case could be made that Henry owed me something for his deception, yet . . . I did the math in my head . . . four hundred thousand dollars? I thought of Honor. Of Jilly. I would take the money. I would set up some sort of trust for Jilly once I received the funds. I certainly couldn't make those arrangements through Byron Dare—the man who had prosecuted Henry's friend Gaston and his colored wife. I'd have to find a lawyer outside of Hickory. One who wouldn't have known Henry or the Kraft family. One who wouldn't ask questions.

Mr. Dare got to his feet. "I'll be on my way, ladies, and let you two absorb this news," he said. "And again, to both of you, my condolences."

Ruth and I remained quietly seated until we heard the front door open and close. Then she looked across the room at me.

"I suppose you're happy now," she said.

I was startled by the question. "Happy?" My skin prickled with sudden anxiety. Could she possibly know about Vincent and me? "That Henry is dead?" I asked. "How can you ask me that?"

"My son was so foolish," she said. "Why couldn't he have taken a couple of hours out of his busy day to write a will? This division of his money, his property—it's not right. Surely you can see that."

I let out my breath in relief. She knew nothing about Vincent. "I agree," I said, attempting to be conciliatory. "I don't need that much. Maybe Mr. Dare can help us figure out a way to—"

"You tricked my son into marrying you," she said.

That was too much. "I did *not* trick him, Ruth. I—"

"Then you move into my home like you own it." She gripped the arms of her chair, her fingers white, and I saw sudden fire in her eyes. "You, who come from some common . . . Italian neighborhood in Baltimore. You don't belong here. You insinuated yourself into my life. Then you cost me my two children."

I gasped. "Ruth, I never meant to—"

"What you meant or didn't mean to do doesn't matter." Her voice held a deceptive calm in spite of my own rising anger, and I felt a shiver run up my back. "You cost me my daughter and son," she said. "You might as well have shot Lucy through the heart. And Hank?" Her chin quivered and I tensed. I didn't think I could bear it if she cried. "Well, all I can say is, he was alive before you came to Hickory and now he's dead, just like my beautiful daughter. Our lives—mine, Lucy's, and Hank's—they were perfect before you came along. And now look at them. My children are gone and you're still here. Is that fair?"

I was stunned. I opened my mouth to speak without knowing what I would say, but she plowed ahead before I could get a word out.

"Now you want to move into the beautiful house Hank designed and live a life of leisure with his money." She raised one bony hand and pointed her finger at me. "I want you to leave," she said. "I want you to get out of my house. Today. I don't want to have to look at you another instant."

"This is your grief talking, Ruth." I tried to speak calmly. "Things have been so much better between you and me. Please don't . . . I know you're upset. I know you're grieving and I am too. But it's not fair for you to—"

"Hank was so foolish not to protect his assets from your greedy hands."

My cheeks burned and I stood up. I'd had enough. "I never wanted to hurt Henry or you or Lucy and I certainly never asked him to leave me so much money," I said. "But the truth is, Ruth"—I looked her directly in the eye—"I didn't get *myself* pregnant."

I turned on my heel and left her in the living room as I stormed up the stairs. *She's a sad, grieving old woman,* I reminded myself once I reached the bedroom and shut the door behind me. I leaned against it. She was right: I needed to get out of this house as soon as possible. I didn't think she and I could live under the same roof another day.

I sat on the edge of the bed thinking of all I needed to do before I could extricate myself from Ruth and her house. I had to speak to Byron Dare about how to get that "small sum" he said I could have to tide me over. Suddenly, I thought of the armoire. I had access to more than two thousand dollars in cash, right at my fingertips.

I stood up and crossed the room to the armoire, catching my reflection in the mirrored door as I turned the key in the lock. I was as pale as Ruth. It had been a hard few days. I pulled open the door and saw that the armoire's false bottom was askew. The fabric-covered board sat at an angle, one side higher than the other. I gripped the leather strap. Lifting the board, I let out a gasp. The money was gone and in its place was a single manila envelope, this one quite bulky. Written on the white mailing label were three initials, and it took me a moment to realize they were mine. *T.D.K.*

I sat on the edge of the bed, the envelope in my lap as I undid the clasp.

I spilled the contents onto the bed and nearly screamed. Ten fifty-dollar bills. A red C gasoline ration sticker. A booklet of C coupons.

And *bones*.

Three chalk-white skeletal fingers.

I stared at the contents of the envelope for a long time, and then I couldn't help myself: I laughed.

Henry was alive.

81

I put the envelope and false bottom back in place in the armoire, grabbed my handbag, and went downstairs to call for a cab. I was relieved to discover that Ruth was in her room. I wouldn't bother to tell her I was going out. Instead, I walked outside into the darkening night to wait for the cab, thinking about my discovery. Henry had planned this whole charade and he'd intended me to know. He'd left the bottom of the armoire askew in case I hadn't already thought to look for the money. And he'd known exactly where he could find a skeleton to leave in the fire as his "charred bones."

The taxi pulled up in front of me and I slipped into the backseat, breathless and excited, and gave the driver Reverend Sam's address.

"*What?*" he exclaimed. "You want to go to Ridgeview *now?*"

"Yes," I said. "I do. And I'd like you to wait for me. I may be as long as an hour. All right?"

"You'll pay for the wait time?" he asked.

"Yes, of course." I had the feeling he'd be telling his buddies that Hank Kraft's widow went to Colored Town after dark, but I didn't really care. I watched Hickory sail by outside the window. I couldn't wait to see Reverend Sam.

"Ah!" Reverend Sam said when he answered his door. "I've been expecting you, child." He stepped aside to let me in.

"You have?" I asked.

"Yes, I was certain you'd want to try to connect with your husband. I was sorry to hear of his passing. Even though he didn't think much of me, did he?"

I didn't bother responding. I was too anxious to get to the anteroom, and I nearly plowed ahead of him down the hallway. I let him catch up to me. Let him be the one to open the anteroom door. As I'd expected, the skeleton was gone.

"Where is it?" I asked. "Your skeleton?"

"It was stolen," he said, hands on his hips. "Very strange. I came down here a couple of mornings ago and it was gone." We stood in the center of the small anteroom, staring at the empty place where the skeleton used to stand. "That was the only thing missing as far as I could tell." He swept his arm around the room, taking in the other artifacts. "Very odd, don't you think?" He walked toward the open door to his office.

"Very odd," I agreed, following him into the smaller room. "You said your power came from your artifacts," I said as I sat down opposite him. "So have you lost your power without the skeleton here?"

He shrugged. "Doesn't seem to have affected my ability to connect at all," he said. He reached across the desk, motioning for my hands. "Let's put it to the test, shall we?"

For twenty minutes or longer, we sat across from one another as he tried and failed to contact my husband.

"I'm sorry, Tess," he said finally. "It seems your husband is still not too fond of me."

"It's all right," I said, sitting back in the chair. If anything, I believed in Reverend Sam and his abilities more than ever now. After all, it was impossible to connect with the spirit of someone who was still alive.

"I don't think it has anything to do with my missing skeleton affecting my powers though," he said, getting to his feet. "I had a couple of good readings this morning."

"Henry's just being stubborn." I smiled at him as we walked out of his office and into the anteroom. I wondered if he thought I sounded quite flip for a new widow, but he returned my smile.

"Yes, I believe he is," he said, and either he winked at me or he had something in his eye.

I stopped walking and studied him curiously. "Did you call the police about the stolen skeleton?" I asked.

"No," he said, looking at the empty spot in the room where the skeleton had been. "I've always believed that if a person steals something from me, he needs that something more than I do. That's probably the case with my skeleton. What do you think?"

He knows, I thought, and I wondered if Henry had stolen the skeleton or if it had been a gift.

"What I think," I said, leaning forward to give him a kiss on the cheek, "is that you're a good and generous man, and I'm very glad I met you."

82

I could barely concentrate on my work the next morning at the hospital. It was my first day back since the fire, and I'm sure my coworkers thought my distraction had to do with grief. They had no idea what was really going through my mind: where was my husband and what did he have up his sleeve?

I was also exhausted. I'd called Grace Wilding when I got home from Ridgeview the night before to ask if I could stay with her for a while.

"Of course," she'd said. She'd asked no prying questions and I was grateful, both for a place to stay and for her kindness. I moved my things to her apartment in the middle of the night, leaving a curt note for Ruth about where I'd gone. It was a relief to be out of that house.

People were so kind to me at the hospital that morning. "You should have taken more time off," they all said. "It's so soon, and you must still be so upset about Mr. Kraft."

I gave each of them my stock answer. "Thank you, but it's best for me to keep busy."

Grace had taken over most of Amy Pryor's care in my absence, but we had many new patients and they kept me occupied. While I bathed them and fed them and wrapped their limbs in hot wool, I was constantly looking through the screened windows for Zeke. I needed to talk to him. I was sure he knew the truth, in spite of his bravura performance at the house the other night when we were anxiously waiting for news about Henry's fate. They were as close as brothers, those two.

Late that morning, I finally spotted Zeke walking from the stone building toward his truck, and I knew I needed to catch up with him quickly before he drove off. I was in the middle of feeding a two-year-old girl, but I called to one of the volunteers and asked if she could take over for me.

"Of course, Mrs. Kraft," she said, and she took the spoon from my hand and gave me a little push toward the door. She probably thought my grief had suddenly gotten the better of me and I needed a break. I thanked her and nearly flew out of the building. I caught up with Zeke as he was opening the door to his truck.

"I need to talk to you," I said as I neared him.

"What about?" he asked, his hand on the door handle.

"Where is he?" I asked quietly. "Where's Henry?"

"I reckon he's with his maker," he said, and for a fleeting moment, I was afraid I'd guessed wrong and Henry really *hadn't* told him his plan. But then I saw a flicker of light in his long-lashed eyes. "Why would you think anything else?" he asked.

"I know he's alive," I said. "And I know he wanted me to figure it out."

He looked away from me and I saw his Adam's apple bob in his throat. He wasn't sure he could trust me.

"You don't need to worry," I added. "I understand this was his way of setting me free."

He nodded then, and I saw relief in his eyes. "Yes," he said. "That's exactly right."

"What I don't understand," I said, "is how this sets *him* free."

He glanced behind me as though trying to see if anyone was around to overhear us. "Get in the truck," he said.

I walked around to the other side of the truck and climbed in. He started the truck and we drove along the dirt road until we came to the clearing where the National Guard had cut down trees to use in building one of the wards. The expanse of stumps had an eerie feel to it, a sea of light and shadow, and I shivered. Zeke turned off the engine.

"He's goin' out west," he said, facing me. "Right now he's on a bus somewhere in the middle of the country on his way to Washington State."

"Oh my God," I said. "Washington? Where his friend Gaston is?"

He nodded. "He'll stay with Gaston and Loretta."

"But what about Honor?" I asked. "What about Jilly? Does Honor think he's . . . does she know he's alive?"

"Yes, she knows," he said. "The plan is for her and Jilly to follow him, soon as I can figure a safe way to get them there."

"Could she take the train?" I asked. "Or a bus?

He smirked at my ignorance. "Those trains are full to the gills and there ain't no room for a colored gal and her child," he said. "Even if there was, she'd be in the Negro car with the colored soldiers drinkin' it up and talkin' about how they got lucky on leave." He shook his head. "I know all about that 'cause I used to be one of them. I wouldn't let her do it. And the bus? That'd be worse." He looked at me, raising his eyebrows. "You have any idea what that's like?" he asked. "Sitting in the back, if there's any seats at all. Having to get out every time you come to a new state line 'cause you're colored. Fight for a seat on the next bus if you can get on at all, because all the seats are already filled with white folks. No place willing to feed you when you stop in a town. They can't make that trip out there alone."

"Could you possibly drive them?" I asked, although I knew it would take forever with gasoline rationed.

He shook his head. "Negro man driving 'cross the country?" he asked. "It wouldn't be safe for me to try." He looked past me, scratching his cheek, and I thought he was imagining something I couldn't possibly comprehend. "Colored folk have a way of disappearing on the road," he said. Then he looked squarely at me, the slightest smile on his face. "He left you that C gas sticker for a reason," he said.

"Me?" I was shocked. "I can't possibly!"

"Can't you?" he asked. "He left you his car too."

"What if we had a flat or . . ."

"I'll get you another spare," he said. "And a copy of the *Green Book*."

"The green book?"

"It tells you safe places you . . . Honor and Jilly . . . can get food and a room for the night. The sundown towns to steer clear of."

"What's a 'sundown town'?"

"Places where she and Jilly wouldn't be safe after sundown."

"Oh," I said. "Once we were out of the South, though, they'd be okay, right?" I couldn't believe I was actually considering this.

He shook his head. "You read the *Green Book*, you'll see. You'll do it?"

"I'm needed here right now, Zeke," I said. The trip would take weeks. I thought of Vincent. He was here and I was now free. I didn't want to leave.

"Hank had faith in you," he said.

"What about Adora? How can Honor leave her?"

"I'll take care of Mama," he said. "Right now she thinks Hank is dead, but she's good at keeping secrets. She'd like knowing Honor and Jilly are safe with him, wherever they are." He looked toward the tree stumps, rubbing his jaw with his hand, thoughtful. "Maybe in time me and Mama can go out there too," he said. Then he shook his head, letting out his breath as though he knew he was getting ahead of himself. "We got to just take things one step at a time," he said.

I thought of the money Hank had been socking away in the armoire. Had he been saving for his escape long before I came on the scene? "He hid money in our room," I said. "Was this his plan all along?"

"He was savin' up, but he didn't rightly know what he was savin' for except to have money for Butchie and Jilly. He couldn't use factory money. Miss Ruth kept a tight grip on that, goin' over the books with a fine-tooth comb. He had to find another way to get money." He clamped his mouth shut, and I knew he thought he'd said too much.

"The money has something to do with the gasoline rationing coupons, doesn't it."

He hesitated. "Everything to do with it," he said finally. "But you don't need to know. It's better you don't."

"Yes, I do need to know," I said. "He owes me that. He owes me the truth."

He ran his hands over the steering wheel and a few seconds passed before he spoke again. "They were counterfeit, those coupons and stickers," he said finally. "He printed them at the factory, then he'd sell them to some local people, and Lucy would take them to . . . I guess you'd call them middlemen. The middlemen would buy a slew of 'em, raise the price and resell them."

"Lucy!" I thought of the manila envelope she'd wanted to deliver to someone across the river the day of the accident. Then there was that cryptic note Teddy Wright had left for Henry. "Was Teddy Wright involved?" I asked.

Zeke gnawed his lower lip as he decided how much to tell me. "Teddy was the eyes and ears in the police department," he said finally. "He let Hank know if the police were gettin' suspicious, which didn't happen for a long time. Lately, with those agents comin' 'round, Hank knew it was time to get out."

"What about you, Zeke?" I asked. "How did you fit in?"

"I had nothin' to do with it," he said sharply. "Nothin', 'cept that I knew too much. But he was making the money for Honor and the kids. I kept that in mind."

I stared at the field of tree stumps in front of us. I thought of the many thousands of dollars I would have to live on for the rest of my life. I thought of how much Henry loved Honor. How he'd spent most of his life having to love her in secret. I thought of how he had freed us both.

I looked at Zeke. "All right," I said, a shiver of both excitement and fear running up my spine. "I'll do it."

MARCH 10, 1945

83

From the open window of the Cadillac, I waved to Adora and Zeke where they stood on the porch of Adora's house. They smiled and waved back, but I knew Adora's happy expression masked her tears. I'd stayed in the Cadillac keeping the heat on, while Honor and Jilly walked to the car, lugging their suitcases, Jilly clutching her doll Nursie in her free arm. I hadn't wanted to be in the house for the good-byes. It would have been unbearable to witness that scene.

I got out of the car to open the trunk.

"Hi, Miss Tess!" Jilly said, trying to lift her small suitcase over the bumper.

"Hi, sweetheart," I said, taking the suitcase from her and slipping it between my own suitcase and one of the spare tires.

I rested my hand on Honor's back as she slipped her suitcase into the trunk. "How are you holding up?" I asked.

"I'm fine." She smiled at me to let me know she meant it.

I closed the trunk and the two of them got into the backseat, Jilly clambering in on her hands and knees. They called out their good-byes, Honor's voice not betraying the mix of emotions she had to be feeling. She was leaving her family and Hickory, heading across the country on a long uncertain journey toward a future she yearned for but hadn't dared to imagine.

I turned to look at my passengers. "All set?" I asked.

"Yup!" Jilly said, her little legs sticking out straight from the seat, Nursie on her lap. She had no real idea what she was in for. Honor had done a good job of convincing her she was going on a great adventure. Indeed, she was.

Honor leaned forward to squeeze my shoulder. "Let's go, Tess," she said quietly, and I knew she needed to get away from her mother and brother, away from Ridgeview and everything familiar, before she broke down.

I steered the Cadillac into the street, and for the hundredth time that morning, I thought over everything we had with us, hoping we'd forgotten nothing. I didn't ask Zeke where he had gotten that second spare. I already knew too much I would need to lie about if we were stopped. We had chicken sandwiches Adora had packed for us, bags filled with apples, biscuits, and molasses cookies, and a big thermos of cold tea. I had the *Green Book* and I'd marked possible places, most of them private homes, where we—or at least Honor and Jilly—could safely stay along our route. I had a map of the country as well as maps for Tennessee and Kentucky, the first states we'd drive through. I'd affixed the red C sticker to the windshield and had the gasoline coupons safely in my handbag. At Zeke's suggestion, I'd packed a pail we might need on the road if we couldn't find a bathroom Honor and Jilly would be able to use. I hoped and prayed I'd thought of everything.

I had five hundred dollars in my handbag, the money Henry had hidden for me in the armoire. I also had cash in the bank from the stipend intended to tide me over until I received my inheritance. One worry I would never have for the rest of my life was money. I planned though to find a way to give some of that "inheritance" to Henry and Honor. I wanted Honor and Jilly to have a much better life than the one they'd had so far, and Henry could use some money himself. He was no longer the owner of a prestigious factory. Instead, he was training to be a ship builder in a town near Seattle, starting out as an apprentice, keeping the fact that he'd lived and breathed woodworking all his life a secret. He didn't want anyone poking into his background. I was sure his supervisors were finding him a quick study.

I drove out of Ridgeview, heading toward Lake Hickory, our last stop before we started our journey. We passed the small building where I'd been living with Grace since moving out of Ruth's house. Grace was funny and kind and it was all I could do to keep myself from telling her the truth about Henry, but I wisely stayed silent and feigned my grief. I'd yet to see that wild side of Grace that Ruth had told me about long ago. I found her lively and positive, qualities that had made her a wonderful nurse in the polio hospital.

I saw the sparkle of the lake through the trees and turned onto the road leading to the hospital. It felt strange to be driving up that narrow rutted road in a skirt and blouse rather than my nurse's uniform. Four days ago, the Hickory Emergency Infantile Paralysis Hospital closed its doors. During the nine months we'd been in existence, we'd treated four hundred and fifty-four inpatients. We lost twelve of them, and though we grieved each one, our losses were the lowest percentage of any polio treatment facility in the country. We'd still had eighty-seven patients at the time we closed, Amy Pryor being one of them. Twelve ambulances and seventy cars driven by our tireless volunteers drove every one of those patients to a new treatment center in Charlotte. As they left, the patients cried. The staff cried. I cried.

I pulled into the parking area near the stone building. Only a few cars and trucks were there this morning, and I saw workers carrying boxloads of equipment out of the wards. The Fresh Air Camp's days as a hospital were over.

I drove as close to the stone building as I could get, and Jilly suddenly let out a shout from the backseat.

"There's Doctor Vince!" she yelled. "In real-people clothes!"

Honor laughed, and I smiled. Yes. There he was, standing near the front of the building, looking handsome in tan trousers and a camel-hair coat, a brown plaid scarf at his neck. He walked toward us as I stopped the car in front of him.

He got into the Cadillac, taking off his fedora. Leaning across the bench seat, he kissed me, then turned to look behind him at Honor and Jilly. "Ready for the grand journey?" he asked.

"Yes!" Jilly said with all the joy of a child who had no idea what it was going to be like to spend the next nine days cooped up in a car.

Vincent looked at me as I put the car in gear. "Want me to drive?" he asked.

"I'll drive first," I said as I pulled out of the parking lot.

"We have a million apples and cookies," Jilly told Vincent.

"Well, we're very lucky people," he said.

I thought of what lay ahead of us. More than a week on the road with counterfeit rationing coupons and a fake C sticker. Only the two tires to replace any flats we might have. The worry of being stopped by the police or maybe harassed by bullies, wanting to know what we were doing with Honor and Jilly in our car.

The day before, I'd sat in Adora's house, ticking off all my worries to Honor as we talked about what we needed to pack.

"I'll put up with nine difficult days to get a lifetime of happiness," Honor'd said simply. I thought she was very brave.

It wasn't only Honor and Jilly who were embarking on a grand new adventure this morning though. When Vincent and I left Washington State, we would head home to Baltimore. After eight months away, Vincent no longer had his job at the Harriet Lane Hospital, but he planned to open his own pediatric office with me working by his side. We'd had plenty of practice learning how to work together over the past few months. Plenty of time to fall in love all over again too. Very quietly, of course. Very carefully. Once again, we were waiting impatiently until we could be together, out in the open, as husband and wife. We would be married in May, one year later than we'd originally planned. I'd had to do some soul-searching about getting married when I was still technically married to Henry, but it was the only way to have a life with Vincent. It was impossible to get a divorce from a dead man.

In my mirror, I saw Jilly get to her knees in the backseat and turn around to look out the rear window, Nursie clutched under one arm.

"Bye-bye, Hickory!" She waved with her free hand. "Bye-bye!"

We were quiet, Honor, Vincent, and myself, all of us, I thought, touched by her words. *Bye-bye, Hickory.*

I remembered the article that had appeared in the *Hickory Daily Record* the day the hospital closed its doors. *So ends the final chapter of the "Miracle of Hickory,"* the reporter had written. It had been my miracle too, I thought now. I'd arrived in Hickory broken and frightened and filled with shame, but I had a strength inside me now I'd never known I possessed.

I turned onto the main road that would take us out of Hickory, and in my rearview mirror, I watched the buildings grow smaller and smaller until they disappeared altogether, and we were left with the open road ahead of us and a cloudless blue sky.

"Good-bye, Hickory," I whispered to myself, my gaze on the mountains in the distance. "Good-bye," I said, "and thank you."

APRIL 12, 1955

EPILOGUE

Little Italy, Baltimore, Maryland

I was about to enter LoPresti's Butcher Shop when the bells at St. Leo's started ringing and the siren at the fire station blared. A couple of car horns joined in the cacophony and the other shoppers and I stopped walking and simply stared at one another. What on earth was going on? The war was long over, yet I was sure every one of us was reminded of how the church bells tolled that day as well. I had no idea why they'd be ringing today.

I walked into the butcher's to find the customers talking excitedly to one another. Old Mrs. Bruno grabbed my arm.

"Did you hear, Tess?" she asked, nodding toward the big radio on the shelf behind the meat counter. "That new Salk polio vaccine's been approved! They just announced it!"

"Oh!" I said. The bells and sirens suddenly made sense. I stood in the middle of the crowded shop, the women chattering around me and Mr. LoPresti asking his familiar "who's next?", but I was no longer truly there. The raw, meaty smell of the shop was gone. Instead, the air filled with the scent of freshly cut lumber, antiseptic, and hot wet wool. I heard the sound of saws and hammers. The whoosh of the iron lung and the cries of a frightened child. They took my breath away, those sounds and smells.

"Can my kids get the vaccine from Dr. Vince?" Rose Merino asked.

I shook off my memories and gave her my attention.

"I'm sure he'll have it soon," I said. "You can call the office and ask." No one wanted that vaccine more than my husband.

"Imagine a summer without polio hanging over our heads!" Michelle

Abruzio said. One of her children was asleep in her arms. Another dozed in the stroller at her feet. I'd lost track over the years of how many she had.

"I miss when you used to work in Dr. Vince's office, Tess," Rose said, a mournful look in her big brown eyes.

I smiled at her. "I'll be back in the office again before you know it," I said.

I'd thought Vincent was crazy when he suggested I go to medical school, but he knew me better than I knew myself. He knew I needed to be challenged and he was right. I loved my classes. One more year in school, followed by my internship and residency, and I'd be working with Vincent again, this time as his partner.

"A lady doctor." Mr. LoPresti shook his head as he pulled a roast from the glass-fronted case and began wrapping it for Mrs. Bruno. "That's as wrongheaded as a lady butcher," he said, but he winked at me over the top of the counter and I knew he was teasing, at least in part.

"I don't know how you manage to keep house and go to school at the same time, Tess," Michelle said. "At least you only have the one kid. My five keep me hopping."

"I bet they do," I said. There was a time when her comment would have stung, but Vincent and I had long ago made peace with the fact that we could have only one child. Maybe that was a good thing, since Philip was such a little pistol. Last Tuesday was his eighth birthday and to celebrate he drew mustaches on every picture in our new *Life* magazine and broke his arm when he fell out of the dogwood tree—the tree we'd planted in my mother's memory. He was full of energy and hard to keep in one piece, but he was a good boy. He had his daddy's brains and kind heart.

Vincent and Philip were already home and in the kitchen when I walked in the door with the groceries and the mail. Our three-story brick house was only a few blocks from where Vincent and I had grown up, but it was three times the size of our childhood homes and, best of all, we owned every inch of it. I set the groceries and mail on the table, gave Vincent a kiss, and hugged my son more tightly than he would have liked. I ruffled his thick, jet-black hair. He was already shying away from my displays of affection, so I would get them while I still could.

"What's that?" he asked, pointing to the mail on the table as I let go of him.

"What's what?" I followed his gaze. On the top of the stack of mail was a postcard with some sort of illustration on it. I picked it up and saw that it was a drawing of a skull entirely composed of intricate floral designs. The image was both spooky and beautiful and the three of us looked at it with knitted brows.

"I think it's supposed to be a sugar skull," Vincent said.

"What's a sugar skull?" Philip asked the question I was thinking.

"It's Mexican," Vincent said, resting his hands on Philip's shoulders. "A symbol of Mexico's Day of the Dead festival. Who sent it?" He reached for the card and flipped it over. "Postmarked Mexico City," he said, but I was already reading the few lines of neat, slanted handwriting.

Tess and Vincent,

We're in Mexico City and when H spotted this card, he said he thought you'd appreciate it. You can tell he's gotten a sense of humor in the last few years! Sincerely, H, H, J, F, C, and P.

I smiled. Every couple of years we'd get a postcard from them, each one with a new initial at the bottom. Their family was expanding.

"Who's H, H, J, and . . . all those letters?" Philip asked.

"Old friends of ours," Vincent said. "A husband and wife and their children."

"What do the letters stand for?" Philip asked.

Vincent looked at me and I gave a small shake of my head. The likelihood anyone would ever come around asking us questions about Henry and Honor at this late date was not strong, but I didn't want to take chances.

"They just like to go by their initials," I said to Philip.

"Dopey," Philip said, backing away from us. "Can I go to my room?"

"Dinner in half an hour," I said. "Wash up, all right?"

He mumbled a response and disappeared down the hall. I was still holding the card, and once Philip was out of our hearing, I said, "I don't understand. Why did Henry say I'd appreciate this card?"

Vincent turned the card over so that the skull was facing us again. "He was probably thinking of Reverend Sam's skeleton," he said.

"Oh!" I laughed. "I bet you're right. Do you think they're visiting Mexico City or living there?"

"You can never tell with those two," Vincent said, walking to the cupboard near the sink and taking out a glass. Over the years, Henry and Honor's postcards had come from Seattle, North Dakota, Dallas, and now Mexico City. We didn't know if Henry was using his own name or some other in the places they lived. The less we knew, the better.

"They're together," I said. "That's all that matters." I set down the card with a shake of my head. "It's such a coincidence that this came today," I said. "I've been thinking about Hickory all afternoon."

"The polio vaccine," he said, filling the glass with water from the tap.

I nodded. "It's wonderful news, isn't it?" I said. "When will you get it?"

"Should be Monday," he said, then smiled. "The summer of '55 will be a worryfree summer."

I began unloading the groceries from the bag on the table. "Do you ever think about all those kids we treated?" I asked.

"Often," he said, leaning back against the sink as he sipped the water.

"It's hard to believe they're all ten years older than when we knew them." I added a few oranges to the fruit bowl on the table. "Some of them are probably married with kids of their own by now," I said. "Jilly Johnson is fourteen. Amy Pryor's baby is ten." I shook my head. "I hope they're all leading wonderful lives."

Vincent put his glass in the sink, then smiled at me. "You're a romantic, do you know that?" he asked.

I barely heard him. For the second time that day, I was lost back in memories of 1944. "Hickory changed me for the better," I said soberly. "I was falling apart when I got there and it slowly made me whole again."

Vincent was loosening his tie, heading for the hallway and the stairs, but he stopped walking to look at me.

"You always say that, Tess," he said. "But have you ever stopped to think about how *you* changed Hickory?"

I stared at him, puzzled.

"Look what you did for Henry and Honor and Jilly, not to mention for the hundreds of patients at the hospital, some of whose lives you literally saved. I can personally testify to that." He walked over to me. Kissed me on the lips. "Hickory's the better for you having been there, sweetheart," he said.

I watched him turn and walk down the hallway. Heard him climb the stairs. I felt a little choked up. I looked down at the postcard and the intricate floral designs on the skull. I smiled, remembering Reverend Sam and his crazy anteroom and his skeleton. I remembered the day he told me I was kind. No one else had ever asked him if his gift left him tired, he'd said. I remembered Adora telling me I'd saved Henry from "something terrible." I remembered endlessly tucking hot wool around the thin, useless legs of frightened children, and breathing life into Amy Pryor's baby. And I would never forget the journey across country, the nine days that turned into two treacherous weeks, and the very real dangers faced by a little girl and her anxious mother.

I stood next to the table, my hand pressed to my cheek and my eyes stinging. No, I hadn't thought about how I changed Hickory, but from now on, I would. I'd remember how, during that year so long ago, Hickory changed forever.

And I was a part of it.

AUTHOR'S NOTES AND ACKNOWLEDGMENTS

Yes, it really happened. The people of Hickory built, outfitted and staffed a polio hospital in fifty-four hours. Ultimately consisting of thirteen wards, the hospital evaluated six hundred and sixty-three patients over its nine months in existence. The hospital is long gone now, only existing in our imaginations.

I heard about Hickory and its polio hospital when I moved to North Carolina twelve years ago and I'm glad I had this opportunity to write about it. Although the hospital itself did exist, the patients and their situations described in *The Stolen Marriage* are purely products of my imagination. As is always the case when writing about an actual event, I needed to come up with a way to fictionalize the real-life story. That's when Tess and her devastating personal situation came into existence. Like many of us, Tess begins her story with a crisis and self-doubt and grows stronger through adversity. I wish that for all of us!

As you can imagine, *The Stolen Marriage* was a research-heavy book. I began my research with a visit to the Catawba County Museum of History, where I spent a day reading old copies of the *Hickory Daily Record*. After eight hours immersed in 1944, it was a strange experience to walk out-side and discover it was still 2016! On that initial research trip, I realized that, while Hickory is a charming town to visit, I was seeing it through a modern-day lens and had no idea what it had been like during the war years. To complicate matters, the town is impossible to navigate by map, having street names like "44th Avenue Court NE." To make matters even worse, as I tried to learn what the town was like in 1944, I discovered that the street names were different back then. The joke is that the town gov-ernment changed the names during the war in case of invasion—the en-emies would never be able to find their way around. The reality is that the street names were changed in the fifties, apparently because they were even more confusing prior to that time. Whatever the reason, I knew as I drove around that I was going to need some help in discovering Hickory during the war years.

I found that help in Peggy Mainess. Peggy is the genealogy assistant at the Hickory Public Library and an enthusiastic expert on the history of the area. For several hours, she and I drove around Hickory as she helped me see it through 1944 eyes. I'm grateful to Peggy for taking the time out of her schedule and for sharing her wealth of knowledge with me.

There is a good deal of information online about Hickory and the po-lio hospital. One of the problems I had as I sorted through site after site was the discovery of contradictory information. When exactly did the ward for the African American patients open? Was there a meeting in the high school or wasn't there? I did my best with the information I had. I altered a few of the dates and events slightly to mesh better with my story, but for the most part, I stuck to the facts as I discovered them.

My "bible" as I researched the story was Alice Sink's book *The Grit Behind the Miracle*. Ms. Sink has written an extraordinary account of the hospital, informed by her interviews and exchanges with former patients.

Joyce Moyer, the author of the award-winning children's novel, *Blue*, shared some of her research with me early on. She whetted my appetite to learn more, and I'm grateful for her generosity.

Not only did I need to research the polio hospital and life in Hickory during the war, I also needed to educate myself to North Carolina laws regarding marriage in the forties. Interracial marriage was prohibited and punishable by up to ten years in prison, and getting out of a marriage was close to impossible, as Tess discovers.

While I'm not much of a believer in the supernatural, Tess's encounters with Reverend Sam are based on a similar experience I had personally, an experience I've never been able to satisfactorily explain to myself or anyone else. In a way, an explanation isn't necessary. What matters is what I took away from that experience—and what Tess takes away from hers. Reverend Reed Brown, formerly of the Arlington Metaphysical Chapel in Arlington, Virginia, has no idea he helped in the writing of this novel, but he did. Although I met with him only briefly years ago, his influence on me remains strong and positive and I'm grateful for that connection.

Thank you to my amazing research assistant, Kathy Williamson, for her ability to track down whatever information I need, even when the task seems impossible. She can find the most obscure resources for me in a heartbeat. She's also a Jill-of-all-trades as she updates my website, sends out my newsletter and takes care of sundry other business-related tasks so I'm free to write.

To all the folks at St. Martin's Press, a big thank you for everything you do. Special thanks to my editor, Jen Enderlin. It's rewarding, exciting and sometimes scary working with Jen, because I can never predict her reaction to the book I turn in. She sees things in my work that I'm too close to see, and her perspective and suggestions are always right on.

My publicist at St. Martin's, Katie Bassel, deserves her own shout out. Katie not only sets up my events and keeps everything running smoothly, she does so with a calm professionalism I hugely admire.

I'm also grateful to the rest of the folks at St. Martin's who get my books into the hands of my readers. Thank you Sally Richardson, Brant Janeway, Erica Martirano, Jeff Dodes, Lisa Senz, Kim Ludlam, Malati Chavali, Jonathan Hollingsworth, Anne Marie Tallberg, Tracey Guest, Olga Grlic, Lisa Davis, and all those hard workers in the Broadway and Fifth Avenue sales department.

I was so happy to finally meet the folks at my UK publisher Pan MacMillan this past year so I could thank all of them in person. I'm especially grateful to my charming UK editor, Wayne Brooks; my UK agent, Angharad Kowal; and Pan Macmillan publicist, Francesca Pearce, who saw to it that I had the chance to meet with many of my readers while I was in London. What a treat that was!

Thank you to my agent, Susan Ginsburg, who simply rocks as an agent, friend, and human being. It was my lucky day when she took me on as a client. Thanks, too, to everyone else at Writers House who works hard to get my books published in various formats around the world.

As always, I'm grateful to my writing friends, the Weymouth 7. I don't think I could complete a book without the brainstorming lunches, emails, and retreats I share with these women. Thank you Mary Kay Andrews, Margaret Maron, Katy Munger, Sarah Shaber, Alexandra Sokoloff, and Brenda Witchger. I look forward to many more years of our friendship.

My significant other, John Pagliuca, has been his usual supportive self during the writing of *The Stolen Marriage* and as always was my first reader. He's insightful, knowledgeable, and sharp as a tack, and I'm always grateful for his input, even when it means serious rewriting. John is also an awesome dog-walker, grocery shopper, vacuum operator, and all-around helpmate. I'm lucky to have him.

For those who would like to read more about Hickory's Emergency Infantile Paralysis Hospital, here are some of the research materials I used:

Eller, Richard | The Miracle of Hickory | TEDxHickory TEDxTalks - https://www.youtube.com/watch?v=z1UzRVOLsmo

Elliott, Marvin L. "Miracle of Hickory: Mass Media and the 'Miracle'." (2007), North Dakota State University.

Hickory Daily Record: Various articles in the 1944 editions.

Hostetter, Joyce Moyer. *Blue*. Honesdale, PA: Boyds Mills Press, Inc., 2006.

Hughes, C. "The Miracle of Hickory." *Coronet*, February, 1945, pp. 3–7.

"Infantile paralysis: Child victims fill beds of an emergency hospital as epidemic hits rural counties of North Carolina." *Life*, July 31, 1944, pp. 25–28.

Sink, Alice E. *The Grit Behind the Miracle*. Lanham, MD: University Press of America, 1998.

DEAD WOMAN WALKING

www.**penguin**.co.uk

Also by Sharon Bolton

Sacrifice
Awakening
Blood Harvest
Now You See Me
Dead Scared
Like This, For Ever
A Dark and Twisted Tide
Little Black Lies
Daisy in Chains

For more information on Sharon Bolton and her books,
see her website at www.sharonbolton.com